George Meredith

Richard Cronin

George Meredith

The Life and Writing of an Alteregoist

palgrave
macmillan

Richard Cronin
University of Glasgow
Glasgow, UK

ISBN 978-3-030-32450-6   ISBN 978-3-030-32448-3   (eBook)
https://doi.org/10.1007/978-3-030-32448-3

This Palgrave Macmillan imprint is published by the registered company Springer Nature Switzerland AG.
The registered company address is: Gewerbestrasse 11, 6330 Cham, Switzerland

To Alys, Isadora, Matilda and Ruaridh

PREFACE

In 1904, reporting Meredith's unconventional view that the marriage contract should bind the parties who enter into it for a fixed term only, the *Daily Mail* confidently described him as 'our greatest novelist'.[1] Throughout his career he had thought of his work as unpopular. He had maintained for upwards of 40 years an embattled relationship with the reading public, but now the battle seemed won. The following year, 5 years before Hardy and 11 years before Henry James, he became the first man of letters to be awarded the Order of Merit. By then he was not just read, he was studied. In 1906 G. M. Trevelyan published *The Poetry and Philosophy of George Meredith*, a book still worth reading; Richard Curle's *Aspects of George Meredith* followed in 1908, and the next year, the year of Meredith's death, James Moffatt's *George Meredith: Introduction to His Novels* appeared. It was not an interest confined to England. In 1910 the French critic Constantin Photiadès produced the first of his studies of Meredith, and studies of Meredith's work also appeared in Germany.[2] Meredith's place in literary history seemed assured. In the event, Meredith's death proved to be the high water mark of his reputation. Within two decades his critical fortunes were on the decline, and the decline has continued ever since. It has been interrupted on occasion. In

---

[1] 'The Marriage Handicap. Views of Our Greatest Novelist. Ten-Year Marriages: A Revolutionary Suggestion'. *Daily Mail*, September 24, 1904, p. 5.

[2] Constantin Photiadès, *George Meredith: sa vie, son imagination, son art, sa doctrine*, Emil Wrage, *Die Psychologie der charactere in der Romanen George Meredith's* and Ernst Dick, *George Meredith: Drei Versuche* all appeared in 1910.

1975 Judith Wilt remarked, 'There is something of a Meredith renaissance going on in the seventies.' Gillian Beer had published her fine study of Meredith, Ian Fletcher had collected a volume of essays, C. L. Cline had edited Meredith's letters in three volumes and Ioan Williams had contributed a volume on Meredith to Routledge's *Critical Heritage* series.[3] It did not amount to a renaissance perhaps, but there were at least signs of renewed critical interest. In the event it came to nothing. Meredith's reputation continued to plummet. Those who have written on him since have persisted in predicting a turn in his critical fortunes. In 2012 Jacqueline Banerjee was still detecting 'welcome signs of renewed critical interest' in a writer 'more relevant than ever to us today'.[4] But such claims seem merely wistful. Two years later, in 2014, in a piece for *The Guardian* headed 'Literary Hero to Zero', D. J. Taylor was still able to offer the case of 'the forgotten Victorian titan George Meredith' as an exemplary instance of a lost literary reputation.[5]

Meredith had been a key figure in the distinction that began to emerge in the closing decades of the nineteenth century between general fiction and literary fiction, between the novels that the British public liked to read and the novels that they felt they could congratulate themselves on having read. Meredith, as George Gissing remarked, was 'too difficult for the British public'. 'What good thing is not?' he added. *Diana of the Crossways* was 'Shakespeare in modern English; but, mind you, to be read twice, or, if need be, thrice'.[6] Once novels had to be read two or three times before they could be understood they might safely be admitted to the syllabus. That is how it seemed at least at the beginning of the twentieth century. By the beginning of the twenty-first the syllabus had changed. Students of Victorian literature were far more likely to be invited to read novels by Wilkie Collins or Mary Braddon or Bram Stoker or Rider Haggard than any novel by George Meredith. Meredith would have been doubly pained.

---

[3] Judith Wilt, *The Readable People of George Meredith* (Princeton: Princeton University Press, 1975), 3; Gillian Beer, *Meredith: A Change of Masks: A Study of the Novels*; *Meredith Now: Some Critical Essays*, ed. Ian Fletcher (London: Routledge and Kegan Paul, 1971); *Meredith: The Critical Heritage*, ed. Ioan Williams (London: Routledge and Kegan Paul, 1971). Judith Wilt might also have mentioned V. S. Pritchett, *George Meredith and English Comedy* (London: Chatto and Windus, 1970).

[4] Banerjee, *George Meredith*, 4.

[5] https://www.theguardian.com/books/2014/may/10/literary-reputations-zero-hero-dj-taylor.

[6] Coustillas, 2, 253 and 257.

In the 1860s Arthur, his eldest child, had developed a taste for sensation novels. He had not thought it a promising sign.

D. J. Taylor's example of a modern writer who has suffered a decline in reputation almost as catastrophic as Meredith's is Iris Murdoch, but when I ask myself what warrants attention to a writer so unfashionable as George Meredith it is one of Iris Murdoch's philosophical essays that I turn to. In 'The Idea of Perfection' Murdoch takes the case of a mother who has thought of her daughter-in-law slightingly, as a vulgar, silly young woman, but over the years learns, by dint of paying her patient attention, to regard her more generously, and succeeds at last in arriving at a proper appreciation of her daughter-in-law's real virtues.[7] Iris Murdoch is pursuing a disagreement with her friend Stuart Hampshire. She supposes that throughout this process the mother-in-law's behaviour is unchanged. It is from the first and always remains impeccable. Her change of attitude has not resulted in any change in the way that she acts, and yet, Murdoch argues, the purely mental activity in which she has been engaged ought properly to be thought of as an ethical achievement. My point is simpler. Students of literature have a responsibility patiently to attend to the work of significant writers even, perhaps especially, when they have become unfashionable. They are under an obligation to do so, and the obligation, like the obligation that the woman in Iris Murdoch's essay recognises to her daughter-in-law, is at bottom ethical.

Literary biography may of course be a way of escaping rather than accepting that obligation. In his 1977 biography of Meredith David Williams announced his intention to 'hive off Meredith's voluminous writings' into two chapters in order to minimise the risk that attention to the books might distract from the life.[8] A reviewer of a more recent biography went further. He judged Meredith's novels 'almost unreadable' but took the view that 'even if we were to abandon the work completely, Meredith the man would still be well worth reading about'.[9] But it is hard to see why the lives of writers, so much of which, as Meredith was given to

---

[7] 'The Idea of Perfection' is the first essay in Iris Murdoch's *The Sovereignty of Good over Other Concepts* (London: Routledge and Kegan Paul, 1970).

[8] See David Williams, *George Meredith: His Life and Lost Love* (London: Hamish Hamilton, 1977). The best biography of Meredith is still Lionel Stevenson's *The Ordeal of George Meredith*.

[9] https://www.telegraph.co.uk/culture/4718402/Eminently-unreadable.html. The book under review was Mervyn Jones's *The Amazing Victorian: A Life of George Meredith* (London: Constable, 1999).

complaining, is spent at their desks, should be of much interest if the life the writers lived sheds no light on the books that they wrote. This is not a biography addressed to those willing to be interested in everything about Meredith apart from the books that he wrote. It is a biography in which the books take centre stage. It is written on the principle that the only events in Meredith's life worth recording are the events out of which he wrote his novels and his poems.

Meredith's was a long life. He was 81 when he died on May 18, 1909, but the life with which I am concerned ended 45 years earlier, on September 20, 1864, on the day that Meredith married his second wife. By then he was 36, and the events that had made him the man he was were behind him: the upbringing in Portsmouth as the son of a tailor, the marriage to the beautiful widowed daughter of Thomas Love Peacock, his humiliation when she left him for the painter, Henry Wallis, his ruthless decision to remove his son from his wife's care, and the years when he cultivated a love for his son so fierce and exclusive that it left no room, or so he believed, for the love of a woman. Meredith was content in his second marriage and he had two more children. He was saddened when his second wife died in 1885 after two unsuccessful operations for cancer, but his life after her death did not greatly change. It was, from the time he remarried, a writer's life, a life lived, as he described it to an old friend, between his pen and his books. He published his last novel, *The Amazing Marriage*, in 1895, and after that he confined himself to poems, but all through that long life of his he found all the materials that he needed in the events of his early life, in the events of his first thirty-six years. I examine that early life in my central chapters. In the second chapter I focus on Meredith's boyhood, in the third and fourth on his first marriage and in the sixth on his troubled relationship with Arthur Meredith, his son by that marriage, but in each case my interest is not so much in what really happened, as in how Meredith recalled and re-worked those events in novels and in poems sometimes written decades afterwards. I present these chapters in a roughly chronological order, but here and throughout the book is organised thematically. In the first chapter I point out Meredith's contradictory impulses to confess and conceal that organise the whole book. In the central chapters I treat the topics that gave later nineteenth-century novelists their principal themes. The second focuses on class. In the third and fourth I explore what Henry James calls 'the great relation', the relationship between men and women, and in the sixth I examine parenthood. In the fifth chapter I reflect on novelists as novel readers. In the seventh I examine Meredith's title to be regarded as one of the leading male feminists of the nineteenth century, the characteristic of his work on which claims for his contemporary relevance most often rest.

When Meredith described himself as living between his pen and his books, he made it clear that the two most important activities for him were writing and reading. An oddity of my account of Meredith is that I pay almost as much attention to the books Meredith read as to the books that he wrote. I do so in part because I want to offer my book not just as a portrait of Meredith but as a portrait of the novel in the closing decades of the nineteenth century. But it is not just that. Meredith was a great reader. He has claims to have read more books, and more novels in particular, than any other Victorian novelist. But all of the novelists of his generation were novel readers. They were, as I put it in the title of my fifth chapter, novel people. Meredith was born in 1828. *The Pickwick Papers* began appearing in monthly instalments when he was eight years old. He grew up reading novels, and so did all of his contemporaries. I argue in my fifth chapter that this was one of the things that made novelists of his generation different from Dickens and all the novelists that had come before them. They were novelists formed as much by the novels that they had read as by the experiences that they had undergone. In my final chapter I focus on Meredith, the writer, and in particular on the question of why he should have chosen to cultivate a style of such extreme idiosyncrasy.

J. B. Priestley long ago pointed out that Meredith confronts us with a contradiction. He was an unusually secretive man, and yet he was also a man willing to exploit in his novels his own family history without feeling constrained even by 'the customary reticences of fiction'.[10] That contradiction in Meredith is the topic of my first chapter, but it is, I want to add, no more than an extreme instance of a cast of mind that novelists and novel readers had in common. Novels offered them the opportunity to find themselves, and also, just as valuably, the opportunity to escape from themselves, and in the novels that meant most to them those two ambitions were in unusually close relationship. In Meredith's very first novel, for instance, Meredith, the son of a snip, brought up above his father's tailoring shop at 73, the High Street, Portsmouth, takes as his hero the son and heir of 'Sir Austin Absworthy Bearne Feverel, Baronet, of Raynham Abbey, in a certain Western county folding Thames'. Imaginatively if not

---

[10] Priestley, 2.

geographically Raynham Abbey and Portsmouth High Street are very far apart. But it soon emerges that the Baronet's 'somewhat lamentable history' rather closely follows Meredith's own. Sir Austin 'had a wife, and he had a friend'. Sir Austin's friend was 'a sort of poet' rather than a sort of painter,[11] but the outcome for both men is the same, and Sir Austin is allowed to feel all the shame and bitterness that Meredith felt when his first wife left him for another man. Sir Austin is an invention that allows Meredith at once to turn his back on his own shamefully undistinguished family origins and to confront with unusual candour the still more shameful history of the breakdown of his own first marriage.

Meredith, although he pretended otherwise, clearly rather liked having his photograph taken. He preferred to be taken in profile, rightly persuaded that his profile, like Nevil Beauchamp's in his novel *Beauchamp's Career*, 'suggested an arrow-head in the upflight'.[12] My own portrait of Meredith is, in comparison with those photographs, likely to strike the reader as unflattering. The Meredith that emerges is a self-absorbed man, and a man capable of treating those closest to him cruelly, but he was also a man who showed an unusual capacity to see himself for what he was. There is no criticism that one might be inclined to make of Meredith that he has not already made of himself, and made with a harshness that even the most unsympathetic commentator would struggle to match. That is not only Meredith's most striking virtue, it is also the ability on which his special contribution to English literature depends. He is the first exponent in the English novel of 'alteregoism' (the coinage is his own)[13]: that is, he has the rare ability to write about himself as if he were another person. It is a technique that, as I suggest in Chap. 5, he may have learned from his reading of Stendhal, and it is the technique that made it possible for him to write *Modern Love*, his greatest poem, and *The Egoist*, his most finished novel.

For the *Telegraph* reviewer, Meredith's work remains 'almost unreadable', and the verdict cannot be dismissed as the judgement of a lazy or an inexperienced reader. No one who has read his *Companion to Victorian Fiction* can doubt John Sutherland's appetite for nineteenth-century novels, but even he is defeated by 'the peculiar unreadability of George

---

[11] *The Ordeal of Richard Feverel*, chapter 1.
[12] *Beauchamp's Career*, chapter 26.
[13] In *The Tragic Comedians*, chapter 4.

Meredith'.[14] It is why in my final chapter I do not, like most biographers, trace the last years of my subject, the years that brought him to his death. I turn instead to Meredith's style. It is a style that Meredith's contemporaries were almost as likely to object to as readers are today. Still more remarkably, it is a style that Meredith very often objected to himself. His novels are punctuated by abrasive attacks on the verbal tics that characterise Meredithian prose. But, I will argue, the value of Meredith's novels is not separable from the prose in which they are written. The contortions of the prose reveal Meredith's pained sense that he was writing for a novel-reading public unfit or unwilling to appreciate the kind of novels that he wanted to write. But that was a feeling that he shared with contemporaries such as Hardy and James who remain much more widely read than he is. His prose is more contorted than theirs because his uneasy relationship with the reading public was supplemented by a still more uneasy relationship with himself.

Meredith has been fortunate in his admirers. J. B. Priestley, Siegfried Sassoon[15] and V. S. Pritchett have written lively introductions to his work. Gillian Beer and Judith Wilt, both exceptionally fine literary critics, have produced more specialised studies. But Meredith's work, like Meredith himself, remains difficult to like. It is why Iris Murdoch's essay, 'The Idea of Perfection', is so important to me. The mother-in-law's achievement in learning to appreciate the virtues of the young woman with whom she had at first found herself so completely out of sympathy is exactly proportionate to the difficulty that she experienced in struggling to discard her first impressions and arrive at a proper appreciation of her daughter-in-law's merits. Meredith as a man demands of us a similar exercise of patience, and so too do his books. My only ambition is to persuade my reader that such an effort might be worthwhile.

Glasgow, UK   Richard Cronin

[14] See John Sutherland, 'A Revered Corpse: The Peculiar Unreadability of George Meredith', *Times Literary Supplement*, September 5, 1997, p. 5.
[15] Siegfried Sassoon, *Meredith* (London: Constable, 1948).

CONTENTS

ABBREVIATIONS

Banerjee   Jacqueline Banerjee, *George Meredith*
                      (Tavistock, Devon: Northcote House,
                      2012)

Bartlett   *The Poems of George Meredith*, ed. Phyllis
                      B. Bartlett, 2 vols (New Haven and
                      London: Yale University Press, 1978)

Bibliography   Maurice Buxton Forman, *A Bibliography of
                      the Writings in Prose and Verse of George
                      Meredith* (Edinburgh: Bibliographical
                      Society, 1922)

Butcher   Lady Butcher, *Memories of George
                      Meredith, O. M.* (London: Constable,
                      1919)

Clodd   Edward Clodd, *Memories* (London:
                      Putnam, 1916)

Coustillas   Pierre Coustillas, *The Heroic Life of George
                      Gissing*, 3 vols (London: Pickering and
                      Chatto, 2011)

Edel   Leon Edel, *Henry James: A Life* (London:
                      Collins, 1987)

Ellis   S. M. Ellis, *George Meredith: His Life and
                      Friends in Relation to His Work* (London:
                      Grant Richards, 1920)

Hammerton   J. A. Hammerton, *George Meredith: His
                      Life and Art in Anecdote and Criticism*
                      (Edinburgh: J. Grant, 1911)

Hardman   *A Mid-Victorian Pepys: The Letters and Memoirs of Sir William Hardman, M. A., F. R. G. S.*, ed. S. M. Ellis, revised second edition (London: Cecil Palmer, 1928)

Hyndman   H. M. Hyndman, *The Record of an Adventurous Life* (London: Macmillan, 1911)

Johnson   Diane Johnson, *The True History of the First Mrs Meredith and Other Lesser Lives* (New York: Alfred A. Knopf, 1972)

Le Gallienne   Richard Le Gallienne, *The Romantic 90s* (London: Doubleday, Page and Co., 1925)

Letters   *The Letters of George Meredith*, ed. C. L. Cline, 3 vols (Oxford: Clarendon Press, 1970)

Letters of Henry James   *The Letters of Henry James*, ed. Leon Edel, 4 volumes (London: Macmillan, 1974–84)

Letters of Mary Wollstonecraft Shelley   *The Letters of Mary Wollstonecraft Shelley*, ed. Betty T. Bennett, 3 vols (Baltimore and London; Johns Hopkins University Press, 1983)

Nicoll   W. Robertson Nicoll, *A Bookman's Letters* (London: Hodder and Stoughton, 1915)

Notebooks   *Notebooks of George Meredith*, ed. Gillian Beer and Margaret Harris (Salzburg: Salzburg Studies in English Literature, 1983)

Priestley   J. B. Priestley, *George Meredith* (London: Macmillan 1926)

Rousseau   John Morley, *Rousseau*, 2 vols (London: Chapman and Hall, 1873)

Sencourt   Robert Sencourt, *The Life of George Meredith* (New York: Charles Scribner, 1929)

Shaheen   *Selected Letters of George Meredith*, ed. Mohammad Shaheen (Houndmills, Basingstoke: Macmillan, 1997)

Squire   J. C. Squire, *Life and Letters* (London: Hodder and Stoughton, 1920)

Stevenson   Lionel Stevenson, *The Ordeal of George Meredith* (New York: Charles Scribner's Sons, 1953)

Wharton   Edith Wharton, *A Backward Glance* (New York: Appleton-Century, 1934)

CHAPTER 1

Meredith and the Personal

CONCEALING

Meredith hated the thought that he might become the subject of a biography. 'Horribly will I haunt the man who writes memoir of me,'[1] he wrote to Edward Clodd, the agnostic and evolutionist. It was a pointed threat. At the time Clodd was engaged in a biography of a fellow agnostic and evolutionist, the novelist Grant Allen. Meredith was 71 by then and already knew that the biography he dreaded was inevitable. A year later, in 1900, he explained to a young correspondent that he was careful to write only 'blunt letters', letters that gave away little of himself, as a shield against 'the memoir or biography few can now escape'.[2] I doubt if he was acting simply out of policy. Even when he was writing to close friends, even when he was being bawdy or loving, Meredith's letters remain oddly impersonal. The Egoist, Sir Willoughby Patterne, acknowledges, 'I am not completely myself in my letters.'[3] Meredith might have said the same. His letters suggest a man who was never at his ease when what he was supposed to be doing was being himself. But Meredith was certainly sincere in his wish to deter biographers, and Clodd at least was deterred. He did

[1] *Letters*, 3, 1342.
[2] *Letters*, 3, 1356.
[3] *The Egoist*, chapter 7.

© The Author(s) 2019
R. Cronin, *George Meredith*,
https://doi.org/10.1007/978-3-030-32448-3_1

not attempt a biography of Meredith. He confined himself to a brief article in the *Fortnightly Review*, 'George Meredith: Some Recollections',[4] published a few weeks after Meredith died.

Meredith's anxiety was longstanding. In 1891 the journalist Clement Shorter had suggested that he might include a chronology of Meredith's life and writings as a preface to a new edition of his novel, *The Tragic Comedians*. Meredith was appalled. 'This "Chronology" must be quashed,' he wrote: 'Here is the citation of pieces of work which I wish to forget and see forgotten. And personal matter too!' 'There is no excuse', he insisted, 'for heading the book with such stuff.'[5] In 1901 he was astonished by rumours that he was writing his own life: 'I see in the papers that I am writing an autobiography. I would as soon think of composing a treatise on the origin of Humpty-Dumpty.'[6] He was chief reader for the publishing firm of Chapman and Hall, and in 1899, when the manuscript of Janet Ross's autobiography, *Early Days Recalled*, was submitted to him, he grudgingly recommended publication. Forty years before, in 1859, while he was writing *Evan Harrington*, Meredith had been in love with Janet Ross, then Janet Duff Gordon, or imagined that he was. But the letter that he wrote to her was less than encouraging:

> It is the kind of book done by volatile German ladies. You will be discreeter, and yet the book must necessarily be of that kind of skeleton-cupboard and desk-drawer prattle; the artless prattler archly appealing to a gracious audience and picking up her bouquets. She becomes a figurante.[7]

A figurante was a ballet dancer, a woman whose art consisted in an indecorous display of her own body to the public gaze. Meredith sharply refused Janet Ross's permission to make use of his own letters to her. They were 'entirely private communications; there is nothing in them for the public'.[8] Ten years later, Edward Clodd asked him whether he had kept any letters from Grant Allen that might be of use to him as Allen's biographer, and Meredith responded just as sharply: 'In this matter of letters I treat my friends as I wish they should treat me and reserve not one for the public maw.'[9]

[4] *Fortnightly Review*, 86 (July 1909), 19–31. Clodd recycled the material in his *Memories*. Clodd's *Grant Allen: A Memoir* was published by Grant Richards in 1900.

[5] *Letters*, 2, 1048.

[6] *Letters*, 3, 1411.

[7] *Letters*, 2, 981.

[8] *Letters*, 2, 995.

[9] *Letters*, 3, 1342.

He brusquely rebuffed correspondents who wrote asking for personal information. 'I cannot refer you to any published account of the personal me,' he told one of them.[10] With a German critic who planned to write a book about him he was still more emphatic, 'All that is needed to say of me should be found in *Men of the Times*. I do not minister to gossip.'[11] Meredith does not specify which edition of *Men of the Time* he has in mind, but all editions are uninformative. The 1879 edition, for example, describes him as a 'novelist, born in Hampshire about 1828, and educated partly in Germany'. He was 'brought up to the law, which he quitted for literature'. There follows a list of his publications, pretty accurate except that it includes *Mary Bertrand*, a novel of 1860 the author of which was a Francis Meredith (no relation).[12] Entries on other writers are almost as terse, but the entry on Meredith is exceptional in that it makes no reference at all to his parentage or to his marriages.

Meredith was reminding his German admirer somewhat tartly to confine her interest to the books. George Gissing, a novelist that Meredith has a claim to have discovered, responded similarly to requests for information about his life: 'My work is my autobiography, which those may read who care to do so.'[13] Gissing's was a view that Meredith often took himself:

> Our books contain the best of us. I hold that the public has little to do with what is outside the printed matter beyond hearing that the writer is reputedly a good citizen.[14]

The tone is a little lofty, but it is easy to sympathise with the sentiment. Meredith took it very far, and maintained it to the very end. Richard H. P. Curle wrote to him after agreeing to contribute the entry for Meredith in Alfred Miles's splendid anthology *The Poets and Poetry of the Nineteenth Century*. Each poet's work was represented by a selection of characteristic poems preceded by a brief biographical introduction. It was the introduction that worried Meredith: 'I should counsel you to keep from anything personal to me—my portrait, the walk up hill to see the dawn and look over the valley, etc. etc. When I read that form of eulogy I am not

---

[10] *Letters*, 3, 1255.

[11] *Letters*, 3, 1314.

[12] *Men of the Time: A Dictionary of Contemporaries, containing biographical notices of eminent characters of both sexes*, 10th edn (London: Routledge, 1879), 704.

[13] Coustillas, 3, 243.

[14] *Letters*, 3, 1255.

impressed.'[15] Most men would allow their habits of rising early and taking a walk up Box Hill to be put before the public without protest, but not Meredith. He was 77 when he wrote to Curle, and he had kept up that reluctance to allow the public access to his private life for more than 50 years. It was not a foible peculiar to him. Henry James expressed his 'utter and absolute abhorrence' of any attempted biography. He issued 'a curse no less explicit than Shakespeare's own on any such as try to move my bones', and stipulated that all his private papers should be burnt: 'Then, the pale forewarned victim, with every track covered, every paper burnt and every letter unanswered, will, in the tower of art, the invulnerable granite, stand, without a sally, the siege of all the years.'[16] Thomas Hardy was more pragmatic. Aware that he could not prohibit biographers he decided to forestall them. The studiously reticent biography published under the name of Florence Hardy, his second wife, had been almost all of it dictated by Hardy himself. But Meredith's reticence was more extreme than James's or Hardy's.

The first biographer to break Meredith's embargo, S. M. Ellis, published *George Meredith: His Life and Friends in Relation to His Work* in 1920, 11 years after Meredith's death. Ellis was a close relation. The youngest of Meredith's aunts, Catherine, had married Samuel Burdon Ellis of the Royal Marines. S. M. Ellis was their grandson, which makes him Meredith's second cousin. Ellis begins with a dramatic flourish: 'During his lifetime an impenetrable veil of reticence, and, in consequence, of mystery also, hid the facts of George Meredith's origin and family history and his own early days from public knowledge.'[17] Meredith had been born in February 1828, the son of a tailor, a naval outfitter, Augustus Urmston Meredith, who lived above the shop at 73, Portsmouth High Street, and he was ashamed of it. His 'tailoring parentage was', according to W. S. Blunt, 'the secret trouble of his life'.[18] His mother died when he was only five. Then, when he was 21, he married Mary Ellen Nicolls, the daughter of Thomas Love Peacock and the widow of Captain Edward Nicolls of the Royal Navy. Eight years later, in 1857, four years after the

[15] *Letters*, 3, 1512.
[16] Edel, 560–1.
[17] Ellis, 13.
[18] W. S. Blunt, *My Diaries: Being a Personal Narrative of Events 1888–1914*, 2 vols (London: Martin Secker, 1919–20), 2, 246. Blunt makes the suggestion on the authority of Wilfred Meynell, the husband of the poet Alice Meynell. The Meynells were friends of Meredith.

birth of their son Arthur, his wife left him. She was pregnant by the painter, Henry Wallis. Her second son was born in April the following year. By then Meredith had removed Arthur from her care. He seems to have decided that his wife should never be permitted to see her son again. He relented only in the autumn of 1861, when his wife was dying of Bright's Disease. It was not just chance that brought Humpty Dumpty to Meredith's mind when he wanted to explain how unlikely it would be for him to write an autobiography. He and Humpty had something in common. Both of them had a great fall that left them shattered, and Meredith found it just as impossible as Humpty to put his pieces together again.

Meredith decided very early that the best way of coping with his past was to turn his back on it. As he went through life he rolled up his past behind him. In 1849, just before Meredith married, his father emigrated to South Africa, where he set up a tailoring business in Adderley Street in Cape Town. For years Meredith lost all contact with him. His father did not return to England until 1863, by which time he had saved enough to give up business. He and his second wife took a house in Southsea, not far from Portsmouth where he had been born. But there was no renewal of intimacy with his son. In October 1870 Meredith mentioned in a letter to his own son, Arthur, that he had called on 'your Grandpa Meredith'.[19] He had dropped in while on his way to stay with his friend Captain Maxse. It was evidently a rare visit, although when his father died, on June 18, 1876, Meredith attended the funeral. Meredith broke off relations with his wife still more emphatically. After she left him in 1857 he seems never to have seen her again. He allowed their son to visit her in her last illness but did not go with him. After he removed Arthur from his mother, he took the boy's care upon himself. His friends were impressed by the intensity of his devotion. But it did not last. When Arthur was 13 Meredith sent him away to school in Switzerland. Two years later in 1869 he escorted his son who was just turned 16 to Stuttgart where he enrolled him in the gymnasium, the town's grammar school, and after that he did not see Arthur again for ten years. Arthur died in 1890 without ever quite repairing his relationship with his father.

In 1864, shortly after Meredith had remarried, he reassured an old friend, William Hardman, that a man who had entered 'a new state' should not '(short of Beatitude) cast off his byegone self utterly',[20] but all through his life Meredith cast off bygone selves more ruthlessly than most of us.

[19] *Letters*, 1, 430.
[20] *Letters*, 1, 298.

Like Edward Blancove in his novel *Rhoda Fleming* his instinct was 'to shut the past behind a brazen gate'.[21] Almost five years later, he wrote to his second wife while he was on a visit to Hardman. He wanted to tell his wife that he was missing her, but he expressed the thought oddly: 'Unless I move on I regret what I have left.'[22] The remark seems too pregnant for the occasion, as if Meredith were revealing more of himself than he intended. Meredith's *Diana of the Crossways* takes as her second husband Thomas Redworth. Redworth is not at all like Meredith. He is a businessman who has made a fortune in railway speculation, but he retains at least one point of similarity with the novelist who created him: 'He belonged to the class of his countrymen who have a dungeon-vault for feelings that should not be suffered to cry abroad, and into this oubliette he cast them, letting them feed as they might, or perish.'[23] Captain Kirby, the heroine's father in Meredith's last novel, *The Amazing Marriage* speaks for the novelist when he makes it a principle not to brood lingeringly on the past. His daughter remembers one of his sayings: '*No regrets,* her father had said; *they unman the heart we want for tomorrow.*'[24] Captain Kirby, author of *Maxims for Men,* is an authority on masculinity, and real men, it seems, keep their gaze fixed on the future.

Meredith was a determined, even a desperate optimist. It was, he announced to the husband of the poet Alice Meynell, just two months before he died, an article of faith: 'my religion of life is always to be cheerful.'[25] He told Edmund Gosse in 1905, when he was laid up after a fall, that he felt himself 'afflicted' by Thomas Hardy's pessimism, by his 'twilight view of life',[26] and Gosse wrote to Hardy to ask whether he had himself not been 'saddened' by Meredith's 'optimism':

> There is something to me almost flighty in his cheerfulness. You know he has broken his ankle? He appears to be quite cheerful about that too. What a very curious thing temperament is there seems no reason at all why G. M. should be so happy, and in some irrational way one almost resents it.[27]

---

[21] *Rhoda Fleming*, chapter 16.

[22] *Letters*, 1, 385.

[23] *Diana of the Crossways*, chapter 6.

[24] *The Amazing Marriage*, chapter 46.

[25] *Letters*, 3, 1684.

[26] *Letters*, 3, 1529.

[27] Evan Charteris, *Life and Letters of Sir Edmund Gosse* (London; Heinemann, 1931), p. 297.

That temperament, the determined cheerfulness, became a central plank of what Meredith and the more earnest of his disciples thought of as his philosophy. In 1888 Meredith was visited by one of his American admirers, the journalist William Morton Fullerton, who was incautious enough to suggest that the autumn leaves were 'suggestive of the dying year':

Mr Meredith had no place for sentimentality of that sort. What was there in the thought of the passing years that should be sad? It was life, more life and fuller, for which men should be ever seeking, to be sure. But life was not to be had by whining into a past that had turned tail and fled. Rather, men must look up bravely, planted on the honest present, to the problems of the pressing future, never content to rest in a fool's paradise, but always courting activity, and making use of moments as they came, so bravely, so well, that such moments would be quite transformed into the energy of character, not left behind to haunt like sloughed chrysalises of vanished butterfly hopes and impulses.[28]

But even as Fullerton recalls the thought, the 'pressing future' is made to seem insubstantial in comparison with the 'sloughed chrysalises of vanished butterfly hopes' that 'haunt' the man who does not resolutely turn his back on them (the metaphor is surely Meredith's rather than Fullerton's). It leaves one wondering how far Meredith's optimism was a defence mechanism. Perhaps he resembled his own Victor Radnor, the central character in *One of Our Conquerors*, who tries to preserve an appearance of cheerfulness because it is his pride to appear 'woundless and scarless, a shining surface, like pure health's, in the sight of men'.[29] Only the severely wounded and the deeply scarred are likely to entertain any such ambition. One especially perceptive observer recognised Meredith's public manner as turning to the world just the same kind of shining surface that Meredith credited to Victor Radnor. In June 1893 Henry James remarked, 'Meredith I saw three months ago—with his charming *accueil*, his impenetrable shining scales, and the (to me) general mystery of his perversity.'[30]

[28] From Fullerton's report of the visit in the *Boston Advertiser*, December 17, 1888, as quoted in Hammerton, 60.
[29] *One of Our Conquerors*, chapter 12.
[30] *Letters of Henry James*, 3, 415.

The religion of cheerfulness and the determination to turn his back on the past informed Meredith's aesthetic sense too. Meredith, like Wordsworth, was a 'lover of the meadows and the woods / And mountains; and of all that we behold / From this green earth'. But the natural world offered Wordsworth a 'picture of the mind'. Meredith did not turn to nature in search of an access of self-consciousness, but in quest of an escape from it. For Wordsworth, experience and memory are always intimately connected, and when the experience is of nature they become all but inseparable. But Meredith went to nature in flight from painful recollections. He liked windy days, days when the branches bent and the clouds scudded across the sky. He enjoyed 'Hard Weather', as he described it in the title of one of his poems, because the 'savage whirr' of the wind taught the salutary lesson that 'contention is the vital force'. More than that, the wind, 'The South-Wester' for example, gave out an invitation to live in the present: it had the power to 'make evanescence permanent'. By discountenancing softer feelings the natural world offered a chastening rebuke to those inclined to self-pity. As he puts it in a poem robustly entitled 'Whimper of Sympathy', 'All round we find cold Nature slight / The feelings of the totter-kneed.' The wind in its onward rush teaches, like the song of 'The Thrush in February', 'the rapture of the forward view'. In Meredith's nature poems an urgent appeal to embrace the future that derives from Shelley is oddly compounded with a brisk, sometimes brutal, dismissal of the gentler feelings that comes from Thomas Carlyle. Meredith's thrush singing in February may have given Hardy a clue for his 'Darkling Thrush', but Hardy's thrush would never, like Meredith's, have come out as an outspoken advocate for rearmament, teaching a proper scorn of 'the ventral dream of peace'.[31]

Meredith's nature poems now seem not so much weighted as weighed down by his philosophy, and 'The Woods of Westermain' is more heavily weighed down than most, which is why the poem is no longer as admired as it once was.[32] To enter the woods is to find a world of creatures, of 'mossy-footed squirrels' and 'yaffles' (green woodpeckers) skimming 'on a chuckle', each of which has 'business of his own'. Even the plants, the

[31] 'Hard Weather', 'The South-Wester' and 'The Thrush in February' were published in *A Reading of Earth* (1888); 'Whimper of Sympathy' in *Ballads and Poems of Tragic Life* (1887).
[32] 'The Woods of Westermain' was the opening poem in *Poems and Lyrics of the Joy of Earth* (1883).

wild strawberry for instance, are bent on their own purposes. The woods, according to Meredith, have important lessons to teach: they have the power to 'wed the thought and felt'. But their real value seems more personal. The animals and plants are too intent on their own business to be concerned with his. The woods are an enchanted space because they free those who enter them from the intrusive, captious scrutiny to which, outside them, everyone is subjected by his neighbours. In the world outside the woods there are a 'thousand eyeballs under hoods' from which the trees offer temporary and precarious respite. In the woods, introspection, usually so painful a business, is freed from its horrors. In the woods light and darkness coexist, but the darkness of the woods is a darkness that can be embraced: 'You must love the light so well / That no darkness will seem fell.' The woods offer a world in which the self has no need to bruise itself against other selves. They make available a world which is perfect because it is a world of one, a place where 'Love, the sole permitted, sings / Sovereignly of ME and I'. It is an enchanted place, and one condition of the enchantment is that it is a place freed from the past, a place which only exists in the present tense in which almost the whole of the poem is written. The natural world offered Meredith an escape from the past, and still more importantly it offered him an escape from his own past self. Wordsworth turned to nature to find himself, and Meredith went in search of what he calls in 'The Lark Ascending' 'self-forgetfulness divine'.[33]

Meredith did not only set about ridding himself of the past by escaping into the ever-present of the lark's song and of lyric poetry. He also went to work more practically. C. L. Cline had no need to castigate himself for so flagrantly flouting Meredith's wishes by publishing his letters because two volumes of letters had already been published in 1912, just three years after Meredith's death, by Will Meredith, his son from his second marriage.[34] But the letters are unrevealing. Only 52 of the 2600 letters Cline collected were written before Meredith turned 30 and his first wife left him for Henry Wallis, and very few have come to light since then.[35] There are more than 260 surviving letters from the period between 1858 and September 20, 1864, when Meredith remarried, but the great bulk of the

[33] 'The Lark Ascending' like 'The Woods of Westermain' was published in *Poems and Lyrics of the Joy of Earth* (1883).

[34] *Letters of George Meredith, collected and edited by his son* (London: Constable, 1912).

[35] In his *Selected Letters of George Meredith*, Mohammad Shaheen includes just six letters unpublished by Cline written in this period.

surviving letters were written in the second half of Meredith's life, the period during which he wrote most of his novels and poems. Meredith's later life, the period in which at long last he became a literary celebrity, was also the period in which nothing much happened to him. He was contented in his second marriage, and his new wife gave him two more children. On September 17, 1885, Marie Meredith died. Meredith mourned her and wrote two poems in her memory, but after her death his way of life was not much different. He took holidays, and visited friends more often, and invited them to dine with him at Flint Cottage on Box Hill, the house that he moved into with Marie late in 1867 and the house that he was to occupy for the rest of his life.

The life he lived in all those years was a writer's life, the bulk of it spent at his desk. As early as 1861, three years before his second marriage, he wrote to Janet Ross, 'The truth is, my experiences are all mental—I see nothing of the world, and what I have to say goes into my books.'[36] As the years passed, and especially after he was widowed for the second time, he came more and more to live in his own head. 'I go nowhere, do nothing but read and write', he wrote in 1889, 'with thoughts of friends, and hopes amounting to prayers, that in their daily pecking at the pleasures of London, they will not take up too much of the dust which chokes.'[37] In 1899 Meredith wrote in the same vein to Frederick Maxse, his best friend. Maxse was intimate with Georges Clemenceau, and Meredith asks about the Dreyfus affair in which Maxse and Clemenceau were both deeply involved, but his own life, he acknowledges, was very different: 'I have no news, have declined all invitations, and live between my pen and my books, in wait for the final tap on the head—our one certainty in life.'[38] In the event, it was Maxse who was tapped on the head first, just the following year, in 1900. Meredith lived on. After Maxse's death his closest friend was John Morley, but Meredith did not see much of him in his last years. Morley was a busy man, a member of cabinet in successive Liberal administrations, first as Chief Secretary for Ireland, and then from 1905 as Secretary of State for India. Meredith's life was much less active. By 1907 his literary career was all but over. 'I write some little verses,' he told Morley, 'and, the thing done, confess it to be only another form of

---

[36] *Letters*, 1, 79.
[37] *Letters*, 2, 951.
[38] *Letters*, 3, 1335–6.

idleness.'[39] Morley, like Meredith, had achieved literary fame: he was Gladstone's great biographer. But his active, public life had been very different from Meredith's. 'I have lived all my time in imagination,' Meredith told Morley, and the purely imaginative life he had lived had left him, so close to its end, with 'an unsatisfied yearning'.[40]

Meredith's biographer is confronted with an odd paradox. In the period when Meredith's life was of interest, there are almost no records of it. When he remarried in September 1864 his life, the life out of which he wrote his novels and poems, came to an end. He lived on for almost 45 years, and as he grew older the documentary evidence becomes fuller and fuller. The record of the life becomes rich exactly at the time when there is less and less that it seems worthwhile to record. J. A. Hammerton brought out his *George Meredith: His Life and Art in Anecdote and Criticism* in 1911, just two years after Meredith died. Meredith's career up to 1864 is dealt with in 20 pages that might almost have satisfied Meredith himself by the meagreness of Hammerton's commentary on 'the personal him'. Hammerton notes his marriage to his first wife, Mary Ellen Peacock, and remarks that 'happiness did not characterise their wedded life'. He disposes of that life, of the years in which Meredith and Mary Peacock remained husband and wife, in two sentences, the second of which seems designed to mislead (Meredith and his wife had been married for eight years before they separated):

> In 1860 Mrs. Meredith died. For a great part of the twelve years of their married life she and her husband had lived separately.[41]

Hammerton knew that Meredith would have detested his enterprise, and defends himself on the grounds that 'no man has a right to make a public appeal who is not ready to face the consequences of having awakened interest in himself'. Furthermore, 'all who pretend that the personality of an author is no-one's business but his own are either ignorant or posturing critics.'[42] But Hammerton does remarkably little to satisfy public interest in the young Meredith and still less to conjure up his personality. Things are quite different as Meredith gets older. A single day in his life, February 12, 1908, warrants a whole chapter. It was admittedly Meredith's 80th birthday.

---

[39] *Letters*, 3, 1606.
[40] *Letters*, 3, 1606.
[41] Hammerton, 19.
[42] Hammerton, 1–2.

Meredith always rose early, and on that morning, as on most others, he began the day by climbing Box Hill. He had been a famous walker once, but now he made the ascent in his donkey cart, pulled by Picnic, who was led by Meredith's long-serving manservant, Frank Cole. He followed his usual custom and took with him Sandie, the latest in a sequence of dachshunds. Meredith's daughter Mariette was abroad with her husband and so Frederick Maxse's daughter, Lady Edward Cecil, walked by his side. Maxse himself had been dead for eight years. Meredith's son, Will, and his wife also spent the day with him. Later that morning Clement Shorter and his wife, the poet Dora Sigerson Shorter, arrived with Edward Clodd. They brought with them a congratulatory address, mounted on vellum and bound in dark blue crushed morocco, with Meredith's monogram worked in gold on each corner. The memorandum was signed by 250 distinguished names, some of whom, such as Hardy, Morley and Swinburne, had signed the more modest testimonial presented to Meredith ten years earlier, on the occasion of his 70th birthday. Oddly, the leader of the Tory opposition, Arthur Balfour, signed, but Asquith, the Liberal Prime Minister, did not. Meredith was a Liberal and Asquith was a friend, but Asquith disapproved of Meredith's prose style. Meredith was thanked for the 'example' he had 'set to the world of lofty ideals embodied not only in books but in life'. There was also an address from 14 'American men and women of letters': Henry Adams, Oliver Wendell Holmes, Julia Ward Howe, Charles Eliot Norton and so on. There were dozens of telegrams laid out on the tables in Meredith's cottage, and bouquets of flowers displayed in the hall. Meredith was President of the Society of Authors and in the afternoon a delegation arrived to offer the Society's congratulations. All of these comings and goings were reported and photographed by a gathering of the world's press. Meredith invited some of the reporters inside and allowed himself to be interviewed. The fullest report appeared in the *Telegraph*. 'When a man has climbed the steps of eighty years,' Meredith began, 'he should not use them as a pulpit.' He went on to do just that. 'The great delineator of female character' declared his wholehearted support for the 'Suffragists', but denounced their methods: 'These rowdy scenes!' He approved the bill establishing the Territorial Army passed just a year earlier by his 'dear friend' Viscount Haldane, the Secretary of State for War, but was inclined himself to go further: 'I believe that universal service should be adopted.' He invited the assembled journalists to report that they found him sitting in his chair, and delivering himself 'freely of very Radical sentiments'. But he seems not to have repeated on this occasion his suggestion that marriage should become a ten-year contract renewable only by the agreement of both parties, nor to have given voice to any of his more unorthodox religious opinions. All day long, as the reporter for the *Daily News* noted, crowds of Meredith's admirers made a 'silent pilgrimage' to Box Hill, and 'stood for a minute outside Flint Cottage, registering their tributes in their hearts', unseen by the poet who was busy inside receiving his distinguished visitors. It is the day in all of Meredith's life of which the fullest biographical record has been preserved, and it tells us remarkably little about the writer that all those who visited him that day claimed to admire so much. It leaves one wondering, like Henry James after finishing the first volume of Meredith's *Lord Ormont and His Aminta*, how it could be possible to tell 'the reader less of what the reader needs to know'.[43]

Revealing

The life out of which Meredith wrote his novels and his poems had ended more than 40 years before. It ended on September 20, 1864, when he married Marie Vulliamy, his second wife. After that, as he put it to John Morley in 1907, he lived his life 'in imagination'. Even before he remarried, in 1861, he reported that his experiences were 'all mental', and since then he had spent his time writing and reading, 'between my pen and my books', as he put it to Maxse,[44] and a life spent reading and writing leaves no records, except, of course, for the books that Meredith read and the books that he wrote. Meredith sought to remove all traces of his life before 1858 when his first marriage ended, but in novel after novel all through his life he continued to revisit it. 'We shall never now have an intimate biographical portrait of George Meredith as a young man,' John Sutherland once remarked,[45] which in one sense is true, but there remains the most intimate portrait of all, the portrait that Meredith composed in the novels and poems that he wrote all through that long life of his.

There are 13 novels, not counting the early romances *The Shaving of Shagpat* and *The Legend of Farina* and not counting the unfinished *Celts and Saxons*, and there are seven volumes of poetry. There is the once

[43] *Letters of Henry James*, 3, 485.
[44] *Letters*, 3, 1904.
[45] John Sutherland, 'A Revered Corpse: The Peculiar Unreadability of George Meredith', *Times Literary Supplement*, September 5, 1997, p. 5.

famous lecture, 'On the Idea of Comedy and the Uses of the Comic Spirit', there is an unfinished play, there are short stories, essays and reviews, and there is the journalism, most of which remains uncollected—for years Meredith contributed two articles a week to the *Ipswich Journal*. But despite all those leading articles and the interest in the politics of the day that is just as evident in the novels, the world that Meredith inhabited, as John Bayley once pointed out, remained throughout his long life curiously solipsistic.[46] His writings, even when he pretends to be looking around him, resemble those of Colney Durance, another of Meredith's alter egos, the satiric fabulist of *One of Our Conquerors*. Durance's 'picture of the country is a portrait of himself by the artist'.[47] It is as if all events for him were like the figures of speech that he describes in *Vittoria*: 'all similes followed out are mazes: they bring us back to our own face in the glass.'[48] A character in Meredith's unfinished play, *The Sentimentalists*, remarks, 'a young man sees the index of himself in everything spoken!' If that is the proper measure of youth Meredith stayed a young man all through his long life. He lacked the colossal vanity of Sigismund Alvan in *The Tragic Comedians*, a character closely modelled on the French socialist leader Ferdinand Lassalle, but he addresses his readers in rather the same manner. When Alvan, who has retained into late middle age his reputation as a philanderer, speaks to a young woman, 'he slid off to some chance bit of likeness to himself in every subject he discussed with her'.[49] Meredith was acutely aware of the same tendency in himself, ruefully noting it in an early notebook: 'You see, we live so much with ourselves some degree of egotism is necessary to make life endurable.'[50] It seems an unpromising cast of mind for a novelist. As Meredith observed in another notebook: 'The first point in studying others is to be disengaged from ourselves.'[51] So it might seem, but in this as in much else Meredith resembled his own Egoist. Sir Willoughby Patterne is almost wholly self-absorbed, and yet his 'intensity of personal feeling struck so vivid an illumination of mankind at intervals' that he almost succeeds in achieving

[46] See John Bayley's review of *The Poems of George Meredith*, ed. Phyllis Bartlett, *Times Literary Supplement*, October 7, 1978, pp. 1246–8.

[47] *One of Our Conquerors*, chapter 31.

[48] The thought, included in the serialisation of the novel, was omitted when *Vittoria* was published as a book. See *Fortnightly Review*, 6 (September 15, 1866), 322.

[49] *The Tragic Comedians*, chapter 4.

[50] *Notebooks*, 36.

[51] *Notebooks*, 62.

wisdom. Self-absorption, if it is intense enough, becomes an exercise that may conduct by an unlikely route to a knowledge of other people. After all, as Meredith remarked in another notebook entry, 'The book of common humanity lies in our own bosoms.'[52]

Meredith was an unusually self-absorbed man, but he knew as much himself. When his first wife had left him, when her pregnancy by another man could no longer be disguised or denied, Meredith removed his own son from her care, and settled down to write his first novel, *The Ordeal of Richard Feverel*, in which a cuckolded husband, Sir Austin Feverel, devotes himself to the education of his son unaware that all his care will prove unavailing, because the love he showers on the son is in truth only his way of giving vent to his hatred for the wife who has betrayed him. Sir Austin, like Meredith, is an author, his principal work a collection of aphorisms, 'The Pilgrim's Scrip' (Meredith was already an admirer of the aphoristic qualities of his own prose). Sir Austin's closest friend, Lady Blandish, who has ambitions for much of the novel to become his second wife, remembers one of these aphorisms and thinks to herself, 'He must have written it when he had himself for an example—strange man that he is.'[53] Meredith wrote his novels in much the same way. One of Sir Austin's nephews, Adrian Harley, the 'Wise Youth' of the novel, describes 'The Pilgrim's Scrip' as Sir Austin's 'abstract portraiture of his surrounding relatives'.[54] The same description might serve for *The Ordeal of Richard Feverel* and still more obviously for the novel that followed it, *Evan Harrington*. Meredith's father read his son's second novel in Cape Town, as it was being serialised in *Once a Week*. 'I am very sore about it,' he is remembered as saying, 'I am pained beyond expression, as I consider it aimed at myself, and I am sorry to say the writer is my own son.'[55] Meredith's reticence about his family origins was matched by a need just as imperative to publish those origins to the world. His need to conceal himself was matched by a need just as strong to stand revealed.

Meredith's horror of self-revelation, the horror that he shares with Adrian Harley of 'being turned inside-out to the rabble' and having his 'machinery made bare to them',[56] is matched by an equally strong compulsion to offer

[52] *Notebooks*, 36.
[53] *The Ordeal of Richard Feverel*, chapter 44.
[54] *The Ordeal of Richard Feverel*, chapter 34.
[55] Ellis, 137–8. Ellis is quoting the reminiscence of B. T. Lawton, a Cape Town acquaintance of Augustus Meredith's, that was published in the *Cape Times* in 1909.
[56] *The Ordeal of Richard Feverel*, chapter 25.

himself up for public inspection. Even more transparently than he portrays his family in his novels, he offers portraits of himself. He may portray himself sympathetically as Evan Harrington or, in female form, as Diana of the Crossways, but more often the self-portraits are caustic, as in the case of Sir Austin Feverel or the Earl of Fleetwood in *The Amazing Marriage* or, most tellingly of all, in the case of the Egoist, Sir Willoughby Patterne. In Meredith's third novel, *Emilia in England*,[57] there are three socially aspirant young sisters who have as their mortal enemies an all but identical family of three socially aspirant young women. It is as if, Meredith remarks, they need to examine 'their features hideous, but real, in a magnifying mirror'.[58] It is a need that Meredith understood very well. Many of his most interesting characters, even his women, are best thought of as self-portraits. Diana of the Crossways, for example, is like Meredith a novelist, and she speaks for him when she exclaims, '"O self! self! self! are we eternally masking in a domino that reveals your hideous old face when we could be most positive we had escaped you?" Eternally! the desolating answer knelled.'[59] Meredith turned to the novel because the novel offered him a way of looking at himself as if he were someone else. It was the easiest, perhaps the only way in which he could bear to look at himself. He practises in his novels a kind of 'alteregoism'. He uses the word to describe the comfort that Clothilde in *The Tragic Comedians* finds in her relationship with Marko, her naive young fiancé. She finds in him an 'alteregoistic home'. She can contemplate him and think to herself, 'That is like me: that is very like me: that is terribly like: up to the point where the comparison wooed her no longer with an agreeable lure of affinity, but nipped her so shrewdly as to force her to say: "That is he, not I."' He allows her a rare pleasure, 'the probing of herself in another, with the liberty to cease probing as soon as it hurt her'.[60] Meredith was very like Clothilde. He examined his characters as a way of examining himself. He found in his characters what Emilia, the heroine of his third novel, finds when she looks into the mirror, a face 'so familiar in its aspects, so strange when scrutinized studiously'.[61] But he did not, like Clothilde, cease his probing as soon as it began to hurt, which is why he was able to arrive at the last at a bleak, pitiless self-knowledge. It was an achievement of

[57] The novel was later re-titled *Sandra Belloni*.
[58] *Emilia in England*, chapter 1.
[59] *Diana of the Crossways*, chapter 4.
[60] *The Tragic Comedians*, chapter 5.
[61] *Emilia in England*, chapter 38.

a sort, although, as Sir Willoughby Patterne finds, it was not an achievement that allowed him to change the kind of man he was. Sir Willoughby feels on occasion that he 'stood above himself, contemplating his active machinery' only to find that although he could 'partly criticise' that machinery, he was entirely powerless to bring it to a stop.[62] Meredith, to a remarkable degree, succeeded in seeing himself as he was. He could have contemplated unabashed the words written on the forecourt of the temple of Apollo at Delphi, 'Know thyself'. But he found that it was a good deal easier to know himself than to change himself.

Meredith's strongest work in prose and in verse is produced by violently conflicting impulses. He was, as he recognised, far from unusual in this. As he puts it in *Evan Harrington*, 'few feelings are single on this globe, and junction of sentiments need not imply unity in our yeasty compositions.'[63] He insists on looking resolutely to the future and insists on it so strenuously that it at once becomes apparent how strongly he is drawn towards the past. 'Whining into a past that had turned tail and fled' struck him as weak, unmanly, sentimental, and it was also, as he occasionally admitted, something in which he was all too inclined to indulge himself. He was much more than he was always ready to admit like his own Sir Willoughby Patterne, 'a man who lived backward almost as intensely as in the present'.[64] He was Welsh after all—at least he claimed to be—and, as he put it in *The Amazing Marriage*, the Welsh, if they are examined closely, will usually be found to be 'in the heart of the injury done them thirty years back'.[65] Widowed for the second time, and about to turn 60, he wrote as much to his friend, Captain Maxse: 'Living so much alone, as I do, I am at the mercy of the haunting demonry.'[66] His novels are a record of those hauntings and they are also his attempts to exorcise his demons; they are haunted by the ghosts of his father and of his first wife, by the ghost of the son he rejected, and, most pressingly of all, by the ghost of his own past self.

Meredith was in the grip of two powerful urges, the one demanding that he conceal all the most pertinent facts about himself, and the other demanding that he confess them. In this he rather resembles the Earl of

[62] *The Egoist*, chapter 34.
[63] *Evan Harrington*, chapter 3.
[64] *The Egoist*, chapter 3.
[65] *The Amazing Marriage*, chapter 28.
[66] *Letters*, 2, 901.

Fleetwood, the richest young man in all England and the central character of *The Amazing Marriage*, the last novel that Meredith ever published. Fleetwood is as much at the mercy of the 'haunting demonry' as Meredith. 'Did you ever tell any one', he asks Gower Woodseer, his writer friend, a character that Meredith thought of as an affectionate portrait of Robert Louis Stevenson although he is better understood as yet another portrait by Meredith of himself, 'that there's not an act of a man's life lies dead behind him, but it is blessing or cursing him every step he takes?'[67] Meredith admired Olive Schreiner's *Story of an African Farm*. There were things in the book to which he would have responded: 'If you wound the tree in its youth the bark will quickly cover the gash; but when the tree is very old, peeling the bark off, and looking carefully, you will see the scar there still.'[68] Fleetwood has married an Englishwoman of embarrassing origins, a young woman who had been brought up abroad, so distanced from her own country that when she spoke she talked 'the language of early Exercises in English',[69] a woman uncouth in her manners, and, what seems hardest of all for Fleetwood to bear, not conventionally beautiful. He cannot rely on her physical appearance to offer English society a compelling excuse for the eccentricity of his choice. Fleetwood, insulated from public opinion by his fabulous wealth, prides himself on his rugged independence, and, like many men who make similar claims, lives in thrall to the opinions even of those he most despises. On the day of his marriage he escorts his wife to a prizefight. He already thinks of his marriage as a 'freak', and he understands that the proper response to a freak is to exaggerate its freakishness, so that you may 'win a name for yourself as the husband of such a wife; a name in sporting journals and shilling biographies'.[70] But Fleetwood's wife, Carinthia Jane, refuses the role he imagines for her. She is, like several other Meredith heroines, like Emilia in England, for example, terrifyingly indifferent to social appearances and quite immune from irony. Cast off by Fleetwood she goes to live with Gower Woodseer's family and helps out in the family greengrocer's business. Her blindness to conventional social distinctions makes her into a figure out of legend, 'the Whitechapel Countess', and inflicts on Fleetwood

---

[67] *The Amazing Marriage*, chapter 40.
[68] Olive Schreiner, *The Story of an African Farm*, Part 1, chapter 13, (London: Chapman and Hall, 1892), p. 108.
[69] *The Amazing Marriage*, chapter 37.
[70] *The Amazing Marriage*, chapter 15.

'the solitary tortures' that he suffers all through the novel 'behind the pleasant social mask'.[71] Meredith knew the pain of preserving an impassive exterior despite inward agonies. When his older wife abandoned him for an even younger man, he kept his feelings to himself. He never allowed the social mask to slip. It must have been scarcely tolerable for him. Most men (the thought occurs in *The Amazing Marriage*) live like this. They live their lives in armour, so fearful are they of exposing themselves to the world's scorn. That is the Earl of Fleetwood's case, and it was Meredith's, and in both cases the stratagem was unavailing because 'their armour' proved 'more sensitive than their skins'.[72]

When Fleetwood says that no act of a man's life lies dead behind him, Gower Woodseer recognises at once that he is quoting Lord Feltre, the new friend who has begun to rival Woodseer in his influence over Fleetwood. The most important thing about Lord Feltre is that he is a Roman Catholic. Fleetwood dallies with the thought of turning Catholic himself, and the chief inducement seems to be that Catholicism offers the luxury of confession. In the end Fleetwood decides that it permits that luxury to be purchased too cheaply, in the privacy of the confessional. Fleetwood knows very well that the 'complete exposure of past meanness is the deed of present courage certain of its reward without as well as within'. He knows that if he could only bring himself to tell his wife how badly he has treated her and how much he regrets it, he might win her forgiveness: her feelings for him would have 'subsided into the channel of duty, even tenderness, had he been resolutely able to strip himself bare'. But he cannot bring himself to do it. He could bring himself to make such a confession to a priest, 'under seal, and in safety', but not to his wife, who is the person to whom the confession is due. He cannot bear the thought of offering himself up 'hideously naked to her mercy': 'A confession! It could be to none but the priest.' The men of today, his Catholic friend, Lord Feltre, tells him, have abandoned religion for philosophy, and they have found that it will not do, because philosophy is 'an untenanted confessional': it cannot offer absolution.[73] In his later years Meredith cultivated friendships with a number of Catholics, the poet Alice Meynell and her husband, for example, but *The Amazing Marriage* suggests that he could never bring himself to believe that a readiness to strip himself bare

[71] *The Amazing Marriage*, chapter 23.
[72] *The Amazing Marriage*, chapter 43.
[73] *The Amazing Marriage*, chapter 43.

before God might compensate for the failure to find the much greater resolution necessary to strip himself bare before the real victims, before those who had actually suffered from all his 'past meanness'.

Of all John Morley's books, Meredith was most stirred by the 1873 study of Rousseau: 'It has moved me as few books have done'; it is 'one of the most precious of studies', 'one of the wisest of books'. Meredith claims that, although he has only 'a poor knowledge' of the subject, no one is better able to appreciate Morley's achievement than he is because Meredith 'penetrates to the man, hating this in him, warming to that, alternately'.[74] His confidence that he understands Rousseau better than anyone is clearly founded on a belief that he and Rousseau are uncannily alike. Rousseau, like Meredith, lived all his life 'profoundly enwrapped in the brooding egoism of his own sensations'. At his worst Rousseau stands convicted of 'a monstrous and diseased love of self', but that self-absorption is also the quality on which his achievement is founded.[75] His love of self finds one expression in Rousseau's capacity for caustic self-knowledge, a capacity that Morley explains as 'egoism standing on its head and not on its feet'.[76] By an even stranger paradox egoism is what made Rousseau into a novelist. *La Nouvelle Héloïse* is an expression of 'vicarious or reflected egoism',[77] a novel in which Rousseau's understanding of other people issues from an intense preoccupation with himself. Rousseau ruthlessly cut himself loose from his own past: 'His heart, completely occupied with the present, filled its whole capacity and entire space with that, and except past pleasures, no empty corner was ever left for what was done with.' But even Rousseau could not always succeed in turning his back on his own past self: '"It is not," he says in words of profound warning, which we verify in those two or three hours before the tardy dawn, that swell into huge purgatorial æons, "it is not when we have just done a bad action, that it torments us; it is when we recall it long after, for the memory of it cannot be put out."'[78] Meredith recognised himself even in the self-contradictions of Morley's Rousseau, perhaps especially in them. For Morley, who would later publish his own *Recollections*, an autobiography that seems almost pathologically unself-

[74] *Letters*, 1, 506.
[75] *Rousseau*, 1, 200 and 43.
[76] *Rousseau*, 1, 212.
[77] *Rousseau*, 1, 259.
[78] *Rousseau*, 1, 57–8.

revealing (as Morley's biographer observes, 'it does not admit the reader to a single secret of the writer's heart'[79]), the *Confessions* was Rousseau's most startling achievement. He is particularly struck by Rousseau's willingness to publish his shabbiest misdemeanours, as when he falsely accused one of the servants of stealing a ribbon that he had in fact taken himself: 'It led him to conceive a long train of ruin as having befallen Marion in consequence of his calumny against her, and this dreadful thought haunted him to the end of his life.'[80] Meredith would have seized on this when he read it because he had been struck by exactly the same incident 18 years before, when he was writing *The Ordeal of Richard Feverel*. Austin Wentworth, Richard's saintly uncle, 'as true a Christian and kindly a spirit as ever walked the earth', who lives in social disgrace because he had insisted on marrying the housemaid who had seduced him, offers his nephew Rousseau's treachery as an instance of cowardice, before adding that it was Rousseau himself who had published the fact. 'Would you have done as much?' he asks Richard, and when Richard admits that he 'never could have told people', Austin asks him, 'Then who is to call that man a coward?'[81] In *Rousseau*, Meredith told Morley, he had shown 'the Heroic coward complete in his contradictions'.[82]

Meredith, like Morley, lacked Rousseau's particular kind of courage. Just as much as his own Lord Fleetwood he flinched from appearing 'hideously naked' in public. He feared the fate of the Egoist who is 'condemned to strip himself stark naked' before all his friends and acquaintance.[83] More than 30 years after Morley published his *Rousseau*, Meredith wrote to tell him that the book had been cited in an article in the *Atlantic Monthly* on 'The Nude in Autobiography'. The article has 'some rather good things', Meredith remarks, especially on 'the effect on the writer of his own nudities of revelation'.[84] Meredith lingers on the term, nudities, at once so seductive and so horrifying.

In the novels Meredith introduces again and again characters who find it within themselves to publish their confessions. As a boy, Richard Feverel yields to his uncle Austin's persuasion and confesses to Farmer Blaize that he had revenged himself for the whipping the farmer had given him by

[79] J. H. Morgan, *John, Viscount Morley* (London, John Murray, 1925), 160.
[80] *Rousseau*, 1, 40.
[81] *The Ordeal of Richard Feverel*, chapter 7.
[82] *Letters*, 1, 506.
[83] *The Egoist*, Prelude.
[84] *Letters*, 3, 1586.

suborning Tom Bakewell to fire the farmer's rick. He finds it in him to be true to the code of schoolboy ethics: he owns up. As a man he makes a harder confession. He confesses to his wife that he has been unfaithful to her. The Countess of Saldar in *Evan Harrington* is more slippery. She thinks of the young curates she meets at Beckley Court and almost wishes 'it was Protestant to speak a word behind a board to them and imbibe comfort'. She 'could see a haven of peace in that picture of the little brown box with the sleekly reverend figure bending his ear to the kneeling Beauty outside, thrice ravishing as she half-lifts the veil of her sins and her visage!'[85] When at the end of the novel she at last becomes a Catholic convert it is 'the charms of confession' that have seduced her.[86] In *Diana of the Crossways* Diana shows a bravery more like Rousseau's because the action that she confesses is so humiliatingly mean-spirited. She curdles Percy Dacier's love for her when she confesses that after having dinner with him she left her house at midnight, and went to the *Times* offices where she sold to the editor the secret that Dacier had let slip that evening, that the Cabinet had agreed on an immediate repeal of the Corn Laws. 'You sold me to a journalist for money?' Dacier asks, and 'the shutting of her house-door closed for Dacier that woman's history in relation to himself'.[87] Unlike the Countess, the comfort that Diana finds in confession comes at a high price. Then there is Edward Blancove, the lover of Dahlia Fleming in Meredith's *Rhoda Fleming*. He tires of the woman he has seduced and bribes the unspeakable Nic Sedgett to marry her, only to realise belatedly that Dahlia is the woman he truly loves. He proves his love by making a full confession not just to Dahlia but to her father, and to her sister, Rhoda:

> 'Has he—can he have confessed in words all his wicked baseness?' she thought, and in her soul the magnitude of his crime threw a gleam of splendour on his courage.[88]

Edward Blancove at that moment achieves the odd, flawed and paradoxical heroism of Rousseau. Meredith had once imagined that he might himself write a book rather like Rousseau's confessions. 'Every man', he wrote in his Red Notebook, 'has in him the materials of writing, from his

---

[85] *Evan Harrington*, chapter 19.
[86] *Evan Harrington*, chapter 47.
[87] *Diana of the Crossways*, chapters 35 and 36.
[88] *Rhoda Fleming*, chapter 46.

own personal experience, positive and experimental the most extraordinary book ever yet given to the world.'[89] He never wrote that book, but in the novels that he did write, Meredith came back again and again to the idea of confession, and as he did so he walked all the way around it, examining it from different sides, seeing it in different lights.

As he grew older, and especially after his marriage failed, Meredith became as intent as Morley was when he wrote his *Recollections* on preserving every secret of the writer's life—except that, unlike Morley, Meredith wrote novels. The novels are best understood as produced out of Meredith's contradictions. They were impelled by his need at once to confess and to conceal everything in his life that he was most ashamed of. In this he recalls Lord Ormont, the old soldier in *Lord Ormont and His Aminta*, a character closely modelled on Lord Cardigan who nevertheless manages to strike, as so many of Meredith's characters do, at least a passing resemblance to Meredith himself. 'No man so secret',' says his sister of him, and yet 'what his mouth shuts on, he exposes in his hand'.[90]

'I do not minister to gossip' was Meredith's lofty response to the German admirer who had asked him for some personal information.[91] He was not always so high-minded. His letters are often gossipy. In the 1880s he became friends with Louisa and Mary Lawrence, the unmarried sisters of his local MP. They gave musical evenings in London to which Meredith was always invited. His letters to Louisa regularly purvey the gossip that she obviously enjoyed. She 'may not have heard of poor Jack Clayton's ill luck with the legitimate dove of his bosom'. Clayton was a well-known actor. His wife had left him for 'a Captain Claremont of bad repute and some attractions for your fish-at-fly sex'.[92] It was 1883, Meredith's own ill luck with the legitimate dove of his bosom was a quarter of a century in the past, and unknown, he probably imagined, to Louisa Lawrence. But it was not only Miss Lawrence who brought out the gossip in him. His letters to his friend William Hardman are similarly gossipy and a good deal more scabrous. A Mrs Vaux, for example, is reported as complaining vociferously of her husband's impotence, a disability that, it is true, Meredith cloaks in the decent obscurity of a dead language: he describes it through

[89] *Notebooks*, 4.
[90] *Lord Ormont and His Aminta*, chapter 3.
[91] *Letters*, 3, 1314.
[92] *Letters*, 2, 717.

a quotation from Catullus.[93] Meredith repudiated gossip, and he practised it, which is not a very rare inconsistency, but it is an inconsistency that goes to the heart of his practice as a novelist.

In the novels, Meredith sometimes deprecates gossip almost as fiercely as in his reply to his German correspondent. His Diana is treated wholly sympathetically when she falls victim to 'Dame Gossip', a fate that she could scarcely have avoided after being accused in court of adultery with Lord Dannisburgh, a senior politician. She speaks for the novelist when she condenses her hatred of gossip into a Meredithian aphorism, 'Gossip is a beast of prey that does not wait for the death of the creature it devours.'[94] But the Regency gossip, John Rose Mackrell, in *The Amazing Marriage* is a character not without charm. *The Amazing Marriage* is the novel in which Meredith elevates Dame Gossip into a principal character. She is the narrator demanded by the contemporary reading public, the public that Meredith despises. She has no time for 'the moderns' whose method involves 'a frequent arrest of the actors in the story and a searching of the internal state of this one or that one of them'. She is the vociferous enemy of the psychological novel, which is the kind of novel that Meredith aspired to write: 'Her one idea of animation is to have her *dramatis personae* in violent motion', and she has 'the world to back her in protest against all fine, filmy work of the exploration of a young man's intricacies or cavities'. She has a particular animus against the novelist who threatens to take a step towards 'the lecturing-desk'.[95] The novelist as gossip is the mortal enemy of the novelist as philosopher, which is the role that Meredith hankers after. And yet Meredith knew very well that no novelist can allow himself to eschew gossip. Henry James is the proper type of the novelist when he bends his ear at dinner to the woman sitting next to him, knowing that a few stray gossamer threads of scandal may give him all the clue he needs for the weaving of his next tale. In *The Amazing Marriage*, Meredith gives over the first three chapters of the novel to Dame Gossip and in those chapters he shows how gossip can take facts and make them shimmer. These are the chapters in which he tells the history of the parents of Carinthia Jane, the young woman that the Earl of Fleetwood decides in an impulsive moment to make his bride.

---

[93] *Letters*, 1, 433.
[94] *Diana of the Crossways*, chapter 29.
[95] *The Amazing Marriage*, chapters 35 and 38.

When she is 23 Carinthia's mother leaves her husband and runs away with Carinthia's father, a naval man of 65. She is Fanny, the Countess of Cressett, and he is John Peter Kirby, the Old Buccaneer, and their story is told through gossip, and all the various aids on which gossip depends. Fanny, the runaway bride is not seen directly, but as she is reflected in the nation's 'Galleries of Art', as a nymph 'gazing at her naked feet', or under a broad-brimmed hat, 'tipped ever so slightly' to expose a roguish eye, or dressed in innocent blue and white but standing near a table on which lie a hefty pair of pistols. Or there is the Countess Fanny as she appears in a volume of Regency letters by Nymney, who seems from his name to have been an effeminate, gentlemanly trifler, 'a hater of women and the clergy', 'one of the horrid creatures who write with a wink at you'. Far better the Fanny whose exploits won her commemoration in a ballad:

> My family my gaolers be,
>   My husband is a zany;
> Nought see I clear save my bold Buccaneer
>   To rescue Countess Fanny.

The Buccaneer too shows at his best when his exploits are commemorated in popular song: '"What's rank to me!" cries Kirby.' Dame Gossip shows in these three chapters that she has a magic wand that allows Kirby to live his whole life as grandly as he lives in that song. Kirby lives happily with his young wife for 25 years, and Fanny dies before him. 'On the last night of her life this old man of past ninety carried her in his arms up a flight of stairs to her bed.' He survives her by just one week.

After those first three chapters, chapters that might stand alone as a brief, romantic novella, Dame Gossip is dismissed, put out as casually as if she had been a candle. But she proves to be one of those joke birthday-cake candles that refuse to be blown out and reignite themselves. Chapter XIII is entitled 'An Irruption of Mistress Gossip', Chapter XXIII is 'In Dame Gossip's Vein', and the novel ends 'With a Concluding Word by the Dame'. All the way through the novel Dame Gossip seizes every opportunity to leap onto stage, push the philosopher aside and take over the narrative. The novel could not survive her banishment—not this novel, nor any novel. In Meredith's novels the gossip and the philosopher are allowed to tussle with one another. Meredith likes to present himself as the champion of the philosophical novel or the psychological novel, but he knows very well that if that tussle ever came to an end, if the philosopher were to win an outright victory, the casualty would not just be Dame Gossip. The novel as a literary form would be dead. 'I do not minister to gossip,' he told his German correspondent, but he did. He was a novelist, and so he had to. In his novels he repeatedly retails gossip about his friends and acquaintances, his family and most of all he retails gossip about himself.

Writing novels allowed Meredith to return again and again to the key events in his own life; to the shame of being a tailor's son, to the loss of a mother before he could claim ever really to have known her, to the hero-worship of his father that soured over the years into contempt, to his first wife, Thomas Love Peacock's daughter, who remained for him all through his life the type of all that was most seductive in women, to her unfaithfulness, to his decision to remove their son from her and forbid her any access to him, and to his relationship with that son that so precisely and so sadly rehearsed his relationship with his own father. Meredith's nature was, as John Bayley has remarked, 'solipsistic'. It seems an odd disposition for a novelist, except that, as Meredith shows, one way of finding out about other people might be by finding in them some image of oneself. And in any case, as Bayley goes on to remark, Meredith's solipsism was not peculiar to him, 'perhaps we are all like that really'. It can seem so at any rate while we are reading George Meredith's novels.

CHAPTER 2

Tailordom

Hybrid Monsters

On the night of March 31, 1901, Edward Clodd was staying with Meredith at Flint Cottage and offered to fill in Meredith's census form. When he asked Meredith where he was born, Meredith responded, 'Is that necessary?' Told that it was, he replied, 'Well, put Hampshire', and when asked to be more specific he added, 'Well, say near Petersfield'. Clodd did not believe him. Meredith was born, Clodd thought, on February 12, 1828, 17 miles south of the little market town of Petersfield, at 73, High Street Portsmouth, where his father kept a tailor's shop.[1] Portsmouth was the great naval town of Britain, and the Merediths were naval outfitters. Meredith may have told Clodd the truth. His mother, Jane Eliza Macnamara, was the daughter of a publican who kept the Vine, in Broad Street, just yards from the Merediths' shop. Perhaps she preferred her only child to be born in rural Hampshire rather than in the centre of a busy town. Perhaps, as her confinement approached, she went to stay with relatives. But even so the information Meredith offered Clodd so reluctantly seems intentionally misleading. S. M. Ellis begins his biography of Meredith by pointing out how all through his life Meredith hid his 'origin and family history' beneath an 'impenetrable veil of mystery'.[2] He was so

[1] Edward Clodd, 'George Meredith: Some Recollections', *Fortnightly Review*, 86 (July, 1909), 19–31.
[2] Ellis, 13.

© The Author(s) 2019
R. Cronin, *George Meredith*,
https://doi.org/10.1007/978-3-030-32448-3_2

reluctant to tell Clodd where he had been brought up because, Ellis believes, he was ashamed of it. Evan Harrington's sister in Meredith's second novel, the novel in which he deals most directly with the circumstances of his own upbringing, recalls Evan coming home from school, a lisping schoolboy, and exclaiming in despair, 'I'm the thon of a thnip'. 'Oh!', she remembers, 'it was hell-fire to us then.'[3] According to some of his friends, it was a scorching from which Meredith never recovered. It was, according to W. S. Blunt, 'the secret trouble of his life'.[4]

It was certainly one of the troubles out of which Meredith wrote his novels. It might be said, of course, that the Victorian novel itself was born of a sense of shame. It had its origin in that morning in February 1824 when Dickens left his family home in Gower Street and walked the three miles to Warren's Blacking Factory where he was employed to stick labels onto the blacking pots for ten hours a day. 'No words', Dickens wrote, 'can express the secret agony of my soul as I sunk into the companionship of common men and boys', no words could express 'the shame of [his] position'.[5] There is no reason to doubt him, but it is a story known to us, as it was known to many of Dickens's contemporaries, because it was a story that Dickens enjoyed telling. It was the story that allowed him to present his own early life as the necessary prequel to his novels, and to identify himself as the prototype of his best-loved characters, of Nicholas Nickleby and David Copperfield and Pip in *Great Expectations*. It was rather different for a later generation of novelists, for Meredith and for his younger contemporaries.

George Gissing would never have become the novelist he was, and might never have become a novelist at all, had his brilliant academic career not been abruptly terminated. In 1876 he was expelled from Owen's College, Manchester. He had been found rifling the coat pockets of his fellow students. Gissing's exposure as a thief deprived him of his place in the social world. He became, to borrow the title of his second novel, one of *The Unclassed*, and, like Osmond Waymark, the hero of that novel, his lack of a social place confined him to the company of women like Nell Harrison, the woman whose importunities had driven Gissing to theft. Waymark could encounter 'refined and virtuous' women only in

[3] *Evan Harrington*, chapter 44.
[4] W. S. Blunt, *My Diaries: Being a Personal Narrative of Events 1888–1914*, 2 vols (London: Martin Secker, 1919–20), 2, 246.
[5] John Forster, *Life of Charles Dickens* (London: Chapman and Hall, 1893), 18.

'the sanctuary of his imagination'. It seemed impossible to bridge 'the hopeless gulf fixed between his world and that in which such creatures had their being'.[6] Gissing's was an extreme case. Henry James found his relations with women amazing: 'Why will he do these things?'[7] Thomas Hardy did not have so wide a gulf to bridge in 1874 when he married the middle-class Emma Gifford, but the difference in their social status remained a source of shame and it impelled Hardy's fiction. He called on Emma's father at his house in Bodmin just once before the marriage and never communicated with him again. John Gifford was a solicitor and could not accept as a son-in-law a man whose father was a stonemason and whose mother had been in service. Hardy exploited the circumstance in much of his fiction, most directly in his third novel, *A Pair of Blue Eyes*. But the separation from his own parents was still more shaming than his separation from Emma's. Hardy and Emma stayed with his parents in 1876 when they met Emma for the first time, but the visit seems never to have been repeated. Jemima Hardy lived to be 90, dying only in 1894, but she was never invited to Max Gate and Emma did not attend her funeral. His parents seem to have prompted in Hardy the same embarrassment suffered by the heroine of *The Hand of Ethelberta* who becomes a successful novelist and finds herself a guest at a smart dinner party at which her father is waiting at table. He is a butler. Dickens could speak openly of the shame of his position in the blacking factory, but Gissing and Hardy experienced a different kind of shame, a shame that made them into novelists precisely because it remained unspeakable. Meredith may or may not have guessed something of that history when he read the manuscripts of their first novels for Chapman and Hall, but he decided to encourage them, and he continued to feel an affinity for Hardy's and Gissing's fiction all through his life.

Meredith, Hardy and Gissing all wrote from the perspective of what Hardy calls the 'hybrid monster in social position'.[8] The central character of Hardy's first novel, *Desperate Remedies*, is Edward Springrove, who is, like Hardy, a young architect. Hardy claims for him what he would surely have claimed for himself: 'though he is not a public school man he has read widely, and has a sharp appreciation of what's good in books and

[6] George Gissing, *The Unclassed*, chapter 11.
[7] Edel, 543.
[8] Thomas Hardy, *Desperate Remedies*, chapter 9.

art.'[9] Springrove has learned 'to view society from a Bohemian stand-point', by which we are to understand that he has acquired 'all a developed man's unorthodox opinion about the subordination of classes'.[10] It is the standpoint from which Hardy tries to write his novel, which accounts in large part for how remarkably awkward a novel it is. The Bohemian stand-point that Hardy tries to assume is not yet available to him, and it never would be. The social position from which he wrote his novels was always, as it was for Gissing and Meredith, less Bohemian than monstrous. They were novelists of social class more pervasively, more intricately and more ashamedly than their Victorian predecessors. They had a particular fond-ness for characters drawn from what Hardy calls 'the metamorphic classes of society',[11] characters such as Martha Garland in *The Trumpet-Major* who 'occupied a twilight rank between the benighted villagers and the well-informed gentry',[12] or Swithin St Cleeve of *Two on a Tower* who found himself 'in the unhappy case of deriving his existence through two channels of society' with the result that 'he seemed to belong to either this or that according to the attitude of the beholder'.[13] The 'peculiar situa-tion, as it were in mid-air between two planes of society',[14] occupied by Grace Melbury in *The Woodlanders* is peculiar because it offers nothing to stand on, but it is the stance from which the late Victorian novelist very often chose to write.

Henry James, who could not claim for himself the social ambiguity that Meredith and Hardy and Gissing shared, managed to achieve a similar perspective by writing not from mid-air but mid-ocean. In 1878, after he had become a permanent resident in England, he wrote to Grace Norton, 'In one sense I feel intimately at home here, and in another sense I feel—as an American may be on the whole very willing, at times, very glad, to feel, like a complete outsider.'[15] When he came to write *Princess Casamassima*, his first thoroughly English novel, he chose as his central character Hyacinth Robinson, the illegitimate child of a French grisette and her aristocratic English lover, a peculiarity of birth ensuring that his fate was

[9] Thomas Hardy, *Desperate Remedies*, chapter 2.
[10] Thomas Hardy, *Desperate Remedies*, chapter 11.
[11] Thomas Hardy, *The Hand of Ethelberta*, chapter 39.
[12] Thomas Hardy, *The Trumpet-Major*, chapter 6.
[13] Thomas Hardy, *Two on a Tower*, chapter 28.
[14] Thomas Hardy, *The Woodlanders*, chapter 30.
[15] *The Complete Letters of Henry James, 1876–1878*, ed. Pierre A. Walker and Greg W. Zacharias, 2 vols (Lincoln and London: University of Nebraska Press, 2013), 2, 165.

'to be divided, to the point of torture, to be split open by sympathies that pulled him in different ways; for hadn't he an extraordinarily mingled current in his blood, and from the time he could remember was there not one half of him that seemed to be always playing tricks on the other, or getting snubs and pinches from it?'[16] In Hyacinth Robinson James fashions a character that allows him to see the world as it was seen by his contemporaries amongst the English novelists, by novelists such as Meredith and Hardy. The Princess herself, an American woman distantly married to an Italian aristocrat, insists that she has 'very little respect for distinctions of class— the sort of thing they make so much of in this country',[17] but Captain Sholto is an Englishman and sees very clearly, although he is not an astute man, that in England the central issue is 'the whole matter of the relations of class with class, and all that sort of thing, you know'.[18] As it was for the country, so it was for the country's novelists.

Hyacinth has 'a kind of double identity', and Henry James too, his biographer remarks, lived 'a double life': 'he courted Europe, and he never forgot America.'[19] The double life was the life characteristic of the late nineteenth-century novelist. Meredith points out in *Diana of the Crossways* that Diana lives 'the double life of the author' by which he means that she lives at once in the drawing room, the setting for her social life, and in the pages of the fictions that she writes. The life of the nineteenth-century poet too was double. In *Aurora Leigh* the poet is defined by her 'double vision',[20] by her power to see the thing under her eyes as if she looked at it from a distance, and to see the distant thing intimately, which is precisely the way in which Meredith most often sees his characters. They maintain what Robert Louis Stevenson calls in *Prince Otto* 'a double scale': they are 'so small to the eye, so vast to the imagination'.[21] For E. B. Browning it is double vision that allows the poet to escape gender categories and to understand with equal sympathy both men and women, which was again an ability claimed more commonly by the novelist than the poet. In *The Ordeal of Richard Feverel* it is even granted to Richard's misogynistic father, who signs his book, *The Pilgrim's Scrip*, not with his name but with

[16] Henry James, *The Princess Casamassima*, chapter 11.
[17] Henry James, *The Princess Casamassima*, chapter 17.
[18] Henry James, *The Princess Casamassima*, chapter 15.
[19] Edel, 175.
[20] Elizabeth Barrett Browning, *Aurora Leigh*, 5, 184.
[21] Robert Louis Stevenson, *Prince Otto: A Romance*, Book 3, chapter 1.

the griffin from his family crest, which the ladies amongst his admirers take 'to mean that the author was a double-animal, and could do without them',[22] that is, that he was hermaphroditic. For Meredith doubleness is strongly associated with youth, when it figures the inability of the young to reconcile soul and body, although it may survive into mature years. It is 'The Sage Enamoured' who tells 'the Honest Lady', 'For us the double conscience and its war, / The serving of two masters, false to both'.[23] Chapter XXX of *Emilia in England*, 'Of the Double-Man in Us', focuses on Wilfred Pole. 'The two men composing most of us at the outset of our lives', we are told, have just begun 'their deadly wrestle within him'. Nevil Beauchamp is in the same predicament: 'He was trying to be two men at once.' When 'circumstance' fuses those two men into one he will have reached maturity.[24] But Meredith is the novelist of immature men, of double-men, and their doubleness is most often signalled by their class, by their 'twilight rank'. For such men, for men who belong to two classes at once, as Gissing points out in *Born in Exile*, there is no alternative to 'the cultivation of a double consciousness'.[25]

The preoccupation with class leaves its stamp on the vocabulary of these novelists. In *Evan Harrington* Meredith writes of 'class-prejudice' and 'class-barriers'.[26] In *Beauchamp's Career* there are class-traitors: Cecilia Halkett has no intention of imitating Nevil Beauchamp and 'playing traitor to one's class'.[27] Beauchamp must be the first character in all of English literature to make the claim, 'I've no class',[28] and it is no more convincing when he makes it than when the claim came to be repeated by so many of his successors. The focus on class difference intensifies in the late Victorian novel not, as might be supposed, because the distance between the classes was widening but because it was becoming increasingly difficult to tell the different classes apart. All classes seemed to be converging towards the middle. Meredith disliked Hall Caine's novel *The Prodigal Son* because it introduced an episode transparently based on D. G. Rossetti's exhumation

---

[22] *The Ordeal of Richard Feverel*, chapter 1 (in the first edition).
[23] 'The Sage Enamoured and the Honest Lady', 229–30. The poem was first published in 1892.
[24] *Beauchamp's Career*, chapter 42.
[25] George Gissing, *Born in Exile*, Part 1, chapter 3.
[26] *Evan Harrington*, chapters 3 and 12.
[27] *Beauchamp's Career*, chapter 15.
[28] *Beauchamp's Career*, chapter 19.

of his wife's body to retrieve the manuscript of his poems,[29] but he would have recognised the description of the gamesters in a Monte Carlo casino. Gathered together in the room are 'the middle-class financier, the middle-class millionaire, the middle-class peer, the middle-class baron, the middle-class duchess', even the 'middle-class prostitute'.[30] As the classes converged, it became still more important to distinguish between them. Godwin Peak explains the matter in Gissing's *Born in Exile*: the 'classes are getting mixed, confounded. Yes, but we are so conscious of the process that we talk of class distinctions more than of anything else,—talk and think of them incessantly.'[31]

The crucial distinction was between the gentleman and the tradesman, and it was crucial precisely because it was a distinction that was becoming ever more difficult to maintain. In *Diana of the Crossways* there is Mr Cramborne Wither, a lawyer, a member of the professional classes and hence a gentleman, but Wither 'sprang (behind a curtain of horror) from tradesmen'.[32] His case was increasingly common. The horror that it excited had become, as Meredith's phrasing indicates, theatrical, but that served only to intensify it. Meredith's novella, *The House on the Beach*, concerns Mr Tinman, a successful shopkeeper who retires from trade at the age of 40 and sets about making himself into a gentleman. He is presented as a ridiculous figure engaged in a ridiculous enterprise, but the ridicule extends from him to his nation, because Britain, like Mr Tinman, espouses a class system that hinges on the upper-class contempt for trade despite the fact that it is trade on which the country's prosperity is founded. It is 'the shop which has shot half their stars to their social zenith', and yet the shop remains 'what verily they would scald themselves to wash themselves free from'.[33] In England the gentlemanly class defines itself by the distance it maintains from commerce, and it continues to do so even though, as Meredith points out in *One of Our Conquerors*: 'These are the deluge days when even aristocracy will cry blessings on the man who procures a commercial appointment for one of its younger sons offended and rebutted by the barrier of Examinations for the Civil Service.' Lady

[29] Meredith thought the incident 'too sacred for allusion', and Hall Caine's use of it in his novel a 'base and cowardly trick' when perpetrated by a man who had 'posed as Rossetti's friend'. See *Letters*, 3, 1508.

[30] Hall Caine, *The Prodigal Son* (London: Heinemann, 1904), 289.

[31] George Gissing, *Born in Exile*, Part 5, chapter 2.

[32] *Diana of the Crossways*, chapter 14.

[33] *The House on the Beach: A Realistic Tale*, chapter 10.

Blachington is delighted when Victor Radnor appoints her third son to
'the coveted post of clerk in the Indian house of Inchling and Radnor'.[34]
The irony is more easily appreciated by a foreigner. The German professor
in *The Adventures of Harry Richmond* understands very well that in Britain
the aristocracy has only been able to maintain its substance by forging an
alliance with the merchant class, but he also recognises that this has
resulted in an increase rather than a diminution of the reverence with
which it is regarded by all the other social orders. It is a paradox that the
professor relishes. In Britain the aristocracy has to be worshipped 'in order
to preserve an ideal of contrast to the vulgarity of the nation'.[35]

GENTLEMAN GEORGY

All this fascinating material was made available to Meredith through the
accident of being born, or if not born brought up, at 73 High Street,
Portsmouth, above his father's tailor's shop. It was important that it was
a tailor's shop rather than a chandler's or a bookseller's or a shop of some
other kind, because tailoring was a peculiarly despised profession. In
Trollope's *Lady Anna*, Lord Lovell, when he is forced to consider the
possibility that Lady Anna might choose to marry Daniel Thwaite,
exclaims, 'But think of the disgrace of such a marriage—to a tailor'.[36]
Why marriage to a tailor should be peculiarly disgraceful is hard to say. It
must owe something to the proverb according to which it takes nine
tailors to make a man. The original meaning of the proverb remains
obscure. Some trace its origin to the passing bell or teller which tolls nine
times to mark the death of a man, six times for a woman and three times
for a child. For others, it simply marks the unusual number of workmen
needed to furnish a fashionable male wardrobe. The character modelled
on Beau Brummel in Bulwer-Lytton's *Pelham* recalls that he employed
three tradesmen just to make his gloves, 'one for the hand, a second for
the fingers, and a third for the thumb!'[37] But whatever its origin the
proverb has come to signify that a tailor is less than a man. Tailoring
requires no physical strength. It is a trade open to the physically feeble,
which is presumably why the tailor in *A Midsummer Night's Dream* is

[34] *One of Our Conquerors*, chapters 17 and 15.
[35] *The Adventures of Harry Richmond*, chapter 29.
[36] Anthony Trollope, *Lady Anna*, chapter 18.
[37] Edward Bulwer-Lytton, *Pelham*, chapter 33.

Robin Starveling. The posture that tailors traditionally assumed might be thought peculiarly demeaning. All of Evan Harrington's disgust at the thought of becoming a tailor is compressed into the image of 'sitting with one's legs crossed, publicly stitching, and scoffed at!'[38] There is too the undignified jargon of the trade. The bride of a tailor, as Evan Harrington's benefactor points out, is obliged to swallow 'goose, shears, cabbage, and all!' (the goose is the smoothing iron, and cabbage is remnant cloth).[39] But most of all it has to do, surely, with the physical intimacy of the relationship between the tailor and his gentlemanly clientele, a physical intimacy that makes it the more necessary to insist on social distance. Meredith's 'Old Chartist', a cobbler who has been transported as a political agitator, is a democrat, but even he cannot help but look down on his son-in-law, a linen draper: 'I feel superior to a chap whose place / Commands him to be neat and supple.'[40] The call on tailors to be neat and supple is even more pressing than the call on linen drapers.

Evan Harrington was serialised in *Once a Week* in 1860 where it appeared under the title *Evan Harrington, or, He Would Be a Gentleman*. When the novel was published in three volumes by Bradbury and Evans the following year the subtitle had disappeared. Perhaps Meredith worried that it might be too revealing. In Hardy's *A Pair of Blue Eyes* Mrs Troyton warns Elfride that we 'mustn't say "gentlemen" nowadays': 'We have handed over "gentlemen" to the lower middle class.'[41] Perhaps he feared that it brought the novel too close to home, because becoming a gentleman was exactly the ambition that had been entertained for that other tailor's son, the young George Meredith. The local boys called him 'Gentleman Georgy'. One of them, James Price, lived next door. His father was a printer and bookseller, but James Price, Jem as he was called, had a clear sense of his social inferiority. James Price furnished S. M. Ellis, Meredith's first biographer, with his recollections of the young George Meredith. Price was two years older, and never knew Meredith well, but he provides the only surviving accounts of Meredith's childhood that bring the boy to life. When George was two or three, not yet out of frocks, Jem was invited to play with him. 'The boy did not seem to care much

[38] *Evan Harrington*, chapter 10.

[39] *Evan Harrington*, chapter 28.

[40] 'The Old Chartist', 76–7. The poem appeared in *Once a Week* on February 8, 1862, before Meredith included it in *Modern Love and Poems of the English Roadside* later that year.

[41] Thomas Hardy, *A Pair of Blue Eyes*, chapter 14.

about playing with me,' he recalled, 'and I was rather shy.' But George showed Jem his books and toys. Jem remembered being 'mightily pleased' with 'a horse and cart (not like the many cheap ones that I had seen)—a beautiful lifelike white horse, and the cart of superior make, and as George drew it along it made music as the wheels went round'. The boys spent the afternoon together, but, Jem reported, 'we did not get on much together as he assumed a sort of superiority'. A year or two later Jem was invited to a party given to celebrate George's fourth or fifth birthday. He remembered it as a strikingly grisly occasion. Jem, his elder brother and his two sisters were the first guests to arrive, and they were shown into the drawing room where they sat side by side on a sofa until the other guests began to come in, at which point they were removed to a bench. There were about 50 guests in all, most of them adults. There was tea and coffee and cakes, and then dancing in the next room. Jem was partnered by an adult who tried to push him though the figures, but to little effect: 'I was such a failure that I had to sit the rest of the evening—a mere spectator.' But he was given 'quarters of oranges, almonds and raisins, and weak negus' and became 'very sleepy'. There was a rush to the dining-room when supper was announced, and Jem and his brother and sisters had tart and cake. Then 'the lady' (George's mother presumably) said, '"It is time those children went home," so my brother took us home, and as regards myself I was very glad to be there.' After that Jem and George often met, as they were bound to do, living next door to each other, but they 'did not fraternise much': 'He used just to say, "How de do," and nod. I did the same.'[42]

Not long after the birthday party, on July 11, 1833, Meredith's mother died. She was just 31. George was five years old. Many years later, in 1870, John Morley's mother died, and Meredith wrote him a letter of condolence. 'I had this shock when I was a little boy', he recalled, 'and merely wondered.'[43] 'Wondered' seems a mild word, as if Meredith only dimly remembered his pain and bewilderment, which may help to explain, although it can scarcely excuse, Meredith's response when his own son lost his mother. Arthur Meredith was eight when Mary died. Meredith had not allowed him to see his mother since she had given birth to Henry Wallis's son three years before. He relented only when she was on her deathbed. He wrote to his friend William Hardman with news of her death, and added, 'My dear boy fortunately will not feel the blow as he might have under dif-

[42] Ellis, 37–9.
[43] *Letters*, 1, 416.

ferent circumstances.'[44] George Meredith was an only child, unused to playing with other children, brought up to think himself superior to boys like Jem Price. His mother's death confirmed him in his loneliness.

There were female relatives. His aunt, Anne Burbey, lived nearby, on the other side of the High Street, and her grown-up daughter, Mary Burbey, helped look after little George. Another aunt, Catherine Ellis, was often in Portsmouth, and she too took an interest in George, even though she had children of her own. He was a motherless boy, but his father remained determined that he should be raised as a gentleman. When he was nine he was sent to St Paul's School in Southsea, not to the local school, Frost's Academy in St Thomas's Street that Jem Price and the other boys of the neighbourhood attended. The headmaster of St Paul's was the Reverend William Foster, a Cambridge man, a graduate of Trinity, who published his school textbooks; *Elements of Algebra, for the use of St Paul's School, Southsea*, *Rudiments of the Greek Language, for the use of St Paul's School, Southsea*. Frost's Academy had no such pretensions. 'The boys of St Paul's looked down upon us Frost's boys,' Jem Price recalled, 'but George Meredith and I when we met always exchanged salutations: "How de do, Price," in his usual drawling, patronising way':

> He was certainly a good-looking youth, with bright blue or grey eyes, and a nice, light, curly head of hair, and always well dressed, much better than any of us boys, all sons of tradespeople. We were, however, a jolly lot of boys— trundled hoops, played at marbles, whip and peg-tops, rounders, prisoner's base, pitch-hat, and on winter nights at 'nickey-night,' with flint and steel to strike when told to 'show your light.' To these sorts of things George Meredith never stooped, and, in consequence, he got the name of 'Gentleman Georgy' amongst us boys. We often waited for the Convict Guard to come to the Guard House on the Parade, where the soldiers had to draw their cartridges, and we boys collected the powder and made what we called 'Devils' by mixing our saliva with the powder and working it into a pyramid, and then set light to it at the top—it was really a pretty bit of fireworks. Need I say George Meredith did not join in this?[45]

It is hard to imagine that the fine clothes and cultivated drawl always seemed adequate compensation for missing out on the games of 'nickey-night' and the chance to set light to a pyramid of gunpowder.

[44] *Letters*, 1, 108.
[45] Ellis, 45.

Jem Price last saw Meredith in 1839. The boys from Frost's Academy were chatting together after their sports day. Meredith joined them and remarked to one of the boys, Joe Neale, whose father kept a race horse as well as a coffee house, 'I was at Stokes Bay races last week and I saw your father's horse come in *second*, but I think he is a grand horse. By George! he's got some blood in him!' Meredith was 11 and was already playing a role. He was the tailor's son as young swell.

It was a role that ran in the family. His father, Augustus Urmston Meredith, had been destined for the medical profession, but in 1814, when Augustus was 17, his father died, and Augustus was obliged to take over the family business. The circumstance gave Meredith the plot for *Evan Harrington* in which Evan's mother insists that he join her in the shop and work to pay off his father's debts. Ten years after taking over the business Augustus married Jane Macnamara whose father had kept the Vine, a prosperous public house in Broad Street, just yards from the Merediths' shop. It was an entirely appropriate match for a tailor. Jane Macnamara, a good-looking young woman in her early 20s, brought with her a dowry of £1000. But Augustus Meredith had higher aspirations. He was a skilled chess player, a leading member of the Portsmouth and Portsea Literary and Philosophical Society, and he entertained lavishly. He was, as a friend of his reported to S. M. Ellis, 'a perfect gentleman and not in the least like a tailor'.[46] He was himself what Hardy calls a 'monstrous hybrid in social position', and he passed on the hybridity to his son.

The hybridity had been bequeathed to Augustus, along with substantial debts, by his own father, the founder of the tailoring business, Melchizedek Meredith (Melchizedek is the 'priest of the most high God' of the 14th chapter of Genesis), who was known in the family as 'the great Mel'. He died more than a decade before George Meredith was born, but young George spent his childhood in the shadow of the great Mel's legend. It is an effect that he reproduces in *Evan Harrington*. The death of Melchisedec Harrington is announced in the first paragraph of the novel, but his doings and sayings are remembered all the way through the book, retailed by his wife, his daughters, by the men who had been his friends, and the women who had succumbed to his attractions:

> This had been a grand man, despite his calling, and in the teeth of opprobrious epithets against his craft. To be both generally blamed, and generally liked, evinces a peculiar construction of mortal. Mr. Melchisedec, whom

---

[46] Ellis, 43.

people in private called the great Mel, had been at once the sad dog of Lymport, and the pride of the town. He was a tailor, and he kept horses; he was a tailor, and he made gallant adventures; he was a tailor, and he shook hands with his customers. Finally, he was a tradesman, and he never was known to have sent in a bill. Such a personage comes but once in a generation, and, when he goes, men miss the man as well as their money.[47]

This is not so much a gentleman's outfitter as the hero of a family romance. It is not at all clear how widely the romance circulated outside the family. The great Mel makes an appearance in Captain Marryat's novel, *Peter Simple*. Peter, then a young midshipman, docks at Portsmouth but is unable to report to the admiral because he has nothing to wear, 'But we called at Meredith the tailor's, and he promised that, by the next morning, we should be fitted complete'. This speaks to the great Mel's professional efficiency but does nothing to present him as a striking anomaly, as someone who contrived at once to be a tailor and a perfect gentleman.[48] Mel became a freemason and he served twice as churchwarden at St Thomas's, the local church, now a cathedral, where his children were baptised. He and his fellow warden presented two silver alms plates to the church. But there is nothing in this that suggests he was anything more than a respectable tradesman. When he died on July 10, 1814, it was as a tradesman that his death was recorded in the *Hampshire Courier*: 'Died on Sunday, 10th inst., much respected, Mr. M. Meredith, aged 51, who for many years carried on a respectable trade in the Men's Mercery line in this town.'[49] The romance of the great Mel may have been a romance confined to the family, but it was the family romance that determined the kind of novelist that George Meredith became. The dream that the great Mel inspired, the dream that class difference might somehow be evaded or transcended or defied, inspires much of his fiction.

It was the romance that produced in *The Amazing Marriage* the fast friendship between the Earl of Fleetwood, the richest nobleman in all England, and Gower Woodseer, the son of a cobbler who had been to school with 'hawkers, tinkers, tramps and ploughmen, choughs and

[47] *Evan Harrington*, chapter 1.
[48] *Peter Simple*, chapter 26. Marryat's failure to notice the great Mel's gentility is the more remarkable because it comes just after a conversation in which one naval lieutenant describes a midshipman as a 'remarkably genteel, well-dressed young man' only for it to emerge later that, despite appearances, he is the son of a tailor.
[49] Quoted in S. M. Ellis, *George Meredith: His Life and Friends in Relation to His Work*, 31.

crows'.[50] In the same novel it produced Carinthia Kirby, who marries Fleetwood and, when she lodges with Woodseer's father in London's East End, becomes known to the world as the 'Whitechapel Countess'. *The Tale of Chloe* begins with Beau Beamish's ballad inspired by the Duke who had married a dairymaid. The romance prompted Meredith's fiction from the first. In *The Shaving of Shagpat*, a barber becomes a king and takes as his wife Noorna bin Noorka, the beautiful daughter of the Vizier. In his second story, *Farina*, there is Gottlieb Groschen, the wealthy Cologne merchant, who, for all that his money comes from trade, was 'easy with the proudest princes of the Holy German Realm'.[51] In the first of the novels Richard Feverel falls in love with Lucy Desborough and marries her, even though, as her uncle, Farmer Blaize, points out, 'baronets' sons were not in the habit of marrying farmers' nieces'.[52] It is, of course, the dream that lies behind a rather large proportion of Victorian fiction from Tennyson's ballad in which a landscape painter wins and woos a village maiden before revealing that he is in fact 'The Lord of Burleigh' to Dickens's *Our Mutual Friend* in which Lizzie Hexham, the daughter of a waterman and corpse-robber, ends the novel married to Eugene Wrayburn, a barrister and a gentleman.

In England, Carinthia Kirby's brother remarks in *The Amazing Marriage*, 'you meet people of your own class; you don't meet others.'[53] One result of the social separation of the classes was a demand for novels that allowed their readers to enjoy in fiction the encounters that they were denied in their lives. The wide social panoramas of the Victorian novel met the needs of readers who found their own social experience cramped and narrow. Another consequence was the extraordinary importance attached in the late Victorian period to sport. Sport, the notion was, had the power to undo social distinctions, or at any rate to suspend them for as long as the match lasted. In Meredith's *Lord Ormont and His Aminta* Matthew Weyburn is acknowledged by all his fellows to be at the head of Cuper's school. Matthew (rather unfortunately known as Matey) was 'a lad with a heart for games': 'The son of a tradesman, if a boy fell under the imputation, was worthy of honour with him, let the fellow but show grip and

[50] *The Amazing Marriage*, chapter 8.
[51] *Farina*, chapter 1.
[52] *The Ordeal of Richard Feverel*, chapter 23.
[53] *The Amazing Marriage*, chapter 6.

toughness.'[54] The village cricket match in which squire and blacksmith share a stand for the last wicket became a staple of English fiction that retained its potency for the Edwardians and beyond. It was so popular not despite but because of the fact that cricket was the most class-ridden of games. In 1863 Meredith became friendly with Henry Hyndman, the early socialist, who was already playing cricket for Sussex while he was an undergraduate. But Hyndman was exceptional. Cricket and socialism were not easily reconciled. The English team could only be captained by an amateur and a gentleman, a rule that remained in place until 1952, when the claims of the great Len Hutton were accepted as indisputable, and a distinction between professional and amateur cricketers ('players' and 'gentlemen') persisted for ten more years. The cricket field and the novel, the national sport and the nation's favourite kind of literature, worked together to uphold the fantasy of a nation in which class distinctions might be effortlessly dispensed with. It was a fantasy that the late Victorian novelists with whom Meredith had most in common, James, Hardy and Gissing, repudiated. The fantasy meant more to Meredith than it did to them, but he too rejected it.

In *The Adventures of Harry Richmond* Harry, for all that his father is little better than a fraudster, wins the love of a German princess, but in the end Harry does not marry his Ottilia. He marries Janet Ilchester, his grandfather's favourite, whom he has known all his life. Richard Feverel does marry Lucy Desborough, the farmer's niece, and his father is at last reconciled to the match, but there is no happy ending. Lucy succeeds in marrying the son of a baronet, but her marriage proves, quite literally, the death of her. Carinthia Kirby does even better. She marries an earl, only for her husband to alienate her so successfully that she loses all the love she once had for him. In Meredith's novels, in contrast to the avowed romances, *The Shaving of Shagpat* and *Farina*, the romance does battle with the novel and loses. Meredith almost yields to the temptation to create a fictional world in which class difference is annulled only in the end to resist it. He flirts with the possibility entertained by his own Nevil Beauchamp that an individual might escape from class, but when Nevil renounces his class he finds that he gives up along with it not just the young woman that he had hoped to marry but the possibility of finding anything meaningful to do with his life at all. The title of the novel, *Beauchamp's Career*, is ironic, finding a career is precisely what always

---

[54] *Lord Ormont and His Aminta*, chapter 1.

proves beyond him. Meredith is attracted to the notion that the great novelist might, by virtue of his genius, transcend the class system in which his characters are enmeshed. He would like, one feels, to make for himself the claim that he only allows himself to make ironically, on behalf of Beau Beamish, a character in *The Tale of Chloe* modelled on Beau Nash, the most famous of the Bath Masters of Ceremony. Beamish 'had neither ancestors nor descendants: he was a genius'.[55] But, unlike Beamish, Meredith knows that all such claims remain fantastic. Nevil Beauchamp was modelled on Meredith's best friend, Captain Maxse, and Maxse, like Beauchamp, sometimes claimed that he had no class. His political opinions, he claimed, had a special authority as those of a man who had lived 'from childhood in an upper class atmosphere' and yet had been led 'by the irresistible force of conscientious conviction to espouse—as the cause of human justice—the Democratic cause'. This is from a lecture, 'The Causes of Social Revolt' that Maxse gave in 1872, prompted by the defeat of the Paris Communards. But Maxse did not claim that his own example supported the claim that class difference was an empty fiction. Any credible analysis of the state of the nation must, he insisted, be 'founded upon a recognition of Class divisions'.[56]

The same might be said of Meredith's novels, all of which recognise, however much they may regret it, the insuperable reality of the division between classes, all of them, that is, except one, *Evan Harrington*, which is the novel in which Meredith confronts most directly his own family circumstances. In *Evan Harrington* romance trumps the novel. Evan falls in love with Rose Jocelyn, the only child of Sir Franks and Lady Jocelyn, and his love is returned, even though he is the son of a tailor and Rose has 'little thought' she 'should ever love one sprung from that class'.[57] The novel ends when she agrees to marry Evan even though she has already accepted the proposal of the entirely suitable Ferdinand Laxley, and has even—a significant matter for her—allowed Ferdinand to kiss her lips. But in *Evan Harrington* Meredith espouses the romance only at the end of a novel in which it has been very thoroughly exposed as a sham.

Unsurprisingly, there is a cricket match in *Evan Harrington*. The match pits Beckley against Fallowfield: 'The sons of first-rate families are in two

---

[55] *The Tale of Chloe: An Episode in the History of Beau Beamish*, chapter 4.

[56] Captain Maxse, R. N., *The Causes of Social Revolt: A Lecture* (London: Longman, Green, Reader, and Dyer, 1872), 3.

[57] *Evan Harrington*, chapter 25.

elevens, mingled with the yeomen and whoever can best do the business.' The two villages have chosen their teams 'without regard to rank', in proof of which Nick Frim, the gamekeeper's son, joins Tom Copping, son of Squire Copping of Dox Hall, in a thrilling last-wicket stand. It takes Beckley to a total that seems beyond Fallowfield's reach, but long before the stand is broken the spectators, all of them except the boys, have lost interest: 'the ladies were beginning to ask when Nick Frim would be out', and even Nick himself begins to 'suffer from the monotony of his luck'. We never learn how Fallowfield fare in their reply to the Beckley innings. Even the result of the match remains unreported.[58] Meredith's silence on the matter is itself a tart comment on the power of cricket to repair the class divisions that, as Captain Maxse thought, best defined the nation.

The match is played the day after a dinner that Tom Cogglesby, brother of Evan's uncle Andrew, gives each year at the Green Dragon Inn in Fallowfield to celebrate his birthday. The peculiarity of the birthday dinner is that 'no names' are permitted. The company consists of 'jolly yeomen, tradesmen, farmers, and the like', but there are also 'three young gentlemen-cricketers' who are in Fallowfield for the match the next day. There are Harry Jocelyn, Rose's brother, Ferdinand Laxley, and Drummond Forth, a close friend of Lady Jocelyn's. Evan and his old school friend Jack Raikes are also guests. The rule that no names should be used is designed to eliminate social distinctions. The dinner table becomes a privileged space, like the wood of no names in *Through the Looking-Glass*, a book that Lewis Carroll published ten years after *Evan Harrington*. In the wood Alice meets a fawn but neither of them can remember their names, and so they walk through the wood together, 'Alice with her arm clasped lovingly round the soft neck of the Fawn', until they emerge into an open field and 'a sudden look of alarm' comes into the animal's eyes. At once the fawn 'gave a sudden bound into the air' and 'in another moment it had darted away at full speed'.[59] In *Through the Looking-Glass* the magic works, if only briefly, under the cover of the trees. At the Green Dragon it never works at all. For one thing the yeomen have trouble remembering the rule. They repeatedly refer to their host as Mr Tom. But the chief problem is the presence of the gentlemen-cricketers, not the yeomen's forgetfulness. The young gentlemen behave with 'a certain propriety' when their attention is fixed on the rustic guests. Then they simply conduct themselves 'as if they were at a play,

---

[58] *Evan Harrington*, chapter 13.
[59] Lewis Carroll, *Through the Looking-Glass*, chapter 3.

and the rest of the company paid actors'. But when Jack Raikes claims to be the son of a gentleman, Ferdinand Laxley and Harry Jocelyn are irked. Raikes, who has drunk too much ale on an empty belly, rises to address the company. 'Gentlemen,' he begins, and repeats the address twice more before proceeding. Laxley throws himself 'weariedly' back in his chair, and exclaims, 'By the Lord; too many gentlemen here!' Raikes calls Laxley a puppy, and Laxley calls Raikes a snob (Laxley is using the word in its older sense, in which it signifies someone who has no breeding). It might all have passed off easily enough if Laxley had not assumed Evan to be 'a gentleman condescending to the society of a low-born acquaintance' and sought to register as much by directing towards Evan 'sundry propitiations, intelligent glances, light shrugs, and such like'. This prompts Evan to announce that he has no claims to 'blue blood, or yellow', that he is 'the son a tailor', but that he is very willing to give Harry satisfaction if he 'will deign to challenge a man who is *not* the son of a gentleman, and consider the expression of his thorough contempt for [his] conduct sufficient to overlook that fact'. Evan only makes the admission because he is half drunk himself: 'the more ale he drank the fiercer rebel he grew against conventional ideas of rank, and those class-barriers which we scorn so vehemently when we find ourselves kicking against them.' But he has an odd way of kicking. His language is never more lordly than when confessing his lack of gentlemanly status. The confession prompts Harry to an outburst less remarkable for its rudeness than its vulgarity. 'We'll come to you when our supply of clothes runs short,' he says, 'A snip!'[60] The dinner with no names at the Green Dragon offers lively confirmation that in England class divisions may be complicated, they may even be inverted, but they can never be evaded.

Evan, obliged after his father's death to take his place in the shop, is in the same predicament as Meredith's father, who was forced to take over the family business on the death of the great Mel, but the outcome for Meredith's father was very different. Augustus Meredith remarried after his first wife died. He took as his second wife the woman who had come to live with him as his housekeeper after he was widowed. Evan Harrington marries Rose Jocelyn: Augustus Urmston Meredith, when he married again, chose Matilda Buckett. The name and the woman who bore it rankled with Meredith, and he despised himself for it. He reveals as much in his third novel, *Emilia in England*, in which a Mr Pole disappoints his socially aspirant daughters by choosing as his second wife 'a lady of the

[60] *Evan Harrington*, chapter 12.

name of Mrs. Chump'.[61] Mrs Chump has only one advantage over Matilda Buckett: she is the widow of a rich merchant. Even Pole's fastidious daughters are obliged at last to recognise that, despite her name and her lapses in grammar and pronunciation, she is a good-natured woman. Meredith would perhaps have allowed his own stepmother as much, but, tellingly, Meredith's father did not marry Matilda Buckett until July 3, 1839, after he had left Portsmouth for London. Before then their relationship was, it seems likely, unofficial. Meredith kept his silence on the matter, and yet, as was his habit, still found a way quietly to introduce the circumstance into his novels. In *Beauchamp's Career* Nevil Beauchamp, whose parents are dead, is brought up by his uncle, Everard Romfrey, son of the Earl of Romfrey, who has an estate on the border of Hampshire and Wiltshire, and another, Steynham, in Sussex, which is where he generally resides. Romfrey, like Meredith's father, has a housekeeper, Mrs Rosamund Culling, the widow of an army officer, and after he succeeds his father as Earl he marries her. There are only the most delicate references to the nature of their relationship before their marriage. We are told, for example, that 'Rosamund would not present herself at her lord's dinner-table when there were any guests at Steynham'.[62] But the telling evidence is Romfrey's response when he is told, mistakenly and probably maliciously, that the nature of his relationship with Mrs Culling has been impugned. Romfrey beats the man he holds responsible to within an inch of his life with his gold-headed horsewhip, a savagery explicable only if the insinuation is true. In *Beauchamp's Career* it may be the wide social distance between Romfrey and his own father that prompted Meredith to allow their domestic circumstances to coincide. Augustus Meredith and Matilda Buckett were not so distant from Mr Pole and Mrs Chump of *Emilia in England*, but in that novel too Meredith accommodates his father's situation. One of Pole's daughters, Arabella, tries to explain the relationship in a letter to her brother, but she is a young woman of 'fine shades and nice feelings', and cannot bring herself to be explicit: '*The step he desired to take*, WHICH WE OPPOSED, *he has anticipated*, AND MUST CONSUMMATE.' She trusts to the italics and capitals to clarify her meaning, adding only, 'You comprehend me I am sure! I should have said "*had* anticipated."'[63]

[61] *Emilia in England*, chapter 4.
[62] *Beauchamp's Career*, chapter 34.
[63] *Emilia in England*, chapter 36.

Everard Romfrey ends the novel as an earl, an elevation that he had not expected because he is a younger son. Augustus Meredith's progress was less fortunate. One of the names included in the list of bankrupts in *The Times* for November 17, 1838, is 'Augustus Urmston Meredith, Portsmouth, draper'. The business had been debt-ridden when he had inherited it from his father, and he had failed to turn it around. The 11-year-old George Meredith who congratulated Joe Neale on the quality of his father's horse—'By George, he's got some blood in him!'—already knew that he was the son of a bankrupt. The comic energy in *Evan Harrington* is generated by the brio with which Evan's sisters, especially Louisa, the Countess of Saldar, deny their origins. They simply refuse to acknowledge that their father was a tailor. By the time he was 11, Meredith was already almost as adept in denying the reality of his social status.

After Augustus had lost his business he left Portsmouth for London. He left his son in the care of his Portsmouth relatives, but he took Matilda Buckett his housekeeper with him, and in July they were married. On the marriage certificate Augustus Meredith designated himself 'gentleman', but it was the last gesture of the kind that he made. He never again yielded to the temptation to live his life as if he were above his profession. He needed to support himself and his new wife, and he took employment as a journeyman in the shop of a London tailor. Later he seems to have gone into business on his own account, but he would never again pretend, as he had at Portsmouth, to be a gentleman who tailored in his spare time. In 1844, when he was thinking of apprenticing young George to a bookseller, he submitted to the Court of Chancery a document in which he declared that since his bankruptcy he had not had and did not now have 'any income except what is derived from his business as a tailor'. George saw his father only sporadically after he left Portsmouth, and in 1849, just before George married, his father emigrated to South Africa, sailing on April 15 for the Cape of Good Hope. Soon after disembarking, he took out an advertisement in the Cape Town newspapers to announce that he was setting up in business. In the advertisement he designated himself 'Tailor and Professed Trouser Cutter, from St. James's Street, London' and begged to announce 'to the Gentry and Public of Cape Town' that he was newly arrived from England 'with a well-selected Stock', had taken over the business of a Mr Hume, and could 'from long experience in all the branches of his trade' guarantee 'Style, Fit, and Comfort, combined with the economy of his predecessor'. He adds a note promising that he was 'not so bigoted in his own style but that he willingly yields to gentlemen's own peculiarities'.[64] There is no reason to believe that it ever came to George Meredith's attention, but the advertisement encapsulates with unusual force everything that persuaded him that it was peculiarly shaming to acknowledge himself the son of a tailor. 'We do not get to any heaven by renouncing the Mother we spring from,' Meredith remarks in *Lord Ormont and His Aminta*,[65] but he came close to renouncing his own father. He was left feeling for him the kind of love that a minor character in *Emilia in England* feels for his parents, 'a fitful love … that was not attachment; a baffled natural love, that in teaching us to brood on the hardness of our lot, lays the foundation for a perniciously mystical self-love'.[66] After 14 years in Cape Town Augustus Meredith retired from business and came back to England with his wife. They took a house in Southsea, not far from their old home, but George saw them only rarely. Augustus Meredith died on June 18, 1876, and his son went down to Southsea for the funeral, but he remained unforgiving. Even in his old age his judgement of his father was crisply dismissive; he was 'a muddler and a fool'.[67]

George was not left destitute when his father left for London. He had inherited £1000 from his mother, and when an aunt died in 1840 he inherited almost as much again. It may have been the second inheritance that allowed him to leave St Paul's in Southsea for a boarding school somewhere in the south of England. He once mentioned to Captain Maxse's daughter that he had attended a school in Lowestoft.[68] He seems to have made no other reference to it, but the accounts of a boarding school in *Lord Ormont and His Aminta*, and still more in *The Adventures of Harry Richmond* seem founded on personal experience. Harry Richmond is escorted to his school by his father, who gives the head boy money to treat all the boys. Mr Rippenger, the headmaster, is so impressed that he marks the occasion by granting the boys a half holiday. Rippenger is soon disillusioned. The school fees are not forthcoming and he summons Harry to tell him that 'Surrey House was not an almshouse, either for the sons of gentlemen of high connection, or for the sons of vagabonds'.[69] Augustus

[64] *Bibliography*, xvi.

[65] *Lord Ormont and His Aminta*, chapter 14.

[66] *Emilia in England*, chapter 55.

[67] Clodd, *Memories*, 141.

[68] Viscountess Milner, 'Talks with George Meredith', *National Review*, 131 (1948), 449–58.

[69] *The Adventures of Harry Richmond*, chapter 5.

Meredith was not so colourfully impecunious as Harry's father, Richmond Roy, although the incident may reflect George's anxious awareness that his financial position at school was precarious. A casual remark in *Evan Harrington* is more revealing. When Evan meets an old school friend, the friend recalls, 'You said your father—I think I remember at old Cudford's—was a cavalry officer, a bold dragoon?' 'I did,' Evan replies. 'I told a lie.'[70] The staunch admission is wholly in character for Evan, the lie that prompted it less so. It seems entirely possible that George Meredith passed through boarding school in disguise, representing himself as the son of an army officer rather than as the son of a tailor. If so *Evan Harrington* is the appropriate novel in which to make the confession. It is a novel born out of Meredith's shame at being the son of a tailor, and out of shame that he had ever felt such shame, and out of shame that he should continue to do so.

THON OF A THNIP

It may seem odd to describe *Evan Harrington* as born out of shame because it is a novel in which Meredith exposed his own family history more recklessly than any nineteenth-century novelist before him had dared. He sometimes refuses even to change the names either of the members of his family or of his Portsmouth neighbours. In *Evan Harrington* the character based on his grandfather is given the grandfather's extraordinary forename Melchisedec and he too is known as 'the great Mel'. Amongst his friends and neighbours are Mr Kilne the publican, Mr Barnes the butcher and Mr Grossby the confectioner. Robert Kilne kept the Wellington Tavern on Portsmouth High Street directly opposite the Merediths' shop, Barnes was the name of the local butcher, and the confectioner, whose shop was two doors down from the tailor's, was not Mr Grossby but Mr Grossmith. This was indiscreet, but the indiscretion is as nothing when compared with Meredith's introduction of his own aunts as characters in the novel. Meredith's father had five sisters, but by the time that Meredith was born only three survived. Of these Harriet married John Hellyer, whose family owned a brewery, Louisa married John Read and Catherine, the youngest of the daughters, married Samuel Burdon Ellis, a Lieutenant in the Royal Marines. Louisa was the most remarkable of them. Her husband, John Read, died in 1821, and in 1829 Louisa married his elder brother, William Harding Read, British Consul-General in

[70] *Evan Harrington*, chapter 17.

the Azores, and a close friend of Pedro I, the Emperor of Brazil, who became briefly, in 1826, before abdicating in favour of his daughter, King of Portugal. Louisa had three sons and a daughter, named Luiza after her mother, and in 1834, Luiza married Antonia da Costa Cabral, a Portuguese nobleman who went on to become Queen Maria II's most trusted minister. Meredith does not bother to change the names of two of his aunts. Harriet Harrington, like his Aunt Harriet, marries a brewer, Andrew Cogglesby. Louisa Harrington is even more successful than her namesake. She marries a Portuguese nobleman and becomes the Countess de Saldar. Catherine becomes Caroline Harrington and marries Lieutenant Strike of the Royal Marines, who has subsequently been promoted to Major. Catherine's husband was promoted to major in 1841, and became a general the year after *Evan Harrington* was published. Meredith changes the name of his aunt Catherine, perhaps, because Caroline's husband is characterised as a wife-beater, who is properly requited when his wife has an affair with a Duke who has been smitten by her beauty. Meredith appropriates his own family history with a recklessness that makes nonsense, or seems to, of the suggestion that he was ashamed of his origins. But the contradiction was, as J. B. Priestley recognised, central to the kind of novelist he was.[71] In *Evan Harrington* he announces as much by passing on the contradiction to his hero. For most of the novel Evan is torn between the impulse to conceal his family origins and an equally strong impulse to confess them.

'He Would Be a Gentleman', the subtitle to *Evan Harrington* that Meredith discarded when the novel was published as a book, alerts the reader to the novel's theme. The novel was serialised in *Once a Week* from February 1861. Dickens's *Great Expectations* began to appear in *All the Year Round* in December of the same year. Both are novels that examine the idea of the gentleman, a word which, as Chillon Kirby points out in *The Amazing Marriage*, 'conveys in England a special signification'.[72] In *Great Expectations* Joe Gargery, a blacksmith who cannot even read until he is taught to do so by Biddy, is presented by Dickens as the ideal gentleman. 'O God bless this gentle Christian man,'[73] Pip whispers when Joe comes to tend him in his sickness, and the word 'Christian', when it is allowed to interrupt the word 'gentleman', transforms it. The term no longer refers to

<hr/>

[71] Priestley, 2.
[72] *The Amazing Marriage*, chapter 6.
[73] *Great Expectations*, chapter 57.

a set of social accomplishments but to a moral disposition, an active benev-
olence that is far more appropriately exemplified by the village blacksmith
than by the so-called gentlemen of the novel, by people such as the
unspeakable Bentley Drummle or Compeyson, the gentleman criminal, or
the man Pip changes into when he acquires all the gentlemanly accomplishments and acquires along with them a sense of shame at his relationship with Joe. Meredith's novel is so different because Meredith, unlike
Dickens, remains wedded to the traditional idea of the gentleman that the
whole of his novel is designed to repudiate. The idea of the gentleman is,
the novel shows, an incoherent idea, an idea riddled with impossible contradictions, and yet it is an ideal that Meredith cannot bring himself to
relinquish.

Gentlemen and tradesmen occupy different worlds. Gentlemen live in
the upper air: tradesmen are confined to an underworld. When they grow
up Evan's three sisters sever all connections with the tailor's shop. They
become Eurydices who have successfully escaped 'the gloomy realms of
Dis, otherwise Trade'.[74] Tradesmen remain below, confined to a world
ruled over by Pluto, the god of wealth. Gentlemen by contrast never concern themselves with money. Evan's father, the great Mel, established himself, invented himself it might be better to say, as a living anomaly, a
gentleman tailor, and he assumes the character not just by keeping horses
and riding to hounds but by cultivating a gentlemanly carelessness about
money: 'he was a tradesman, and he never was known to have sent in a
bill.'[75] But that carelessness, a carelessness that he has to cultivate if he is
to maintain his gentlemanly demeanour, results in his disgrace as a tradesman. He dies in debt to the tune of £5000, and this, as his wife understands, is to die with a stain on his character that can be expunged only if
his debts are discharged. 'You have £5000 to pay to save your father from
being called a rogue,' she tells Evan. The honour of a tradesman, as she
knows very well, unlike the honour of a gentleman, demands an exact
keeping of accounts. 'Very well,' Evan replies to his mother, 'I will pay it.'
But he has no idea how. He has been educated as a gentleman, but that is
not in itself a position to which a salary attaches. He had thought of the
army, but knows that he does not have the means for it. He has been living
with his sister, the Countess, in Portugal, and for ten months has served as
private secretary to the 'celebrated diplomat' Melville Jocelyn, on the

[74] *Evan Harrington*, chapter 3.
[75] *Evan Harrington*, chapter 1.

strength of which he thinks he may be offered a government appointment. He has written half of a history of Portugal. His mother listens to his suggestions and dismisses them. He will only be able to pay off his father's debts if he takes over the family business. Evan retires to his bedroom overcome with 'horrible sensations of self-contempt'.[76]

There is the world of trade, a world centred on money, and there is the gentlemanly world, a world which is above money. The two worlds pretend to be opposites, each the antipode of the other. But it is not really so. The two worlds are interdependent. In the term that Meredith uses in the novel, the two worlds rhyme. There is the gentlemanly kingdom with its aristocracy and, rhyming with it, is 'tailordom' with its 'snipocracy'. Reigning over the first is the Prince Regent, the first gentleman of Europe, and reigning over the second the great Mel, who is, according to Lady Jocelyn, the Regent's 'twin-brother'.[77] It is not only Melchisedec Harrington, the tailor, who is known as the great Mel. It is also the nickname of the Honourable Melville Jocelyn, the diplomat, Rose's uncle and Lady Jocelyn's brother-in-law: 'they call him the great Mel.'[78] The two men rhyme with one another. Melville Jocelyn expertly maintains the 'Balance of Power' in Europe: the expertise of tailors, like Melchisedec Harrington's colleague Mr Goren, is not shown in maintaining a balance of power but a 'Balance in Breeches'.[79] The rhyming may be literal. A woman of birth is outraged by the proposal that the great Mel, a tailor, might be invited to her country house, 'Dox Hall', and protests that Dox Hall should not be mistaken for Vauxhall.[80] George Uplift is engaged to Lady Jocelyn's cousin, Louisa Carrington. Uplift had as a young man been so struck by the beauty of a tailor's daughter that he was in some danger of marrying foolishly. Her name was Louisa Harrington, the girl who grew up to become the Countess de Saldar. The novel begins as the ship carrying the Countess and Evan back to England nears shore. The ship also carries Rose Jocelyn and she and Evan consolidate on board the romantic attachment that they had first formed in Portugal. But before the ship docks it is boarded by a dark-suited man, Mr Goren, a London tailor, who brings news of the death of Evan's father. The secret of Evan's ancestry, the fact

[76] *Evan Harrington*, chapter 7.
[77] *Evan Harrington*, chapter 20.
[78] *Evan Harrington*, chapter 14.
[79] *Evan Harrington*, chapter 16.
[80] *Evan Harrington*, chapter 22. Vauxhall Gardens, the London pleasure garden, closed finally in 1859, but long before then the once fashionable resort had gone downmarket.

that he is the son of a tailor, would certainly have been exposed at that moment if the Countess had not noticed listed among the deaths in the newspaper, 'Sir Abraham Harrington, of Torquay, Baronet, of quinsy', and decided at once to shed her tears not for the deceased tailor but the dead baronet.[81] It is not simply a coincidence that two men named Harrington should die at the same time, the Countess insists. It is 'Providence', the Providence, as she thinks, that comes to her aid whenever she is in danger of being revealed as a tailor's daughter. In fact, Providence is all through the novel busy pointing out that the genteel world and the shop, the aristocracy and the snipocracy, cannot be kept apart. Sir Abraham, although the Countess does not know it, inherited his estate, Ryelands Park, from Burley Bennet, a notorious gambler, who had won it from a royal duke in a game of cards. The great Mel always swore that, had he not somehow offended Bennet, the property would have been left to him.[82] Melchisedec and Abraham Harrington are distinguished not by an accident of birth but by a still more accidental legacy. The belief that defines the gentlemanly world, the belief that it is above money, is, the novel reveals, an illusion, and an illusion that only money can sustain.

All three of Mel's daughters make their escape from tailordom, Caroline by marrying an officer in the Royal Marines, Louise by marrying a Portuguese Count, and Harriet by marrying Andrew Cogglesby, a brewer. A brewer, it might be objected, is just as much a tradesman as a tailor. In fact, Cogglesby has a yet lower origin, he is the son of a cobbler. But a brewer, unlike a tailor, is rich, and wealth, especially if the wealth is fabulous, always has the power to confer gentlemanly status on its possessor. The Jocelyns live in Beckley Court, their country house, but they do not own it. It belongs to Rose's grandmother, 'rich old Mrs. Bonner', and Mrs Bonner's husband made his wealth, as Harry Jocelyn admits to the Countess, through speculation in oil. The Countess is shocked. She conceives oil to be a kind of 'grocery', 'So, you are grocers on one side!' 'You should', she warns Harry, 'ever be careful not to expose the grocer.'[83] It is a fine example of the Countess's effrontery, but it is also the case, as the Countess knows very well, that there was hardly a family in England, no matter how well bred, that did not have a grocer to conceal. As she points

---

[81] *Evan Harrington*, chapter 9.
[82] *Evan Harrington*, chapter 22.
[83] *Evan Harrington*, chapter 15.

out, 'Half the aristocracy of England spring from shops!'[84] When her uncle describes an acquaintance as 'the son of a small shopkeeper of some kind in Southampton', Rose Jocelyn exclaims, 'Oh, I can't bear that class of people', and Evan who overhears her is mortified.[85] But, as Rose later explains, she responds as she does not because that class of people is so distant from her but because it is so close: 'It happened through my mother's father being a merchant; and on that side of the family the men and women are quite sordid and unendurable; and that's how it came that I spoke of disliking tradesmen.'[86] But it is Mrs Bonner, her mother's mother, not her father Sir Franks Jocelyn who owns Beckley Court, and it was Mrs Bonner's husband who made the money that supports the Jocelyns in their contempt for the merchant classes. Lady Jocelyn tells Evan that she has 'no Republican virtues',[87] which is why she will not recommend her daughter to marry the son of a tailor. But when she was Miss Bonner she was a playmate of Tom and Andrew Cogglesby, the sons of a cobbler, and inspired in Tom Cogglesby a devotion that has kept him a bachelor all his life. Rose overcomes at the last her repugnance at the notion of marrying the son of a tradesman, but she is able to do so only because old Tom Cogglesby, the immensely rich brewer, has taken to Evan and made him his heir. It is the tradesman who supplies the wealth that allows Evan to rise above trade.

When Rose is told that Evan has lied to her, she replies superbly, 'Do you think my lover could tell a lie?'[88] Rose admits that she told lies herself when she was a girl. When Lady Jocelyn found it out she branded her daughter on the palm of her hand with the letter L. 'I have never told a lie since,' she tells Evan.[89] An inability to lie is as much a class marker as a refusal to take any interest in money. The Earl of Fleetwood in *The Amazing Marriage* prides himself above all else on never breaking his word when once it has been given: he is 'the prisoner of his word'.[90] But in fact all the Jocelyns, despite Rose's protestation, tell lies. Rose's brother Harry, for example, proclaims his love for his wealthy invalid cousin, Juliana, 'It isn't a lie! I say, I do love you', and as he speaks the words, he

[84] *Evan Harrington*, chapter 44.
[85] *Evan Harrington*, chapter 4.
[86] *Evan Harrington*, chapter 25.
[87] *Evan Harrington*, chapter 28.
[88] *Evan Harrington*, chapter 35.
[89] *Evan Harrington*, chapter 25.
[90] The title of chapter 11 of *The Amazing Marriage*.

is almost able to persuade himself that he is speaking the truth: 'for an instant he thought and hoped that he did love her.'[91] Lady Jocelyn lies when a violent husband demands an interview with his errant wife. 'Evelyn is not here,' she tells him.[92] Rose breaks her word when she accepts Ferdinand Laxley's proposal and afterwards decides that she would rather marry Evan. Evan lives a lie for most of the novel. He has, as his mother tells Lady Jocelyn, 'been playing the lord in your house' when he was all along 'no more than a tailor's son'.[93] He has systematically misled the Jocelyns as to his social status. His sister, the Countess of Saldar, lies so consummately that she achieves a kind of magnificence. She is the tailor's daughter from Lymport-on-the-Sea who has made herself into a foreign noblewoman and can entrance almost any man she meets by tilting up to him a face 'that had all the sugary sparkles of a crystallised preserved fruit of the Portugal clime'.[94] She inhabits the role she has chosen so completely that she speaks a heavily accented, unidiomatic English, and even manages to find the rules of cricket mystifying: 'Indeed, it is an intricate game!'[95] Lying for her has become a virtuoso performance rather than a moral failing. One crucial mark of the gentleman is that he cannot tell a lie, and yet the genteel world, as Meredith's novel reveals, is only sustained by the systematic deployment of untruths.

Evan is the great Mel's true son. He does not take on his father's debts, but he does take on his mission: to prove that it is possible at once to be a tailor and a gentleman. He gives two large demonstrations of the nobility of his character. The very first is to tell a lie. He confesses to Lady Jocelyn that he is the author of a forged letter. He is willing to besmirch his own character in order to protect the reputation of the real culprit, his sister, the Countess. Evan proves that he is a gentleman by telling a lie, which is not at all a paradox in a world in which gentlemen define themselves by their difference from tradesmen even though it is trade from which, directly or indirectly, the gentlemen derive the wealth that secures their status. The second demonstration is still grander. Juliana Bonner inherits Beckley Court from her grandmother, and when she dies (prompting the tart remark, 'diseased little heroines may be made attractive, and are now

[91] *Evan Harrington*, chapter 29.
[92] *Evan Harrington*, chapter 31.
[93] *Evan Harrington*, chapter 31.
[94] *Evan Harrington*, chapter 4.
[95] *Evan Harrington*, chapter 13.

popular'[96]) she leaves the house to Evan, the man that she has all along secretly loved. Evan responds to this somewhat theatrical turn of events with a still more theatrical gesture. He refuses the legacy and returns Beckley Court to the Jocelyns, rendering them indebted for the house in which they live to the man they had despised. It is a gesture through which Evan demonstrates how truly a gentleman he is by rising so grandly above all mercenary considerations. In the first case Evan shows himself a gentleman by telling a lie. In the second he shows himself a gentleman by underwriting the lie on which the idea of gentlemanliness is founded.

In April 1873, the new serial in the *Fortnightly* was Trollope's *Lady Anna*. Meredith would have noticed it, because he read the *Fortnightly*. It was edited by his friend, John Morley. Lady Anna, disowned as illegitimate by her father who has cast off his wife, is dependent all through her early life on the generosity of a radical tailor. Thomas Thwaite supports Lady Anna and her mother as a way of expressing his contempt for the aristocracy (Anna's father is an earl). Anna shares her childhood with the tailor's son, and so it is unsurprising when Daniel Thwaite, who follows his father's profession, falls in love with her, proposes and is accepted. But then Lord Lovel dies, and Anna and her mother are recognised as his heirs. A male cousin inherits the title, but almost nothing of the late earl's large fortune. His friends decide that rather than dispute the will the new Lord Lovel would do better to marry his cousin. It seems a sordid bargain, but the young Lord Lovel is a winning specimen of his class and makes Anna feel what it would be to live the life that he offers her. His courtship is enthusiastically encouraged by all the Lovel family, and by Anna's mother, whose treatment by the late earl has entirely failed to moderate her respect for the aristocracy. Daniel Thwaite is an upright, principled, and generous young man, but he is also 'ambitious, discontented, sullen, and tyrannical',[97] and he shares with his father a narrow, ideological disapproval of the upper classes. When she is kissed by the young earl, captivated by the winning softness of his manners still more than by the softness of his lips, Anna finds her love for the journeyman tailor all but evaporate. But Thwaite refuses to give up his claim to her hand even when advised to do so by Wordsworth (the poet who gives the advice is unnamed but his identity is clear). In his old age the poet has come to disapprove of unequal marriages.

---

[96] *Evan Harrington*, chapter 42. Dickens's *The Old Curiosity Shop* had established the fashion 20 years before.

[97] Anthony Trollope, *Lady Anna*, chapter 21.

Thwaite does offer to free her from the engagement but only if she asks him to do so, and this, he knows, she will never do, because she is a young woman of her word. Her own mother would rather her daughter die than bring disgrace on the family by marrying a tailor, but in the end she compromises and settles on the death of her daughter's fiancé. She shoots him, but Daniel Thwaite survives, and at the last Anna marries him. The young earl agrees to give away the bride, even though she has 'preferred to his own the addresses of a low-born man, reeking with the sweat of a tailor's board',[98] the earl's uncle, the Rector of Yoxham, performs the ceremony, and the Rector's daughter Minnie acts as bridesmaid, even though the thought of Lady Anna marrying a tailor strikes her as 'almost as bad as the story of the Princess who had to marry a bear'.[99] The sane verdict on the marriage is offered by the young earl's lawyer, Sir William Paterson, the Solicitor-General, who points out that the tailor is clearly a man of ability. Given the fortune that his wife brings him he will be a member of parliament in five years, and Sir Daniel Thwaite in ten, and, after all, 'How many peers' daughters marry commoners in England?'[100]

It may be that Trollope took the idea for his novel from Meredith. He may at least have glanced at *Evan Harrington* when it was appearing in *Once a Week*. On the face of it, Trollope's Lady Anna, who chooses to marry Daniel Thwaite, the tailor's son, rather than Lord Lovel, seems close kin to Meredith's Rose Jocelyn, who chooses Evan Harrington rather than Ferdinand Laxley, Lord Laxley's son and heir to the title. But the novels are not really very alike. *Lady Anna* may have been published 12 years after *Evan Harrington*, but Trollope is a novelist of an earlier generation, born in 1815, almost 13 years before Meredith. Trollope invites the reader to share Lady Anna's fascination with Lord Lovel, to be all but seduced by a manner that seems still more winning by its contrast with the abrasive, dictatorial manner of the young tailor. Trollope's well-born friend, Lady Wood, wrote to him hoping that he would allow his heroine to marry the lord, but Trollope refused ('Of course the girl has to marry the tailor. It is very dreadful but there was no other way'). Lady Anna must be true to her word and marry the man whose proposal she

---

[98] Anthony Trollope, *Lady Anna*, chapter 17.
[99] Anthony Trollope, *Lady Anna*, chapter 48.
[100] Anthony Trollope, *Lady Anna*, chapter 40.

had accepted.[101] In Trollope's novels identities are fixed, in Meredith's they are fluid. The Solicitor-General expects Daniel Thwaite to become an MP. and to be knighted, but whatever the future brings he will retain the harsh manner of a tradesman from the north of England. Evan Harrington is quite different. He is not less but more of a gentleman in his manners than the son and heir of Lord Laxley. He has after all been taught his manners by his Portuguese sister. Her special ability is to maintain two identities and to keep them quite separate one from another. She is both Louisa Harrington and the Countess of Saldar. When she meets George Uplift, an old flame of hers, he recognises her at once as the daughter of the tailor, but instead of fleeing him, she engages him in conversation, and her performance as the Countess is so convincing that he finds himself disbelieving the evidence of his own eyes. Evan lacks his sister's bravura, but he shares her ability to maintain two identities. At Beckley Court he is the complete gentleman, and yet thoughts of his dead father still have for him the power to 'cast a sort of halo over Tailordom'.[102] Those thoughts prompt him to approach the insufferably rude gentlemen-cricketers and confess to them that his father was a tradesman, but even at that moment he retains his dual identity, because the manner in which he makes his confession is so completely the manner of a gentleman. Harry Jocelyn, one of the cricketers, finds himself quite unable to decide whether Evan is a tailor pretending to be a gentleman, or a gentleman who has taken it into his head to pretend for reasons of his own to be a tailor.

Evan Harrington is a novel about mimicry. The Countess, its most vivid character, is also its greatest mimic. She performs her role as a foreign countess with the gusto of the female impersonator who seems almost to mock the femininity to which he aspires. The great Mel's pet monkey, who has survived his master, is introduced early in the novel. Jacko squats at the foot of his master's coffin, 'with his legs crossed, very like a tailor!'[103] Jacko is given human form when Jack Raikes, Evan's old school friend, is introduced into the novel. He reminds the Countess of a Brazilian ape.[104] Unlike the monkey, Raikes imitates a gentleman rather than a tailor. Old Tom

---

[101] *Letters of Anthony Trollope*, ed. John H. Hall, 2 volumes (Stanford: Stanford University Press, 1983), 2, 589.

[102] *Evan Harrington*, chapter 6.

[103] *Evan Harrington*, chapter 2.

[104] *Evan Harrington*, chapter 33.

Cogglesby humiliates him by persuading him for a cash recompense to wear a tin plate on his back inscribed 'John F. Raikes, Gentleman'. When he looks at Raikes Evan cannot help seeing 'something of himself magnified'.[105] Raikes has tried to make a career for himself on the stage, but failed. Evan's misgivings are produced by an anxious sense that the difference between the two might simply be that he is the better actor. It may be that the only difference between them is that he is Raikes's superior in the art of mimicry. He looks at Raikes and bursts out in bitter laughter at 'this burlesque of himself'.[106] But mimicry cuts both ways: the ridicule it excites might attach itself either to the mimic or the mimicked. After she has listened to anecdotes of the great Mel over dinner Lady Jocelyn, for all that she recognises something fine in him, describes him as a 'buffoon imitation of the real thing'. But she also recognises him as the 'embodied protest against our social prejudice', the man who 'measures your husband in the morning', and 'in the evening makes love to you, through a series of pantomimic transformations'.[107] The tailor who shows he can pass as a gentleman makes himself into a buffoon by wishing to be taken for something he is not, by becoming a mimic man, like one of Naipaul's colonials, but he also makes buffoons of the gentlemen, by showing how the social accomplishments on which they pride themselves can be perfectly mastered by a tailor. The same is true of the Countess, a 'heroine who is combating class-prejudices' and a woman who acts at the same time as 'the champion of the opposing institution misplaced'.[108] In her frantic ambition to pass for an aristocrat, she strikes a shrewd blow against all aristocratic pretension. She occupies like the great Mel, the father whose memory she worships, that strange indeterminate position that Evan, her brother, occupies so much more quietly and decorously, and it is from the same position that Meredith writes his novel. He writes from what Hardy calls the 'peculiar situation, as it were in mid-air between two planes of society'. It is why *Evan Harrington* is so different a novel from *Lady Anna*. Trollope finds a firm footing from which to tell his story: Meredith tells his from mid-air.

The novel did not please his father. Augustus Meredith, a Cape Town customer of his recalled, asked him whether he had seen *Evan Harrington*, which was being serialised at the time in *Once a Week*. 'I am very sore about

[105] *Evan Harrington*, chapter 32.
[106] *Evan Harrington*, chapter 36.
[107] *Evan Harrington*, chapter 22.
[108] *Evan Harrington*, chapter 30.

it,' Augustus said; 'I am pained beyond expression, as I consider it aimed at myself, and I am sorry to say the writer is my own son.'[109] It is easy to see why he should have reacted as he did. The novel recklessly betrays family confidences, and no man would like to see his profession represented by his own son as emblematically humiliating. 'Oh, Evan,' the Countess exclaims, 'the eternal contemplation of gentlemen's legs!'[110] *Evan Harrington* is Meredith's treacherous burlesque of his own family's history, but it is also his love letter to his family. The plot relies on such well-worn devices that it creaks. Meredith falls back, as he often does when he is trying to write in a manner that will please the reading public, on weak imitations of Dickens. His Cogglesby brothers, for example, are such close imitations of the brothers Cheeryble of *Nicholas Nickleby* that it almost constitutes a case of plagiarism. But the novel keeps its vitality because Meredith gives his hero so many of his own contradictions; his love and contempt for his family, his need to conceal and to confess his origins, his claim to be as good a gentleman as anyone and his fear that he will only ever be a burlesque imitation of the real thing. Just after *Evan Harrington* was published Meredith wrote to the woman who had been his model for Rose, Janet Duff Gordon, now Mrs Janet Ross. He told her how he had recently met a friend of hers, a man that they refer to between themselves as the 'Perfect Gentleman'. 'He has a pleasant way of being inquisitive', Meredith writes, 'and has already informed me, quite agreeably, that I am a gentleman, though I may not have been born one.' He seems amused, insouciant, but he adds, 'Some men are always shooting about you like May flies in little quick darts, to see how near you they may come.'[111] Jem Price recalled the ten-year-old Meredith's 'drawling, patronising' intonation. Richard Le Gallienne first met him when he was an old man, but Meredith's voice struck him very much as it had struck young Jem: it seemed to him 'slightly theatrical, almost affectedly bravura'.[112] It is the voice that he gave to the Countess of Saldar who lapses into the vernacular only when excited, and at all other times favours 'a deliberate delicately-syllabled drawl'.[113] Meredith was born a tailor's son. It was an identity that he left far behind him and yet still contrived to carry with him all his life.

[109] *Bibliography*, 138.
[110] *Evan Harrington*, chapter 33.
[111] *Letters*, 1, 111.
[112] Le Gallienne, 40.
[113] *Evan Harrington*, chapter 3.

GOTT IST DIE LIEBE

At his English boarding school, wherever it was, Meredith may, like Evan Harrington, have pretended that his father was in the army. But it was a deception that he did not have to maintain for long. On August 18, 1842, he was enrolled at the Moravian School at Neuwied, the principal town of the tiny German principality of Wied-Neuwied, just seven miles downstream from Koblenz. It seems unlikely that Meredith left his English boarding school, like Harry Richmond, because his fees were not paid. The year before, in 1841, Meredith's father had surrendered the guardianship of his son to the Macnamara family solicitor. The boy was dependent for his financial support on his legacies from his mother and her sister. Perhaps Augustus Meredith gave up his guardianship of young George as a way of ensuring that George's modest inheritance did not become tangled up in his own financial embarrassments, perhaps his wife's family insisted on it, but in either case Charles Binstead, the solicitor, would have made sure that the school fees were paid. It must have been decided, though, that the fees were too high, and that by the time he left school not enough would be left of the money George had inherited to set him up in a profession, because the principal reason for transferring George from the English boarding school to the school at Neuwied can only have been that the German school was cheaper. The bill that the school sent back to England was, as Henry Morley, who enrolled in the school nine years before Meredith, put it, 'a moderate one'.

Meredith offered no first-hand account of the two years he spent at Neuwied any more than of his time at St Paul's, Southsea, or the English boarding school that he seems to have attended after his father moved to London, but Henry Morley published his own vivid recollections of the school in Dickens's *Household Words*.[114] The school was run by the Moravian Brothers, a missionary order that had been expelled from Moravia during the counter-reformation and had established itself in German states such as Wied-Neuwied that practised religious toleration. Henry Morley looked back on his two years at the school as the happiest time of his life. At Neuwied, unlike the English schools he had attended, corporal punishment was unknown. The Brothers lived in simple fellowship with the boys they taught, and the teaching they offered was moral rather than academic. There were about 150 pupils, half of them English,

---

[114] 'Brother Mieth and His Brothers', *Household Words*, 9 (May 27, 1854), 344–9.

the others drawn from various European countries. Discipline was relaxed. The boys were encouraged to play in the school grounds and to roam abroad. At Whitsun they went on week-long rambles, sleeping in barns and farmhouses. The boys were divided into groups of 20 of similar age who slept together, and all 20 birthdays were celebrated as well as the birthdays of the two Brothers who had special charge of the group, one of them responsible for minds of the boys, the other for their bodies. The Brothers offered their pupils what Morley calls 'the liberty of growth'. 'I had been used at English schools to strictness of rule with laxity of principle,' he writes. The Moravian brothers offered 'strictness of principle with laxity of rule'. The Brothers were remarkable for their simple piety, but they made no attempt to impose their own beliefs on the pupils. They relied simply on the force of their example. Morley was impressed by the churchyard in which the grave of each brother was marked by an identical flat stone. It was a place in which 'all rested as equals': there were none of the 'colossal tea-caddies in stone, and the stone tea-urns without spouts, that indicate, in English cemeteries, where the respectable dead bodies have been placed'. Morley's father was a London apothecary. The family lived in Gower Street, and Morley recalls how he made a drawing of his family home to show the Brothers and his school friends. He made 'a rude pen-and-ink sketch of a spacious turreted castle with four corner towers of such height as it would enter only into the mind of Mr. Barry to conceive', and the sketch was quietly examined by the Brothers with 'not a trace of doubt'. 'Against this quiet trustfulness,' Morley writes, 'no child's spirit of untruth could maintain itself.' When he arrived at the school, he was 'a little rascal'. The Brothers taught him the lessons he most needed to learn, and they did so by allowing him to cultivate rather than combat the instincts that he had been born with. Morley wrote his essay for *Household Words*. His recollections are self-consciously idyllic: they conform to a genre that Dickens and his readers enjoyed. But they give some sense of the school at which Meredith arrived in August 1842.

Henry Morley travelled to Germany alone.[115] His father saw him safely over 'the worst part of the journey—London Streets', and left him at the docks in the care of a steward for the voyage to Rotterdam. Morley had a letter of introduction to a Rotterdam family. He found that there were several families of that name in the city, but he eventually found the family

---

[115] Morley gives his account of the journey in 'Ten Years Old', *Household Words*, 7 (May 14, 1853), 245–8.

that he was looking for. The family recommended a hotel where he slept the night, and the next morning he embarked on a Rhine steamer. He slept on board that night and at Neuwied on the following day a Brother from the school was waiting on the jetty to meet him. As Morley puts it, 'From St Katherine's Docks it was all plain sailing, and a boy of ten must be a dunce indeed if he could not find his own way up the Rhine.' Meredith may well have travelled alone like Henry Morley. He was four years older, and his father is unlikely to have had the time or the money to escort him. But he may have travelled with another boy as a companion. In *The Adventures of Harry Richmond* at any rate Harry travels to Germany accompanied by his school friend, Gus Temple. The circumstances of the voyage are fantastic enough. Gus and Harry, alone in London, are given a berth for the night by the mate of a merchantman, and wake after a drunken evening to find that the ship has embarked. The Captain, a born-again Christian, refuses to put the boys ashore, trusting that in the course of the voyage he will be able to reclaim them for God. Harry had come to London in search of his father. The father had cut a typically grand figure when he arrived with Harry at Mr Rippenger's school, but Harry has seen nothing of him since. 'My dreams of my father were losing distinctness,'[116] he recalls, and the sentence erases the distance between young Harry and young George. After his mother died in 1833, when he was five, his life had revolved around his father, Augustus Meredith. And then on July 3, 1839, accompanied by Matilda Buckett, he left Portsmouth for London, and all but disappeared from his son's life.

Harry is looking for his father when he and Temple take a train to London, and, as in a dream, when they are kidnapped by Captain Welsh and disembark in a German port they find that Harry's father has preceded them, and that he too is in Germany. Meredith lends Harry the ache left by his own father's absence, and the absence has the same cause, debt. Harry takes the train to London because he has learned that his father is in the Bench, the debtors' prison in Southwark. He pictures the place to himself as an exotic palace. When he imagines the building he tops it with 'a multitude of domes of pumpkin or of turban shape, resembling the Kremlin of Moscow, which had once leapt up in the eye of Winter, glowing like a million pine-torches, and flung shadows of stretching red horses on the black smoke-drift'.[117] In his imagination he yields to the same impulse that led Henry Morley to add crenellations to his family house in

---

[116] *The Adventures of Harry Richmond*, chapter 5.
[117] *The Adventures of Harry Richmond*, chapter 11.

Gower Street. Morley allows his ten-year-old self to travel through Europe with undisturbed insouciance: 'There are some men of fifty a great deal less fit to travel unprotected than the majority of boys at ten.' Harry and Temple travel through London fog, quite ignorant of the whereabouts of the prison they are seeking, and find themselves as if by magic outside the Bench, with the fog lit luridly by a house beside the prison that is in flames. The journeys that children go on when they travel alone are phantasmagoric journeys through a world that has lost its sharp contours, and is always threatening to melt into a dream. Meredith found that out, it seems likely, when at the age of 14 he was sent to Germany.

In his old age Meredith told Edward Clodd that he had once suffered 'a spasm of religion which lasted about six weeks', during which he made himself a nuisance by 'asking everybody whether they were saved'.[118] He gave a rather different account to the Reverend Augustus Jessopp, his first son's headmaster, when he regretted Jessopp's practice of having the boys attend services three times each Sunday:

> I remember, at that age, how all love of the Apostles was laboured out of me by three Sunday services of prodigious length and dreariness. Corinthians will forever be associated in my mind with rows of wax candles and a holy drone over-head, combined with the sensation that those who did not choose the road to Heaven, enjoyed by far the pleasantest way.[119]

His habit, he claimed, was to take to church a serial story recounting the adventures of St George and read it during the sermon. Meredith must have been recalling the time when he had attended an English boarding school, but the tedium was not so lethal to his faith as he pretended. His earliest surviving letters were written from Neuwied in 1844, after he had been a pupil at the school for almost 18 months. All three of the letters are extravagantly pious, quite unlike any letters that he wrote afterwards. The first of them, to a fellow pupil, R. M. Hill, recalls the 'fellowship' the two had enjoyed at school, and warns that 'true fellowship is not to be had without Christianity; not the name but the practice of it'. He wishes Hill 'the greatest of all things, "God's blessing", which comprehends all I would or could otherwise say'.[120] The second, written in German, is to Brother Adolph Hermann Jannasch who seems to have been one of his

[118] Clodd, 153.
[119] *Letters*, 1, 181.
[120] *Letters*, 1, 1.

teachers.[121] Meredith apologises to Jannasch if he has ever behaved badly towards him and assures him of his full conversion to the religion of love, 'Wer nicht lieb hat, der ist nicht von Gott, denn Gott ist die Liebe' (Who has not love is not of God, for God is love). The third advises a friend that it is impossible to change 'without help from above': 'May you receive that power that you may be beloved by all that know you and enjoy all inward happiness.'[122] Less than five years before the 11-year-old Meredith had congratulated Joe Neale on the quality of his father's racehorse, 'By George! he's got some blood in him!' He was 15 now, and seems at last to have become a child. Henry Morley recognised for the first time at Neuwied how his 'puerility had been, at other schools, discouraged and repressed'. Neuwied allowed him to become a child again. It seems to have done something of the same for Meredith. It allowed him at any rate to become the kind of boy he would never have dared to be at Saint Paul's, Southsea, or at whatever English boarding school he attended afterwards. He had not quite changed character though. When he was talking to Joe Neale he was acting the young swell. In the letters that he wrote five years later he is performing a very different role, the earnest young Christian. It is the sense that he is giving a performance that stays the same.

Neuwied left its mark on Meredith as it had on Henry Morley. Morley remained grateful to the school all through his life. Meredith's feelings were more complicated. The Brothers' teaching was more repressive than Morley registers. They forbade the reading of novels and plays. Even copies of Shakespeare were confiscated. The boys were restricted, as even Morley complains, to 'edifying stories about Easter eggs and other holy things'. Meredith explores the mixed feelings that the school prompted in him in the debates in which Harry Richmond and his friend Temple engage with Captain Welsh when the two boys are unwilling passengers on Welsh's ship, the Priscilla, bound for Germany. The boys pit their classical education against the Captain's Bible learning. Irritated by 'the dogmatic arrogance of a just but ignorant man' they counter Welsh's scriptural texts with 'bits of Cicero, bits of Seneca' which 'did service on behalf of Paganism'. The Captain is unmoved. He only 'groaned heartily to hear that our learning lay in the direction of Pagan Gods and Goddesses, and

[121] Jannasch is listed in the *Periodical accounts relating to the missions of the Church of the United Brethren, established among the heathen* (London: 1844), p. 510, as having been appointed to serve in the South African Mission.
[122] Shaheen, 17–8.

heathen historians and poets'. Welsh is quite unimpressed by the boys' public school education. There is only one book that he believes it necessary to know. If he envies the boys their Greek it is only because 'the New Testament was written in Greek, and happy were those who could read it in the original'.[123] As Henry Morley admits, at Neuwied he 'learned the German language, and unlearned everything else'. He took with him to Germany a 'good stock of Latin and Greek' and found that in his two years at the school he forgot his Greek and was permitted 'to dwindle down from a precocious bolter of Virgil to a bad decliner of rex regis'. He valued his German education because it taught him lessons he thought more important. He learned in Germany to recognise and to value the Christian virtues. But it was the classical learning that he lost that was still in the middle of the nineteenth century the defining badge of the gentleman. How can we keep up our Greek on board your ship, Temple asks Captain Welsh, and, if we cannot, 'how can we be graduating for our sphere in life?' He will not take Welsh's word for it that 'Greek and Latin authors are bad' for him, although he would have accepted the advice if it had come from the Archbishop of Canterbury, 'because he's a scholar'. Like Morley, Meredith would have lost at Neuwied most of the Greek and Latin that St Paul's and his English boarding school had drummed into him, and that was not simply by accident. Classical learning, like the tea-caddies in stone, and the stone tea-urns without spouts that identify where the respectable bodies lie in English churchyards, marked a class division, and class divisions were banished from Neuwied where every brother was buried under the same flat stone. Meredith remembered all through his life that German romance of simple fellowship between people who lived together without any distinction of rank, but once he was back in England he worked hard to recover his Latin and his Greek.

On board ship Richmond and Temple counter Captain Welsh's Biblical texts with quotations from Plutarch. 'Do not despise a virtue purely Pagan,' Meredith advises in *Evan Harrington*. He is prompted to the remark when Evan defends the honour of his sister by falsely confessing that it was him rather than her who had forged a letter. He makes the confession even though he knows that it may cost him Rose's love. Meredith goes on to claim that there are advantages in beginning life as a pagan: 'The heathen ideal is not so easy to attain, and those who mount

---

[123] *The Adventures of Harry Richmond*, chapter 12.

from it to the Christian have, in my humble thought, a firmer footing.'[124] When he is not just exposed as a tailor but believed on his own confession to be a forger, Evan is supported in his humiliation by his heathen pride, which, Meredith supposes, will graduate as he grows older into true Christian virtue. But by 1860, when he wrote *Evan Harrington*, Meredith thought no such thing. He offers the suggestion only as a sop to his Christian readers. His first novel, *The Ordeal of Richard Feverel*, had attracted complaints. Its hero, newly married, allowed himself to be seduced by a notorious demirep, Mrs Bella Mount. Charles Mudie listened to representations and cancelled the order for the novel he had already placed. Not to be stocked in Mudie's circulating library was a distinction in which a combative young novelist might take some pride. Does the Rev. Augustus Jessopp's wife know, Meredith asks, that his 'literary reputation is tabooed as worse than libertine in certain virtuous Societies?' Is she aware that 'there have been meetings to banish me from book-clubs? And that Pater familias has given Mr. Mudie a very large bit of his petticoated mind concerning me?'[125] But it was a satisfaction that came at considerable financial cost. Meredith was anxious not to repeat the offence in his second novel. The inclusion of such thoroughly Dickensian characters as the Cogglesby brothers is compelling evidence that in *Evan Harrington* he was making a determined attempt to please the readership to which throughout most of his career he claimed to be truculently indifferent. The plot, in which the Jocelyns are persuaded at the story's end to make a family pilgrimage to Evan at the tailor's shop in Lynmouth to thank him for restoring them to Beckley Court and formally to recognise his claim to be a gentleman, is another indication of an anxiety to please. By making that visit the Jocelyns acknowledge Evan as their equal. In surrendering to them the house that has been bequeathed to him he has vanquished them by a display of gentlemanly grace that they cannot match. The tailor has proved himself a fit match for their daughter. He has even proved himself their superior. And yet Meredith has already established that the gentlemanly code can be sustained only by a virtuoso display of precisely the capacity for lying of which gentlemen are supposed to be incapable. The Victorian gentleman and the Victorian novelist found themselves in much the same position, because they can both of them maintain themselves only by telling lies. The novelist is a realist, under an

---

[124] *Evan Harrington*, chapter 34.
[125] *Letters*, 1, 130.

obligation to describe the world honestly, and yet he writes for a reader-ship who will only be content if he upholds their illusions, if he pretends that the Jocelyns will learn to be entirely happy for their daughter to marry a tailor's son, and that the heathen virtues that Evan displays will ripen in time into the Christian humility that he so clearly lacks.

When Meredith came back to England from Germany early in 1844, he returned rather like Evan Harrington who stands on deck watching as his ship, the Jocasta, approaches the white cliffs, wearing a dusky sombrero, a cloak dangling from his shoulder, and sporting a thin, dark moustache. Meredith's clothing would have been German and less elegant, but like Evan he came home wearing a foreign disguise, and it was a disguise that he maintained all through his life. As Henry James remarked after meeting Meredith at a dinner party, 'He hates the English, whom he speaks of as "they".'[126] But the costume was not just adopted to disguise his national-ity. It worked, as the Countess of Saldar recognises when she looks approv-ingly at her brother, to disguise his class. The Countess is distressed even when Evan shaves off that thin, foreign-looking moustache of his, fearing that a naked upper lip might expose the tailor's son. But Meredith also brought back with him to England the values that the Moravian Brothers had instilled in him. In particular, he had learned the value that attached to 'true fellowship', a fellowship that did not recognise social distinctions, a fellowship 'not to be had without Christianity; not the name but the practice of it'. His Christian phase lasted longer than the six weeks he admitted to, but it did not last long. Two years later he fell in love with the daughter of Thomas Love Peacock, who had been the close friend of the atheist Shelley and took great pleasure in declaring himself a pagan. By then Meredith had become what he was to remain all his life, what he admired the poet James Thompson for being, 'an open-mouthed despiser of the parsonry'.[127] Meredith may have rejected the lessons that he learned from the Moravian Brothers at Neuwied, but he never forgot them. They stayed with him, and produced an alternative self, a self that he chose not to be, but a self that he nevertheless carried with him all through his life just as much as he carried with him the secret knowledge that he was the son of a tailor.

---

[126] *The Complete Letters of Henry James, 1878–1880*, ed. Pierre A. Walker and Greg W. Zacharias (Lincoln, Nebraska: University of Nebraska Press, 2015), 72.

[127] *Letters*, 2, 677.

In March 1844, just weeks after Meredith arrived back in England his
father applied to Chancery asking that £400 be realised from George's
estate so that he could be bound apprentice to John Williams, a bookseller
and publisher. Williams had a business at 44, Paternoster Row, but he
planned to emigrate to Hong Kong, and set up business there as a bookseller and publisher 'together with the business of taking portraits, landscapes, and other representative objects by the Photogenic System and of
precipitating metals by Galvanic electricity'. Williams proposed to take
George Meredith with him, to which, Augustus Meredith added, 'the
deponent's said son is desirous so to do if he can be supplied with the
necessary funds for that purpose.' It was an exciting suggestion.
Photography by the daguerreotype process had only been commercially
viable since 1839, and it was only in 1842 that Hong Kong became a
Crown Colony of the British Empire after the defeat of China in the First
Opium War. But it must have seemed to Meredith, who had only just
turned 16, that his father, almost as soon as he had arrived back in England
from Germany, was intent on sending him away again. It must have
seemed like another rejection, and a still more brutal rejection than those
that had preceded it. In the event nothing came of the plan. Nothing is
known of where Meredith lived or of how he lived until 1845. It seems
most likely that he spent the year at an English boarding school. The
boarding schools in *The Adventures of Harry Richmond* and *Lord Ormont
and His Aminta* suggest first-hand knowledge of what an English boarding school was like for an older pupil, and Meredith's Latin was good,
which suggests that he had somehow managed to repair the deficiencies of
his Neuwied schooling. In 1845 there were more applications to the
Court of Chancery after which the Court ordered that a sum of £630
should be realised from Meredith's legacy from his aunt. £500 was to be
paid to Richard Stephen Charnock, a solicitor of Paternoster Row. The
remaining £130 would supply Meredith's living expenses. The Law
Society's register records that on February 3, 1846, George Meredith was
articled to Charnock for five years.

CHAPTER 3

Mary (Courtship)

THWACKINGS

The Shaving of Shagpat, Meredith's first prose fiction, was published at the end of 1855, when Meredith had been married to his first wife, Mary, for more than six years. It is like nothing else he ever wrote. Meredith presents it as a story that was left out of the *Arabian Nights*. It tells of the protracted ordeal through which Shibli Bagarag, a young barber, grows to man's estate, an achievement that he marks by shaving the tailor, Shagpat, whose supreme hairiness has made him an object of reverence in his city. But beneath the eastern veneer it is a version of the story that Meredith rehearses in various forms in a number of his novels, in *The Ordeal of Richard Feverel*, in *Evan Harrington*, in *The Adventures of Harry Richmond*, and in *The Amazing Marriage*. In all these stories young men pass through an ordeal. They find, like Shibli Bagarag, that the only way to grow up is to put up as best they can with the 'thwackings' to which life subjects them. The goal to which the story drives, Shibli's shaving of Shagpat, like the unmasking of Sir Willoughby Patterne in *The Egoist*, is an exhibition of how vacuous the qualities may be that command popular admiration. But Shibli himself, the barber who becomes a King, engages triumphantly in the project of bettering himself that, as Meredith ruefully recognised, was his own project too, and the project that he lends to Evan Harrington, the hero of his second novel. Shagpat's family, like Evan's, have been 'clothiers for generations'. When Shagpat is pictured 'lolling in his shop-front', giving all the townsfolk the opportunity to gaze on their

© The Author(s) 2019
R. Cronin, *George Meredith*,
https://doi.org/10.1007/978-3-030-32448-3_3

idol, Meredith has in mind his own grandfather, the great Mel, the tailor who made himself into an object of general admiration by sheer force of personality. Shagpat and Shibli, who unmasks him, have a lot in common. Meredith's novels regularly end in an unmasking, but, as in *The Shaving of Shagpat*, the unmasker and the unmasked seem often to be different versions of the same person.

The Shaving of Shagpat did not sell, but it did establish Meredith's literary reputation. George Lewes in the *Saturday Review* concluded that Meredith, 'hitherto known to us as a writer of graceful, but not very remarkable verse, now becomes the name of a man of genius.'[1] His enthusiasm was shared by his common-law wife. George Eliot noticed the book twice. In *The Leader* she called it 'a work of genius, and of poetical genius', and in the *Westminster Review* she gave it a prominent place in her round-up of the year's fiction.[2] But even George Eliot admitted to feeling 'rather a languishing interest towards the end of the work', and she was a far more patient reader than the story is likely to find these days. The more wondrous the story's events and the more exotic its prose, the harder it becomes to stifle a yawn. The reviewer in *The Critic* seems more prescient when he suggested that Meredith's talents would be better employed if he would agree to 'write an English story in the English manner, laying his scenes among places familiar to him, and making his personages of those whom he has met in the actual world about him'.[3] That was the advice Meredith took when he came to write his first novel *The Ordeal of Richard Feverel*, or so it might seem. But in fact neither that novel, nor any of its successors is quite written 'in the English manner'. In the novels, Meredith's prose remains almost as densely figurative as in his Eastern tale. He continued all through his career to write English almost as if he were writing in a foreign language. His characters may dress like nineteenth-century English people, but many of them remain spectral presences, scarcely more solidly established than Shibli and Shagpat. Something changes but something that cannot quite be explained by Meredith's abandonment of Arabian fantasy for the realist conventions of the nineteenth-century novel.

Meredith retained all through his literary career a hearty belief in the salutary effect of 'thwackings'. Richard Feverel's ordeal begins when Farmer Blaize finds him poaching on his land and gives him a whipping. In

[1] *Saturday Review*, 1 (January 19, 1856), 12.
[2] *The Leader*, 1 (January 5, 1856), 15–6; *Westminster Review*, 65 (April 1856), 658–9.
[3] *The Critic*, 15 (January 1, 1856), 16.

one of the last novels, *One of Our Conquerors*, there is a clerk called Skepsey who believes that the nation will be renewed if all the young men are taught boxing and accustom themselves to giving and taking a pummelling in the ring. The aged crone that Shibli agrees to marry speaks for Meredith at any point of his career when she tells Shibli that he should be grateful for his thwackings, the fruit of which is 'resoluteness, strength of mind, sternness in the pursuit of the object!'[4] But the word itself refuses the weight that Meredith places on it. 'Thwackings' is a schoolboy word, and Meredith's insistence on using it shrinks the world to a schoolyard, which would not matter so much if it were a real schoolyard. But 'thwackings' are schoolboy punishments disinfected of pain and fear and shame. They are the beatings that Billy Bunter suffers at the story's end ('Yarooh!'), or the slipperings administered by Denis the Menace's father in the last frame of the unreformed strip. Cries of pain are morphed into screams of laughter. In the novels Meredith is altogether less willing to refuse the reality of pain.

When Farmer Blaize gives Richard Feverel and his young friend, Ripton Thompson, a good whipping, the incident is presented as truculently humorous, but that is not how it feels to Richard, who has never attended a boarding school, and hence has never learned, like his friend Ripton, to accept such treatment with manly indifference. Instead he feels a 'horrible sense of shame, self-loathing, universal hatred, impotent vengeance, as if the spirit were steeped in abysmal blackness, which comes upon a courageous and sensitive youth condemned for the first time to taste this piece of fleshly bitterness, and taste what he feels is a defilement'.[5] It seems to him that his 'blood' has been 'poisoned'. Something had happened to Meredith in between writing *The Shaving of Shagpat* and *The Ordeal of Richard Feverel*, something that brought home to him, more forcefully than his experience of an English boarding school, how real pain was. His wife had left him for another man. As John Bayley puts it, for him 'the marriage break-up was decisive, more productive than Emma's death was for Hardy'.[6] It was a disaster from which it took Meredith years to recover, if he ever quite did, but it was the making of Meredith as a writer. 'The greatest social difficulty in the England of today', Justin McCarthy writes in the *Westminster Review* (he was reviewing, amongst other novels, *The Ordeal*

---

[4] *The Shaving of Shagpat: An Arabian Romance*, Book 1.
[5] *The Ordeal of Richard Feverel*, chapter 2.
[6] John Bayley, review of *The Poems of George Meredith*, ed. Phyllis W. Bartlett, *Times Literary Supplement*, October 7, 1978, 1246–8.

of Richard Feverel and *Emilia in England*), 'is not that which is created by the relations between wealth and poverty.' The relations between the rich and the poor are susceptible to 'a gradual adjustment' and, in McCarthy's optimistic view, his countrymen seemed to be 'in the right way' towards making that adjustment. 'A much more complicated difficulty', he went on, 'is found in the relation between man and woman.'[7] It was the relation, 'the great relation' as Henry James called it,[8] that gave the novelists of the later nineteenth century their principal theme, and it was a theme that was given to Meredith at some time in 1857, at the moment when his wife left him.

Articled Clerks

On February 3, 1846, a week before he turned 18, Meredith was articled to Richard Stephen Charnock of Paternoster Row for the term of five years. He was to be trained for the law. Charnock was an expert on bankruptcy, which may be what brought him to the attention of Meredith's bankrupted father.[9] He was also a scholar, who became a Fellow of the Society of Antiquaries and a leading member of the Anthropological Society of London. He even contrived to acquire a doctorate from the University of Göttingen. He had a special interest in the history of words, and published books on the etymology of rare words, and on the etymology of Christian and surnames. He wrote on the origin of the Etruscans and their language. He was interested in local customs and local dialects, especially those of Essex. He was, like Meredith and his friends Leslie Stephen and John Morley, a hill-walker. In 1857 he brought out a guide to the Tyrol, and in 1865 he published his most widely known book, *Bradshaw's Illustrated Hand-Book to Spain and Portugal.* He was a more interesting man than the general run of London solicitors. In his only surviving reference to Charnock, Meredith remarked that 'he had neither business nor morals'. The curt dismissal is entirely characteristic. It recalls his description of his own father as 'a muddler and a fool'.[10] But he may have had solid grounds for his opinion of Charnock.

---

[7] 'Novels with a Purpose', *Westminster Review*, 26.1 (July 1964), 24–49, p. 40.

[8] Henry James, *The Future of the Novel: Essays on the Art of Fiction*, ed. Leon Edel (New York: Vintage Books, 1956), 39.

[9] See Richard Charnock, *On the New Bankrupt and Insolvent Acts* (1845).

[10] Clodd, *Memories*, 142 and 141.

By 1846 Charnock's interest in the law was already waning, its place taken by his other interests, in anthropology, in etymology, and in Continental travel. In 1863, when James Hunt left the Ethnological Society and set up the Anthropological Society of London as a rival organisation, Charnock sided with Hunt. The outbreak of the American Civil War had made Hunt's refusal to accept that negroes and Europeans were members of a single species a more pressing issue. The Anthropological Society, as might be expected, was loud in its support for the Confederacy, as, rather more surprisingly, was George Meredith. The Cannibal Club was formed as an offshoot of the Anthropological Society, and Charnock became the club treasurer. It had famous members. Besides James Hunt, there were Monckton Milnes, Richard Burton, Swinburne and the atheist Charles Bradlaugh. Cannibal Club members were interested in racial characteristics and in the customs of primitive societies. They were freethinkers, scornful of Christian orthodoxy, but their strongest interest was in pornography.[11] The club met in a famous London restaurant, Bertolini's, and there was a club song, written by Swinburne:

> Preserve us from our enemies;
> Thou who art Lord of suns and skies;
> Whose meat and drink is flesh in pies;
> And blood in bowls!
> Of thy sweet mercy, damn their eyes;
> And damn their souls!

Charnock's office must have been a startling place for a young man not quite 18 who had so recently been under the influence of the teachings of the Moravian Brothers at Neuwied. Meredith may make a sly allusion to the character of the office in *The Ordeal of Richard Feverel*. Richard's friend, Ripton Thompson, is articled to his father. When Sir Austin Feverel visits the office, Mr Thompson, anxious to impress him with the progress his son is making in the study of the law, directs Sir Austin's attention to Ripton, who is studiously reading, but the volume that he is studying turns out to be a book detailing 'the entrancing adventures of Miss Random', 'a strange young lady' who 'smiled bewitchingly out' from the book's coloured frontispiece.[12] Sir Austin Feverel, although he insists that

---

[11] See John Wallen, 'The Cannibal Club and the Origins of 19th Century Racism and Pornography', *The Victorian*, 1. i (August 2013), 1–13.

[12] *The Ordeal of Richard Feverel*, chapter 17.

his own son remain pure, is not greatly shocked. He even comes at last to accept that 'Miss Random' might be a 'necessary establishment' even if a regrettable one.[13] Richard Charnock would have been still less disconcerted to find a pupil reading a racy novel at his desk rather than making notes on Blackstone.

Charnock encouraged the literary interests of the young men in his office. In 1848 he brought out the first issue of a monthly magazine, the *Monthly Observer*, that was printed for private circulation, and ran to 15 issues, 5 of which are preserved in Harvard's Houghton Library. The contributors, apart from Charnock himself, were all young men who worked in the city. In addition to Meredith, who is represented only by verse contributions, there were Henry Howes who was a clerk at the Adjutant-General's office in Whitehall, and three clerks in East India House, Hilaire de St Croix, Peter Austin Daniel and Edward Gryffydh Peacock. The young men took it in turns to edit an issue, and the editor supplied a ponderous critique of the contributors' efforts. The standard of the contributions, Meredith's verse included, is not high. The attempts at wit are particularly unfortunate. Charnock, for example, signed his contributions 'Aretched Kooez' (a wretched quiz). One woman was included in this otherwise all-male company, Edward Peacock's sister, Mary Ellen Nicolls, who was staying in London with her brother. She was a young widow, still only 26, with a three-year-old daughter, Edith.

The fascination Mary Nicolls wielded over Meredith, and no doubt over the other young men who contributed to the *Monthly Observer*, was heightened, as Meredith came to understand, by her position as the one woman in a company of men. In *One of Our Conquerors*, Victor Radnor is visited in his offices in the City by Lady Grace Halley. Radnor is in love with Nataly, the woman for whom he left his wife 20 years before, and in any case Lady Grace is not his type: 'She belonged rather to the description physically distasteful to him.' But nevertheless her presence in his office leaves Victor 'uncomfortably ruffled'. It is because a woman in a city office is anomalous. Lady Grace is an 'inflammable' presence in a city office which is a space from which women are commonly excluded. Within that space a woman wields an erotic power that would disappear if the men of the City could somehow contrive so far to 'de-orientalize', or 'dis-Turk themselves' that the presence of women in the City were to become unre-

---

[13] *The Ordeal of Richard Feverel*, chapter 33.

markable.[14] Victor is ruffled even though he is a middle-aged man with a grown-up daughter, a man who goes home every evening to the woman he loves. Meredith, who was not yet 20 when he met the woman who was to become his first wife, was a good deal more than ruffled. Leitch Ritchie, the editor of *Chamber's Journal*, who became a friend of the Merediths after their marriage, observes in one of his novels that 'in respect to female companionship, nine-tenths of the struggling young men of London might as well be in a huge monkery, where no such thing can be enjoyed, except when of a secret and criminal character'.[15] Mary Ellen Nicolls was a young woman of 26, but already a widow and the mother of a daughter not yet three years old. She was old enough for young men to feel they could talk to her easily. As Richard Feverel's uncle Adrian explains to his nephew, young women 'can't be quite natural: they blush, and fib, and affect this and that', and the consequence is that young men can't be quite natural with them. But all that 'wears off when they're women',[16] and Mary Ellen was a 26-year-old woman. It is not hard to imagine the sensation she made in the company of those young men.

At the outset Meredith's relationship with her could only have been unequal. She was a widow of 26, a mother, a woman at her ease in social circles in which Meredith would have been thoroughly abashed.[17] More than 30 years later Meredith introduced into *Diana of the Crossways* a character called Arthur Rhodes, 'an articled clerk of Mr Braddock's' as Meredith was of Mr Charnock. The young man develops a passionate attachment to Diana. When her dog swims out to her row-boat, his eyes beseeching pathetically to be taken on board, Diana has to refuse because his muddy paws put the other women in fear for their muslin dresses. At that moment the dog reminds her of Arthur Rhodes.[18] Rhodes is, as she puts it, 'not much more than a boy'. He is a poet as well as a clerk, but Diana is a famous novelist, whereas Rhodes is only a young aspirant 'who had recently taken a drubbing for venturing to show a peep of his head, like an early crocus, in the literary market'.[19] The slim volume of poems

---

[14] *One of Our Conquerors*, chapter 18.

[15] Leitch Ritchie, *Wearyfoot Common* (London: Bogue, 1855), 135.

[16] *The Ordeal of Richard Feverel*, chapter 38.

[17] In 1845, 18 months after the death of her husband, Mary Shelley reported that Mary was living with her parents-in-law, and that 'they see a good deal of society'. *Letters of Mary Wollstonecraft Shelley*, 3, 258.

[18] *Diana of the Crossways*, chapter 18.

[19] *Diana of the Crossways*, chapter 21.

that Meredith had published in 1851, when he was just 23, had not been very warmly received. Diana's patronage of the young man, who is 'rather good-looking and well built', does not go unnoticed: it 'led to suppositions' amongst some of her female friends.[20] But Thomas Redworth, the man Diana marries at last, knows that Rhodes is no threat to him. Arthur is Diana's devoted pet not her suitor. It is hard not to recognise Arthur Rhodes as Meredith's representation of himself in the first months of his courtship of Mary Ellen Nicolls.

Meredith had no great opinion of *Rhoda Fleming*, the novel he began while he was on honeymoon with his second wife. He had planned a novel in one volume that he could finish quickly, and would bring in enough to cover his immediate expenses. As usual, it took longer than he had anticipated, six months, and, by the time he had done, the single volume had expanded to three. The novel concerns two sisters, Dahlia, the flighty, errant young woman, who tours Europe with her aristocratic lover without insisting that he marry her first, and the upright Rhoda whose moral rectitude can on occasion seem harshly unfeeling. In writing *Rhoda Fleming* Meredith was making a determined incursion into literary territory that George Eliot had made her own. Dahlia is very like Hetty Sorrel in *Adam Bede*, and the two sisters behave on occasion like a same-sex version of Maggie and Tom Tulliver. Meredith even includes a miser who feels for Dahlia something of the tenderness that Silas Marner feels for Eppie. In June 1862, Meredith had announced to Captain Maxse that the first instalment of a new novel by 'Adam Bede' was to appear the next month in the *Cornhill*: 'I understand they have given her an enormous sum (£8000 or more! she retaining the ultimate copyright)—Bon Dieu! will aught like this ever happen to me?'[21] It never would, and *Rhoda Fleming* was a particular disappointment. Meredith wrote it to appeal to the readership that had made George Eliot so successful, and found that Tinsley Brothers, a firm with its finger on the pulse of the market—three years before it had published Mary Braddon's bestseller *Lady Audley's Secret*—would only offer him £400 for it.[22] Newly married to the second Mrs Meredith, Meredith set out to write a potboiler, and ended by writing a novel in which the most arresting presence is a beautiful young widow, Mrs Lovell, a character unmistakably modelled on his first wife. In *Lord Ormont and His Aminta*, there is a character called Mrs Lawrence Finchley who has

[20] *Diana of the Crossways*, chapter 28.
[21] *Letters*, 1, 149. The novel in question was *Romola*.
[22] *Letters*, 1, 307.

recently divorced her husband and finds, 'I begin to understand that husband of mine, now we're on bowing terms.'[23] Perhaps Meredith, like Mrs Finchley, found that he only ever came truly to know his first wife long after they had parted, when he was freshly married to his second. Mary Ellen Nicolls was the widow of a lieutenant in the Royal Navy, Mrs Lovell of an officer in the Indian army. Mrs Lovell is almost extraneous to the plot of the novel. She has no role except to instigate a wicked plot of a kind that suggests she is cut from the same cloth as Lady Waldemar in *Aurora Leigh*. But her impact in the novel is at odds with her actions. At every appearance she impresses herself on the reader almost as forcefully as she impresses herself on the imagination of Dahlia Fleming. When Mrs Lovell first makes her entry into the village church, Dahlia shuts her eyes the better to 'conjure up the image of herself, as she had appeared to the beautiful woman in the dress of grey-shot silk, with violet mantle and green bonnet, rose-trimmed; and the picture she conceived was the one which she knew herself by, for many ensuing years'.[24] Seeing Mrs Lovell does not just stamp her face and her clothes on Dahlia's imagination: it fixes Dahlia's idea of herself. It is an arresting thought, and, it may be, a revealing one. When he met Mary Ellen Nicolls, did Meredith find that the wavering contours of his youthful personality for the very first time achieved definition as they fell under her gaze? Edward Blancove, the man who seduces Dahlia, is smitten with Mrs Lovell and buys her a necklace with an opal pendant, 'a really fine opal, coquetting with the lights of every gem that is known: it shot succinct red flashes, and green, and yellow; the emerald, the amethyst, the topaz lived in it, and a remote ruby; it was veined with lightning hues, and at times it slept in a milky cloud, innocent of fire, quite maidenlike'.[25] He chooses the jewel because it reminds him of the woman he is buying it for. Edward knows that opals are associated with widows, which is why they must never be given to brides, but Mrs Lovell is linked to the jewel by more than a conventional association. It has her 'cold wit', a wit that Edward responds to as a provocation—it 'gave him a throb of desire to gain possession of her and crush her'[26]—and, like the gem, Margaret Lovell is so shifting, so changeable, that she escapes definition. She is a woman who never allows a man to feel securely in possession of her. But, perhaps for this very reason, she is a woman through whom men come to know

---

[23] *Lord Ormont and His Aminta*, chapter 11.
[24] *Rhoda Fleming*, chapter 1.
[25] *Rhoda Fleming*, chapter 16.
[26] *Rhoda Fleming*, chapter 21.

themselves. Mrs Lovell is what Meredith calls 'a crucible-woman',[27] a woman who, if a man has a weakness, will expose it, and then dismiss him, as she dismisses Edward Blancove when she learns how miserably he has treated Dahlia, 'with the inexorable contempt of Nature, when she has tried one of her creatures and found him wanting'. It is not only vain, worldly men like Edward Blancove who are vulnerable to her attractions. The upright lover in the novel, the man who woos and at last wins Rhoda Fleming, is Robert Eccles and even Eccles admits, 'I do, I declare, clean *forget* Rhoda; I forget the girl, if only I see Mrs Lovell at a distance.'[28] Meredith had only just married his second wife. It reads like his confession as much as the young farmer's. Meredith's dream woman, like young Harry Richmond's, was always opal-like. Harry dreams of 'bloom and mystery, a woman shifting like the light with evening and night and dawn, and sudden fire'.[29] He dreams of a woman like Mrs Lovell, like Mary Ellen Nicolls. Meredith was still dreaming of just such a woman even in the first months of his marriage to a second wife who could scarcely have been more different.

CRYSTALLISATION

Meredith sometimes suggested in later life that he had been trapped into marriage by Mary Ellen Nicolls, but Mary's daughter Edith insisted that her mother refused Meredith six times before she at last agreed to marry him, and her version is the more believable. When Mary Nicolls met Meredith she had been a widow only three years and had a young daughter. It seems unlikely that she would have set out to entrap a young man more than six years her junior who was quite without the means to support her. Meredith and Mary Ellen Nicolls were married on August 9, 1849, at St George's in Hanover Square, the parish church for Mayfair. Mary's father, Thomas Love Peacock, was present and signed the register. We cannot know exactly when Meredith fell in love, but we know at least how Meredith understood what falling in love was like. In 1861 he asked his friend, Maxse, what he thought of a book that he had sent him, Stendhal's *De l'Amour*. 'I think de Stendhal very subtle and observant,' he remarked: 'He goes over ground that I know.'[30]

[27] *Rhoda Fleming*, chapter 28.
[28] *Rhoda Fleming*, chapter 30.
[29] *The Adventures of Harry Richmond*, chapter 23.
[30] *Letters*, 1, 121.

For Stendhal, to fall in love is to experience a moment of 'crystallisation'. At the salt mines near Salzburg the miners will throw into one of the abandoned workings a branch stripped by winter of all its leaves, and leave it there for two or three months. When it is retrieved, the whole branch, even the smallest twigs no thicker than the leg of a small bird, will be hung with crystals of salt that glance and dazzle like diamonds. The original branch is no longer recognisable: it has been transfigured.[31] Love, for Stendhal, names the process through which the beloved is transfigured in the eyes of the lover. In Stendhal's little fable the miracle is the work of salt crystals. Balzac borrows the idea, but in *Le Curé de village*, the active agent is not salt but frost. Véronique Sauviat discovers romantic love when she purchases a copy of *Paul et Virginie*, and once she has read the book she is in danger of finding a Paul in the first young man she meets, so ready is she to attach her passionate imaginings to an actual person, 'comme les vapeurs d'atmosphère humide, saisies par la gelée, se cristallisent à une branche d'arbre, au bord du chemin' (as mists of moist air, touched by frost, crystallise on the branch of a tree by the roadside).[32] In Meredith, who knew both Stendhal's essay and Balzac's novel, the miracle is performed by blossom rather than salt or frost, but its origins in Stendhal's salt mines and in Balzac's frost-festooned tree are evident enough. When Richard Feverel reaches puberty, entering what his father calls 'the blossoming season', he finds his dreams freshly peopled by knights and fair ladies. In his dreams he sees himself bending over 'a hand glittering white and fragrant as the frosted blossom of a May night'. That scene is realised for him when he meets Lucy Desborough, Farmer Blaize's niece. She takes her leave of him, holding out to him her hand and the dream sentence is repeated. Lucy's hand is 'white and fragrant as the frosted blossom of a Maynight'.[33] Lionel Stevenson, Meredith's biographer, suggests that Lucy may have had a real-life counterpart.[34] 'An early goddess was a country lass', the husband in *Modern Love* recalls,[35] and young men of a higher social station are attracted to farmers' daughters in *Rhoda Fleming* and *The Adventures of Harry Richmond* as well as in *The Ordeal of Richard Feverel*. Stevenson may be right, but as Meredith knew, and as he signals

---

[31] Stendhal, *De l'Amour*, chapter 14.
[32] Honoré de Balzac, *Le Curé de village*, chapter 1.
[33] *The Ordeal of Richard Feverel*, chapters 14 and 15.
[34] Stevenson, 16–8.
[35] *Modern Love*, XVIII.

when he repeats the sentence about the hand as white and fragrant as frosted blossom, it hardly matters, because in the erotic experience of very young men dream and reality, the young woman imagined and the young woman encountered, are scarcely distinguishable. It is in *The Egoist* that the idea that Meredith found in Stendhal, the idea of crystallisation, is most fully developed. Again the work of Stendhal's salt crystals is performed by blossom. In Sir Willoughby Patterne's grounds there is a double-blossom wild cherry. The tree is 'worshipped' by Sir Willoughby's cousin, Vernon Whitford. Clara Middleton is engaged to Sir Willoughby, but when she comes across Vernon asleep under the tree she falls in love with him at once. Vernon has a book with him. She cranes her neck to see what he is reading, and then

> she turned her face to where the load of virginal blossom, whiter than the summer-cloud on the sky, showered and drooped and clustered so thick as to claim colour and seem, like higher Alpine snows in noon-sunlight, a flush of white. From deep to deeper heavens of white, her eyes perched and soared.

Her first thought is, 'He must be good who loves to be and sleep beneath the branches of this tree!'[36] The tree is a modern hybrid, 'a gardener's improvement', as Clara's father puts it, on 'the Vestal of the forest, the wild cherry'.[37] Its beauty is not natural. It is a product of the gardener's artifice. Love for Stendhal, and for Meredith who took his cue from Stendhal, is always artificial. The beauty of the beloved is a beauty lent by the lover, no more proper to the beloved than the jewel-like crystals belong to the wintry branch retrieved from the salt mine. Lucy Desborough is only 17 when Richard Feverel marries her. Clara Middleton chooses a husband many years her senior, a man who has been married before and is free to marry again only because his wife has died. It is her experience that best mirrors what happened to George Meredith when he first met Mary Ellen Nicolls.

Everyone describes Mary Ellen as beautiful. Of course they do. Her face has come down to us only in a charcoal sketch made by Henry Wallis in 1858, either just before, or more likely just after their son was born. Mary Ellen is drawn in full face, as she turns to the left. Her large eyes and drooping lids gaze calmly just to the viewer's right. The nose is slim and

---

[36] *The Egoist*, chapter 11.
[37] *The Egoist*, chapter 9.

straight, the lips full and wide. She wears a lace cap and her hair falls in waves over strong, softly rounded shoulders. It might be a sketch of a Dickens heroine, of a more mature Bella Wilfer. Mary Ellen was 37, the mother of two children, but the face is unlined. There is only a single crease over each eyelid. It is a sketch of a beautiful woman, but it is a sketch made by a man who was in love with her. We cannot know how far Mary's beauty made Henry Wallis fall in love with her and how far Wallis's love produced Mary's beauty. Mary Shelley was rather less impressed by the 16-year-old Mary Ellen Peacock, but she thought her pretty enough. She was 'a very fine girl—& her pretty face indicates intelligence'.[38] It is a good deal more disconcerting to turn from Wallis's sketch to the description of Mary Ellen offered by one of her closest friends, Anne Ramsden Bennett, who met her in 1860, just two years after Wallis made his sketch. Anne Bennett recalls a 'massive face something like George Elliot's' [sic], a face weighed down by her 'solemnity', although her expression was transfigured when she smiled.[39] Catherine Horne, the young wife of R. H. Horne, who was, it is true, herself a famous beauty, commented that if she had been married to Mary Meredith she would have found her temper insupportable even if she had been 'beautiful, young, affectionate (and everything she is not)'.[40] Meredith was intrigued by women who prompted debates about whether or not they were beautiful. The best example is Carinthia Jane Kirby, heroine of *The Amazing Marriage*. Her own brother judges that, despite her expressive eyes, 'no one could fancy her handsome'.[41] But when Carinthia comes to live in London the city divides over her: there are 'certain whispers of her good looks, contested only to be the more violently asserted'.[42] For Gower Woodseer, the poet of the novel, Carinthia can only be described in paradoxes: she is 'a beautiful Gorgon—a haggard Venus'.[43] He explains that people think women beautiful if they are 'suitable for paintings and statues', but paintings and statues (Wallis's sketch of Mary Ellen is a good example) can only show women's beauty in repose, whereas true beauty is to be found in animation, in 'a breezy tree or ever ruffled waters'. Woodseer is delighted when

[38] *Letters of Mary Wollstonecraft Shelley*, 2, 291.

[39] Nicholas A. Joukovsky, 'According to Mrs Bennett: A document sheds a kinder light on George Meredith's first wife', *Times Literary Supplement*, October 8, 2004, 13–5.

[40] Shaheen, 28.

[41] *The Amazing Marriage*, chapter 4.

[42] *The Amazing Marriage*, chapter 28.

[43] *The Amazing Marriage*, chapter 8.

Madge Winch, the working-class girl that he will marry, struggles to find the words to describe Carinthia's beauty. All she can say is that 'it flashes', like the opal ring in *Rhoda Fleming*, and for Woodseer that is exactly right. Carinthia's flashing beauty proves 'the supremacy of irregular lines', of the 'living face' as opposed to the face in repose, which is why, he explains to Madge, 'we can't hope to have a true portrait' of her.[44] Meredith probably never saw the charcoal sketch of Mary Ellen that Wallis made in 1858, but he certainly saw *Fireside Reverie*, a painting, since lost, that Wallis exhibited at the Royal Academy in 1856, a portrait of Mary sitting dreamily at the hearth for which Meredith supplied the epigraph. But it is unlikely that he would have recognised either as a 'true portrait'. Might his own experience have been more like the Earl of Fleetwood's? He falls in love with Carinthia Jane Kirby and proposes all in one evening, when he sees her at a ball in Baden, and sees her transfigured, threading her way through the throng like a 'rose-crystal'.[45] When he looks at her face after they are married he is only able to see 'the skull of the face' that he had fallen in love with, in which he can glimpse only 'for a twinkle or two, the creature or vision she had been, as if to mock by reminding him'.[46]

On February 12, 1849, Meredith turned 21, and came into possession of his trust fund, about £1000. He left Charnock's chambers and took lodgings in Pimlico. He had decided to give up the law for literature. He wrote to the poet, R. H. Horne, who had made himself famous by writing an epic poem, *Orion*, and selling it for a farthing a copy, inviting Horne's interest. He asked to send Horne some of his poems so that Horne might gauge 'the power of the Poetic Faculty' in him.[47] It must have been at about the same time that he fell in love with Mary Ellen Nicolls and asked her to marry him. She was a grown-up woman, and that was a part of her attraction. He is clearly remembering the effect she had on him when in his first novel he describes Richard Feverel meeting Bella Mount. Bella 'opened a wider view of the world to him'. After meeting her, 'he thought poorly of girls': 'A woman, a sensible, brave, beautiful woman seemed, on comparison, infinitely nobler than those weak creatures.'[48] She seemed to him, as he was to put it in *Modern Love*, the poem in which he chronicled

---

[44] *The Amazing Marriage*, chapter 30.
[45] *The Amazing Marriage*, chapter 12.
[46] *The Amazing Marriage*, chapter 15.
[47] *Letters*, 1, 2.
[48] *The Ordeal of Richard Feverel*, chapter 38.

most faithfully the long disaster of his marriage, 'more sweet than those /
Who breathe the violet breath of maidenhood'.[49] According to Mary's
daughter he proposed six times before at last he was accepted.

THOMAS LOVE PEACOCK, ESQ.

The decisions that Meredith made in 1849 to devote himself to literature
and to Mary Ellen Nicolls were closely related. Meredith had been introduced to Mary Ellen by her brother, Edward Peacock. They were the children of a famous father, Thomas Love Peacock. The poet, Robert Buchanan,
now best known for his attack on D. G. Rossetti and Swinburne, the principal members of what Buchanan named 'The Fleshly School of Poetry', visited Peacock in his retirement at his Thames-side house, and remembered
thinking, 'And this old man had spoken with Shelley, not once, but a thousand times; and had known well both Harriett Westbrook [Shelley's first
wife] and Mary Godwin [his second wife, the author of *Frankenstein*]; and
had cracked jokes with Hobhouse [Byron's closest friend], and chaffed
Procter's latinity [Procter was the poet who wrote under the pen name of
Barry Cornwall]; and had seen, and actually criticised Malibran [the Spanish
mezzo-soprano]; and had bought "the vasty version of a new system to
perplex the sages," [Wordsworth's *Excursion* as described by Byron] when
it first came out, in a bright, new, uncut quarto; and had dined with Jeremy
Bentham; and had smiled at Disraeli, when, resplendently attired, he stood
chatting at Hookham's [the circulating library on Bond Street] with the
Countess of Blessington; and had been face to face with that bland
Rhadamanthus, Chief Justice Eldon; and was, in short, such a living chronicle of things past and men dead as filled one's soul with delight and ever-
varying wonder.'[50] Mary's father 'opened a wider view of the world' to
Meredith just as his daughter had done. Through the Peacocks he found a
connection to the heroic age of English literature, the age that had ended a
quarter of a century before, in 1824, when Byron died at Missolonghi.
When Meredith published his first book, *Poems* in 1851, two years after his
marriage, he chose as an epigraph some lines from Horne's *Orion* and he

---

[49] *Modern Love*, XL. This is a description of the 'lady' with whom the husband solaces
himself after the infidelity of his wife. It says much that this, clearly entirely fictional character, should be modelled, like the wife, on Mary Ellen.

[50] Robert Buchanan, *A Look Round Literature* (London: Ward and Downey, 1887), 165.

dedicated the volume to 'Thomas Love Peacock, Esq., with the profound admiration and affectionate respect of his son-in-law'.

I doubt whether Meredith had read Peacock's novels before he met his first wife. Few people had. Peacock's glamour and the glamour he cast over his children would have come to him as the friend of Shelley. But two years later, when Meredith dedicated his first book to him 'with profound admiration', he would have been familiar with Peacock's own writings, with the poems and the novels. Peacock's work had an influence on his fiction second only to Stendhal's.[51] In Meredith's *Essay on Comedy*, Molière is offered as the supreme example of the comic writer, but Meredith's idea of comedy derives from Peacock's novels more obviously than from Molière's plays. It is a comedy of the head rather than of the heart. It is comedy that allows a 'clear Hellenic perception of facts' to dispel 'the vapours of Unreason and Sentimentalism'. It celebrates common sense, the proponents of which are commonly women. Women are emancipated in comedy where they are allowed 'free play for their wit'. Comedy is inherently social, which is why a misanthropic writer such as Byron cannot be truly comic. The comic writer relies upon 'a society of cultivated men and women', a society in which 'ideas are current and the perceptions quick, that he might be supplied with matter and an audience'. The want of an audience is crucial. Neither Peacock nor Meredith ever succeeded in finding an audience of the kind they felt in need of. They wrote for a readership that they could only imagine. They wrote for it, it is true, very differently. Comic writing, Meredith believed, should be remarkable for its 'beautiful translucency of language', a phrase that might serve as a proper tribute to Peacock's prose. When Peacock sent a copy of *Nightmare Abbey* to Shelley in Italy, Shelley wrote to say how much he admired it. He thought the character of Scythrop Glowry 'admirably conceived & executed', dryly refusing to acknowledge that Scythrop was a caricature of himself, but what he most admired was the prose: 'I know not how to praise sufficiently the lightness chastity & strength of the language of the whole.'[52] Peacock, like Stendhal and like Robert Louis Stevenson, wrote prose of the kind that Meredith admired, but it was the kind of prose that he could not write himself. In other ways Meredith remained throughout his career a disciple of his first father-in-law.

[51] For Stendhal's influence on Meredith, see chapter 5.

[52] *Letters of Percy Bysshe Shelley*, ed. F. L. Jones, 2 vols (Oxford: Clarendon Press, 1964), 2, 98.

Peacock's novels are constructed like plays, and so are Meredith's. 'So ends the fourth act of our comedy,' he writes in *Evan Harrington*.[53] Peacock writes novels of talk, novels in which a group of characters, brought together in a country house, converse with one another, often over the dinner table, all of them so immured within their own particular eccentricity that, however extended the conversation might be, no communication ever takes place. In *The Ordeal of Richard Feverel* Meredith assembles at Raynham Abbey a very similar cast of characters. There is Sir Austin himself, compensating for his wife's infidelity by bringing up his son according to his own system; there are his brothers, Algernon who has lost a leg playing cricket and has ever afterwards devoted himself to the bottle, and Hippias, once thought to be a genius, who suffers so greatly from dyspepsia that he is unable to continue at the bar and has devoted himself to a 'ponderous work on the Fairy Mythology of Europe'.[54] And there are Sir Austin's nephews, Austin Wentworth, whose reputation has not survived a reckless decision to marry his mother's housemaid, and Adrian, the 'wise youth', who remains at an ironical distance from life, his only intimate companions Gibbon and Horace, and takes seriously only such requirements as that an egg should be boiled for 'two minutes and a half, or three-quarters at the outside': 'An egg should never rashly verge upon hardness—never.'[55] It is a novel that Peacock might well have enjoyed, but it is unlikely that he read it because, by the time it was published, Meredith and his daughter had been separated for two years. Meredith did not publish *One of Our Conquerors* until 1891, but *One of Our Conquerors* just as clearly as *The Ordeal of Richard Feverel* is a Peacockian novel. In Peacock's first novel Squire Headlong assembles at Headlong Hall 'men of taste and philosophers' that he has located by 'beating up in several booksellers' shops, theatres, exhibition-rooms, and other resorts of literature and taste', and he assembles too the multitude of items required for their entertainment; 'books, wine, cheese, globes, mathematical instruments, turkeys, telescopes, hams, tongues, microscopes, quadrants, sextants, fiddles, flutes, tea, sugar, electrical machines, figs, spices, air-pumps, soda-water, chemical apparatus, eggs, French-horns, drawing books, palettes, oils and colours, bottled ale and porter',

---

[53] *Evan Harrington*, chapter 38.
[54] *The Ordeal of Richard Feverel*, chapter 1.
[55] *The Ordeal of Richard Feverel*, chapter 34.

and much, much else.[56] Meredith's Victor Radnor caters almost as extravagantly for the guests he invites to his musical weekends at Lakelands, and the guests themselves are similar. Among their number are Miss Priscilla Graves, a meat-eater 'ridiculous in her ant'alcoholic exclusiveness', Mr Pepton a vegetarian wine-bibber, a clergyman who is an enthusiastic smoker and Mr Perison 'who traced mortal evil to that act', a man who 'jeered at globules' and a man who 'mourned over human creatures treated as cattle by big doses'.[57] Lakelands is Meredith's version of Peacock's Crotchet Castle to which proponents of all the arts and sciences are welcome, and where may be found 'music, painting, and poetry; hydrostatics, and political economy; meteorology, transcendentalism, and fish for breakfast'.[58] Meredith's marriage had ended more than 30 years before he wrote *One of Our Conquerors*, and Peacock had been dead for a quarter of a century, but he remained Peacock's son-in-law.

He was as ungrateful as most sons-in-law are. In *The Egoist* Peacock is traduced in the character of the Rev. Dr Middleton, father of the lovely Clara Middleton, the heroine of the novel, who captivates at the young age of 18 Sir Willoughby Patterne and is rewarded at the novel's end when she succeeds in breaking her engagement to him and marrying his cousin, Vernon Whitford, instead. She manages this only by circumventing her father, who would much rather Clara keep her engagement to Sir Willoughby. A broken engagement would cause a fuss and Dr Middleton is always 'apprehensive of a disturbance of the serenity precious to scholars'.[59] Clara tries to tell him that the engagement that she has entered into is making her unhappy. 'He and I', she begins. But then the dinner bell rings, and in any case Middleton has been offended by his daughter's pronunciation:

> 'And let me direct you, for the next occasion when you shall bring the vowels I and A, in verbally detached letters, into collision, that you do not fill the hiatus with so pronounced a Y. It is the vulgarization of our tongue of which I y-accuse you. I do not like my girl to be guilty of it.'[60]

[56] Thomas Love Peacock, *Headlong Hall*, chapter 2.
[57] *One of Our Conquerors*, chapter 8.
[58] Thomas Love Peacock, *Crotchet Castle*, chapter 3.
[59] *The Egoist*, chapter 6.
[60] *The Egoist*, chapter 19.

He will not hear of her breaking her engagement because Sir Willoughby keeps a very good table. Sir Willoughby seduces him with talk of wine, the only topic that has the power to distract Dr Middleton from 'his classics'. The esteem in which Middleton holds Sir Willoughby is founded on a visit to his wine cellar, a cellar that 'bore witness to forethoughtful practical solidity in the man who had built the house on such foundations'.[61] Middleton reserves his highest admiration for a remarkable port, of which, he is impressed to learn, the cellar contains 50 dozen bottles. When his daughter asks him to take her away from Patterne Hall he cannot bring himself to go, because he cannot bear to absent himself from 'Patterne Port'. Sir Willoughby puts a fresh bottle on the table and Dr Middleton is struck by the asymmetry of their relations: 'I have but a girl to give!'[62] Peacock, who had not allowed his scholarly habit of life to be disturbed when his daughter left her husband for Henry Wallis, who had even agreed to sit to Wallis for his portrait, is traduced as a man who would pimp his daughter for a glass of port. Dr Middleton is a vicious caricature of Peacock, but it is, for all that, a Peacockian caricature. The Rev. Dr Middleton is a direct descendant of the Rev. Dr Folliot in Peacock's sixth novel, *Crotchet Castle*, and the Reverend Doctor Opimian in *Gryll Grange*, his last. Folliot and Opimian, unlike Middleton, are wholly sympathetic characters, amused, affectionate Peacockian self-portraits, but they are also happily married men who are always ready to leave their wives at home when they have the opportunity to dine abroad, and men always ready to be distracted from weighty discussion, over, for example, the relative importance of nature and nurture in human development, by 'a slice of lamb, with lemon and pepper' and a glass of 'Vin de Grave'.[63]

When Meredith came into possession of his trust fund, when he left Charnock's chambers and embarked on a literary career, he did not only abandon his profession, he asked Mary Ellen Nicolls to marry him. Mary yielded at last, and on August 9, 1849, they were married, and set off on an extended wedding tour. Meredith took Mary to the Rhine valley. Mary was fluent in French, but in Germany she would have been dependent on her young husband. He knew the language and the area. It was where he had been at school. When Evan Harrington comes home after his father's death, he brings with him half a history of Portugal, and has vague hopes

---

[61] *The Egoist*, chapter 20.
[62] *The Egoist*, chapter 20.
[63] Thomas Love Peacock, *Crotchet Castle*, chapter 4.

of building a career on it. Meredith brought back with him rather less when he returned from his wedding tour in Germany. He brought four sheets of a projected biography of Lajos Kossuth, the Hungarian patriot hero, and some 'Sonnets on Two Kings of England'. He wrote to Leitch Ritchie, editor of *Chamber's Journal* offering both, assuring Ritchie that he was 'at liberty to erase *all* passages which suit not the purpose or politics of the Journal'.[64] It was Ritchie who in July 1849 had been responsible for Meredith's only published work, an unpromising poem of 48 lines, 'Chillianwallah', that had already appeared in the *Monthly Observer*.[65] The poem celebrates a particularly bloody battle fought that January in which Sir Hugh Gough, who remained Commander-in-Chief of the army in India despite being in his 70s, lost 1000 men before making a strategic withdrawal. As Meredith has it, Gough made Chillianwallah a name so famous that it was in no need of a 'chiming word', which was, he must have recognised, just as well (a rhyme would have been hard to come by). He also offered Ritchie 'a sketch of the life' of Johann Gottfried Hermann, a Leipzig professor who had died in 1848. There was as yet, he told Ritchie, 'no English account' of him.[66] Meredith was ill-equipped to assess the work of a classical philologist but no doubt he had brought back from Germany an account of Hermann's life and planned to pillage it. None of these offers tempted Ritchie. When Meredith and Mary Ellen arrived back from their Continental tour, they lodged at Peacock's substantial London house in John Street, but soon moved out and took lodgings in Weybridge, at 'The Limes', a lodging house favoured by literary and artistic young people. There Meredith set about arranging the publication of his poems. The terms he secured were the usual ones. He would be responsible for all costs and the profit, in the unlikely event that the volume made a profit, would be divided with the publisher. As it turned out, the publication of Meredith's first book cost him upwards of £50. The publisher he chose was John W. Parker. He was probably recommended to Parker by his father-in-law. Peacock was a contributor to *Fraser's Magazine* and Parker was the magazine's publisher. It was in *Fraser's* that Peacock serialised his last novel, *Gryll Grange*.

---

[64] *Letters*, 1, 5.

[65] See *Chamber's Journal*, 288 (July 7, 1849), 16. Siegfried Sassoon remarks that the poem 'can safely be classified as the worst he ever published'. Siegfried Sassoon, *Meredith* (London: Constable and Co., 1948), 7.

[66] *Letters*, 1, 6.

Peacock might have been expected to welcome his new son-in-law. Peacock's schooling had ended when he was twelve, and at the age of 14 he had found employment as a clerk in a firm of city merchants. Five years later he gave up his job and dedicated himself to literature. For years he stumbled from one financial crisis to another despite assistance from the Royal Literary Fund, and in 1815 he was arrested for debt in Liverpool. After that, he relied for his survival on an allowance of £120 a year from his friend, Shelley. But men in their 60s do not always look complacently on a son-in-law in whom they recognise a younger self. In 1849 Peacock was no longer the young man who had been befriended by Shelley. Thirty years before, in 1819, tiring of living hand to mouth, he had joined the East India Company as assistant to the examiner, and steadily risen through the ranks at India House until in 1836 he succeeded James Mill as examiner. He was now one of the two highest permanent officials in the East India Company's home service, and drew a salary of £2000. His predecessor and successor were both exceptionally distinguished. James Mill had been co-founder with Jeremy Bentham of the British school of utilitarianism (Peacock was intimate with both men), and was the author of the great *History of British India*. Peacock's successor, when he finally retired in 1856, was James Mill's son, John Stuart Mill. Meredith's father-in-law was one of the most powerful executives in Britain, and his tolerance for wastrels was limited. Two of the India House clerks who contributed to the *Monthly Observer*, Hilaire de St Croix and Edward Peacock, owed their places to Peacock. His son Edward had disappointed him by developing a taste for unsuitable women and for prize fights. 'Edward is rather a despair,' Mary Shelley wrote in 1844. When his father secured a clerkship for him at India House, she hoped that regular employment would be the making of him, but three months later she reported that 'he does not improve in looks or otherwise'.[67] It was through Edward, as Peacock must have known, that Meredith had come to know his daughter Mary. It was not an association that would have endeared him to his father-in-law.

Meredith was not only marrying the daughter of a literary man, he was marrying above himself. The son of a 'Tailor and Professed Trouser Cutter' became the son-in-law of a wealthy, powerful man who had a town house in John Street and a weekend house on the Thames at Lower Halliford that he had made by knocking two cottages together. This was the house in which Peacock, a man who was, as his friend Thomas Jefferson

---

[67] *Letters of Mary Wollstonecraft Shelley*, 3, 102 and 135.

Hogg put it, 'amorous of rivers',[68] felt most at home. In *De l'Amour*, Stendhal identifies four kinds of love, one of which is 'l'amour de vanité', the love for a woman the possession of whom elevates a man's status in his own eyes and in the eyes of the world.[69] It is l'amour de vanité that ensures that a duchess is never older than 30 in the eyes of a bourgeois: youth and beauty are hers by right of her rank. When Meredith married Mary Ellen in 1849 he allied himself with a family wealthy enough and socially prominent enough to give him reason to congratulate himself, and to give him reason too to feel a twinge of unease. It must have been a solace to him that he was a man without close family, and that his father had left England for South Africa some months before. It was in a Cape Town rather than a London newspaper that he advertised himself as a tailor ever willing to yield to 'gentlemen's own peculiarities'. But the family that he was marrying into was not without peculiarities of its own.

According to his cousin, Peacock had as a young man acted as 'a sort of universal lover, making half-declarations to half the young women he knew'.[70] On one occasion he eloped with a woman he supposed to be an heiress before discovering, just in time, that she was penniless. His friends expected him to marry Marianne St Croix, the sister of his friend William St Croix. But in 1819, when his position at India House gave him the means to marry, he wrote a letter proposing marriage to Jane Gryffydh, the daughter of a clergyman, a young woman who had caught his attention on a visit to Wales. But that had been eight years before, and Peacock had had no contact with her since. Amazingly, Jane Gryffydh accepted, and at first the marriage seems to have been happy enough. Mary was born in 1821, and when Peacock made a visit to Wales a few months later he wrote affectionate letters home, always ending with 'love to mother

---

[68] *The Athenians: Being Correspondence between Thomas Jefferson Hogg and His Friends Thomas Love Peacock, Leigh Hunt, Percy Bysshe Shelley, and Others*, ed. Walter Sidney Scott (London: Golden Cockerel Press, 1943), 80.

[69] Stendhal, *De l'Amour*, Book 1, chapter 1.

[70] The cousin was borrowing Miss Ilex's description of the man she had once loved in *Gryll Grange*. Nicholas Joukovsky and Jim Powell discovered a cache of letters written by Meredith to Susan Mary Neill, and argue persuasively that Susan Neill was Peacock's illegitimate daughter. His unusual tolerance when his daughter became pregnant by Henry Wallis may have been encouraged by his own sexual history. See Nicholas Joukovsky, '"Dearest Susie Pye": New Meredith Letters to Peacock's Natural Daughter', *Studies in Philology*, 111.3 (Summer 2014), 591–629.

and darling'.[71] There was a second daughter, Margaret, and a son, Edward. But in January, 1826, when Margaret seemed to be recovering from a serious illness, Peacock went out for a walk with some friends and found when he returned that his younger daughter had died. Peacock wrote a heartrendingly beautiful epitaph for her, 'Long night succeeds thy little day', and characteristically quarrelled with the vicar when he refused on doctrinal grounds to allow it to be inscribed on Margaret's grave. Jane Peacock gave birth to her last child, Rosa Jane, the following year, but she seems never to have recovered from Margaret's death, despite adopting a local girl as a replacement for her dead daughter. Edith, Mary's daughter, tells the story:

> Very soon after Margaret's death, my grandmother noticed a little girl in its mother's arms, at the door of a cottage on Halliford Green; she was much taken with the child, seeing in it a strong likeness to the little one she was so sorely grieving over; she coaxed the little girl, Mary Rosewell into her own house by a promise of some cake, and dressed it in her lost child's clothes. My grandfather, on his return from town, looked in through the dining-room window as he passed round to the door of his house, and seeing the child standing on the hearth-rug in the room, he was so struck by the likeness to Margaret, that he afterwards declared that he felt quite stunned, for the moment believing that he really saw her again before him. My parents finally adopted the child, Mary Rosewell, whose family had lived for generations much respected in the neighbourhood, and a most devoted and unselfish adopted daughter she always proved to be.

It is a disturbing tale, but, to all appearances, it turned out much better than could reasonably have been expected.[72] Mary Rosewell stayed with

---

[71] *The Letters of Thomas Love Peacock*, ed. Nicholas A. Joukovsky, 2 vols (Oxford: Clarendon Press, 2001), 1, 181 and 182.

[72] *The Works of Thomas Love Peacock, with a biographical notice by his granddaughter, Edith Nicolls* (London: Richard Bentley and Sons, 1875), xxxix. Edith Nicolls clearly rehearses the family story, the story as it was told to her. She does not seem to recognise that her grandmother's behaviour suggests that she was already deeply disturbed, nor does she indicate what arrangement, presumably financial, was made with Mary Rosewell's parents. That arrangement must have been negotiated with Peacock rather than his wife. It seems to me just possible that it was Peacock rather than his wife who arranged for Mary Rosewell to be adopted. It seems the action of a husband anxious about his wife's health rather than a grieving mother. It is worth remembering that, seven years before, Peacock's friend Shelley seems to have acquired a young Neapolitan child that he offered Mary Shelley in very similar circumstances, immediately after the death of Mary's child.

Peacock all through his life. She was with him in 1851 when his wife died, when his daughter Rosa Jane died in 1857, and when his first and favourite child Mary died in 1861. When Peacock died himself five years later he left her his entire estate.

After the death of her daughter Margaret, Jane Peacock withdrew into invalidism. Until 1833 Peacock's mother Sarah ran the household, but in 1833 Sarah died. Peacock's habit was to spend the week in London, returning to Halliford only at weekends. His wife stayed in the London house. In 1835 Mary Shelley reported Peacock's domestic circumstances to a friend: 'His wife lives in town—She is quite mad—his children in the country all by themselves except for his weekly visits—His eldest daughter educates herself & reads Paul de Kock's novels in all innocence'.[73]

Paul de Kock, even more commonly than Eugène Sue, author of *The Mysteries of Paris*, was the most commonly cited instance in Victorian England of the risqué French novelist. That status must have owed something to his name. As Joyce's Molly tells Leopold Bloom, when she wants him to change her library book, 'Get another of Paul de Kock's. Nice name he has.' Like all French novelists Paul de Kock was freer than his English counterparts from conventional moral constraints. His most notorious novel was *Le Cocu*, the cuckold. The wronged husband is for de Kock, *le cocu*, a figure of fun, not the demoniacally possessed creature of the English novel, not Mr Dombey or Trollope's Robert Kennedy. In *Le Cocu*, Ernest the dramatist and the working-girl Marguerite live happily together and have two children although they are not married. It is not an arrangement that would have been tolerated in any English novel of the period. French novels allowed glimpses of social behaviour of a kind that English novelists could not admit. In Kock's *La Bouquetière du Chateau d'Eau* we learn that in Paris the restaurants offer private dining rooms. An actress sends her lover on an errand while she and a writer friend of his continue to occupy the room. When he returns her cheeks are as red as cherries and she throws herself into his arms. Everybody was satisfied, we are told. That kind of double entendre is one of Kock's favourite ploys. The actress urges her lover to invite Roncherolle, an experienced roué, to dinner: she is anxious to learn all the 33 ways of drinking champagne that he boasts of knowing. Kock is ribald in a manner not allowed to his Victorian contemporaries, which accounts for his popularity in Victorian England and for Mary Shelley's shocked disapproval. It was Peacock who had brought the novels into the house. In two magazine essays that

---

[73] *Letters of Mary Wollstonecraft Shelley*, 2, 258.

Peacock wrote in 1835 Kock exemplifies for Peacock the writer as épicier, as grocer, the writer who sees the novel simply as a commodity, and who understands only one duty, the duty to provide the public with the article that it demands. Kock is for Peacock 'the embodied spirit of the age', his novels the defining example of the degradation of its literature, but he did not see that as any reason to prevent his 14-year-old daughter from reading them.[74] Mary Peacock had an odd upbringing. She was not at all likely to grow up to become a conventional young woman.

FIGHTING NICOLLS

Mary Peacock's was an unconventional childhood, but when she married in January 1844, her choice was conventional enough. She married Edward Nicolls, an officer in the navy, and went with her young husband to Ireland, where Nicolls took up his post as first lieutenant on H.M.S. Dwarf. It was his first command. H.M.S. Dwarf was a steamship, which was appropriate, because it was steamships that had brought Mary Ellen and Lieutenant Nicolls together. Nicolls's sister was married to Macgregor Laird, the son of William Laird, the founder of the Birkenhead shipbuilding firm. Macgregor Laird was the founder of a company that ran steamships across the Atlantic. Peacock was the champion at India House of the cause of steam navigation to India, and he would have made a point of making Laird's acquaintance. But for everyone other than Peacock, Lieutenant Nicolls was remarkable for his father rather than his brother-in-law. His father, also Edward Nicolls, was known as 'Fighting Nicolls' because in 40 years of active service he was reputed to have been involved in 107 actions. He had retired from the Royal Marines in 1835, but remained one of Britain's most celebrated military men. He was knighted in 1855, the same year in which he was promoted to full general. The historian of the Royal Marines describes him as 'perhaps the most distinguished officer the corps ever had'.[75] When he died in 1865, aged 85, *The Times* catalogued his wounds: 'He had his left leg broken and his right leg severely injured, was shot through his body and right arm, had received a severe sabre cut in the head, was bayoneted in the chest, and had lost the sight of an eye.'[76] He was not an easy father to live up to.

---

[74] 'An Essay on Fashionable Literature' and 'L'Epicier', *Halliford Edition of the Works of Thomas Love Peacock*, 10 vols (London: Constable, 1926), 8, 263–75, and 9, 289–309.
[75] Peter C. Smith, *Per Mare Per Terram: A History of the Royal Marines*, p. 47.
[76] *The Times*, February 9, 1865, p. 12.

Young Edward grew up as the son of such a father might be expected to. He followed his father into the navy, and cultivated a reputation for recklessness. A letter from Mary written, I think, before their marriage warns her 'darling Eddy' against 'a dissipated life', and begs him not to 'quarrel or fight duels with any creature'. It is a letter of farewell. Mary enclosed it in a letter to her father, and the letter to her father is a suicide note.[77] She begins, 'I cannot tell what I wish to say to you and My dear Mama—forget me. I will not speak of myself.' Instead she writes how concerned she is by her younger sister, Rosa's, cough, and warns that 'it is an unfortunate trial to leave a girl by herself'. More startlingly, she writes that Mary Rosewell, the village girl that Peacock had adopted to take the place of his dead daughter, had been 'the evil genius of [her] existence', and begs, 'do not let her be so to dear Rosa'. Her farewell is theatrically magnanimous: 'God bless you My dear, dear father—May Rose and Edward render you that happiness I have taken.' Whether Mary wrote the two letters as an exercise or in earnest is impossible to say, and it is equally impossible to know what prompted her. My guess is that she wrote them in response to an objection, probably by Peacock, to her engagement. She was making a melodramatic threat that, if not allowed her way, she would do away with herself. In comparison with any letters by Meredith, in comparison at least with those that survive, Mary's letters seem recklessly self-revealing. Both Meredith and Mary wear masks when they write, but the mask that Mary assumes is a mask of herself. Hers are the letters of a young woman who will not allow herself to be thwarted, and in January 1844 she got her way. She and her darling Eddy were married at Shepperton, less than a mile from her father's house at Halliford, and on January 26 *The Times* reported that the Dwarf, a steam tender, had sailed from Portsmouth to Cork, 'Lieutenant Commanding J. Nicholls' (the initial was mistaken). Mary sailed with her husband.

Two months later he was dead. He was with Mary Ellen on board the Dwarf when they saw a yacht in trouble. At Mary's urging Nicolls launched his ship's boat and went to assist. The boat capsized and Nicolls and one of his men were drowned. Mary was already pregnant. She stayed on in Ireland. 'She has no desire to leave the place,' Mary Shelley reported, 'where she lost her husband.'[78] But she came home at last. Her daughter

---

[77] Diane Johnson discovered the two letters in the Pforzheimer Collection. The letter to Peacock is a transcription, not in Mary's hand, but it seems authentic. See Johnson, 57–8.

[78] *Letters of Mary Wollstonecraft Shelley*, 3, 132.

Edith was born on October 27, at her father-in-law's house at Shooter's Hill, Blackheath. In *Rhoda Fleming* Meredith introduces his first wife thinly disguised as Mrs Lovell. She has lived for the whole of her life with the remorse she feels for the death of her first husband, who died in a duel that he fought to vindicate the honour of his 'lovely and terrible young wife'.[79] At the very end of the novel Mrs Lovell makes a clipped confession:

> 'The poor boy would go to his doom. I could have arrested it. I partly caused it. I thought the honour of the army at stake.'[80]

Mary Ellen had similar feelings, perhaps, when she remembered standing on the bridge of the Dwarf and urging her Eddy to launch his boat in a storm and go to the rescue of the single-handed yachtsman.[81] Meredith paid his own barbed tribute to darling Eddy at the end of *Beauchamp's Career*. The whole of Nevil Beauchamp's life in which great talents are exerted to so little purpose is summarised in the manner in which that life ends. An eight-year-old boy is larking in his father's boat with his older brother and both boys fall overboard. Beauchamp goes to their aid, rescues the younger boy and drowns trying to save his brother. Beauchamp's uncle and his father-in-law stare at the surviving urchin and read in each other's eyes the selfsame thought, 'This is what we have in exchange for Beauchamp!' The thought is unspoken but it is there to be read 'in the blank stare at one another of the two men who loved Beauchamp, after they had examined the insignificant bit of mudbank life remaining in this world in the place of him'.[82] Meredith, like Keats in *The Eve of St Agnes*, rather liked to leave his reader at the end of a novel with a feeling of pettish disgust. It was the antidote he insisted on offering to the heart-warming endings that Victorian readers preferred. But the final lines of *Beauchamp's Career* seem to serve a more particular purpose. Thirty years after the event Meredith offers his own tribute to the heroism of Mary's first husband, a tribute scarcely distinguishable from a snort of derision.

Edward Nicolls died doing his duty. He was his father's son and he could not have done otherwise. 'Fighting Nicolls' was a hard man to live up to, but so was darling Eddy. It must certainly have seemed so to Mary's

[79] *Rhoda Fleming*, chapter 6.
[80] *Rhoda Fleming*, chapter 48.
[81] Edith Nicolls, unfamiliar with nautical terminology, understood 'single-handed' to mean that the yachtsman had only one arm.
[82] *Beauchamp's Career*, chapter 56.

second husband. Eddy was a man who had to be warned (at least his future wife thought so) not to live a dissolute life, and not to involve himself in duelling, but he was brave, and, what made him quite impossible to compete with, he was dead. He had died a gallant death just two months after his wedding. In *Rhoda Fleming* Edward Blancove is half in love with Mrs Lovell, and he often wonders about her dead husband: 'What sort of a man had Harry been, her first husband? A dashing soldier, a quarrelsome duellist, a dull dog.' Edward is confident that in comparison with Harry he has all the brains. But Mrs Lovell shows him a portrait of Harry that she wears in a locket at her breast. 'Dead Harry was kept very warm', he thinks, and wonders, 'Could brains ever touch her emotions as bravery had done?'[83] It is a question Meredith must often have asked himself in the seven years of his married life. He published *Rhoda Fleming* in 1865, four years after Mary had died, but the question still preyed on his mind.

Mary Ellen remained close to her formidable father-in-law and his wife Eleanor. They were eager to maintain their relationship with their granddaughter and Edith often went to stay with them. But it was not just Eddy's father and mother that Meredith had to find room for. People who marry for a second time do not go into their second marriages alone. They take their first spouse with them, and that first spouse is a still more palpable presence if he happens to be dead. Meredith never met darling Eddy, who died when Meredith had only just turned 16, but Eddy figured largely in his life. Mrs Lovell 'worshipped brains' but she worships bravery too. She would be fully satisfied only by a 'union of brains and bravery in a man', but she doubts whether such a man exists. She recognises Edward as 'the type of brains and Harry of bravery'.[84] We cannot know whether Mary Ellen drew that comparison between Meredith and Eddy, but it is clear that Meredith did. Meredith spent his life sitting at his desk, but that life was always shadowed for him by the life of the man of action. His was a life of thought, but it was always accompanied by a pained recognition of another kind of life, the unthinking life that expresses itself in deeds rather than words. 'Ass that I was', he wrote when he was nearly 50, 'not to go for a conscript when I was a lad!'[85] Frederick Maxse was his greatest friend, and Maxse was an intellectual, but he was also a war hero, aide de camp to Lord Raglan in the Crimea, his gallantry recognised when he

[83] *Rhoda Fleming*, chapter 22.
[84] *Rhoda Fleming*, chapter 22.
[85] *Letters*, 1, 543.

became the youngest captain in the Royal Navy. When Meredith was in his 50s, as he was preparing to write *Diana of the Crossways*, he also had in hand a series of lives of the great military generals. He acted as general editor.[86] He fancied himself something of an expert in these matters, entitled to offer a compliment to Viscount Wolseley on his campaign in the Gold Coast: 'Ashanti will stand forth in History as one of the most perfectly designed and accomplished pieces of work achieved by British arms.'[87] He and Maxse regularly exchanged letters sharing their fears over the parlous state of unpreparedness of the British forces. Meredith trained for his writer's life almost as if it were a soldier's. He performed daily exercises with his 'beetle', his 19-pound hammer, his walks were like route marches, and in Britain and especially on holidays in the Alps he complained loudly if his companions could not keep up his pace. In 1865, when he acted briefly as war correspondent, reporting for the *Morning Post* on the war in Italy, he was able for three months to combine the two lives. He was disappointed that he saw scarcely any action. But for the whole of the rest of his life he remained at an irksome distance from the life lived by men such as Fighting Nicolls and his son.

Meredith at once despised that life and envied it. Edward Nicolls, both the father and the son, shared an unthinking adherence to a masculine code that Meredith could neither bring himself to accept nor to reject. The most striking sign of his ambivalence is the extraordinary prominence allowed in the novels to the practice of duelling. In *Rhoda Fleming* Edward Blancove refuses to resort to that 'decayed method of settling disputes', but he cannot rid himself of the suspicion that by his refusal he forfeits Mrs Lovell's respect. 'Does she think me wanting in physical courage?' he wonders; does she think him 'deficient in personal bravery'?[88] Mary Ellen added a postscript to the suicide letter to Eddy that she enclosed in the letter to her father: 'Eddy one more request and I have done, if you would have my bones rest in peace, oh for the sake of all you hold dearest, do not quarrel or fight duels with any creature. I die in the hope your kindness will grant my soul felt request.' In *Rhoda Fleming* Mrs Lovell, whose husband died in a duel, carries with her the guilt of having encouraged him. Mary Meredith made clear to Eddy her detestation of the practice. But her second husband could not leave the topic alone. Duels had no place at all

[86] *Letters*, 2, 643, note 3.
[87] *Letters*, 3, 1530.
[88] *Rhoda Fleming*, chapter 21.

in the England that Meredith knew (his friend, John Morley, offers as one proof of the liberalism that presides over the nineteenth century that 'duelling has been transformed from folly to crime'[89]), and yet Meredith scarcely writes a novel in which a duel does not take place. The very first of them ends when Richard Feverel is wounded in a duel with Lord Mountfalcon, the man who has attempted to seduce his young wife. In *Evan Harrington* Evan places himself at the service of Harry Jocelyn if Harry 'will deign to challenge a man who is not the son of a gentleman'.[90] In *Vittoria* Captain Weisspriess, an Austrian officer, has a reputation as a deadly duellist until he is killed by Angelo Guidascarpi in 'The Duel in the Pass', a duel in which Angelo, armed only with a stiletto, triumphs against the Captain's sword.[91] In *The Adventures of Harry Richmond* Harry's school friend Heriot challenges the undermaster Boddy, prompting the headmaster to give a sermon on 'the unChristian spirit and hideous moral perversity of one who would even consent to fight a duel',[92] and Harry himself fights a duel with Prince Otto, his rival for the hand of Princess Ottilia, despite the Princess's view that duels are 'the pastime of brainless young men' and that 'only military men and Frenchmen' fight them.[93] The young Nevil Beauchamp admits that duelling is 'sickening folly'.[94] When he was just a stripling he had issued a challenge to the whole of the French Imperial Guard, but as a grown man he thinks differently. 'I never have fought a duel, and never will,'[95] he announces, although he is popularly thought to have interrupted his election campaign to take a trip to France for the purpose of fighting one. In *Diana of the Crossways* there is the comical Irishman Sullivan Smith, who is ready to challenge almost anyone: 'let it be pugilism if their white livers shivered at the notion of powder and ball.'[96] Lord Ormont in *Lord Ormont and His Aminta* is also a notorious duellist, but Matthew Weyburn, who supplants him in Aminta's affections will never accept a challenge even though he is an expert swordsman. In *The Amazing Marriage* Captain Kirby elopes with the Countess Fanny, but not before her husband has 'peppered Kirby with

[89] John Morley, *Recollections*, 2 vols (London: Macmillan, 1917), 1, p. 29.
[90] *Evan Harrington*, chapter 12.
[91] *Vittoria*, chapter 26.
[92] *The Adventures of Harry Richmond*, chapter 5.
[93] *The Adventures of Harry Richmond*, chapter 33.
[94] *Beauchamp's Career*, chapter 1.
[95] *Beauchamp's Career*, chapter 19.
[96] *Diana of the Crossways*, chapter 3.

shot from a fowling-piece'. Kirby who claims to have been 'pickled in saltpetre when an infant', a process that has left him immune to powder and shot, is none the worse. 'Have your shot at me; it's only fair,' Lord Cressett says, and Kirby discharges his pistol 'at the top twigs of an old oak tree'. Lord Cressett and Kirby are reconciled but Cressett's family take up the cause, with unfortunate results for the family member that 'Captain John Peter Kirby laid on his heels at ten paces on an April morning'.[97] Ferdinand Lassalle's ambivalence about duelling may have been what prompted Meredith lightly to fictionalise his history in *The Tragic Comedians*. Lassalle becomes Sigismund Alvan in Meredith's novel. He is so fierce an opponent of duelling that to preserve him from insult an admirer presents him with the walking-stick topped by a heavy metal handle that had once belonged to Robespierre. But when Alvan is jilted he challenges Prince Marko, his young rival, and dies three days later of his wounds. His end, we are told, is 'unheroic', 'a derision', the end of a 'tragic comedian', but, Meredith adds, 'not many are of a stature and a complexity calling for the junction of the two Muses to name them'.[98] Duelling for Meredith is similarly ambivalent, tragi-comic. He repeatedly sides with Mary in repudiating duels and reprehending duellists, but he rarely does so without an admiring glance at those like Eddy who had to be reprehended. He understood that men like Eddy clung to a narrow, antiquated idea of masculinity. He saw through it, but he could not for all that free himself from it, and the best indication of his helplessness is that he, alone of the novelists of the later nineteenth century, introduces duels and the ethics of duelling into almost every novel he wrote.

Mary Peacock was a clever woman, quite clever enough to recognise Meredith's talents, and quite clever enough to understand that by comparison her first husband had been a 'dashing soldier, a quarrelsome duellist, a dull dog', but that need not have spared Meredith a chill sense of his own inferiority. Mrs Lovell has the intelligence to form a very accurate estimate of the men she meets, and yet 'the show of an unflinching courage' still has the power to make her forget all other shortcomings, and the lack of it to render all other virtues null. Mary's first husband had been dead for five years, but he remained a potent presence in Meredith's marriage. So too was the father-in-law who was very much alive.

[97] *The Amazing Marriage*, chapter 1.
[98] *The Tragic Comedians*, chapter 19.

CHAPTER 4

Mary (Marriage)

THE IDEA OF MONEY

Peacock began work at India House in 1819 and did not retire until 1856, by which time he had served for 19 years as Examiner to the Company. The man that Meredith knew was not the young man who had given up his clerk's position to devote himself to literature, the young poet scraping by on grants from the Literary Fund and Shelley's generosity. He was a senior civil servant, perfectly willing to use his influence to assist family members, but the assistance he preferred to give them was help in finding paid work. Peacock secured clerkships in India House for his son Edward and for Hilaire de St Croix. He would have done the same for Meredith, but Meredith refused. He preferred to live the life of the aspiring young writer: 'I have sent you the enclosed Poem in the hope that it may be acceptable to your Journal', 'Would a translation of the life etc. etc. of *Kossuth the Magyar* suit the columns of your journal?', 'I accompany this with some Sonnets on Two Kings of England, which may if you like form a series', 'Let me know about the article on Hermann as early as you can as the sooner that it is printed the better', 'Mr. Horne has had the kindness to speak to you about a volume of Poems which I am desirous of publishing in the style of Tennyson', 'By publishing I scarcely expect any thing but loss', 'Would you accept for *Fraser* some articles on the Austrian Poets?', 'trust me to be quite prepared for all the "merciful" flaying alive so prevalent just now—worse than the worst days of Gifford and *The Quarterly*—Indeed Kingsley and one or two others are the only critics

© The Author(s) 2019
R. Cronin, *George Meredith*,
https://doi.org/10.1007/978-3-030-32448-3_4

whose corrections I should attend to'.[1] He published a volume of poems at his own expense. He busily tempted editors with poems and articles, but without much success. He had been married for six years before he was at last able to announce, 'I have just finished a book which I have sold to Chapman & Hall.'[2] That was *The Shaving of Shagpat*, and whatever Meredith sold it for, it could not have been much. This was the life that Meredith lived all through the seven or eight years that his first marriage lasted. It must have tested Peacock's patience, and it must have tested Mary's too.

Peacock did his best for the young couple. When they came back from their European wedding tour, they moved into his London house in John Street. At the end of the year, they took lodgings with Mrs Macirone at The Limes in Weybridge, but they could not afford it for long. There would not have been much left of Meredith's inheritance of £1000. Mary had a pension of £60 as a navy widow, and the young couple may have earned about as much again, or nearly as much, from their writings. They moved into cheaper lodgings in Weybridge. Early in 1853, with Mary Ellen pregnant again (her first child with Meredith had been stillborn three years before, and after that she had lost a second child), Peacock had them back to live with him at his Thameside house in Halliwell. But sharing a house with a noisy young family did not fit well with the quiet scholarly life that Peacock preferred after his retirement, so he rented a place for them, The Vines, just across the village green from his own house. It must have galled him that his favourite child had married a man who gave no indication that he would ever be able to support his family. It may have been Meredith's failure to earn a living just as much as the attentions of Henry Wallis that cost him his marriage. He carried both failures with him all through life.

Meredith was no better able to incorporate the world of work into his fiction than most of his contemporaries. Tailordom is crucial to his second novel, but the novel has very little to say about tailoring. Evan Harrington is no Seymour Levov. The hero of Philip Roth's *American Pastoral* yields to family pressure and gives up the possibility of a career in sport to enter the family's glove-making business, and Roth's account of how to make gloves is riveting. But for Evan being a tailor is no more than a costume that he wears for a while, a kind of fancy dress that he has to don before

---

[1] *Letters*, 1, 4–9, 12 and 13.
[2] *Letters*, 1, 23.

he can at last be recognised as the gentleman he has always known himself to be. In *Rhoda Fleming* Robert Eccles wins Rhoda's love after he proves himself an expert farmer, but his expertise, unlike Gabriel Oak's in *Far from the Madding Crowd*, is talked about rather than shown. Victor Radnor, the financier of *One of Our Conquerors*, is at his offices in the city almost every day, but there is scarcely any indication of what he does there. All the work seems to be done by his clerk, Daniel Skepsey, who is in constant motion, forever bringing documents to Radnor for his signature or perusal, but the precise nature of the documents remains mysterious. Meredith thought Hugo's *Les Miserables* the great novel of the century. He was less enthusiastic when he read *Les Travailleurs de la mer*, but he admired Hugo's descriptive power, at its finest in the account of the storm that takes up almost the whole of the novel's third book: he had 'never read anything like it'. He continued to think of Hugo as 'the largest son of his mother earth in this time present', and yet Meredith made no remark on the main business of the novel, Hugo's celebration of the workman as hero.[3] The heroic exploit of the novel is Gilliatt's single-handed salvage of the steamship, the Durante, after it is wrecked on the Douvres. Gilliatt's is a labour of love—Mess Lethierry promises the hand of his daughter to the man who can salvage the engine of his ship—but the novel is still more emphatically an expression of Hugo's love of labour. Lethierry is happy to give his daughter to a workman, to a man 'qui travaille, qui est utile', not a man like a soldier or a priest, which is to say a person who knows how to kill or a man who knows how to lie.[4] When Hugo praises 'les calculs de Stevenson',[5] he is not thinking of Robert Louis's experiments, but his father's, and Thomas Stevenson was an engineer, not a writer: he designed lighthouses. Hugo was fascinated by 'les travailleurs', but the only working life that Meredith imagines at all fully is the life of the writer, the life he lived himself, and even in the novel that most fully imagines that life, *Diana of the Crossways*, Diana Warwick is at least as much a society woman as a novelist. But if he did not find a way of getting work into his fiction, he did succeed, after his first marriage was over, in finding a place for it in his life.

Meredith always had half a feeling that swaggering the nut-strewn roads was the life proper to the poet. It is the life he allows Gower Woodseer in

---

[3] *Letters*, 1, 332.
[4] Victor Hugo, *Les Travailleurs de la mer*, Second Part, Book 2, chapter 1.
[5] Victor Hugo, *Les Travailleurs de la mer*, Third Part, Book 3, chapter 6.

The Amazing Marriage, and the life Harry Richmond enjoys for a while when he goes tramping with the gypsy girl Kiomi, the two of them sleeping in ditches nestled in each other's arms. But it was a life Meredith could only live on his walking trips in England and abroad. He kept long into adulthood his love of the open road. In 1862 he published *Modern Love*, his greatest poem, together with *Poems of the English Roadside*, Kiplingesque poems *avant la lettre* in which characters such as 'Grandfather Bridgeman', 'Juggling Jerry' and 'The Old Chartist' are given voices. He told his friend Augustus Jessopp, 'my Jugglers, Beggars, etc., I have met on the road',[6] and perhaps he had. It was at any rate the story that he liked to tell. He might well have claimed, like George Gissing, that he was 'a strange compound of the bohemian and the bourgeois',[7] but for Meredith the bohemian life was a life that he allowed himself only on holiday. For six months, from October 1862, Meredith tried, almost as if he were Algernon or Jack in *The Importance of Being Earnest*, to carve out a double life for himself. All week he stayed in his cottage at Copsham, where he did his work and was sole parent to his nine-year-old son, but he also took a room at 16, Cheyne Walk, in the house that D. G. Rossetti shared with his brother and Swinburne. There Whistler visited, Swinburne slid down the banisters naked, and there were parties in the garden loud enough to prompt complaints from Jane Carlyle. But Meredith's tenancy ended after six months. He could not reconcile himself to D. G. Rossetti's 'bad habits', his penchant, for instance, for substantial English breakfasts, 'eleven a.m. plates of small-shop ham, thick cut, grisly with brine: four smashed eggs on it'.[8] Like Hippias Feverel, Richard Feverel's dyspeptic uncle in his first novel, Meredith was a bohemian who found in the end that he did not have the stomach for it.

Quite soon after his first marriage ended, Meredith conscientiously set about earning a living. The year 1860 was crucial. His first novel had been published the year before, and in 1860 Meredith accepted a position as publisher's reader for Chapman and Hall, a post that he continued to occupy for more than 30 years. In the same year, he agreed to supply a conservative provincial newspaper, the *Ipswich Journal*, with two columns every week. He kept up the task for eight years, persuading friends to stand in for him when he was holidaying abroad. He wrote occasional

[6] *Letters*, 1, 110.
[7] Coustillas, 3, 83.
[8] *Letters*, 1, 376.

pieces too for the *Pall Mall Gazette* and the *Morning Post*. As he wrote to Hardman when he was in his 50s, 'an unpopular author has to work hard'.[9] By 1864, when he married for the second time, he was able to assure his bride's father that he had an annual income of £800. Even so, in 1868, when he was invited to read to an eccentric old lady twice a week, he seized the opportunity. Mrs Benjamin Wood offered the extravagant sum of £300 a year, and she was an interesting woman, the aunt of Kitty O'Shea, who was later to become Parnell's mistress. Meredith safeguarded his self-respect by developing a courtly, chaffing relationship with her that she seemed rather to enjoy, but it remained a role that some literary men would have thought demeaning. The bitter experience of his first marriage had fully apprised Meredith of what W. H. Auden terms 'the amorous effects of "brass"'. It was a lesson that he did not forget when he embarked on his second.

The income that Meredith achieved in the 1860s was as important to his literary well-being as it was to his marital happiness. In 1862, rumours of the 'enormous sum (£8000 or more!)' that George Eliot had received for *Romola* made him wistful.[10] It is true that he always tended to exaggerate his own lack of commercial success. Most of his novels were serialised: *Evan Harrington* in *Once a Week*, *The Adventures of Harry Richmond* in *The Cornhill*, *Lord Ormont and His Aminta* in the *Pall Mall Magazine*, *The Amazing Marriage* in *Scribner's* and no less than four novels in the *Fortnightly*, the journal that was edited for many years by his close friend John Morley—*Vittoria, Beauchamp's Career, Diana of the Crossways* and *One of Our Conquerors*. But only *Diana of the Crossways*, which went through three editions in 1885, the year of its publication, achieved anything like popular success, and that may have had as much to do with public interest in the various scandals associated with Caroline Norton, Meredith's model for Diana, as it did with the novel. Meredith was obliged to adopt the forlorn swagger of the artist reduced to offering his lack of commercial success as proof of the loftiness of his principles. He presented himself as a writer dedicated to serving the interests of his art rather than the demands of his audience, but he was able to do so only because, unlike George Gissing, he managed to make himself independent of New Grub Street. He secured a steady income that did not rely on his sales. It was the disaster of his first marriage that taught him how important that was. It

[9] *Letters*, 2, 614.
[10] *Letters*, 1, 149.

taught him a lesson that he encapsulated in one of his notebooks in a snatch of dialogue: 'Poverty is a very beautiful idea, Sir, but when, Sir, you have not a penny in your pocket, you behold the matter in all its hideous deformity.'[11] He incorporated it, too, in the advice he gave his friend Maxse when Maxse told him that he was thinking of marrying: 'Can you bear poverty for her? Will she for you? Can she, even if she would? … remember that very few women bear it and retain their delicacy and charm.'[12] Maxse came from a wealthy family, and his wife was most unlikely to face any such trials. Meredith's advice came out of his own experience.

'I hadn't an idea of money before I was married,' says a character in *The Amazing Marriage*: 'Now I think of nothing else.'[13] The lack of cash put strains on Meredith's first marriage. But it would have been a strained marriage anyway. Both husband and wife were difficult people. Meredith kept secrets: Mary kept none. After her death, Meredith described her in a letter to his friend, William Hardman, as mad, or almost mad. Hardman had agreed to supply the father of the woman Meredith planned to make his second wife with a character reference. The account Meredith gave Hardman of his first wife was designed to allay the fears of the man whose daughter he wanted to marry. He was not feeling fastidious about the truth. He claimed to be 'eight years' Mary's junior (he was in fact a little less than six and a half years younger).[14] But the suicide letter Mary sent her father, with the letter of earnest advice to Eddy enclosed in it, even if it does not suggests madness, suggests a woman raptly attentive to the drama of her own personal life. So too does a letter to John Cam Hobhouse that she wrote in October, 1848, the year before she and Meredith were married. Hobhouse was a close friend of her father's but Mary Ellen had never met him. Hobhouse, once Byron's closest friend, was then serving in Lord John Russell's cabinet as president of the Board of Control for India. Mary Ellen wrote to him from France. She was probably visiting Eddy's mother and father who had a house in Normandy. She tells Hobhouse that he is 'not merely an ordinary rich man' but a rich man who had proved himself 'the friend of poets and of literature', and then she asks him to relieve her father from 'a heavy pressure of debt' under which he has been labouring for years. When she last saw her father, Mary writes, he

---

[11] *Notebooks*, 36.
[12] *Letters*, 1, 115.
[13] *The Amazing Marriage*, chapter 43.
[14] *Letters*, 1, 162.

'preserved utter silence and kept always one helpless restless posture his head resting on his hand'. He had even threatened to give up going to the opera.[15] Hobhouse was certainly a rich man. His father had been wealthy enough to invest £33,000 in Whitbread's brewery. But so was Peacock. His India House salary of £2000 is the equivalent today of at least £200,000. It is difficult to believe that he was in need of Hobhouse's financial support, and impossible to believe that he would have been other than mortified had he known that his daughter was soliciting it. Mary Ellen admits herself that he would 'never forgive' her if Hobhouse revealed her application to him. As in the case of the suicide letter, one can only speculate as to what was in her mind. She probably went to France to tell her parents-in-law of her intention to remarry (oddly, she claims to Hobhouse that she has been in France for 'one year', which cannot have been the case). It seems likely that her letter is a theatrical response to an objection by Peacock to her marrying a man who did not have the means to support a family. She may have anticipated that Hobhouse would feel obliged to report to his friend that he had received the letter and that Peacock would be shocked into behaving more generously than had been his intention. It is, whether or not I am right, a monstrously indiscreet letter, not a letter that boded well for her marriage to a man so secretive as Meredith.

Meredith was especially secretive about his family origins, and that seems to have been an early cause of friction between the two of them. Mary's mother traced her lineage to Welsh princes, and, according to Anne Bennett, Mary's close friend in the final months of her life, Mary was 'bitterly disillusioned' when she came across a letter from Meredith's father and found that her husband was not, as he had claimed, 'a descendant of an "ancient Welsh family"', but the son of a tailor. The discovery 'produced an entire revolution' in Mary's feelings for Meredith.[16] It may seem unlikely that she would have taken the matter so much to heart. If Meredith had pretended that his family was grander than it was, it seem a harmless enough fiction. But a rueful remark in *The Ordeal of Richard Feverel* may be revealing: 'If we pretend to be what we are not, women, for whom the farce is performed, will find us out and punish us for it.'[17] Harry

[15] Shaheen, 19–20.
[16] Nicholas A. Joukovsky, 'According to Mrs Bennett: A document sheds a kinder light on George Meredith's first wife', *Times Literary Supplement*, October 8, 2004, 13–5.
[17] *The Ordeal of Richard Feverel*, chapter 33.

Richmond's confession in a later novel is just as revealing: 'I was deceiving everybody, myself in the bargain, as a man must do when in chase of a woman above him in rank.'[18]

Class feeling seems to have played its part in the disintegration of the marriage. In August 1851, Mary published an unenthusiastic review of Alexis Soyer's *Modern Housewife, or Ménagère* in *Fraser's*. It is, she insists, much inferior to William Kitchiner's *Cook's Oracle*. The review is for the most part a catalogue of Soyer's deficiencies, but there are some interesting interludes. Mary points out in one of them that the *parvenu* 'cannot escape detection at table': 'The man who is the first of his generation that has attained to good society' will 'clasp the decanter round the body, marring its contents with his hot hand, instead of taking it by the neck as he passes it on'. Even the more established man, if he is unused to the table, 'will be sure to cut ham in large lumps, instead of carving it in thin slices'. 'No man,' Mary warns, 'whose father's daily life did not initiate his earliest years into all the mechanical, physiological, and gastrological intricacies of fish, flesh, and fowl, can escape detection at dinner.'[19] Sharing a table with Mary and her father must have been a daunting experience, still more so for a young man who may have suspected that he was himself the *parvenu* who had given rise to Mary's observations. It was one of the experiences that taught Meredith to find an unnerving likeness of himself in Stendhal's Julien Sorel. Meredith was an early English admirer of *Le Rouge et le Noir*. He might have said of its author exactly what he remarked of Stendhal's *De l'Amour*: 'He goes over ground that I know.' Julien Sorel and Meredith share an acute understanding of the seductive power of a woman who exposes a man's social inadequacies. In Meredith's novella, *The Case of General Ople and Lady Camper*, General Ople falls for Lady Camper, a widow of indeterminate age and the daughter of an earl, because she caricatures him, both literally (she is an accomplished artist) and by mocking his habits of speech. She ridicules all his 'vulgar phrases', his use of middle-class locutions such as 'gentlemanly residence', 'thanks' instead of 'thank-you', 'quite so', 'lady-friend'; she mocks his pronunciation of 'bijou'.[20] He is left 'knowing that he was absolutely bare to this woman, defenceless, open to exposure in his little whims, tricks, incompetencies, in what lay in

[18] *The Adventures of Harry Richmond*, chapter 30.
[19] 'Soyer's Modern Housewife, or Ménagère', *Fraser's Magazine* 44.260 (August 1851), 199–209.
[20] *The Case of General Ople and Lady Camper*, chapter 1.

his heart, and the words that would come to his tongue'.[21] It is what makes him fall in love with her. The story ends when the general proposes and Lady Camper accepts him.

Madame de Renal is of better family than Julien Sorel, socially more easy, sexually more experienced, and she is older. The disparity in their ages and their experience was at first for Meredith, just as it is for Julien, one of Mary's attractions. It made her easier to talk to. It made it possible for him to allow her to take the lead. But Meredith did not continue to hold that view. When he told Hardman that he had been 'eight years the junior' in the marriage, the overstatement suggests that the difference in age had come to seem important to him. In *The Amazing Marriage*, there is a misogynistic flight of fancy in which a woman becomes 'a moon-shade witch' whose business it is to enthral men. The thought suggests another: 'Small is her need to be young—especially if it is the man who is very young.'[22] It is the Earl of Fleetwood who is thinking, but his bride is younger than himself. It is as if he has been suddenly interrupted in his train of thought by a rancorous observation that belongs to the author rather than the character. Meredith's most baleful self-portrait is as Sir Willoughby Patterne in *The Egoist*, and Sir Willoughby, even as he decides to make Lætitia Dale his wife, is always conscious of her faded looks. He finds it easier to think of her as his wife at certain times of the day, 'the light favouring her complexion'.[23] When he compares her with the blooming young Clara Middleton, the woman he had once planned to marry, he is aware of 'the physical contrast of the two'.[24] Mary may have been conscious herself that she was an older woman. In the last months of her marriage, she read and made extracts from Leitch Ritchie's *Wearyfoot Common*, a novel in which Claudia Falcontower falls for Bob Acres, a man much her 'inferior in station' and also a man a good deal younger than her. In their final interview, he looks at her: 'She looked older. The lines of time, whose appearance she had hitherto contrived to repress, were now visible in the unusual paleness of her countenance.'[25]

The young couple had their lack of money to contend with, and class difference, and age difference. They also had their lack of occupation.

---

[21] *The Case of General Ople and Lady Camper*, chapter 6.
[22] *The Amazing Marriage*, chapter 23.
[23] *The Egoist*, chapter 38.
[24] *The Egoist*, chapter 46.
[25] Leitch Ritchie, *Wearyfoot Common* (1855), chapter 19.

Meredith had at least made a decision about his career. He wanted to be a writer, however little progress he seemed to be making towards his goal. It was an ambition that Mary shared, if only half-heartedly. She published two papers on cookery in *Fraser's*, possibly in collaboration with her father, and she collaborated with Meredith on his first volume of poems. For much of the time during the marriage, she was pregnant. She lost two babies before Arthur was born in June 1853. Marriages are private, and we are allowed just one glimpse into the early married life of the Merediths. Catherine Horne came to stay with them in Halliford for three weeks in late October 1852, when Mary, although Catherine Horne would not have known it, was already pregnant with Arthur. Catherine Horne was the wife of R. H. Horne, *Orion* Horne as he was sometimes known, who had been one of Meredith's first patrons. When Horne became a sub-editor for Dickens's *Household Words*, the magazine began to publish Meredith's poems. Catherine had married Horne, who was more than 20 years older than her, in 1847, but earlier in 1852 he had emigrated to Australia, intent on repairing his fortunes in the Australian goldfields. It was in a letter to her husband that Catherine gave a detailed account of her visit to the Merediths. She is far from a disinterested observer of the marriage—her sympathies are wholly with the husband—but the account is vivid.

She begins by remarking, 'Everything is a great deal worse than last year.' Mary 'is much more dictatorial and less affectionate, and he instead of bearing it as he used is often very ill-tempered'. Despite Mary's 'spoilt-beauty airs', 'at times he is as much in love and as infatuated as ever', even though Catherine cannot understand 'how it is that he still cares one grain about her'. Had she been the husband, Catherine would 'have thrown her into the river, for one of the things she says to him, without waiting for any more'. The Merediths, she writes, are 'constantly quarrelling, and she speaking at him, he recognizing it and getting ill-tempered'. She goes on to give a detailed account of the events of Sunday, November 14, the last day of her visit. Catherine was reading downstairs in the library:

> I presently heard the two above disputing; and after about half an hour of this, one evidently accusing the other, there came a series of dreadful screams. I rushed upstairs and met Mr M. at the door, very pale—he begged me to go in, and went down stairs. Mrs M. was sitting in a chair, with her hair all down, crying and screaming and calling out 'Take him away, take him away!' As soon as he shut the door she rushed to it and bolted it and then ran to open the window, which you know is directly over the river. I having never seen anyone in such a devilish passion before thought she was

actually mad and wanted to throw herself in the river, so I prevented her opening it and made her sit down. Presently G. came up again and tried to speak to her and take her hand (fool!) but she said 'no George, never again, you've gone too far this time, I'll never speak to you again.' I left the room then rejoicing at the 'never again' and hoping she really meant it. Presently she went down stairs, and I was so cold that I went into the drawing room again to the fire. M. was sitting very grave and pale, but said not a word about what had happened, only talked a little on indifferent subjects![26]

Had Meredith assaulted his wife? It seems the easiest way to account for the 'series of dreadful screams' and Mary's claim that he had gone too far this time. It may not have been an isolated incident. Anne Bennett, who knew Mary in her last years, wrote that the marriage ended when Mary 'found in a friend one who appeared to her to be all that her husband was not'.[27] This is coyly expressed, but may insinuate that Wallis, unlike Meredith, was not violent. Meredith's Diana says of her first husband, 'he was the maddest of tyrants—a weak one.'[28] Meredith wrote *Diana of the Crossways* in 1884, by which time Mary had been dead for 23 years, but it may be that she voices a truth that he had learned at first hand, in the course of his own tempestuous first marriage. The sequel to the quarrel is just as revealing. Catherine asked Meredith whether they would as usual be dining with Peacock that Sunday, and Meredith said that they would: 'Well I thought this was very funny but went to dress.' She had, she thought, witnessed a scene from a marriage in its last throes. She was imagining 'in the distance a separation, and his after a time returning to his poetry and rejoicing in his release, when suddenly she appeared dressed for dinner and looking as cool and sleek and "jolly" as ever':

I could have screamed with laughter, though I must confess I was disappointed. From that time they went on just as usual. He as attentive to 'dear Mary' as ever, and she as exacting and hard. What a strange nature he must have to bear this, and still retain his affection for her. I suppose these fits of fury are common as they are taken by both so as a matter of course. If I were he, and she was beautiful, young, affectionate (and everything she is not) with that temper I should hate her. I wish you could have seen her. I could scarcely believe it could be the proper, cold hard Mrs M.

[26] Shaheen, 26–9.
[27] Nicholas A. Joukovsky, 'According to Mrs Bennett: A document sheds a kinder light on George Meredith's first wife', *Times Literary Supplement*, October 8, 2004, 13–5.
[28] *Diana of the Crossways*, chapter 14.

'The only remark either of them made to me', Catherine adds 'was, she said "I am afraid I frightened you today, but I hope I did nothing worse."' It seems clear that by 1852 the love that kept the Merediths together was the love that Stendhal terms 'l'amour à querelles', the love that is sustained rather than threatened by quarrelling. Love of this kind, Stendhal remarks, can last longer than passionate love. Every day becomes 'un petit drame', and these productions capture the imaginations of the lovers. Quarrelling is the bond that holds together 'beaucoup de mariages bourgeois', the Merediths' marriage, it seems, amongst them.[29] But it did not hold that marriage together for very long.

In October 1853, when Arthur was only a few months old, Mary began a correspondence with the Christian Socialist, Charles Mansfield. The Christian Socialists ran an institute in Red Lion Square in Holborn that Mary proposed to take over and run as a school for domestic servants. Her husband would stay in Halliford at Vine Cottage, and she 'hopes to be able to come to see him on Sundays'.[30] In the end the plan came to nothing. The building was requisitioned by F. D. Maurice for his Working Men's College. But Mary's proposal shows that after just four years of marriage, she was actively seeking an independent career. She had an acute understanding of the need to train women to earn their own livings, an issue that Gissing addressed 40 years later in *The Odd Women*, alerted to their predicament,

[29] Jacqueline Banerjee has argued persuasively that another glimpse into the marriage is offered in Emilie Maceroni's tale for young people, *Magic Words*. *Magic Words* is a Christmas story loosely modelled on Browning's *Pippa Passes*, in which a series of tales is linked by the decisive effect on the protagonists not of a song, as in *Pippa Passes*, but of some 'magic words'. The framing tale concerns a young writer, Percy, who is separated from his 'imperious' wife, who is much his social superior. Their quarrel has been perpetuated because both are too proud to recognise their faults, but husband and wife are reconciled when the husband attends the wife's New Year's Eve party and hears her rehearse the Christmas message of good will and forgiveness. Emilie Maceroni was the daughter of the Meredith's landlady when they took lodgings at The Vines in Weybridge shortly after their marriage and the model for Emilia in *Emilia in England* and *Vittoria*. See Jacqueline Banerjee, 'George Meredith and Emilie Maceroni: Part of the Background to "Modern Love" and the Italian Novels', http://www.victorianweb.org/authors/meredith/emilie.html.
[30] See Nicholas A. Joukovsky, 'Mary Ellen's first affair: New light on the biographical background to *Modern Love*', *Times Literary Supplement*, June 15, 2007, 13–5. Joukovsky believes that Mary had an affair with Mansfield. This seems extremely unlikely. The correspondence is entirely professional in character. When Mansfield invites his Christian Socialist colleague, John Ludlow, to come to Weybridge for the weekend, he warns, 'I feel bound to tell you that you will meet Mr and Mrs Meredith dining and sleeping here.' This is surely a man speaking of difficult house guests, not of his mistress and her husband.

perhaps, by her recognition that she too was in need of a profession. Mary was an expert cook, skilled in home economics, and the school would have allowed her to build a career on the basis of those skills. In the end her ambition remained unrealised. It would be fulfilled not by her but by her daughter. Edith Nicolls, who became Edith Clarke, is widely recognised as the founder of domestic science as an academic discipline. In 1873 she opened the National Training School for Cookery in London, the first such school in Britain, and she went on to campaign for the teaching of cookery in schools. She was, according to Meredith in 1893, 'one of the women of a wise activity', one of those 'doing real help to move the world, instead of vapouring'.[31] By then he recognised how important it was that women be allowed to live an active life. He began his short story, 'The House on the Beach', in 1861, the year that Mary died, although he did not publish it until 1877. The story recalls the period in 1856 and 1857 when the Merediths were living at Seaford and lodged with the Ockendens. The husband was the village carpenter, and the wife, like Mary Ellen, was famed for her cooking. In the story they become the Crickledons. The wife's domestic skills (Crickledon had tempted her away from Sir Alfred Pooney, who had employed her as 'a forty-pound-a-year' cook) allow them to take in paying guests. The husband practises his carpentry as a vocation rather than as a trade. He is at his bench from morning until night and is somewhat resentful that he is obliged to interrupt his work on Sundays. It makes his life as a carpenter rather like the life of a writer. Together, the Crickledons make the kind of marriage that the Merediths never managed to achieve: 'Each had a profession, each was independent of the other, each supported the fabric.'[32] Meredith imagines another such marriage in the late novel, *Lord Ormont and His Aminta*, in which Aminta overcomes her feeling that schoolmastering is a vulgarly low profession and accompanies Matthew Weyburn when he leaves Britain to set up a school in Switzerland. The school they establish is a joint project. Meredith may have learned by then that one reason for the failure of his marriage was that Mary, like almost all the middle-class women of her generation, had no occupation available to her and no way of earning her own income. In her correspondence with Mansfield, she made a bold attempt to carve out a career for herself, but nothing came of it. Whether she was looking for a profession for its own sake, or whether she was in search of an escape from her marriage, we cannot tell. Neither, perhaps, could she.

[31] Shaheen, 132.
[32] *The House on the Beach*, chapter 11.

HE HAD A WIFE, AND HE HAD A FRIEND

The marriage was already damaged, perhaps irretrievably, before Mary ever met Henry Wallis. It may have been Austin Daniel, one of the contributors to the *Monthly Observer*, who introduced them. It was in his room that Meredith modelled for Chatterton in Wallis's painting of the poet's death. Wallis was even younger than Meredith, eight years younger than Mary. As the years went by, Meredith cultivated his bafflement that his wife should have preferred a humble painter to a writer whom some of his contemporaries, Max Beerbohm, for example, were pleased to rank second only to Shakespeare. It seeps into his account in *The Tragic Comedians* of 'the irony of the fates' that allowed Clotilde, after Alvan, the politician of genius, is killed in the duel, to give her hand to the man who had slain him, the youthful but anodyne Prince Marko.[33] But it was there from the first, in the novel that Meredith began almost immediately after his wife left him. Austin Feverel's wife leaves him not for a painter but for a poet:

> He had a wife, and he had a friend. His marriage was for love; his wife was a beauty; his friend was a sort of poet. When he selected Denzil Somers from among his college chums, it was not on account of any similarity of disposition between them, but from his intense worship of genius, which made him overlook the absence of principle in his associate for the sake of such brilliant promise.

She and the poet 'played Rizzio and Mary together',[34] a historical allusion, the only point of which seems to be that it allows Meredith to introduce into the novel his own wife's name. Somers's early promise remains gratifyingly unfulfilled. By the time that the novel begins, 'his fame has sunk; his bodily girth has sensibly increased'. He has gone into a gin-sodden decline ('the juice of the juniper is in requisition') and is reduced to strumming 'with gouty fingers on a greasy guitar'. His pen is for hire, and the hire is inexpensive. Unable, as he explains to his wife, 'pluming a smile upon his succulent mouth', to keep her in a manner befitting 'her gentle nurture', he petitions the husband he has wronged for an annuity.[35] Henry Wallis also failed to fulfil his early promise, although his decline was gentler.

---

[33] *The Tragic Comedians*, chapter 19.
[34] *The Ordeal of Richard Feverel*, chapter 1.
[35] *The Ordeal of Richard Feverel*, chapter 12.

He exhibited 'The Death of Chatterton' at the Royal Academy exhibition in 1856, the year after he had exhibited his portrait of Mary, 'Fireside Reverie'. 'Faultless and wonderful,' Ruskin remarked, 'a most notable example of the great school' (i.e. the Pre-Raphaelite). In 1858 Wallis's 'Thou wert our conscript' impressed Ruskin as 'the picture of the year, and but narrowly missing being a first-rate of any year'. But by 1875 Ruskin could say of a view of Venice, 'Ponte della Paglia', only that it 'may be useful to travellers' and that 'the Bridge of Sighs is better painted than usual'.[36] In 1859 Wallis inherited his stepfather's wealth and seems to have lost much of his ambition. He continued to paint, but he also became a collector of eastern ceramics and wrote learned monographs on them. But all that was in the future. When he and Mary began their affair, when Mary became pregnant by him and bore his child, Meredith was the author of a slim volume of poems and an Arabian tale that had been quite well received. Wallis was two years Meredith's junior, but *The Death of Chatterton* had already made him famous. In 1857 the painting was taken on tour around Great Britain. In Manchester it was viewed by more than a million people.[37] In the same year Wallis showed at the Royal Academy *The Stonebreaker*, the painting still regarded as his masterpiece, a picture of a labourer in a rural landscape, slumped against a rock, asleep or more likely dead of overwork. Mary left a struggling writer for a painter widely expected to establish himself as one of the great British artists. It could not have made her defection easier to bear.

Meredith met William Hardman in 1861. After Maxse and John Morley, he was Meredith's closest friend, and in 1864 it was Hardman that he turned to when Justin Vulliamy insisted on a referee who could speak to the character of the man who wanted to marry his daughter. 'You are to speak your full conviction of me,' Meredith told him, but it is apparent that there was a great deal about Meredith that Hardman did not know:

There is, or was a child—not mine, who was taken by the father, and of whom I hear and shall hear nothing. You can say the truth that incompatibility of temper separated two people of whom the man was eight years the junior, the woman very clever: her qualities we may leave where they lie. To say that she approached madness without being quite mad is to express her

[36] *The Works of John Ruskin*, ed. E. T. Cook and Alexander Wedderburn, 39 vols (London: George Allen, 1904), 14, 60, 170 and 278.
[37] Paul Farley and Michael Symmons Roberts, *Deaths of the Poets* (London: Jonathan Cape, 2017), Introduction.

mental and moral character. She dallied with responsibility, played with passion; rose suddenly to a height of exaltation, sank to a terrible level. And was
very clever.[38]

That tells us at least as much about Meredith as it tells us about Mary,
and one of the more interesting things that it reveals is that Meredith, who
had been an intimate friend of Hardman's for three years, had told him so
little about his first wife. Hardman was close to Meredith's son, Arthur,
but he seems to have known nothing of Arthur's mother. When Ellis was
writing his great uncle's biography, Hardman confirmed to him that he
discovered the identity of Meredith's first wife only when he inspected a
copy of the *Poems* of 1851 and saw the dedication to Peacock, Meredith's
father-in-law.[39]
In April 1858, Meredith was living in Hobury Street. Arthur was with
him. Mary was at Clifton, near Bristol. She had just given birth to her son
by Wallis. Meredith wrote to a friend, the painter Eyre Crowe. He makes
a brave effort to reply in kind to the spirited letter that Crowe had written
him, and then the mask slips: 'If I speak much, old fellow, I shall get to
speaking of myself, and that is not a cheerful theme.'[40] It was a theme that
Meredith systematically avoided. All his effort in this greatest crisis of his
life, like his own Lord Fleetwood's when his wife leaves him, went into
preserving uncracked his 'white plaster of composure'.[41] What mattered
most of all was that he should not become an object of pity or contempt.
In *The Egoist* he was able to trace so deftly Sir Willoughby Patterne's per-
verse state of mind because it was a state of mind that he shared: 'The
breath of the world, the world's view of him, was partly his vital breath, his
view of himself.'[42] In Sir Willoughby Meredith succeeds as well as he ever
did in fulfilling the novelist's true task, which is, as he explains in *Diana of
the Crossways*, 'to give the Within and Without of us', and he did it by
allowing Sir Willoughby to share his own greatest anxiety, the fear that 'he
and his whole story' might be 'discussed in public'.[43] In *The Tragic
Comedians* that fear is realised for Sigismund Alvan when his banal young
fiancée leaves him and he feels that he has 'called up the whole world in an

[38] *Letters*, 1, 162.
[39] Ellis, 69.
[40] *Letters*, 1, 34.
[41] *The Amazing Marriage*, chapter 35.
[42] *The Egoist*, chapter 37.
[43] *Diana of the Crossways*, chapter 1; *The Egoist*, chapter 45.

amphitheatre to see a girl laugh him to scorn'.[44] Alvan displays the kind of masculinity that Hardy explores in several novels, most fully in *Far from the Madding Crowd*. Sergeant Troy and Squire Boldwood do not so much fear rebuff from the women they love as the sting of shame when their rejection is witnessed by their neighbours. When Fanny mistakes the church she is to come to, Troy waits for his bride, standing upright at the altar 'with the abnormal rigidity of the old pillars around', listening to, or perhaps imagining, the titters of the congregation, before he turns and stalks 'resolutely down the nave'. When Bathsheba rejects Boldwood for Troy, 'the very hills and sky seem to laugh' at him. Boldwood's only wish is that he could have been 'jilted secretly'.[45] Only Gabriel Oak is free from this morbid masculine fear of being made a spectacle, and he is at last rewarded for his immunity. Bathsheba becomes his bride because he is the only one of her suitors who cares more for her than for what other people think about him. Gabriel's is a virtue that Meredith prefers to locate in women, in Emilia Belloni, for example. In both of the novels in which she appears, *Emilia in England* and *Vittoria*, she is heroically careless of what the world thinks of her. Her triumph, as Anna von Lenkenstein acknowledges, lies in her 'ignorance of scorn'.[46] It is the men who, like Sergeant Troy and Squire Boldwood, fear public contempt. Percy Dacier in *Diana of the Crossways* to give just one example is stood up by Diana at a railway station and leaves feeling like 'the fool doubled: so completely the fool that he heads the universal shout'.[47] Meredith published *The Egoist* in 1879, *The Tragic Comedians* in 1880 and *Diana of the Crossways* in 1884. The feelings he had in 1859, in Hobury Street, when he was writing his first novel, were still raw a quarter of a century later.

After Mary left him, Meredith made new friends, Hardman amongst them. He kept up with almost none of those who had known him in the years of his marriage, and it seems clear why he dropped them. His marriage was a thing that he could not bear to talk about, and he could bear still less the thought of it being talked about by others. And then in 1862, just a year after Mary died, Meredith published *Modern Love*. In an age of indiscreet poems—*Pauline, The Prelude, In Memoriam, Leaves of Grass, The House of Life, Poems of 1912–13*—*Modern Love* was surely the most

[44] *The Tragic Comedians*, chapter 17.
[45] Thomas Hardy, *Far from the Madding Crowd*, chapters 16 and 31.
[46] *Vittoria*, chapter 39.
[47] *Diana of the Crossways*, chapter 26.

indiscreet poem of them all. Nothing in Meredith's first volume of poems offers any reason to suppose him capable of writing *Modern Love*. Meredith offered his first volume of poems to his publisher as a volume 'in the style of Tennyson',[48] but Meredith's Tennysonian poems are quite without Tennyson's morbidity, his claustrophobic self-absorption. Meredith included poems in the style of other poets too, but in almost every case the imitations work to divest his models of their personality. The result is an oddly characterless volume. The poems were the products of Meredith's courtship and the early months of his marriage. Meredith had praised Mary's poem 'The Blackbird' when it appeared in the *Monthly Observer*, and he includes in his first volume a poem that retells the same story.[49] It was his way of offering a private acknowledgement of their marriage in print. The sequence of sonnets, *Pictures of the Rhine*, is a souvenir of the landscapes that he and Mary had passed through on their wedding tour. But he chose not to include the most intimate of the honeymoon poems, 'Rhine-Land':

> No longer severing our embrace
>   Was Night a sword between us;
> But richest mystery robed in grace
>   To lock us close and screen us. (45–8)

He was only 23, still a shy young man, but it was not just that. He was still struggling to find an idiom that would allow him to introduce into his poems his experience of married love. It was easier to contemplate love postponed: 'When—ah! when will love's own light / Wed me alike thro' day and night, / When will the stars with their linking charms / Wake us in each other's arms?'[50] The only poem in the volume that is still remembered, 'Love in the Valley', the poem that Tennyson, in a rare moment of generosity, wished that he had written himself, celebrates a love that could scarcely be more different from the young Meredith's love for a woman six years his senior who had a six-year-old daughter. It is addressed to a 'maiden', 'Shy as the squirrel whose nest is in the pine-tops',[51] and the metre of the poem, the metre that makes it memorable, is only congruous

---

[48] *Letters*, 1, 8.
[49] Phyllis Bartlett prints Mary's 'The Blackbird' alongside Meredith's 'The Two Blackbirds', 1, 74–6.
[50] 'Song' ('The Flower unfolds its dawning cup'), 13–6.
[51] 'Love in the Valley', 13.

with the tripping gait of a young woman who has scarcely outlived her girlhood. The women Meredith can accommodate comfortably in these poems are coyly virginal, women like Daphne assailed by Apollo in the longest poem in the volume: 'Timidly the timid shoulders / Shrinking from the fervid hand!'[52] He seems unable in his poems to free himself from the notion that 'the choicest maids are those that hide / Like dewy violets under the green'.[53] He has the young man's fascination with breasts. Daphne's are 'twin-heaving havens'.[54] It was a fascination that Meredith carried with him into his late middle age: in *The Egoist* Meredith is still calling attention to Clara Middleton's bodice and the 'peeps' it offers of 'the veiled twins'.[55] There are very occasional attempts to introduce a franker eroticism, but it is awkwardly done, as when Meredith issues an invitation in hexameters to 'the hot-kissing sun': 'come, tho' he kiss till the soft little upper-lip loses / Half its pure whiteness; just speck'd where the curve of the rosy mouth reddens.'[56] That the poet of the *Poems* of 1851 should ten years later become the poet of *Modern Love* is as unlikely as the author of *The Shaving of Shagpat* going on to write *The Ordeal of Richard Feverel*.

In 'Rhine-Land' Meredith refers to the sword that had once separated the lovers but separates them no longer. That sword reappears in the first sonnet of *Modern Love* in which husband and wife lie side by side; neither of them able to sleep:

> Like sculptured effigies they might be seen
> Upon their marriage-tomb, the sword between;
> Each wishing for the sword that severs all. (14–6)

The knight places a sword between himself and the lady beside whom he lies as a pledge of his chastity, but the sword that separates Meredith's husband and wife is the sharper because it is not forged from steel. It has its only existence in the mind of the man and the woman. In the first sonnet of his sequence Meredith colonises a new space for poetry, the bedroom, not the adulterous room shared by lovers in a poem such as Donne's 'The Sunne Rising', but the far stranger, far more fraught space shared by

---

[52] 'Daphne', 13–4.
[53] 'Song: Spring', 8–9.
[54] 'Daphne', 119.
[55] *The Egoist*, chapter 20.
[56] 'Pastorals', VII, 17–8.

husband and wife. The man and woman in the opening sonnet are inches apart, so close that the wife feels her husband's 'hand's light quiver by her head', and at once 'The strange low sobs that shook their common bed / Were called into her with a sharp surprise'. They are almost touching, and their closeness serves only to remind them how far apart they are. They have become strangers, except that they are as achingly conscious of each other and of each other's bodies as any lovers in the first full flush of their love. To the man the sobs that the woman strangles are 'like little gaping snakes', and those snakes hiss their way all through the sonnet, which finds room for 35 's' sounds, voiced and unvoiced. This marriage is an Eden into which a whole nest of serpents has found its way. All through the night, they lie awake, rigidly, side by side, and yet, like Dante's lovers, like Paolo and Francesca, they are reading from the same book: 'they from head to feet / Were moveless, looking through their dead black years.' As they read of the adulterous love of Lancelot and Guinevere, Paolo and Francesca realise for the first time their own, still more transgressive love. This man and woman read through the night the story of their own marriage, a marriage that the wife's adultery has reduced to a succession of 'dead black years'. They are reading a diary from which all the happy days have been redacted, and all that is left are blank dark spaces.

Victorian architects revived the Gothic, and Victorian poets just as incongruously revived the renaissance sonnet sequence. There are examples by Elizabeth Barrett Browning, by D. G. Rossetti and his sister Christina, by George Eliot and Augusta Webster and by J. A. Symonds, but *Modern Love* is the sequence that recalls most tellingly its renaissance predecessors, Sidney's adulterous *Astrophil and Stella*, Spenser's *Amoretti*, a sequence that uniquely celebrates a love that finds its proper end in marriage, and the greatest sequence of them all, Shakespeare's *Sonnets*, which, like *Modern Love*, give voice to the rancour of a lover who believes himself betrayed. Like Sidney, like Spenser and like Shakespeare, Meredith's sequence is written out of a private history to which its readers are only half-admitted. Like *The Ordeal of Richard Feverel*, Meredith's first novel, *Modern Love*, his greatest poem, was a product of the disaster of his marriage and of Meredith's compulsion at once to conceal that disaster and to confess it. Much of the plot of the poem is invented. It ends with the wife's suicide, the catastrophe that so often brings to a conclusion the career of adulterous wives in Victorian fiction. But Mary Ellen Meredith did not kill herself. She died of kidney failure, most probably from Bright's disease. In the poem the husband, when he discovers his wife's infidelity, retaliates by taking a mistress himself. There is no reason to believe that Meredith did the same. The husband in the poem is more secure both economically and socially than the impecunious tailor's son who wrote it. In *Modern Love* Meredith conceals the facts of his marriage as well as revealing them, but for all that it remains a raw poem, the rawest account in all of English literature of what it feels like to live through a failed marriage.

I have called *Modern Love* a sequence of sonnets. So too did the poem's reviewers. But in fact the 50 poems that make up the sequence are not sonnets at all. *Modern Love* is written in stanzas of 16 lines, each of them made up of 4 quatrains, abba. Each poem begins with the kind of quatrain that begins an Italian sonnet. The reader expects a sonnet, but the sonnet never arrives. Instead, the first quatrain is followed by another and another and another. It seems a clodhopping alternative to the 14-line stanza of Petrarch, but it is Meredith's finest invention. Meredith knew nothing of the greatest of Victorian sonneteers, Gerard Manley Hopkins, his younger contemporary. The beauty of the sonnet like all beauty was for Hopkins produced by a counterpoint of symmetry with asymmetry, 14 lines of equal length divided into 2 unequal parts, octave and sestet, 8 lines and 6. That division is, for Hopkins, 'the real characteristic of the sonnet'.[57] Its asymmetry is what allows the sonnet's two parts to come together; it is what allows them to be forged into a unified poem. Meredith invents a bastard version of the sonnet made up of four quatrains, four symmetrical parts that can never be fused into one. They remain as separate from one another as the bodies of husband and wife in the very first poem of the sequence, who stay separate even as they lie in bed together, never touching, each supremely conscious of the other, each for all that quite alone. In the 45th poem of the sequence, the husband knows that the wife has a lover, and the wife knows that the husband has taken a mistress, but still they stroll together through the garden chatting:

> She joins me in a cat-like way, and talks
> Of company, and even condescends
> To utter laughing scandal of old friends.
> These are our summer days, and these our walks. (13–6)

---

[57] *The Correspondence of Gerard Manley Hopkins with Richard Watson Dixon*, ed. Claude Colleer Abbott (London: Oxford University Press, 1935), 71.

That 'cat-like way' of hers is wholly unexpected in so extravagantly literary a poem, and it is exactly right. She walks by his side but with no loss of self-possession, without a trace of dog-like devotion. Husband and wife talk to one another, they seem intimate, and yet for all that they never join. The quatrains in Meredith's sonnets come together in much the same cat-like way.

In love poems the lovers recognise nothing except their love. They cancel the whole world beyond it. 'Nothing else is', as Donne puts it. Their ambition is to undo their difference from one another, so that (Donne again) the love poem becomes a 'dialogue of one'. *Modern Love* by contrast hymns the 'union' of an 'ever-diverse pair'. It has to do with an unhappy marriage, but the partners in all marriages are diverse. Spouses cannot continue to deny through the years the differences between them, which is why so few love poems celebrate married love. Husband and wife cannot sustain the fiction that they have become one person, and they cannot after the honeymoon obliterate the world outside the bedroom or the people who inhabit it. It is after all the world in which they have to find their place, and its residents are the people they have to live amongst. So, in the 23rd poem, husband and wife find themselves guests at a country house. The bedrooms are all taken. The only room left is an 'attic-crib', but, as it is laughingly pointed out, 'Such lovers will not fret / At that'. The husband retires late, knocks at the bedroom door and catches, as he passes the bed, 'the coverlet's quick beat'. He does not lie down on the bed, but beside it. His kinship is with the animals outside, 'out in the freezing darkness' where 'the lambs bleat' and the 'small bird stiffens in the low starlight'. But during the night, his wife joins him on the floor, and warms his feet with her breasts, and when he wakes he thinks it must have been a dream. In the 15th poem, the world outside intrudes more violently into the marital bed. The husband brings it with him when he comes into the bedroom:

> I think she sleeps: it must be sleep, when low
> Hangs that abandoned arm toward the floor;
> The face turned with it. (1–3)

The husband enters the room armed with two letters, two love letters, one to himself and another more recent letter: 'The words are very like; the name is new.' His new knowledge infects the way he sees his sleeping wife. The arm dangling downwards becomes in a grim pun 'abandoned'.

He wakes her to show her the letters he is carrying and notes with sadistic satisfaction how her 'waking infant-stare / Grows woman to the burden my hands bear'. The bedroom shared by husband and wife, unlike the bedroom shared by lovers, is porous. The husband locks the bedroom door before he wakens his wife, but locking the door cannot keep the world out.

All married people are aware of the difference between how their marriage seems to them and how it seems to their friends. In Sonnet XVII husband and wife give a dinner party and offer at table a performance that dazzles their guests. As Edith Nicolls reported of her mother and stepfather, 'they sharpened their wits on each other.'[58] They are like Philip Roth and Clare Bloom in their London years, and the brilliance of their performance makes them 'enamoured' all over again. But they are lost in admiration not of each other but of the acting skills that each displays. There is a ghost present at their party just as there was at Macbeth's, but it is the ghost of a dead marriage rather than a dead friend. They may exchange 'warm-lighted looks', but what shines in their faces is not love but 'Love's corpse-light'. In the 21st sonnet, husband and wife are walking on the lawn with a friend, and the friend confesses how he has himself at long last fallen in love. He asks that, as a happy couple, they give him their blessing. The eyes of husband and wife meet and 'grow white', and the next moment the wife faints, a happy symptom, their friend assumes, of her pregnancy:

> When she wakes,
> She looks the star that thro' the cedar shakes:
> Her lost moist hand clings mortally to mine. (14–6)

She looks at the star, and she looks like it, and the sonnet ends as husband and wife clasp hands in a line in which almost every word seems to repel its neighbour, 'lost moist hand clings'.

Like most unhappily married couples, the Merediths exaggerated their skill in keeping their unhappiness from their friends. In 1852, when they had been married for little more than three years, Catherine Horne reported, 'Everything is a great deal worse than last year'. A year later, when Charles Mansfield invited his friend John Ludlow for the weekend, he felt obliged to give him a warning: 'I feel bound to tell you that you will

---

[58] Edith made the remark to René Galland, *George Meredith: les cinquantes premières années* (Paris: Les Presses Françaises, 1923), 132.

meet Mr and Mrs Meredith dining and sleeping here.'[59] But in *Modern Love* Meredith shows that he had come to understand himself very well. The poem expertly displays his capacity for alarming, excoriating self-knowledge. When, for example, the husband takes a mistress, he knows that he does so only because his wife's infidelity has 'lessened' him in his own eyes and in the eyes of other men, and if he chooses a beautiful woman, it is so that 'men shall mark you eyeing me, and groan / To be the God of such a grand sunflower!' (XXVIII, 13–4). He is like Keats's Lycius who cannot be happy in the possession of a beautiful woman unless other men are 'confounded and abash'd' by his achievement. There is no evidence that Meredith, like the husband in his poem, retaliated in kind, but every indication that for him, as for the husband, the most pressing concern that his wife's adultery caused him was that he felt himself belittled in the eyes of others by her betrayal.

The traditional role of the wronged husband, the role played by Dickens's Dombey in the 1840s, the role still available to Trollope's Glaswegian millionaire, Robert Kennedy, MP, in the 1870s, is not quite possible for a late Victorian like Meredith. When Meredith's husband enters the bedroom brandishing his wife's letter to her lover, he seems theatrical even to himself. He feels like Othello, like the 'Poet's black stage-lion of wronged love' (XV, 5). He feels still more like a character in a novel than one of Shakespeare's tragic heroes, but it is a French novel, like the novel the wife complains of as 'unnatural' in the 25th sonnet. The errant wife in the novel is forgiven by her husband before ever she sheds a tear. The husband's forgiveness allows her to rediscover her affection for him, and the spurned lover takes to a penitential diet of 'blanc-mange and absinthe' before reverting to 'rosbif' lest his pallor renew the wife's interest in him. 'Unnatural?' the husband interjects, 'My dear, these things are life: / And life, some think, is worthy of the Muse.' But if it is life it is la vie parisienne not the life of the Home Counties. Near the end of the sequence, in poem XLVI, the husband seeks out his wife in 'that old wood' in which he had first declared his love for her: 'There did I see her, not alone.' He offers her his arm, she takes it, and the 'disturbing shadow' of her lover 'passed reproved'. The husband fears that she will feel driven to confess and to stop her mouth he insists that she has his full trust:

[59] See Shaheen, 26, and Nicholas A. Joukovsky, 'Mary Ellen's first affair: New light on the biographical background to *Modern Love*', *Times Literary Supplement*, June 15, 2007, 13–5.

A ghastly morning came into her cheek,
While with a widening soul on me she stared. (15–6)

The poem is set in England, not in Paris, and in England 'She will not speak. I will not ask.' In England, it is the silences that speak, that silent stare, for example, that tells us that the wife has seen her husband as if for the first time. It is a stare of astonishment, of contempt, of horror. When the wife takes the husband's arm, she takes it 'simply, with no rude alarm'. She may have been surprised with her lover but she is unafraid, and yet the phrase hints at possibilities of violence even as it gainsays them. The husband is confident that the 'Poet's black stage-lion of wronged love / Frights not our modern dames' (XV, 5–6), but can he think of Othello without feeling his hands around his wife's throat? The husband is a late Victorian, but, as he admits in the ninth poem in the sequence, he can still feel 'the wild beast in himself' and that beast still seems 'masterfully rude' at times: 'Had he not teeth to rend and hunger too? / But still he spared her.' He finds himself alone with her: "twas dusk; she in his grasp; none near.' 'Have you no fear?' he asks. She laughs and replies, 'No, surely; am I not with you?', and at that moment he feels what it would be like to squeeze the life out of her, 'to squeeze like an intoxicating grape'. The grape comes from Keats, from the 'Ode on Melancholy', where the 'strenuous tongue' bursts the grape of joy against 'the palate fine', but in Meredith's rendering of the thought, the erotic and the murderous impulse are fused. Meredith was a young husband, socially and economically insecure, and insecure men are prone to violence. Catherine Horne thought Mary to blame for the fierce quarrels that punctuated the marriage, but it was rash of her to infer that because so soon after one of the fiercest of them Mary was looking 'as cool and sleek and "jolly" as ever', her screams had been only hysterical. Peacock published his last novel, *Gryll Grange*, in 1860, not long before Mary died. Was he thinking of his daughter's marriage when he has Mr MacBorrowdale say, 'Civilised men ill-use their wives; and the wives revenge themselves in their own way, and the Divorce Court has business enough on its hands to employ it twenty years at its present rate of progression'?[60]

The natural world is governed by time, and human beings are natural creatures, but they differ from other animals, Meredith believes, because they have access to a world of ideas, and ideas are not subject to change.

[60] Thomas Love Peacock, *Gryll Grange*, chapter 31.

People are 'first, animals; and next / Intelligences at a leap'. The problem is the leap, the disjunction between the two identities. Love has the power to bridge that gap. In love time seems entirely consonant with eternity:

> When the renewed for ever of a kiss
> Whirls life within the shower of loosened hair! (XIII, 15–6)

A kiss is for ever, but it is a special kind of for ever, a for ever that can be endlessly renewed. It is a thought that makes a kiss, as Keats recognises in 'Ode on a Grecian Urn', very like a poem. In sonnet XVI, the husband recalls sitting with his wife before the fire, the two of them 'joined slackly'. 'Ah, yes!', he says, 'Love dies!', never believing the truth of that remark less than he did at that moment, and finds to his surprise that his wife's cheek is salt to his kiss, and hears sobs lift her breast. The sonnet ends, 'Now am I haunted by that taste! that sound!' He is haunted because his wife's adultery has proved true what had only been a stray remark, 'Love dies!' But the adultery that proves love is dead also serves to awaken it into a ghostly life, a life that perversely mimics the renewed for ever of the true lovers' kiss. In sonnet VII the husband marvels that a hairdresser's skills should have the power to 'take the eyes from out my head / Until I see with eyes of other men'. But it is not the 'oiled barber' who performs the miracle. It is the knowledge that his wife has a lover that has stripped from her the veil of familiarity, so that he can look at her once more as if he saw her for the first time. The wife calls him to her as she sits at her dressing table:

> Familiar was her shoulder in the glass,
> Through that dark rain. (V, 5–6)

And yet, he thinks, 'a changed eye' may find 'such familiar sights / More keenly tempting than new loveliness'. It is the knowledge of the wife's unfaithfulness that has changed his eye. The dark rain through which he glimpses her shoulder is the fall of her hair, but it is also the dark rain of his jealousy. There is a rather similar moment in *Lord Ormont and His Aminta*. Ormont touches his 'alienated' wife's shoulder, and at the moment she flinches, he becomes newly alert to her body, chillingly 'sensible of soft warm flesh stiffening to the skeleton'.[61] In *The Egoist*, when Willoughby believes that Clara Middleton has been unfaithful to him, the

---

[61] *Lord Ormont and His Aminta*, chapter 23.

thought bestows on her a certain 'bewitchingness', 'a certain black-angel beauty for which he felt a hugging hatred'.[62] In *Modern Love* the husband is holding the wife's letter to her lover when he gazes down at his wife asleep in bed and sees that her eyelid is 'full-sloping like the breasts beneath' (XV, 8). The knowledge that his wife has betrayed him reawakens his erotic interest in her. It is as if his love has been reborn, but the thing that has come to life again is really, he knows full well, only the ghost of a love that has died, 'Love's corpse-light' (XVII, 16).

The husband in *Modern Love* is and is not Meredith. He is a device that allows Meredith to examine himself as if he were another person. As I suggested in my first chapter, Meredith explains the technique best in *The Tragic Comedians* when Clotilde describes her relationship not with Sigismund Alvan, who is so much older and more distinguished than she is, but with Prince Marko, the man she marries after he kills Alvan in a duel. Clotilde finds in Marko an 'alteregoistic home'. When she thinks about him, she is reminded of herself: 'That is like me: that is very like me.' But Clotilde is safe in the knowledge that, whenever she wants, whenever the process becomes too painful, she can disclaim the similarity. She can remember, "That is he, not I." Marko offers her the rare privilege of painless self-analysis. The opportunity he afforded, the 'probing of herself in another, with the liberty to cease probing as soon as it hurt her, allowed her while unhurt to feel that she prosecuted her researches in a dead body'.[63] But in *Modern Love* the body that the vivisectionist dissects is tremblingly alive. Meredith conducts through the husband a self-examination that is never painless. He may insist, as Clotilde insists, 'That is he, not I', but in *Modern Love* the insistence is urgent, almost hysterical. It is like the Voice in Beckett's *Not I*, whose monologue is punctuated repeatedly by a cry in which she denies the first person, 'who? ... no! ... she!...', a cry that becomes on its last occurrence still more emphatic: 'who? ... no! ... she! ... SHE!'

Meredith had already practised the skill of seeing himself in the third person. In his first novel, Meredith takes the recent breakdown of his own marriage and displaces it in time (Sir Austin has been separated from his wife for more than a decade before the novel begins) and displaces it much more radically by examining Sir Austin's behaviour in his predicament with a cold, scornful detachment. The technique culminates in *The Egoist*.

[62] *The Egoist*, chapter 29.
[63] *The Tragic Comedians*, chapter 5.

Sir Willoughby Patterne is a self-portrait conducted throughout in a contemptuous, ironic third person. But it is deployed still more energetically in *Modern Love*, because it is in *Modern Love* that it is at its most volatile. Meredith alternates between a third person that repudiates the husband and a first person that acknowledges the husband as a version of himself. The intricately shifting pattern of the pronouns charts the central action of the poem which is not so much the failure of a marriage as Meredith's effort to understand that failure as if it had happened to somebody else without losing the bitter knowledge that it has happened to himself. In the poem's first line, 'By this he knew she wept with waking eyes', the third person holds husband and wife at arm's length. They become objects of the poet's clinical gaze, like the 'sculptured effigies' to which he compares them. But even in this sonnet the third-person statements seem to yield to first-person importunities. It comes as no surprise when in the third sonnet, as he wonders at his continuing susceptibility to the wife who has betrayed him, a first person ousts the third: 'See that I am drawn to her even now!' (10). Thereafter first, second and third persons map with chilling precision the death dance of the marriage. Poem IX is typical. It begins in a third-person confession of murderous rages. The husband cannot trust himself to accompany his wife 'through certain dark defiles' (4). It continues by recalling a tense conversation in which 'he' asks 'Have you no fear?' (6). This prompts a laughing reply, 'No, surely; am I not with you?' (8). Only in the final lines in which the speaker manages to admit how closely allied his violence is with erotic desire does the first person supplant the third:

> Here thy shape
> To squeeze like an intoxicating grape—
> I might, and yet thou goest safe, supreme. (14–6)

Meredith's chief ambition as a novelist was to see people from the inside and from the outside at the same time, to give the 'Within and Without of us' as he puts it in *Diana of the Crossways*,[64] or, as in *The Amazing Marriage*, 'to see the creature he is with the other's eyes, and feel for the other as a very self',[65] but he never succeeded in doing that so

---

[64] *Diana of the Crossways*, chapter 1.
[65] *The Amazing Marriage*, chapter 41.

finely as in *Modern Love*, the poem in which he addressed most directly the disastrous termination of his own marriage.

When Meredith's wife left him for another man, it was not just that his marriage ended. He felt himself placarded to the world as a cuckold, as a husband who had been unable to command his wife's fidelity. He had felt something similar when his name had appeared on a shopfront, when Meredith was not a name on a title page but on a shop sign, the proprietor of the naval outfitter's at 73, the High Street, Portsmouth. He had been placarded as a tailor's son, and he passed on his embarrassment to Evan Harrington, the hero of his second novel whose aristocratic friends visit him in the tailor's shop that has for its sign his own name. But this was a more painful, a more intimate humiliation. It threatened still more decisively his sense of his own identity. In the 39th sonnet of *Modern Love*, the husband sees two people walking together and notices their hands touch: 'A man is one: the woman bears my name.' The designation of the wife as the woman who bears her husband's name seems an awkward turn of phrase, a phrase carefully designed to pinpoint the husband's sense of his own offended dignity, but it was a phrase that Meredith used repeatedly himself. He used it when his wife died. In the autumn of 1861, as he explained to his friend William Hardman, he had just returned from a visit to Suffolk, 'the *Giles* of counties': 'When I entered the world again, I found that one had quitted it who bore my name.'[66] He had used the same expression to describe Sir Austin Feverel's insistence, when his wife left him for Denzil Somers, that the blow was not so much to himself as to his reputation: 'Her conduct struck but at the man whose name she bore.'[67] By the 1880s Meredith had begun to feel the absurdity of the expression. Sir Lucas Dunstane in *Diana of the Crossways* is married to Diana's best friend, and his clumsy pass at Diana is what prompts her rash decision to marry the odious Augustus Warwick. She hopes that by becoming a married woman, she will protect herself from the advances of men such as Sir Lucas. But even Sir Lucas finds it ridiculous when her husband, who suspects that she has been unfaithful to him, refers to her as 'the lady "now bearing my name"'.[68] In *The Amazing Marriage*, Meredith's last novel, the Earl of Fleetwood introduces his new bride to a friend in words that betray his fear that his choice may open him to ridicule: 'The lady bears my

---

[66] *Letters*, 1, 107–8.
[67] *The Ordeal of Richard Feverel*, chapter 1.
[68] *Diana of the Crossways*, chapter 13.

name, Mr Chumley Potts.'[69] The expression gives Mr Chumley Potts a warning. It carries a threat, and more tellingly it exposes Fleetwood as a callow young man far too concerned with what the world thinks of him. Despite the difference in wealth and rank, Meredith had been much the same kind of young man himself. When his wife left him for another man, it confirmed him in that condition of morbid sensitivity to the opinions of other people from which it took him most of his life, and almost the whole of his writing career, to escape. By 1882 he could offer a charitable verdict on the Carlyles' marriage. She was 'a woman of peculiar conversational sprightliness', 'a woman of the liveliest vivacity', 'they snapped at one another', but 'each knew the other to be honest', and they shared a real affection: 'Only she needed for her mate one who was more a citizen of the world, and a woman of the placid disposition of Milton's Eve, framed by her master to be an honest labourer's cook and housekeeper, with a nervous system resembling a dumpling, would have been enough for him.'[70] One wonders how far that was a verdict that he had at last arrived at on his own marriage just as much as the marriage of the Carlyles. After he published *The Amazing Marriage*, the novel that he had worked on for 17 long years, Meredith wrote no more novels. It was as if when he had at long last made peace with himself, he found that he had nothing left to write about.

[69] *The Amazing Marriage*, chapter 17.
[70] *Letters*, 2, 661.

CHAPTER 5

Novel People

NOVELISTS AND NOVEL READERS

As Victoria's reign grew longer and longer, the need grew to divide it. George Gissing published *The Whirlpool* in 1897. When the central character, Harvey Rolfe, needs a term for 'barbarism or crudity in art, letters, morality, or social feeling', the phrase that comes to his mind is 'early Victorian'.[1] His wife, Alma, who thinks of herself as advanced, is scornful when her mother objects to her pursuing a career: 'I can't bear to hear you talk in that early Victorian way.'[2] In the same year that Gissing published *The Whirlpool*, a paper in *Blackwood's* described Bulwer-Lytton as the last survivor of 'the Early Victorian era'.[3] A year earlier Frederic Harrison had published a collection of essays on Disraeli, Dickens, the Brontës, Dickens, George Eliot and Trollope under the title *Studies in Early Victorian Literature*. Gissing and Meredith thought of themselves as writers of a different generation. Bernard Kingcote speaks for Gissing when he insists in *Isabel Clarendon*: 'It is the latter end of the nineteenth century.'[4] When he walks along the Chelsea pavements, Kingcote pauses to gaze at 'the face of Thomas Carlyle, who had just been set up in effigy on the

---

[1] George Gissing, *The Whirlpool*, chapter 6.
[2] George Gissing, *The Whirlpool*, chapter 9.
[3] *Blackwood's Edinburgh Magazine*, 166 (June 1887), p. 636.
[4] George Gissing, *Isabel Clarendon*, chapter 13.

© The Author(s) 2019
R. Cronin, *George Meredith*,
https://doi.org/10.1007/978-3-030-32448-3_5

Embankment'.[5] For him, Carlyle is a figure out of history, not a man but a monument. Meredith had been invited to tea with Thomas and Jane Carlyle at their house in Cheyne Walk,[6] but by 1886, when Gissing published *Isabel Clarendon*, it would have seemed so even to him. Gissing and Meredith were late Victorians. In *The Wings of the Dove*, Merton Densher is troubled by the furnishings in Mrs Lowder's Lancaster Gate house because he cannot dismiss them as 'Mid-Victorian or Early'.[7] They may be ugly but the sofas and tables are distinctive. They are late Victorian, like himself, and to be late Victorian was to be modern, it was even to be, like Paula Power in Hardy's *A Laodicean*, 'ultra-modern'.[8]

There are many differences between the novels of the first and last decades of Victoria's reign, but I want to focus on just one. The characters in the novels of Dickens and George Eliot may lead rich and full lives, but one pleasure that they are rarely allowed is the pleasure of reading novels.[9] For the late Victorians, novels have become part of the furniture. When Maggie in *The Golden Bowl* sits waiting for the arrival of her father and stepmother, who are coming to tea, she sits 'with her book on her knee'.[10] By 1904 novel characters had become novel readers. Maggie watches her stepmother, Charlotte, her husband's mistress, descending a flight of steps, and notices that she is carrying a book, a single volume of the triple-decker novel that Maggie had lent her after she had shown 'a specious glitter of interest' in it. Charlotte has mistakenly picked up the novel's

---

[5] George Gissing, *Isabel Clarendon*, chapter 15.

[6] See Hammerton, 108. Meredith was invited after Carlyle, on Jane's recommendation, read *The Ordeal of Richard Feverel* and concluded that Meredith was 'nae fule'. Over tea he encouraged Meredith to give up the novel for 'heestory'.

[7] *The Wings of the Dove*, Book Second, chapter 2.

[8] Thomas Hardy, *A Laodicean*, chapter 2.

[9] Ever since the eighteenth century, one important kind of novel, the kind invented by Cervantes in *Don Quixote*, had focused on characters who were readers. But these are people who misunderstand the real world because they confuse it with the world with which they are familiar from books. They are comic characters. Catherine Morland's visit to Northanger Abbey ends so disastrously because she imagines it to be the kind of abbey that she has read about in the Gothic novels she enjoys. Edward Waverley, in Walter Scott's first novel, is more violently discountenanced when he is persuaded to join the second Jacobite uprising in the foolish belief that Charles Stuart's reckless bid for a throne was a chivalric enterprise of the kind that thrilled him in the knightly romances to which he was devoted. Catherine Morland and Edward Waverley learn by painful experience to recognise the difference between reality and fiction. They learn that life is not like the books that they had read. The late Victorians thought differently. They learned about life from their reading.

[10] Henry James, *The Golden Bowl*, chapter 42.

second volume, which gives Maggie the opportunity to set off in pursuit with the missing first volume. There follows the second, edgy, strained confrontation between the two women, and all the way through it the volumes of the unnamed novel offer their own wry commentary on the scene, as the attention of each of the women is caught by those 'two books on the seat'.[11]

In the fiction of an earlier period, novels, when they are mentioned at all, tend to be casually dismissed. In *Northanger Abbey* Jane Austen regrets how, if a novel heroine happens to pick up a novel, she is sure to 'turn over its insipid pages with disgust'.[12] Mary Mitford did not publish *Atherton*, her only novel, until 1854, but she was a contemporary of Austen's. In the novel, she itemises at some length the library of Honor Clive who is her type of the cultivated woman. Honor has on her shelves the works of the English poets. She has Chaucer, Spenser, Shakespeare and Milton; she has Dryden, Pope and Cowley; she has Burns, Crabbe, Cowper and Percy's *Reliques*. She has European literature too: Chénier, Ariosto, Alfieri, Molière. She has Bacon, Isaac Walton and Jeremy Taylor, and she has *Antigone* in the Greek. But the collection includes only two novels, *Don Quixote* and Goldsmith's *Vicar of Wakefield*.[13] The absence of novels from her shelves is the proper index of Honor Clive's cultivation. It was the year before, in 1853, that Charlotte Yonge published *The Heir of Redclyffe*, but Yonge belonged to the younger generation. Guy Morville has been forbidden novels by his grandfather, and when the grandfather dies, his cousins decide at once that this is a gap in his education that must be repaired. They discuss which novel he should begin with, and after considering *Dombey and Son*, they settle on *I Promessi Sposi*.[14]

The habit of denigrating the novel persists even in the novels of some late Victorians. In *East Lynne* (1861), a flighty young woman 'would do nothing all day but read books, which she used to get at the West Lynne library'.[15] It even remained possible to disapprove of fiction on religious grounds, although by the 1870s such objections had become comical. One of Bathsheba Everdene's neighbours in *Far from the Madding Crowd* notes disapprovingly the presence amongst her possessions of 'lying books

---

[11] Henry James, *The Golden Bowl*, chapter 39.
[12] Jane Austen, *Northanger Abbey*, chapter 5.
[13] Mary Russell Mitford, *Atherton*, chapter 12, 'A Young Lady's Bookshelves'.
[14] Charlotte M. Yonge, *The Heir of Redclyffe*, chapter 3.
[15] Mrs Henry Wood, *East Lynne*, chapter 16.

for the wicked'.[16] More often the disapproval marks a sense of cultural superiority. In George Gissing's *In the Year of Jubilee* (1894), there is a room that contains 'half a dozen novels of the meaner kind' with which the young woman who occupies it 'sometimes beguiled her infinite leisure'.[17] Of all the late Victorians, Gissing is the readiest to denigrate the novel. In *The Odd Women* (1893), there is Virginia Madden, companion to a woman who requires that she be read to 'at the rate of a volume a day'. The inevitable result is that Virginia Madden has 'lost all power of giving her mind to anything but the feebler fiction'. Gissing clearly has some sympathy with Miss Barfoot in the same novel who maintains that 'if every novelist could be strangled and thrown into the sea we should have some chance of reforming women'.[18] But Gissing does not really share Miss Barfoot's opinion: it is just that he wants to insist on a hierarchy amongst novelists. The man from *In the Year of Jubilee*, who in one breath 'lauded George Eliot' and in the next was 'enthusiastic over a novel by Mrs. Henry Wood', shows his inability to make proper discriminations. Gissing has more respect for the aspirant novelist who knows that she will never be a Charlotte Brontë or a George Eliot.[19] But it is far more common for novelists of the second half of the century to treat their own medium with a new respect. In Charlotte Yonge's *Heartsease, or the Brother's Wife*, Violet Moss is delighted to find a man prepared to discuss Elizabeth Gaskell's *Mary Barton* with her. Her husband, Arthur, 'calls such books trash', but by 1854 such opinions served only to reveal the stupidity of those who held them.[20] In Wilkie Collins's 1870 novel *Man and Wife*, the library of a country house is divided between 'Solid Literature, which is universally respected, and occasionally read', and 'Light Literature', consisting of 'the Novels of our own day', which is 'universally read' but not much respected. Readers of solid literature are invited to take one of the library's luxurious armchairs. 'Snug little curtained recesses' are also provided in which the novel readers may hide themselves away. But, as Collins is well aware, it is the private space in which novels are consumed, the space figured by those curtained recesses,

---

[16] Thomas Hardy, *Far from the Madding Crowd*, chapter 15.

[17] George Gissing, *In the Year of Jubilee*, chapter 1.

[18] George Gissing, *The Odd Women*, chapters 2 and 6.

[19] George Gissing, *The Odd Women*, Part 4, chapter 1 and Part 6, chapter 5.

[20] Charlotte M. Yonge, *Heartsease, or the Brother's Wife*, chapter 4.

that has become central in the literary culture of the later nineteenth century. The public space occupied by the historian or the philosopher is by comparison peripheral.[21]

It had become possible by then to recognise the novel as offering the best available guide to what the world was like. The character in *The Odd Women* who recommends reading Ouida's novels before taking a trip to France does not, it is true, inspire much confidence. The remark, Gissing dryly observes, 'revealed his acquaintance with English literature'.[22] But far more often novelists are offered as trustworthy guides to the world and the people who live in it. When Caroline Norton wants to describe her heroine's state of mind in *Lost and Saved* (1863), she refers the reader to a novel, to Emile Souvestre's description of his heroine in *Riche et Pauvre*.[23] In a novel by Rhoda Broughton (*Alas!*, 1890), a male character bursts into tears, which prompts her to remark: 'Stevenson says that some women like a man who cries.'[24] In another of her novels, *Cometh Up as a Flower* (1867), a character recommends himself by being so like a novel: 'Hugh reminds one somehow of the tone of Dickens's books; there is a broad, healthy geniality about him.'[25] *Alas!* begins with a talk on Dickens given by James Burgoyne to the Oxford Women's Provident Association. It is an appropriate opening to a novel by a leading member of a generation of novelists whose novels derive from their reading quite as much as from their experience. The novelists of the later nineteenth century had all of them like Azalea, the heroine of Anna Steele's *So Runs the World Away*, grown up 'in the society of the library bookshelves', their thoughts 'ripening in the sun and shade of fiction'.[26]

---

[21] See Wilkie Collins, *Man and Wife*, chapter 17.

[22] George Gissing, *The Odd Women*, chapter 15.

[23] Caroline Norton, *Lost and Saved*, chapter 10.

[24] Rhoda Broughton, *Alas!*, chapter 8.

[25] Rhoda Broughton, *Cometh Up as a Flower*, chapter 14.

[26] Mrs A. C. Steele, *So Runs the World Away*, chapter 3. Meredith read *So Runs the World Away* as it was serialised in *Once a Week* and gave Anna Steele his characteristically unsugared opinion of the novel. He allowed her 'cleverness, literary faculty, glimpses of a power of humour', and 'the capacity for pathos, as well as a trained observation superior to that of many reputed good writers', but accused her of writing a succession of 'tableaux' rather than a complete novel (the same might be said of almost all his own), and of writing too often with one eye on the reader: 'don't make points; it's the same as the cocking of the eye in an actor.' He particularly disliked the manner in which Anna Steele, after revealing the moral of her story, 'pounded it on the head' of her public (*Letters*, 1, 402–4). Meredith neglected to mention Steele's evident debt to *Rhoda Fleming*. Steele's ageing coquette, Lady Diana, is

Marcel Proust did not begin publishing *A la recherche du temps perdu* until 1913, by which time Meredith had been dead for four years, but he is the true heir of the novelists of Meredith's generation. Proust's is the novel of a man who had spent his boyhood just like his narrator, reading. Both know 'plus de livres que de gens et mieux la littérature que le monde', more of books than of people, and more of literature than the world.[27] For Proust, as for his characters, things only become real when they are seen through art. Swann does not see Odette, the woman he will marry, as beautiful; he does not even think of her as his type, until he learns to find in her lineaments the woman he knows from one of Botticelli's frescoes.[28] Proust's narrator worships Madame Swann, but he does not properly see her until he finds in the studio of a great modern painter an early sketch of Odette half-dressed for the britches part that she was playing in a long-forgotten musical comedy, 'une stupide petite opérette'.[29] Music and painting are arts that Proust delights in, but the art that means most to him is his own. He sees life most of all through literature, as his young narrator sees it when he contemplates some trees that he is passing in his carriage, and wonders that they seem so like three trees that he has encountered in a book that he has been reading.[30] He is charmed rather than put off when a lovely young girl tells him that she finds her greatest joy in the hours that she spends translating one of George Eliot's novels.[31] When, as a boy, he is first taken to the Champs-Élysées, he finds the gardens 'insupportable'. They have never been described in a book he has read; they have never been imagined by Bergotte, his favourite author, and so there is nothing that made them come alive for him, nothing that 'les faisait vivre'.[32]

There is a good case for recognising *La Dame aux camélias* as the novel that instigates the fiction of the second half of the century. Dumas's novel commemorates his affair with the courtesan, Marie Duplessis. He published

---

closely modelled on Meredith's Mrs Lovell. Both women prompt duels in India: in Meredith's novel the husband is killed, in Steele's the lover.

[27] *Le Côté de Guermantes*, chapitre deuxième.

[28] 'Il aimait encore en effet à voir en sa femme un Botticelli', *A l'ombre des jeunes filles en fleurs*.

[29] *A l'ombre des jeunes filles en fleurs*.

[30] The trees have for him 'la réalité qu'on retrouve en levant les yeux de dessus le livre qu'on était en train de lire', *A l'ombre des jeunes filles en fleurs*.

[31] Andrée tells him that 'ses meilleures heures étaient celles où elle traduisait un roman de George Eliot', *A l'ombre des jeunes filles en fleurs*.

[32] 'Nom de pays, le nom', *Du côté de chez Swann*.

it in 1848, just a year after Marie's death from consumption. It was written, like Meredith's *Modern Love*, when his feelings were still raw. At the very end of his book, he claims for it only one merit, 'celui d'être vraie', that of being true.[33] Three years later Dumas rewrote his story as a play, which very soon afterwards, in 1852, gave Verdi and his librettist, Francesco Piave, the basis for *La Traviata*. In the novel Marie Duplessis becomes Marguerite Gautier, known, by the flowers she always wears, as la dame aux camélias. But in its English versions, the title of the novel and of the play is *Camille*, and Verdi's heroine is Violetta. Marie Duplessis, the famous courtesan, who had been loved by Dumas and by others, almost as soon as she died was dissolved into a succession of fictions, recreated as Marguerite, as Camille, as Violetta. But that was an outcome that the young Alexandre Dumas, who was only 23 when he wrote his novel, had already imagined.

The story begins after Marguerite's death, when the narrator, who has seen and admired her only from afar, attends the sale of her possessions and buys at an inflated price her copy of *Manon Lescaut*. The book had been presented to Marguerite by her lover, Armand Duval. For Armand the gift was an invitation to Marguerite to recognise herself in the heroine of the Abbé Prévost's novel, and to recognise in him Manon's lover, the Chevalier des Grieux. After Marguerite has left him, Armand finds the novel open, its pages blotched by Marguerite's tears. Armand and Marguerite are modern lovers, lovers of the mid-nineteenth century, because they come to understand their love for one another through the pages of a novel, and that too is how the novel's narrator comes to understand the story he is telling. He buys Marguerite's copy of the novel not only as a memento of the woman he had in her lifetime only glimpsed as she passed by in her carriage on the Champs-Élysées but because it is a novel he has read time and time again. After he has secured the book, he searches out Armand who tells him his love story. It leaves him thinking that Marguerite was still more unfortunate than Manon, because, although Manon died in a desert, she died in her lover's arms, whereas Marguerite died abandoned, in a 'désert du coeur', a desert of the heart.[34] But it is not only through Prévost's novel that he understands the story Armand tells him. He also knows Victor Hugo's play about the seventeenth-century courtesan, *Marion de Lorme*; he knows Alfred Musset's novella, *Frédéric et Bernerette*; and he knows the story of a courtesan, *Fernande*, written by

---

[33] Alexandre Dumas, *La Dame aux camélias*, chapter 27.
[34] Alexandre Dumas, *La Dame aux camélias*, chapter 3.

Dumas's own father. The younger novelists who began writing in the second half of the nineteenth century did not write novels as a way of recording their understanding of life. They wrote novels because writing novels and reading them had become the way in which novelists and their readers understood themselves and understood their world. As Oscar Wilde pointed out, life had become an imitation of art, and in particular it had become an imitation of the novel.

The greatest novelist of the period, Henry James, understood, his biographer suggests, that his predecessors had done almost everything that was to be done in the way of making literature out of life. The task left to him was to 'make literature out of literature'.[35] James understands life a little like Merton Densher in *The Wings of the Dove*, who feels as he stands on a London street corner as if he inhabited the city like 'a sentence, of a sort, in the general text'. He experiences the city as 'a great grey page of print', in which he has his own modest place.[36] In the summer of 1860, Henry James was staying in Paris with his brother, William. Henry was reading seriously, William wrote to his father, not spending too much of his time on *Once a Week*.[37] But it was the weekly literary magazine that had the decisive impact on his career. Meredith's *Evan Harrington; or, He Would Be a Gentleman* was being serialised. In later life James formed a low opinion of Meredith as a novelist, although he liked him well enough as a man, but reading *Evan Harrington* in Paris when he was 17 was one of the experiences that made James into a novelist. Like Edred Fitzpiers in Hardy's *The Woodlanders*, when James sat up at night, his lamp 'lighted rank literatures of emotion and passion as often as, or oftener than, the books and materiel of science',[38] but the taste for novels was not in either man a sign of idleness. Taking an interest in novels had become the proper measure of a man who took an interest in life.

Princess Casamassima, first published in the *Atlantic Monthly* in 1885, was James's first thoroughly English novel, although by then he had already been resident in England for almost ten years. The novel's hero, Hyacinth Robinson, is an apprentice bookbinder who makes his way into upper-class society. Hyacinth is James's homage to the hero so typical of the nineteenth-century English novel, the kind of hero that James had

[35] Edel, 167.
[36] Henry James, *The Wings of the Dove*, Book 6, chapter 1.
[37] Leon Edel, *Henry James*, 5 vols (London: Hart Davis, 1953–72), 1, 159.
[38] Thomas Hardy, *The Woodlanders*, chapter 17.

encountered perhaps for the first time when he read *Evan Harrington*. But Hyacinth is also close to James himself, because the aristocratic world that he enters is for both men a world at once entirely strange and very familiar. It is a world that has hitherto been quite outside their own experience, and yet a world that they already know very well because it is a world they have encountered in their reading. When Hyacinth is invited for the very first time to a gentleman's bachelor chambers, they seem familiar because they 'reminded our hero somehow of Bulwer's novels'.[39] Hyacinth is from time to time mocked for relying so much for his knowledge of upper-class habits on his familiarity with 'the light literature of his country'. Members of the upper classes do not all, as he believes, spend their autumns 'ploughing through northern seas on a yacht or creeping after stags in the Highlands'.[40] But more often than not, his reading serves him in good stead, not just in London but even in Paris. He is unabashed to find himself in Tortoni's because he knows about the café very well 'from his study of the French novel', from Balzac and from Alfred de Musset, and he is unfazed when he visits France by the special French use of the second person singular because he is familiar with its use by the three musketeers when they speak to their lackeys.[41] On his very first visit to an English country house, he surrenders at once to the charm of a landscape that he has never before encountered, but he is able to do so because it is a landscape that he has already experienced so often in his reading. He may not know the names of the flowers, but he is entirely familiar with the vocabulary, the turns of phrase, the rhythms, that can turn a paragraph of natural description into a celebration of Englishness:

> the green dimness of leafy lanes; the attraction of meadow-paths that led from stile to stile and seemed a clue to some pastoral happiness, some secret of the fields; the hedges thick with flowers, bewilderingly common, for which he knew no names; the picture-making quality of thatched cottages, the mystery and sweetness of blue distances, the bloom of rural complexions, the quaintness of little girls bobbing curtsies by waysides (a sort of homage he had never prefigured); the soft sense of turf underfoot that had never ached but from paving-stones.[42]

[39] Henry James, *Princess Casamassima*, chapter 15.
[40] Henry James, *Princess Casamassima*, chapter 20.
[41] Henry James, *Princess Casamassima*, chapters 29 and 22.
[42] Henry James, *Princess Casamassima*, chapter 25.

Hyacinth is already familiar with a social world that he has never known, because he has read about it in books. It was the same for Henry James, who gazed fascinatedly at England rather in the manner that Gertrude Wentworth in *The Europeans* gazes at her European cousin Felix Young. She 'seemed to herself to be reading a romance that came out in daily numbers. She had known nothing so delightful since the perusal of "Nicholas Nickleby".'[43] Milly Theale, the young American woman in *The Wings of a Dove*, recognises Kate Croy when she sees her for the first time, because she is already familiar with her from 'old porings over *Punch* and a liberal acquaintance with the fiction of the day'.[44] She relishes England for its eccentric 'Thackerayan character', and as she makes her entrance into English society, she feels as if all her favourite novels were coming to life. She walks through drawing rooms much as James himself did, always listening out for 'a mixed wandering echo of Trollope, of Thackeray, perhaps mostly of Dickens'.[45]

When James thought of literature, he thought above all of the novel. That had not been true of his predecessors, even of the novelists amongst them. David Friedrich Strauss published the most important nineteenth-century life of Jesus in 1835. It was translated into English in 1846 by a woman who was to become a great novelist, George Eliot. But Strauss for all his interest in the mythical mode of interpretation had no gift as a story-teller, and George Eliot does nothing to supply the deficiency. The Victorians preferred the *Vie de Jésus* published in 1863 by Ernest Renan and translated into English that same year. Meredith thought it 'one of the finest of the works of this generation'.[46] Renan's text is free from scholarly clutter. All references are relegated to the notes. He drafted the book in Palestine as he visited the sites associated with the Christian story, his only reference books the New Testament and a copy of Josephus, and his book was dedicated not to his fellow Biblical scholars but to his sister. The result was a life of Jesus made into a novel, a novel of the kind that Robert Louis Stevenson might have written, a romance, in which Jesus as a young man spends his nights sleeping by the shores of Galilee, 'the dreams of these nights passed in the brightness of the stars, under an azure dome of infinite

[43] Henry James, *The Europeans*, chapter 5.
[44] Henry James, *The Wings of the Dove*, Book 4, chapter 2.
[45] Henry James, *The Wings of the Dove*, Book 4, chapter 3.
[46] *Letters*, 1, 227.

expanse', 'sous un dôme d'azur, d'une profondeur sans fin'.[47] Jesus's triumph is to strip Judaism of its theology, to make of it 'a pure religion, without forms, without temple, and without priest',[48] and Renan, in much the same way, purifies his narrative by stripping his account of the life of Jesus of all its theological trappings. His Jesus preaches a sunny faith, free from the austerities advocated by his cousin John the Baptist. His life is darkened towards its close. He cannot quite preserve his purity of spirit during his residence in Jerusalem. He was a young man from the country, and in the big city he was 'no longer himself'. In Jerusalem, he loses something of his 'original purity', his 'limpidité primordiale'.[49] Renan does not regret his early death, because it pains him to imagine Jesus condemned to 'bear the burden of his divinity until his sixtieth or seventieth year, losing his celestial fire, wearing out little by little under the burden of an unheard of mission', 'perdant sa flamme céleste, s'usant peu à peu sous les nécessités d'un rôle inouï'.[50] Renan's book was so successful because he made the life of Jesus seem real, and he did so by making it into a novel.

Renan reclaims Jesus from the theologians, even from the first of them, St John, whose prose is so 'stiff and awkward', 'raide et gauche'.[51] Renan takes the three gospels that he admires and rewrites them as an enchanted bildungsroman, and for Meredith the achievement gave him a place alongside Montaigne, Molière, Racine and La Bruyère as one of the five exemplary French writers. Renan is remarkable for 'a most delicate irony scarcely distinguishable from tenderness'.[52] Meredith means, I suppose, that Renan invests Jesus with rare charm but only by divesting him of his divinity. In making him the hero of a novel, Renan produces a wholly human Christ. But if the effect is ironic, it is an irony quite unlike Gibbon's. It does not wound. Renan's *Vie de Jésus* was admired by freethinkers such as Meredith and Matthew Arnold, but not just by them. It could not have been so popular as it was had it not also been read by more conventionally pious readers. They were not as attentive as they might have been, perhaps, to the challenges Renan presented to their faith, but it is also the case that they read him as sympathetically as they did because they were novel readers. The habit of novel reading changed those who

[47] Ernest Renan, *Vie de Jésus*, chapter 10.
[48] Ernest Renan, *Vie de Jésus*, chapter 17.
[49] Ernest Renan, *Vie de Jésus*, chapter 22.
[50] Ernest Renan, *Vie de Jésus*, chapter 28.
[51] Ernest Renan, *Vie de Jésus*, Introduction.
[52] *Letters*, 3, 1321.

contracted it by training them in the exercise of sympathy for views that they might not share. It loosened the grip on them of their own opinions.

Meredith often reiterated his contempt for 'Parsondom'. He refused to allow his name to go forward for membership of the Athenaeum because he was rarely in London, and 'besides, the Athenaeum was a nest of the parsonry'.[53] He admitted to Edward Clodd that when 'quite a boy', he had suffered 'a spasm of religion which lasted about six weeks', during which he made himself a nuisance by 'asking everybody whether they were saved'.[54] The spasm lasted longer than Meredith admitted. In the months that he spent in the Moravian school in Neuwied, near Coblenz in Germany, he learned to admire the Moravian Brothers who taught him, but his piety had evaporated long before 1849 when he married Mary Ellen Nicolls. She was the daughter of Thomas Love Peacock, a man who did not care to disguise his contempt for the Christian religion. Peacock never wavered in the view that he shared with a friend when he was a young man of 25 and seems never to have modified the trenchancy with which he asserted it: 'A philosopher, in my opinion, ought not to give even the semblance of a momentary sanction to a grovelling, misanthropical, blood-thirsty superstition.'[55] Meredith came to share Peacock's view, but he was of a different generation from his father-in-law. He was brought up on novels, and he carried his paganism more lightly.

In 1851 Meredith was staying with his wife at The Limes in Weybridge. He was widening his social circle. Tom Taylor, already a successful playwright who later became editor of *Punch*, also lodged in the house, and at Weybridge Meredith got to know the Duff Gordons and their daughter, Janet, then just eight years old. But his life was not without its problems. Mary Ellen had suffered two miscarriages since the marriage. Meredith was trying to establish himself as a writer but as yet his earnings were negligible. The young couple were still financially dependent on Mary's father. It was at this time that Meredith read Charles Kingsley's *Yeast*. It had only just been published in book form although it had been serialised in *Fraser's Magazine* three years earlier. He wrote at once to Kingsley to congratulate him. It seems at first glance odd that Meredith should have been so taken

[53] *Letters*, 2, 894.

[54] Clodd, *Memories*, 153.

[55] *The Letters of Thomas Love Peacock*, ed. Nicholas A. Joukovsky (Oxford: Clarendon Press, 2001), 1, 57. For a discussion of Peacock's most virulently anti-Christian poem, once thought to have been destroyed by Mary Ellen's daughter, Edith, see Nicholas A. Joukovsky, 'The Lost Greek Anapaests of Thomas Love Peacock', *Modern Philology*, 89, iii (1992), 363–74.

with the first novel by the Rector of Eversley. His letter to Kingsley was certainly opportune and may even have been opportunistic. Meredith's first book of poems was in the press, and Kingsley was an influential figure, professor of English literature at London's Queen's College and a prominent reviewer. The letter paid dividends later that year when Kingsley wrote a generous review of Meredith's volume.[56] But I doubt whether Meredith's letter was simply self-serving. There was much in *Yeast* that would have caught his attention. He was after all exactly the kind of young man that Kingsley was addressing in a book designed to offer 'an honest sample of the questions, which, good or bad, are fermenting in the minds of the young of this day, and are rapidly leavening the minds of the rising generation'.[57]

Yeast was one of the founding texts of Christian Socialism, and the young Meredith would have been attracted by the socialism if not the Christianity. Kingsley's hero, Lancelot Smith, who, as his name suggests, is both knight errant and everyman, is, like Meredith, a disciple of Carlyle. He owes much in particular to his reading of Carlyle's *Chartism*. Meredith would have been attracted too by Smith's flouting of class distinctions. As the novel begins, he is on the hunting field, a young man of independent means, but he is a young man able to recognise the radical under-gamekeeper, Paul Tregarva, as his spiritual brother. Meredith would have endorsed just as enthusiastically Kingsley's insistence that religious truth cannot claim to be independent of scientific truth, that 'spiritual laws must be in perfect harmony with every fresh physical law which we discover'.[58] It was a view that he often expressed himself. Just as familiar and just as welcome was Kingsley's recognition that love is a matter of the flesh as much as of the spirit. There was a great deal in *Yeast* that Meredith would have applauded, but there was surely just as much that might have been expected to stick in his craw.

There is, most obviously, the insistent religiosity. Lancelot Smith may begin the novel as an unbeliever, but that is only because it gives Kingsley an opportunity to show him finding God and because freethinking for Kingsley is in any case to be preferred to the merely conventional pieties that most young men of Smith's class profess. Kingsley is deeply suspicious of the nature worship of which all through his life Meredith was an enthusiastic

[56] See 'This Year's Song-Crop', *Fraser's Magazine*, 44 (December 1851), 618–31.
[57] Charles Kingsley, *Yeast: A Problem*, chapter 14.
[58] Charles Kingsley, *Yeast: A Problem*, chapter 5.

exponent. To surrender to 'the mere contemplation of Nature' is to 'become her slave' by allowing 'a luscious scene, a singing bird' to distract from 'the most earnest and awful thoughts'.[59] The distrust of nature extends to a distrust of art, even to the art of novel writing. When Smith looks back on his life, he finds that 'the events of the last few years began to arrange themselves in a most attractive dramatic form', and he thinks of making them into a story. He even begins 'to work out a scene or two'. But Barmakill, the 'prophet' who is introduced to act as his guru (Barmakill is F. D. Maurice in fancy dress), denounces any such project as 'the true hell of genius, where Art is regarded as an end and not a means, and objects are interesting, not in as far as they form our spirits, but in proportion as they can be shaped into effective parts of some beautiful whole'.[60] True to his own teaching, in the last pages of the novel Kingsley all but dispenses with the novel form in favour of a loose, desultory sermon by Barmakill in which he urges the English to undergo a radical religious and political regeneration without making it at all clear quite what form the regeneration should take. But in his letter to Kingsley Meredith voices no misgivings. He writes only of his 'delight and admiration'. Reading the book has been a 'positive "Education"' for him: 'It was the very book I was in want of and likely to do me more good than any I know.' He adds a pious hope, 'May it do a great service in the world.'[61] It would be easy to read the letter as pastiche, the young freethinker taking a mischievous pleasure in reproducing the cadences with which Kingsley and his kind signal their piety and their earnestness. But that would be to misconstrue it. Meredith had just turned 23; he was without any stable source of income, the author of a slim volume of verse about to be published at his own expense. He could not possibly have acquired the confidence needed for such a flamboyant display of disingenuousness. He wrote what he felt, and he felt as he did because he was a man who read novels and had developed the special personality of the novel reader. As he read Kingsley's novel, he became almost without being aware of it, at least for the time of the reading, exactly the kind of reader that Kingsley was addressing.

Even Kingsley recognised that people were formed by their reading, and in particular they were formed by their reading of novels. In *Yeast* Honoria Lavington lives 'in a perpetual April-shower of exaggerated sympathy for all suffering'. Her capacity for sympathy prompts her to make

---

[59] Charles Kingsley, *Yeast: A Problem*, chapter 3.
[60] Charles Kingsley, *Yeast: A Problem*, chapter 17.
[61] *Letters*, 1, 14.

visits to the wretched tenants on her father's estate in their unsanitary cottages. Her sister, Lancelot Smith's beloved, the curiously named Argemone Lavington, contracts the typhus from which she dies when she accompanies Honoria on one such visit. Honoria has cultivated her capacity for sympathy by reading novels, and sympathy is a capacity that can, as Kingsley knew, all too easily be exercised indiscriminately. Honoria extends her sympathy to all sufferers, 'whether in novels or in life; and daily gave the lie to that shallow old calumny, that "fictitious sorrows harden the heart to real ones"'.[62] But Kingsley remains suspicious that novelists, himself amongst them, risk extending to their readers an invitation to indulge in the exercise of a sympathy which is valueless because it is undisciplined. He comes close to yielding to such an invitation himself when he seems almost ready to extend his sympathies to Lancelot's cousin, Luke, a Tractarian who goes over to Rome, and, still more alarmingly, to extend it still further to Luke's spiritual adviser, a thinly disguised portrait of Newman. The invitation, implicit in the form of the novel itself, to the exercise of an unrestricted sympathy is surely one reason why Kingsley was a novelist so sceptical of the value of novels. But the temptation hardest for novel readers to resist is not the invitation to sympathise with the characters in the novels they read but with the novelists who wrote them. As he read Kingsley's novel, the young George Meredith sympathised with the author of the novel so warmly that he became Charles Kingsley for a while, which is why when he wrote to congratulate him it was entirely natural for him to do so in a prose that so clearly carried the mark of Kingsley's own.

According to Keats the poet is a chameleon. He has no personal identity, only a capacity for inhabiting the personality of other people. And it is a capacity that the poet exercises with a reckless irresponsibility. He takes just as much pleasure in becoming an Iago as in becoming an Imogen.[63] My point is that this odd temperament that Keats thinks peculiar to poets became during the course of the century the disposition required of all novel readers, and by the second half of the century, everyone was a novel reader. By then, the novel was not just describing human nature, it was changing it. I will give just one example, but it is a significant one, Mary Ellen Peacock, who became when she married Mary Ellen Nicolls, and then, when she married again, Mary Ellen Meredith.

---

[62] Charles Kingsley, *Yeast: A Problem*, chapter 2.
[63] *The Letters of John Keats*, ed. Hyder Edward Rollins (Cambridge, Mass.: Harvard University Press, 1958), 1, 390.

MARY MEREDITH AS NOVEL READER

In 1856 the Merediths' marriage was on the rocks. It might still have been salvageable; it might not. The Merediths already knew the painter, Henry Wallis. He exhibited his portrait of Mary, *Fireside Reverie*, at the Royal Academy in 1855. The following year he showed the painting that made his reputation, *The Death of Chatterton*. The model for the poet, newly dead in his squalid garret after taking poison, his soul escaping from the grimy reality of his earthly existence through the open window, his right arm dangling to the floor, the pallor of his face heightened by his bright red hair, the corpse sporting, rather incongruously, a pair of bright lilac silk breeches, was George Meredith. By August 1857 Mary was pregnant by Wallis. We cannot be sure when they became lovers. Neither Mary nor Henry Wallis kept a diary. But in 1856 Mary did keep a book in which she copied out extracts from her reading. The year 1856 was the year in which her son, Arthur, turned three and her daughter by her first marriage, Ellen, turned 12. Mary was still on terms of some kind with her husband. Meredith even copied a poem into her book, a lively naval ballad called 'The Sailor's Consolation', a friendly tribute perhaps to Mary's first husband:

> Both you and I have sometimes heard
> How men are kill'd and undone,
> By overturns from carriages
> By thieves, and fires in London.
> We know what risks these landsmen run,
> From noblemen to tailors;
> Then, Bill, let us thank Providence
> That you and I are sailors.

It was Diane Johnson, Mary's biographer, who first drew attention to the notebook.[64] It is preserved in Yale's Altschul collection, a book of 64 lined pages, six and a half inches by ten, with a tortoise-shell cover. As Diane Johnson remarks, it 'is in no sense a diary', but one of the passages that Mary copied out was from an 1855 novel by Anne Manning, *Some Account of Mrs. Clarinda Singlehart*. Clarinda is like so many novel characters in the second half of the century, 'a book-devourer', and she has written a book herself, a little tale as distinctive in its own way, we are told,

---

[64] See Johnson, 106–13.

as *Rasselas* or *The Vicar of Wakefield*. She lends the book to the lover she had disappointed many years ago. His first thought when he reads it is that the book is not at all confessional:

> From her book he gained no insight into herself. There was no character bearing any evidence of self-perturbation, or veiled complaint, or confession. Her fancy had run off to a new, untrodden field, where it could gather fresh flowers at its will; only leaving traces of its whereabouts, like the gypsies—
>
> "You may tell where we have been
> By the burnt spot on the green"

The book may not be Clarinda's confession, but it does leave traces of herself, and in this it is very like Mary Meredith's notebook. The passages that Mary copied into her notebook are, like this passage from Anne Manning's novel, the burnt spots on the green that she leaves behind her. Reading the book one is reminded at times of a haunting Tennysonian quatrain of Meredith's that he preserved in one of his notebooks:

> She threw away the book she read;
> Why this is I, 'tis I, she cried:
> And pressed her hands against her head,
> And in a frenzy stretched them wide.[65]

Mary copied poems into her book, not just the shanty that Meredith added in his own hand but a poem by Béranger and some lines from Burns's 'Country Lassie' (Mary did not recognise their author: she describes them as taken from an 'Old Ballad': perhaps she came across them quoted by Helen Huntingdon in Anne Brontë's *The Tenant of Wildfell Hall*). There is a translation from Sanskrit by Sir William Jones, a passage from Kalidas's *Sakontala*. There are extracts from periodicals; from the *Edinburgh Review*, the *St. James's Chronicle*, *The Spectator*, the *Illustrated News* and the *Dublin University Magazine*. More surprisingly there are passages from a volume of sermons by the fashionable Brighton clergyman Frederick W. Robertson, although the passages that Mary copies out speak as tellingly to the unhappily married as to Robertson's Christian congregation:

[65] *Notebooks*, 74.

The philosopher tells us that no atom in creation touches another atom—
they only approach within a certain distance; then the attraction ceases, and
an invisible something repels—they only seem to touch. No soul touches
another soul except at one or two points, and those chiefly external—a fearful or a lonely thought, but one of the truest of life. Death only realizes that
which has been fact all along. In the central deeps of our being we are alone.

But most of all, there are passages from novels, novels in French and
English, most of them recent, although some such as Disraeli's *Henrietta
Temple* had been published years before.

In the later nineteenth century, social life was narrower than it had ever
been. British society was divided by gender, by occupation, by political
sympathy, by cultural interests, above all by class. The novel had a special
importance in these years because it offered the principal means by which
middle-class readers, readers like Mary Meredith, might come to know
something of a wider world than they would ever come across in their
ordinary social lives. Mary travelled in her reading more widely than she
travelled in her life. She travelled to Sweden when she read in translation
Emile Carlen's *The Birthright* and all the way to Australia when she read
Charles Reade's *It Is Never Too Late to Mend*. The novel connected opposite sides of the world. It also brought together those placed on opposite
sides of the social spectrum. In Frédéric Soulié's *Huit jours au château*,
another of the novels from which she took extracts, the plot, in which
adultery and murder figure largely, begins when a feral gipsy makes the
acquaintance of the wife of a banker, and the two discover that they are
near relations. Nineteenth-century novels are full of such unlikely discov-
eries. They feature so often in fiction, one suspects, because they occurred
so rarely in life. Chillon Kirby in Meredith's *The Amazing Marriage*
explains to his sister who is new to the country that in England 'you meet
people of your own class; you don't meet others'.[66] The opportunity that
the English in the nineteenth century were denied in life was given them
by their novels. Mary read racy French yellowbacks by novelists such as
Frédéric Soulié and Paul de Kock, whose novels seem to have been particular favourites. But she also read novels by the Tractarian Charlotte
Yonge and the evangelical Irish novelist, Selina Bunbury. Reading novels
gave her the opportunity to live more variously in her imagination than
she could ever have done in her life.

[66] *The Amazing Marriage*, chapter 6.

Men and women, men and women of the middle classes at least, lived more separately in the later nineteenth century. More and more men spent their evenings in their clubs. Women were confined to their homes. More men than ever chose not to marry, with the result that a new social group came into being, the group that George Gissing calls *The Odd Women*, the surplus of women that remained after all the men prepared to marry had chosen their partners. It was the novel that gave men and women their best opportunity to get to know one another. In 1856 Mary was reading novels about women such as Dumas's *Olympe de Clèves* and his son's *La Dame aux camélias*, and she also read novels about men such as George Sand's *Mauprat* and Charles Reade's *It Is Never Too Late to Mend*. Reading novels was so important in the second half of the nineteenth century because novels offered their readers access to areas of the world that they would otherwise have known next to nothing about. In particular it was the novel that gave nineteenth-century women their best opportunity to learn about men and gave nineteenth-century men their best opportunity to learn about women.

But readers do not only turn to the novel to discover lives different from their own. They are just as likely to read as a way of finding out about themselves, and Mary Meredith, a novel reader whose life was in crisis, had more reason than most to be preoccupied with her own situation. What are 'political revolutions', Disraeli wonders in *Henrietta Temple*, 'compared with the moral mutations that are passing daily under our own eye; uprooting the hearts of families, shattering to pieces domestic circles'.[67] Mary wrote the passage down. In *It Is Never Too Late to Mend*, the upright George Fielding and Tom Robinson, an ex-convict, travel to Australia and become fast friends. It is a novel of male comradeship, the very first celebration in fiction of the Aussie ideal of mateship. Australia gives Tom Robinson the chance to escape from his own past and make himself anew. It was not, it must have struck Mary as she read the novel, a possibility available to women. George Sand's *Mauprat* also has a hero who recreates himself. George Sand explains in a preface (Mary copied the passage out) that *Mauprat* was written while she was pursuing a legal separation from her husband. That may have been what drew Mary to the novel. Edmée is torn between two men, Monsieur de le Marche, her fiancé, a cool, Voltairean lover, and the passionate, Rousseauesque Mauprat. In the end, she chooses Mauprat, but not before she has kept both men dangling for

---

[67] Benjamin Disraeli, *Henrietta Temple*, Book 5, chapter 1.

years. Her behaviour often seems outrageously capricious. Perhaps Mary suspected that the same might be said of her own as she struggled to choose between her husband and her young lover. But *Mauprat* also offered her a tutorial on masculinity. Mauprat, George Sand's hero, needs to be reclaimed. 'Il y a deux hommes en moi,' he claims, 'qui se combattent à mort et sans relâche', to the death and without respite.[68] That combat is the story of the novel. Mauprat has to undergo a seven-year trial before proving himself worthy of Edmée's love. He first meets Edmée when he rescues her from a gang of cutthroats and extorts a promise of marriage from her by threatening rape. His task is to become the kind of man whose character allows her to redeem that promise. He has to change himself from one kind of man to another, and in order to do that 'il faut que l'homme souffre', a man must suffer.[69] We cannot know how much of Mauprat Mary saw in the husband that she was soon to leave, but it was the diagnosis that Meredith arrived at when he thought about himself. He too thought that young men such as himself were divided. He entitled the 30th chapter of *Emilia in England*, his third novel, 'Of the Double Man in Us, and the Great Fight When These are Full Grown'. The story of *Mauprat*, the story of a young man's painful struggle to make himself into a man worthy of the woman he loves, is the story that Meredith tells in the novel he wrote immediately after Mary left him, *The Ordeal of Richard Feverel*, and that he continued to write in different versions all through his career.

The most intriguing of the novels about women that Mary read in the year that she kept her notebook are *Olympe de Clèves* (1852) by Alexandre Dumas the father and *La Dame aux camélias* (1848) by Alexandre Dumas the son. From the novel by the son, Mary chose to transcribe the passage praising *Manon Lescaut* as 'le plus beau livre de coeur que l'on écrit', the finest book of the heart ever written. Olympe in the father's novel is an actress. When a Jesuit novice called Bannière glimpses her in the street, he abandons the Jesuit order and follows her onto the stage. Olympe chooses to marry Bannière preferring him to M de Mailly, her wealthy married lover, and even to Louis XV who wants to make her his mistress. Their story ends tragically when Olympe dies gazing at the corpse of her executed lover, but her death is also her triumph. Olympe is a famous actress, and her profession underwrites her claim to be the woman she chooses to

[68] George Sand, *Mauprat*, chapter 21.
[69] George Sand, *Mauprat*, chapter 11.

be rather than simply a woman who agrees to fulfil the roles that the men in her life offer her. *Olympe de Clèves* is a historical novel, set in the same period as *The Three Musketeers*, but Olympe is a nineteenth-century heroine. Molière, Dumas observes, describes as cuckoldry ('cocuage') what the nineteenth century terms adultery. The comic term has become inappropriate. To some this may suggest that the nineteenth century is a more moral age, but Dumas doubts it. Cuckoldry became adultery, he believes, as soon as all a man's legitimate children were allowed to share his estate. Marital irregularity became a crime not because it inspired a new moral horror but as a way of offering an additional protection to property rights. It was a passage that impressed Mary Meredith. She copied it out.

Mary, it seems clear, was already Wallis's lover, his Olympe, his Marguerite, if only as yet in imagination. Her heady excitement is plain enough in her choice of reading, in some of her reading at least. But in these months, she also read *Little Dorrit* as it was serialised in *Household Words*. She only chose to copy out two snippets from the novel. One of them describes Arthur Clennam who has come back to his solitary room after a pleasant dinner with the Meagles, and muses 'that it might be better to flow away monotonously, like the river, and to compound for its insensibility to happiness with its insensibility to pain'.[70] Arthur Clennam is 40 years old and has just decided that it would be best not to fall in love with Mr Meagles' 20-year-old daughter. It is a poignant passage in the novel and still more poignant in Mary Meredith's notebook. The passage comes in the fifth instalment of the novel which appeared in April 1856. Henry Wallis had just turned 26; Mary Meredith would be 35 that July.

Nineteenth-century readers found their own lives in the novels they read. Mary Meredith found herself in Olympe and Marguerite, in women who bravely fashioned themselves rather than allowing themselves to be fashioned by the men around them. When Marguerite leaves Paris for a village, she gives up her profession as a courtesan. She re-makes herself and becomes a chaste young wife. It is her lover's father who persuades her that she should leave the man she thinks of as her husband, because it is only by leaving him that she can restore him to his family. She returns to Paris and her rich middle-aged lover. She becomes a courtesan again, but she resumes the profession just as she had abandoned it, by an exercise of her own will. Mary read the stories of Olympe and Marguerite in the months when she was wondering whether to remain Mrs Meredith or to

[70] Charles Dickens, *Little Dorrit*, chapter 16.

leave her husband for Henry Wallis and forge a new identity. Her reading, her reading of novels in particular, informed her decision, and she was not special in this. For many nineteenth-century novel readers, the decisions they took about how to live their lives were informed by their reading.

Novels gave their nineteenth-century readers the opportunity to imagine their own lives, but just as importantly they gave them the opportunity to imagine alternative lives, the lives they might have lived if they had made different choices or if they had been different people. Mary Meredith was her father's daughter, the daughter of Thomas Love Peacock, 'Greeky Peaky' as Thomas Taylor called him. When she read a paper on Saul of Tarsus in the *Edinburgh Review* (she misremembers when she assigns the piece to the *Quarterly*), it was the tribute to the Greek language that struck her: 'In no other tongue of heaven, can the minutest shiftings and distinctions of the mental feeling be expressed with so much precision.'[71] Her father, like Thomas Taylor, thought of himself as a man out of his time, a Hellenic pagan surviving into the nineteenth century. He was outspoken in his contempt for Christianity. It was one of the few things on which he saw eye to eye with his son-in-law. Mary agreed with both. She was impressed by a review in *The Spectator* that described mysticism as 'rather a mood of the mind than a theological creed'. It might appear 'in almost any form of belief when fancy and enthusiasm run riot over reason'. Even an unbeliever may be mystical. The reviewer takes as his example a close friend of her father's: 'a man with a mystical mind may glow in negation, as was the case with Shelley's atheism in Queen Mab.' Even atheism, it seems, might be unacceptably religiose. It is a Peacockian sentiment. But in her reading, Mary felt free to accommodate very different points of view. She read racy French novels, but she read just as attentively novels by pious British women. In *Some Account of Mrs. Clarinda Singlehart*, Anne Manning is more interested in the help that Clarinda gives her clergyman brother in the exercise of his parish duties than in her disappointment in love. *Our Own Story* is a loosely autobiographical novel in which Selina Bunbury maps the route which ended in her becoming one of the Religious Tract Society's most popular authors. Her womanly ideal was, one would have thought, at a far remove from Mary Meredith's: 'How much like the moon when she walketh in brightness, was designed to be the pathway of a woman through life—noiseless, pure, and beautiful, keeping her own orbit; performing her own soft ministry.' But novels encouraged their

[71] See 'Saul of Tarsus', *Edinburgh Review*, 97 (January 1853), 87–118.

readers to surprise themselves. There was something in Mary Meredith that responded to the passage. She copied it out.

Even the French novels she read might be pious. She read *Le Curé de village*, Balzac's celebration in the person of the Abbé Bonnet of the saintly Christian priest. It was an odd choice of novel for a woman about to embark on her affair with Henry Wallis. The central character is not the Abbé but Véronique Graslin, married off by her miserly father to a rich banker. Véronique's capacity to love lies dormant until she reads *Paul et Virginie* and meets Jean-Francois Tascheron, a young workman. She and Tascheron become lovers, and Véronique, as Mary Meredith was soon to do, falls pregnant. Tascheron, driven by the need to support his lover, becomes a robber and murderer and dies on the scaffold. Véronique keeps secret the identity of her child's father, even though her testimony might have saved Tascheron's life. In consequence she is able to raise her child as her husband's. After his death, she devotes herself to good works, transforming Tascheron's poverty-stricken native village into a prosperous and thriving township. But all the while, she inflicts on herself a terrible penance, wearing a hair shirt and subsisting only on bread and water, and on her deathbed she makes a public confession of her sins. When Mary Meredith gave birth to Wallis's child, it was not because she had not imagined how grave the consequences might be of bearing a child outside wedlock.

Charlotte Yonge's *Heartsease, or the Brother's Wife*, from which Mary made more copious extracts, is a still more interesting choice. *Heartsease* is a Tractarian novel, a novel designed to point out especially to women the need to discipline vagrant desires and to accept suffering as the cross that all true Christians should gladly embrace. Charlotte Yonge was a devoted follower of John Keble. She submitted her novels to him before publication. The heartsease of the novel is Violet, who marries on her 17th birthday a man much above her in station, the second son of a lord, and by sweetly submitting to his neglect, cruelty and reckless extravagance succeeds in reclaiming him at last for Christ. Her brother-in-law's fiancée had died before they were able to marry and he gives Violet an amber cross that he had intended for his bride. The amber cross is the novel's most potent symbol, signifying how, for a woman, the cross that she is called upon to bear is most often to be found in domestic life rather than in grander, more publicly heroic feats of endurance. But, as the novel's title indicates, its central character is not Violet but her brother's wife, her sister-in-law, Theodora.

Violet, as her name implies, is shy and retiring. Theodora by contrast cannot 'bear not to reign supreme'.[72] Theodora is a young woman of extravagantly high principle whose virtues are thoroughly compromised by her pride, her refusal to accept the duty of submission, either to her parents or to her future husband. Violet's reclamation of her own husband is less central to the plot than her reclamation of Theodora, a process that the novel explicitly compares to the taming of the shrew.[73] The trick is not worked by Percy Fotheringham, the writer of genius that Theodora marries. 'You are taming me,' Theodora tells Violet.[74] When Percy Fotheringham attempts the feat, all that results is the breaking off of their engagement. 'All you value is a slave with no will of her own,' Theodora tells him. 'One who has a will, but knows how to resign it,' he replies. Percy Fotheringham points out to her a passage from *The Baptistery* by Keble's close associate, Isaac Williams, and Theodora at once understands the point he is trying to make, 'Are humility and submission my cross?' she asks, and Percy tells her, 'if you would only so regard them, you would find the secret of peace.'[75] Mary Ellen copied the passage into her commonplace book. It is a lesson that Theodora can more easily accept from Violet than from her robustly assertive fiancé. Theodora has been carelessly brought up, and there must have been times that Mary Ellen thought that her own upbringing had been similarly neglectful. She had no mother, and her father, though fond, was often absent, and in any case had his mind on other things. Like Theodora she had been left to fend for herself, not materially but morally. She had been left to find for herself the principles that she would live by. Reading *Heartsease* allowed Mary to imagine what her life might have been had she chosen to live by quite other lights, if she had chosen the path of submission rather than the brave and lonely independent life that she chose instead.

Novels allowed their readers to continue to entertain the possibilities that in their own lives they had refused. When Oscar Wilde speaks in *The Ballad of Reading Gaol* of the man 'who lives more lives than one', he has in mind the man like himself, the imaginative artist, who lives his own life and lives too all the lives that he has imagined. But in the nineteenth century, the novel gave all its readers the chance to live more than one life. It

[72] Charlotte M. Yonge, *Heartsease, or the Brother's Wife*, chapter 5.
[73] Chapters 13 and 20 have epigraphs taken from Shakespeare's play.
[74] Charlotte M. Yonge, *Heartsease, or the Brother's Wife*, chapter 20.
[75] Charlotte M. Yonge, *Heartsease, or the Brother's Wife*, chapter 16.

gave that chance to Mary Meredith, and it gave it to her husband too. Meredith spent the Christmas of 1857 alone in his lodgings in Hobury Street. Mary Ellen, six months pregnant, spent Christmas with her father in Lower Halliford. Wallis was with her. He was painting Peacock's portrait.[76] That Christmas Meredith was much struck by a little book by Max Müller, *German Love*, and he sent it to his friend Eyre Crowe, the painter, as a belated Christmas present: 'The writing is beautiful ... so German!'[77] It is a story told in eight 'recollections' of the love of a young man of humble parentage for the Countess Maria, the invalid eldest daughter of the ruler of a little German princedom. Its setting and its sweetly simple piety took Meredith back to his schooldays at Neuwied, and the love story it told had the extra virtue of transporting him far away from the much more modern, more brutal love story that he was living through. Müller echoes a conviction of Meredith's own that body and soul are inseparable: 'There is no spirit without a body unless it be a ghost, and no body without a spirit unless it be a corpse.' But the bodies of the lovers in Müller's novella scarcely press the ground: they are all but weightless. The Countess and the young man meet together and they talk. Just once, at their very last meeting, they share a 'soft kiss', and that same night she dies, after sending the young man one last message, 'As God wills'. The message is accompanied by her first gift to him, a ring.[78] Meredith tells Eyre Crowe that he has written no inscription in the book so that, if Crowe does not like it, he can give it to 'some woman who will': 'It is a book women *must* like.'[79] It is at any rate a book that Meredith enjoyed, and one reason he enjoyed it so much is surely that Müller's Countess allowed him to retain a notion of what women were like that his own wife was at that very moment so vigorously contesting. That Christmas Meredith, who was still married but married only in name, found consolation in a novel about two young people who were married in everything but. It was only a few months earlier that Meredith had read a much greater novel, Flaubert's

---

[76] Peacock was far more accepting of his daughter's situation than most Victorian fathers would have been, with good reason. It seems probable that he had at least one illegitimate child himself, a woman with whom Meredith corresponded. See Nicholas A. Joukovsky, '"Dearest Susie Pye": New Meredith Letters to Peacock's Natural Daughter', *Studies in Philology*, 111.3 (2014), 591–629.

[77] *Letters*, 1, 33.

[78] Max Müller, *German Love: from the Papers of an Alien*, trans. Susanna Winkworth (London: Chapman and Gall, 1858), 'Last Memory'.

[79] *Letters*, 1, 33.

Madame Bovary, but it did not affect him so deeply. All he could find in Flaubert's provincial adulteress was 'wickedness'. Flaubert's only feeling for his heroine, he imagined, was the feeling of 'an anatomist for his subject'.[80] That year Meredith's wife had left him for another man, and he was not yet capable of registering how Flaubert's disdain for his heroine might coexist with intimacy: 'Je suis Madame Bovary', as he famously remarked. That would come later, when he first read Stendhal.

Novels changed human nature by allowing their readers to escape the hard outlines of their own characters. That was true not just of novel readers. It became increasingly true of the characters in the novels that they read. Novel characters become 'flexuous'. It is the word Hardy uses in 'The Sheep-Boy' to describe curls of mist, and in *Tess of the d'Urbervilles* it is a word he uses to describe Tess.[81] As D. H. Lawrence puts it in his *Study of Thomas Hardy*, characters begin to flicker, burning 'brighter or dimmer, bluer or yellower or redder, rising or sinking or flaring according to the draughts of circumstance or the changing air of life'.[82] Lawrence was thinking perhaps of the men grouped around a bonfire in Hardy's *Return of the Native*, their faces lit by the flames:

> All was unstable, quivering as leaves, evanescent as lightning. Shadowy eye-sockets, deep as those of a death's head, suddenly turned into pits of lustre: a lantern-jaw cavernous, then it was shining; wrinkles were emphasized to ravines, or obliterated entirely by a changed ray.[83]

As Hardy points out in the same novel, 'a face may make certain admissions by its outline; but it fully confesses only in its changes.'[84] When Meredith republished his third novel in 1886, he gave it a new title. *Emilia in England* became *Sandra Belloni*. In the novel itself, the heroine goes by both names. She is Sandra to her father, named for the young Italian woman who saved his life when he was on the run from the Austrians, and Emilia to her mother and to all her English friends. In the sequel that

---

[80] See Meredith's review of recent 'Belles Lettres and Art', *Westminster Review*, 68 (October 1857), 585–604. Meredith includes in his review a moderately favourable notice of his own *Farina*.

[81] Thomas Hardy, *Tess of the d'Urbervilles*, chapters 13 and 14.

[82] D. H. Lawrence, *Study of Thomas Hardy and Other Essays* (Cambridge: Cambridge University Press, 1985), 186.

[83] Thomas Hardy, *The Return of the Native*, chapter 3.

[84] Thomas Hardy, *The Return of the Native*, chapter 6.

traces her career in Italy, she becomes *Vittoria*, the celebrated soprano, not just an opera singer but the heroine of a life that she chooses to live as if it were an opera. Vittoria is the nation embodied, a flesh and blood version of the statues of the nation in the likeness of a beautiful young woman that were being erected all over Italy in the 1860s. But even when she becomes Vittoria, she refuses to freeze into a marble likeness of herself. She continues to flicker. Diana in *Diana of the Crossways* is also Antonia, the pseudonym that she uses when she publishes her novels, and to her best friend she is always Tony. Proust's narrator thinks that he should have given Albertine a different name for each of the different ways in which she appeared to him, and that is what Meredith does. He gives his heroines more than one name as a signal of his willingness to allow them to flicker between different identities. It is a trait that they share with many of the chief characters of the late nineteenth-century novel. The novel allowed its readers to live out in their imagination the lives they had chosen not to live, and the characters in the novels began to live rather similarly. Hardy's Tess carries with her into her life as an agricultural labourer that other life as a teacher that she might have led had her father been less feckless. When in her Sandbourne lodgings she presents herself to Angel, newly returned from South America, 'loosely wrapped in a cashmere dressing gown of gray-white', her fashionable déshabille marks her as a kept woman,[85] but she still retains within her the maiden in the white frock with the red ribbon in her hair that the young Angel noticed at Marlott and failed to dance with. She murders Alec d'Urberville to keep alive that other self, because it was the maiden in the white frock that Angel had fallen in love with.

Victor Hugo was for Meredith 'the largest son of his mother earth in this time present', and *Les Miserables* was his great achievement, 'the master work of fiction of this century'.[86] He admired the novel's epic breadth. 'My love', he told Maxse, 'is for epical subjects.'[87] Hugo could write a novel that contained all of France from Waterloo to the uprising of 1832, a novel so capacious that it could pause for disquisitions on the metropolitan *gamin*, the character of Louis Philippe, Paris's sewage system and much else. And Hugo's is a democratic epic. The Wellington column in Liverpool would, he claims, be truer if it bore aloft a statue of a people

[85] Thomas Hardy, *Tess of the d'Urbervilles*, chapter 55.
[86] *Letters*, 1, 332 and 152.
[87] *Letters*, 1, 323.

rather than a statue of the Duke.[88] But *Vittoria*, Meredith's one attempt to write an epic novel, is a failure. 'My strength', Meredith was obliged to admit 'lies in painting morbid emotion and exceptional positions', for unravelling 'cobwebs in a putrid corner'.[89] Hugo so impressed him because Hugo could do all the things that Meredith would have liked to do himself and could not. But even Hugo recognised, as Wordsworth had before him, that the epic spaces that remained for the nineteenth-century writer to explore were internal. The true epic, 'le poème de le conscience humaine', will explore the world within each one of us. *Les Miserables* was for Meredith the novel that best defined his century not only, nor principally, because it is the great novel of Paris, which was, second only to London, the great city of the age, but because it is a novel that tells the story of a single individual, Jean Valjean, and finds in him the hero proper to the century.

Valjean is a man over whom a good and a bad angel wrestle. He is a divided man because the representative man of the nineteenth century has to be at odds with himself. Louis Philippe is the century's representative monarch because he too is a composite, a sign that figures at once revolution and stability. Every man contains within himself Cain and Abel, an elevated self and another subterranean self, just as the street map of Paris is mirrored in another map, known only to the few, the map of Paris's sewage system. The nineteenth-century hero, the representative man, places those two selves in communion one with the other. So it is that Hugo nominates as the true hero of Waterloo neither Wellington nor Napoleon nor any of their generals but Pierre Cambronne who, when invited by Maitland to surrender, replied with a single word: 'Merde!'[90] He becomes the true hero of the battle by making the lowest word the loftiest, just as Jean Valjean becomes the hero of the novel when he trudges through the sewers of Paris, all but drowning in the foetid ooze, bearing on his shoulders the inert and bloodied body of the man that his daughter Cosette is in love with. The representative man of the later nineteenth century is of necessity divided, which is one reason why, to Stevenson's consternation, *The Strange Case of Dr Jekyll and Mr Hyde*, should have become his most celebrated novel. When in *Beauchamp's Career*, Meredith wants to fashion a hero 'walking in the complete form proper to his budding age', he

---

[88] Victor Hugo, *Les Miserables*, Volume 2, Book 1, chapter 16.
[89] *Letters*, 1, 322–3.
[90] Victor Hugo, *Les Miserables*, Volume 2, Book 1, chapter 14.

imagines Nevil Beauchamp, who is a man 'in two halves'.[91] Hugo's hero like Beauchamp is self-divided and so too is the novel's chief villain, Thenardier. His is a double nature. He might just as easily have become a criminal psychopath or a bourgeois shopkeeper. He is only able to reconcile these two identities at the very end of the novel when he emigrates to America and sets himself up as a slave-trader.

But Hugo goes further than this. Human identity, he sometimes suggests, is still more radically unstable. Thenardier assumes in the novel multiple identities. He is a workman called Jondrette, he is Fabantou the actor, Genflot the poet, he is even Madame Balizard. The criminals with whom he consorts strip off their personalities as easily as one might remove a false nose at a masked ball. But so much might have been expected. The devil, as James Hogg recognises in *Confessions of a Justified Sinner*, is a shape-shifter. Hugo's special virtue is that he understands that the good man is just as polymorphous. Jean Valjean becomes a convict when he steals a loaf of bread rather than starve. He keeps his name when he recovers his liberty, but his service in the galleys has made a different person of him. He has become the feral outlaw that the judge who first sentenced him to the galleys mistook him for. He robs his benefactor Monseigneur Bienvenu, a man who has achieved the difficult feat of being both a bishop and a Christian, and steals from a little ten-year-old Savoyard a forty-sou piece which is all that he has in the world. Thereafter he changes his name. He becomes Monsieur Madeleine, who earns a fortune by devising a new method of manufacturing costume jewellery and serves as the well-loved mayor of his town. He confesses his true identity only when another man is identified as Jean Valjean, the escaped felon, and is about to be convicted in his stead. But, even as he makes the confession, and at last brings himself to tell the truth, the truth feels like a lie, because he no longer feels like Jean Valjean. After that he takes or has conferred on him a number of names. He is sometimes Ultime Fabre. To his daughter's lover, he is called, after his white hair, M. Leblanc. Most know him as Ultime Fauchelevent, brother, and for several years assistant, of the Fauchelevent who is gardener at the Convent on the Rue Petit-Picpus. When his daughter marries, he confesses to her husband that he is not really Cosette's father at all, and neither is he Monsieur Fauchelevent. He is Jean Valjean, convicted thief and escaped felon. He feels he has to make the confession, because to go under a false name is to go through the world as the flesh and blood

<hr>

[91] *Beauchamp's Career*, chapter 3.

equivalent of a forged signature. It is to be 'infamous within the *I*', 'infâme au dedans de moi'.[92] He confesses who he really is, but Marius, Cosette's husband, cannot brook the confession. He separates Valjean from his daughter, and Valjean cannot live without her. His situation is oddly like that in which his nemesis, the police officer Javert, finds himself when he finally apprehends Valjean. As a policeman he is bound to take Valjean into custody, but Valjean has saved his life, and Javert cannot bring himself to condemn the man who has saved him to the fate of the escaped felon. Throughout the novel Javert has founded his entire identity on the zeal with which he carries out his duties. He has forged himself, in Hugo's striking phrase, as a monstrous Saint Michael, God's chief commander in his war against the devil.[93] When he lets Valjean go free, he loses that identity, and he finds that he can no longer live with himself. He climbs the parapet of a bridge and casts himself into the Seine. His crisis is not ethical so much as existential. He cannot live with the plural identities that the nineteenth century requires that all its citizens assume. Valjean's predicament seems just the same. When he confesses to Marius that he is not M. Fauchelevent but Jean Valjean, the escaped felon, he reduces himself to a single identity. He finds that he no longer has a daughter to love and to be loved by, and the loss kills him. But, and this is what makes him so very different from Javert, not before he has regained his happiness. Marius discovers that it was Valjean who saved him from death on the barricade; it was Valjean who carried him on his shoulders through the sewers. He reunites Valjean with Cosette and Valjean dies happy, not just because he has his adopted daughter with him once again but because he recognises at the last that the 'I' is less stable than he had supposed. He is still, as he confesses to Marius, Jean Valjean, the convict, but he is also and just as truly the rich, benevolent mayor, M. Madeleine, and the humble convent gardener, Ultime Fauchelevent, and he is also the Christ-like figure who walked through the sewers carrying Marius on his back.

That acceptance of multiple identities is what makes the late Victorian novelists so different from George Eliot. F. W. H. Myers records a striking memory of the novelist:

> I remember how, at Cambridge, I walked with her once in the Fellows' Garden of Trinity, on an evening of rainy May; and she, stirred somewhat

[92] Victor Hugo, *Les Misérables*, Volume 5, Book 7, chapter 1.
[93] Victor Hugo, *Les Misérables*, Volume 1, Book 8, chapter 3.

beyond her wont, and taking as her text the three words which have been used so often as the inspiring trumpet-calls of men—the words *God, Immortality, Duty*—pronounced, with terrible earnestness, how inconceivable was the *first*, how unbelievable the *second*, and yet how peremptory and absolute the *third*.[94]

It is because duty is so peremptory and so absolute that George Eliot's characters are never allowed to evade responsibility for their actions. Arthur Donnithorne will always be the seducer of Hetty Sorrel, Maggie Tulliver can never atone for allowing herself to drift downriver in the boat rowed by Stephen Guest, and Doctor Lydgate must live all his life with the consequences of the moment of weakness in which he proposed to Rosamond Vincy, vanquished by the tear swelling in her lovely eye. But the later Victorians preferred not to think of character as inexorable. Instead of Arthur Donnithorne, Gissing has Lionel Tarrant of *In the Year of Jubilee*: 'Faithful in the technical sense he had not been, but the casual amours of a young man cause him no self-reproach.'[95] The philosopher of the later Victorians was William James, Henry's brother, for whom personal identity was only a process of 'continuous transition'.[96] Rhoda Broughton puts a question that exercises many of her contemporaries: 'Is it possible that one is through the whole course of one's life the same individual being? Is one possessed of but one individual soul?'[97] In Gissing's *Isabel Clarendon*, Bernard Kingcote offers a decisive answer, 'How can one be held responsible for the thoughts and acts of the being who bore his name years ago? The past is no part of our existing self; we are free of it, it is buried.'[98] Gissing had much the same thought when he contemplated his own past: 'Of course *that man* and *I* are not identical. He is a relative of mine, who died long ago.'[99] Meredith tended to agree. It was one reason, he told Robertson Nicoll, who had once served as a Church of Scotland minister, that he could not countenance a belief in a life after death: 'I have never felt the unity of personality running through

[94] F. W. H. Myers, *Essays Classical and Modern* (London: Macmillan, 1921), 494–5.

[95] George Gissing, *In the Year of Jubilee*, Part 5, chapter 5.

[96] William James, 'A World of Pure Experience', *The Journal of Philosophy, Psychology and Scientific Methods*, 1 (September 29, 1904), 533–43, p. 536.

[97] Rhoda Broughton, *Cometh Up as a Flower*, chapter 9.

[98] George Gissing, *Isabel Clarendon*, Volume 1, chapter 10.

[99] Coustillas, 2, 212.

my life. I have been six different men, six at least.'[100] Such thoughts loosened the connection between people and their actions. A man might take
a bribe, a woman might commit adultery, Meredith remarked, and yet, 'if
we are assured of their being in character honest', their failings will 'appear
more chargeable to accident than criminality'.[101] It is a cast of mind that
produces in the novels a benevolent scepticism about the relationship
between characters and their doings, a scepticism that George Eliot could
never have countenanced. When Rhoda Fleming is under unusual strain,
'her acts and words', we are told, became 'remoter exponents of her character'. That is, the way she behaved began to be less like herself. The Earl
of Fleetwood in *The Amazing Marriage* betrays his weakness when he
refuses fully to own his ill-treatment of his wife: 'Glimpses of the pictures
his deeds painted of him since his first meeting with this woman had to be
shunned. He threw them off; they were set down to the mystery men
are.'[102] For George Eliot that thought would have prompted a decisive
judgement about the Earl's character, but not so for Meredith. He is ready
to agree that Fleetwood may be right to protest that the picture painted of
us by our deeds is not always a very faithful likeness. Meredith recognises,
as he remarks in *Evan Harrington*, that 'we are now and then above our
own actions: seldom on a level with them'.[103] People may be better than
they behave, or worse. In *Diana of the Crossways*, when Diana is at her
lowest moral ebb, she has 'the vision of a puppet so unlike herself in reality, though identical in situation'.[104] She understands how badly she is
behaving, but she does not quite identify the person behaving so badly as
herself. She is guilty of self-deception, of course, but that is a more difficult verdict for those who suspect that we may have multiple selves. It can
seem harsh, even reductive, to judge us for how we behaved if we would
no longer behave in the same way, or if we feel that even at the time we
might just as well have behaved quite differently. Meredith is a novelist
especially interested in callow young men, in men like Wilfred Pole in
Emilia in England, and it is typical of young men like Wilfred that there
is a gap between what they do and who they are. It is why Emilia finds
Wilfred so puzzling: 'She wanted a reason to make him in harmony with

---

[100] W. Robertson Nicoll, *A Bookman's Letters* (London: Hodder and Stoughton, 1913), 14.
[101] *Letters*, 3, 1431–2.
[102] *The Amazing Marriage*, chapter 28.
[103] *Evan Harrington*, chapter 6.
[104] *Diana of the Crossways*, chapter 13.

his acts, and she could get none.'[105] In *Rhoda Fleming* Meredith remarks, 'Our deathlessness is in what we do, not in what we are,'[106] which seems a remark that George Eliot might subscribe to, except for the suggestion that a person and his acts might be quite independent of one another. Meredith and Gissing are both products of what Hardy calls in *A Laodicean* the 'modern ethical schools'. Early Victorian novelists made their characters, Hardy contests, by 'mechanical admixture of black and white qualities without coalescence'. Their 'theory of men's characters' was based on 'moral analysis'.[107] The late Victorian novelists freed themselves from the theory, and one result is that their major characters only ever have a provisional identity. They flicker. And if that is true for their more important characters, it is especially true for the most important character of all, which is in all novels the character of the novelist.

READING STENDHAL

Meredith like Clarinda Singlehart was a book-devourer. For much of his life, he was a professional reader. In 1860 he succeeded John Forster as principal reader for the publishers Chapman and Hall. Every week he received a parcel of manuscripts, and every Thursday he went to London, to Chapman and Hall's offices, to submit his reports. The £250 a year that Chapman and Hall paid him was an important addition to his income. He became slowly more prosperous over the years, but he did not feel able to give up the position until 1894. In 34 years as principal reader for the firm Meredith must have read, in whole or in part, several thousand manuscripts, many but not all of them novels. In 1863 he felt so insecure financially that he agreed to read for a second firm of publishers, Saunders and Otley, even though, as he knew, to act in this capacity for two firms might be thought unethical.[108] But he did not just read the books on which he was paid to give an opinion. He read for pleasure too, he read his friends' books, and he read because he thought of reading other novelists as one of a writer's professional duties. In March 1882, for example, when he was 54, he was reading Daudet's *Numa Roumestan*. It was a novel that 'would bear study'.[109] Daudet's lively contrast between Parisians and the people of

---

[105] *Emilia in England*, chapter 38.
[106] *Rhoda Fleming*, chapter 16.
[107] Thomas Hardy, *A Laodicean*, Book 3, chapter 4.
[108] *Letters*, 1, 235: 'Of course, this is a secret.'
[109] *Letters*, 2, 654.

the Midi gave him a clue that he took up in his unfinished novel, *Celt and Saxon*. He did not only read books in English. Like Purcell Barrett, the organist in *Emilia in England*, he read 'foreign books, too'. In the novel it is a habit thought of as 'not so particularly improving to his morals',[110] but that is one of Meredith's little jokes. I suspect that by the end of his life, Meredith had read more novels than any other nineteenth-century novelist. He gave away few personal details in his entry in the 1909 edition of *Who's Who*, but he did admit to being 'a great reader', and he added, 'especially of French literature'. A visitor to Flint Cottage in Meredith's old age remembered his as a 'workman's library'. It was 'pleasantly cosmo-politan', and found room for 'classics of all ages and countries, not exclud-ing English', but, he added, 'French works are conspicuous'.[111] The bookshelves were packed with yellow-jacketed French novels.

For a man who read so many novels, Meredith refers to them surprisingly rarely in his fiction. He was deterred, like Gissing, by his contempt for the work of his more popular colleagues, a contempt that in his more jaundiced moments he even extended to Dickens and George Eliot. French novels play a part in *The Adventures of Harry Richmond*, but the part is scarcely dignified. In the library of the German prince whose daughter Harry is courting, some dusty books are piled on the sofa so that 'the yellow Parisian volumes, of which I caught sight of some new dozen, might not be an attraction to the eye of chance-comers'. When Harry contrives a midnight meeting with the Princess in the library, the conversation is interrupted when one after another 'the fatal yellow volumes thumped the floor'.[112] Baroness Turkems has hidden underneath the books to overhear the con-versation, and reveals herself just at the moment when the Princess is on the point of pledging herself to Harry. In *Diana of the Crossways* the heroine is herself a successful novelist, but she fails to mention the work of any of her contemporaries, and few specimens of her own fiction are given. But even if Meredith rarely mentions novels, he reminds his readers even more fre-quently than his fellow novelists that in the later nineteenth-century litera-ture was made out of literature more often than it was made out of life. Diana, for example, is presented to the reader not as most novelists would have introduced her, as the 18-year-old Diana Merion who captivates every-one at the Dublin ball given to celebrate Lord Larrian's return to Ireland

---

[110] *Emilia in England*, chapter 21.
[111] The visitor was John A. Steuart. His account is recorded by Hammerton, 126.
[112] *The Adventures of Harry Richmond*, chapters 34 and 35.

after his heroic exploits in India. That is postponed to the second chapter. The first is entitled 'Of Diaries and Diarists', and it surveys the figure Diana cuts in the pages of the memoirists of the eighteenth century, in such volumes as *Leaves from the Diary of Henry Wilmers*. Diana makes her entry into the novel out of the pages of books. The first story that Meredith ever published, *The Shaving of Shagpat*, is introduced as if it were an uncollected tale from the *Arabian Nights*, and the prose is interrupted by fragments of oriental verse, quotations from an author known only as 'the poet'. His first novel, *The Ordeal of Richard Feverel*, is an even more extravagantly literary fiction. Richard has ambitions to be a poet himself until his father discovers his secret and demands that he burn all his manuscripts: 'Farewell from that day forth, all true confidence between Father and Son.' Just one poem survives on a 'fire-stained scrap of paper', preserved by Lucy Desborough, the woman Richard will marry, a sonnet to the stars of which two lines are quoted, rather good ones: 'Through sunset's amber see me shining fair, / As her blue eyes shine through her golden hair.'[113] Another literary text features far more prominently, *The Pilgrim's Scrip*, the collection of aphorisms into which Richard's father, Sir Austin Feverel, has distilled all his bitter wisdom. This is the book with which the novel begins:

> Some years ago a book was published under the title of "The Pilgrim's Scrip." It consisted of a selection of original aphorisms by an anonymous gentleman, who in this bashful manner gave a bruised heart to the world.

Quotations from the book punctuate the novel, as do quotations from the work of Denzil Somers, who publishes under the name of Diaper Sandoe poems 'so pure and bloodless in their love-passages, and at the same time so biting in their moral tone, that his reputation was great among the virtuous, who form the larger portion of the English book-buying public'. Somers had been Sir Austin's greatest friend until he ran away with his friend's wife. The unflattering estimate of his poetic gift is belied by the examples given in the novel:

> An Age of petty tit for tat,
> An Age of busy gabble:
> An Age that's like a brewer's vat,
> Fermenting for the rabble!

---

[113] *The Ordeal of Richard Feverel*, chapters 12 and 15.

> An Age that's chaste in Love, but lax
> To virtuous abuses:
> Whose gentlemen and ladies wax
> Too dainty for their uses.[114]

More than 20 years later, Meredith replied to a correspondent planning an anthology of verse that had first been published in novels that he might find better poems than those that he planned to include 'in a novel of mine called *The Ordeal of Richard Feverel*'.[115]
Meredith went back to the model he had established in his first novel throughout his career. *The Egoist* too begins with a book, although the book is imaginary rather than real. It is:

> the biggest book on earth; that might indeed be called the Book of Earth; whose title is the Book of Egoism, and it is a book full of the world's wisdom. So full of it, and of such dimensions is this book, in which the generations have written ever since they took to writing, that to be profitable to us the Book needs a powerful compression.

The Book of Egoism like *The Pilgrim's Scrip* is the ur-text of the novel, the scripture on which the novel acts as a commentary. It is the system reduced to a collection of aphorisms of which the novel is an extended illustration: 'In the hundred and fourth chapter of the thirteenth volume of the Book of Egoism it is written: Possession without obligation to the object possessed approaches felicity.'[116] In *The Amazing Marriage* the novel's pre-text is once again a real book, a published text, and once again it is introduced in the very first chapter of the novel. Captain Kirby, the father of Carinthia, the Earl of Fleetwood's bride, has published a book entitled *Maxims for Men*, 'a very curious book, that fetches a rare price now wherever a copy is put up for auction'. *The Amazing Marriage* is a novel about masculinity, and so *Maxims for Men* is its proper pre-text. But it is a novel about women too. Carinthia's mother, the Countess Fanny, is also the author of a 'little volume', 'Meditations in Prospect of Approaching Motherhood'.[117] Meredith knew just as well as Henry James that in the later nineteenth century literature could only be made out of literature.

[114] *The Ordeal of Richard Feverel*, chapter 6.
[115] *Letters*, 2, 676.
[116] *The Egoist*, chapter 14.
[117] *The Amazing Marriage*, chapter 3.

He allows the thought to infiltrate the novels. He would rather present his novels as produced out of diaries, or poems, or books of aphorisms than out of other novels, but he would never have been the kind of novelist he was had he not himself been a devoted novel reader. He wrote the kinds of novels he did because of the kind of life he lived but also because of all those yellow-backed French novels that stuffed his shelves. His biggest debt of all was to three French novels in particular.

Meredith met Captain F. A. Maxse, a naval hero retired on half-pay, in 1859. Both men had published their first novels that year. Meredith had published *The Ordeal of Richard Feverel*, and Maxse under the pseudonym Max Ferrer had published *Robert Mornay*. Maxse was to become Meredith's greatest friend, and it was an early expression of that friendship when two years later, while both men were working on their second novels (Maxse's remained unpublished), Meredith tried to interest Maxse in his favourite novelist. He had sent to Paris for a copy of *De l'Amour* and wanted to know Maxse's opinion, 'How do you like de Stendhal? … Let me hear.' 'I think Stendhal very subtle and observant,' he tells Maxse: 'He goes over ground that I know.'[118] In 1861 Stendhal had been dead for almost 20 years. He was known in France, but still not widely known. He appealed only, as he wryly conceded, to 'the happy few'.[119] He quotes the phrase in English, remembering not so much Shakespeare's *Henry V* as Goldsmith's *Vicar of Wakefield*. Dr Primrose consoles himself for the failure of his monograph on the illegitimacy of second marriages by the thought that his writings are addressed only to 'the happy few'. Stendhal was a great admirer of English literature, but in the middle years of the nineteenth century, the admiration was not returned. In England Stendhal was all but unread. In *Roderick Hudson* James's hero remarks to his patron, Rowland Mallett, that he had never got farther than Stendhal's 'book-covers'.[120] In 1875 that was still an erudite joke. But it was more than ten years earlier, in 1864, that Meredith urged the young novelist, Jennett Humphreys, to 'read de Stendhal (Henri Beyle) in French'[121] (Humphreys would have had no choice: Stendhal's novels were as yet untranslated). Meredith gave Anna C. Steele the same prescription:

[118] *Letters*, 1, 121.
[119] The dedication that concludes *La Chartreuse de Parme*.
[120] Henry James, *Roderick Hudson*, chapter 7.
[121] *Letters*, 1, 296.

If you know not De Stendhal's *Chartreuse de Parme* and *Le Rouge et le Noir*,
get them and study them. They are the models of a clear style and the intelligent manipulation of character. The public may go hang for him—even the
French public. His machinery is just a trifle intrusive perhaps, but it is a running analysis, the men and women move on—[122]

Stendhal's characters are not fixed but fluid: his 'men and women move
on'. That was the great secret that Stendhal had to teach, and it was the
lesson that Meredith took from him.

These are the only references to Stendhal in all of Meredith's surviving
letters except for a brief commendation in a letter to his younger son
('Honour to Stendhal, by all means'),[123] until, as an old man of 78, he
recommended to John Morley two essays on Stendhal by Ernest Seillière
in *Revue des Deux Mondes*.[124] It seems thin evidence to support the view
that Stendhal was the most important of all novelists to Meredith. But
Stendhal is the great novelist of young men, of supremely self-conscious
young men, young men who inspect curiously their every feeling, young
men, that is, very like Meredith himself and very like the young men
Meredith preferred to write about. One of the most important ways that
Meredith came to understand himself was by reading Stendhal's novels. If
he refers to those novels rather seldom, even the reluctance is best
explained by Stendhal. In *Armance*, Stendhal's first novel, the novel that
Meredith did not recommend to Anna Steele, Octave de Malivert is reluctant to allow his servant to dust his room not just for fear that the servant
might read his own writings but fearful that she might see what books he
had on his shelves and that his choice of books might enable her to guess
his thoughts (it might allow her to 'deviner mes pensées par le choix de
mes livres').[125] Octave is a neurotic young man, a man with secrets, but so
too was George Meredith.

It is possible, of course, that Meredith did not recommend *Armance* to
Anna Steele because he had not read it. It remains the least read of Stendhal's
novels. But in this case, the possibility can be discounted. It is inconceivable
that Meredith could have written *The Ordeal of Richard Feverel* if he had not
first read *Armance*. *Armance* was the kind of novel, 'based on character and
continuous development', that Meredith wanted to write. When he used

[122] *Letters*, 1, 404.
[123] *Letters*, 3, 1540.
[124] *Letters*, 3, 1553.
[125] Stendhal, *Armance, ou quelque scènes d'un salon de Paris*, chapter 2.

the phrase, he was referring to his third novel, *Emilia in England*, which, he admits, 'has no plot, albeit a current series of events'.[126] In *Armance* Stendhal refuses still more emphatically to burden himself with a plot, and even the 'current series of events' on which he pins his story is slighter than Meredith ever dared to rely on. Octave de Malivert, just 20 years old and not long graduated from the Ecole Polytechnique, loves his cousin, the half-Russian Armance Zohiloff, and she returns his love. The two lovers encounter the most traditional of obstacles. Armance is penniless, and Octave's aristocratic family has been dispossessed by the Revolution. But the Bill of Indemnity restores the family to wealth, and at once Octave's manners in the salons where the two cousins meet are transformed. He becomes self-assertive and abrupt, which persuades Armance that he might indeed have 'l'âme vulgaire', the vulgar soul, caring only for money, from which she had thought him exempt.[127] But Armance is mistaken. If Octave has changed, it is only in disgust at how his new wealth has changed attitudes towards him. He is as he always was and so are his feelings for his cousin. Both Octave and Armance expect his mother to object to the match, but, in fact, as she reveals to Armance, the marriage is her dearest wish. Even the obstacle of Armance's poverty is at last removed. Three of her Russian uncles die, all three 'par le suicide', and leave her a modest fortune.[128] And yet Octave and Armance still seem unable to come to an understanding. Octave thinks Armance indifferent to him because Armance, scared that he may guess her feelings, pretends to have accepted another suitor. For the same reason Octave pretends to be the lover of the lively Madame d'Aumale. When he joins Madame d'Aumale in her box at the opera, a rival for her affections (the opera appropriately enough is *Otello*) insults him by claiming that he has disturbed the performance by talking too loudly, and Octave issues a challenge. He is delighted to be given the opportunity to die in a duel that he has not provoked. In the first exchange, he is wounded in the thigh and insists on another exchange despite the protests of the seconds. This time he is badly wounded in the arm but after being bandaged manages to take his own shot. His rival, M. de Crêveroche, is hit, and 'deux minutes après' he is dead. Octave's immediate concern is that Crêveroche's beautiful dog might be neglected after the death of his master.[129]

[126] *Letters*, 1, 247.
[127] Stendhal, *Armance*, chapter 3.
[128] Stendhal, *Armance*, chapter 25.
[129] Stendhal, *Armance*, chapter 21.

The weeks that Octave spends recovering from his wounds, closely attended by Armance, are the happiest of his life, but it is a happiness that withers when his mother overcomes his father's objections, removing the final obstruction that stands in the way of his marriage. His problem is that he cannot marry without confessing to Armance a secret so terrible that it cannot be communicated save in writing. At this point Stendhal finds himself for the first time in need of a conventional plot device. Octave is envied by a rival who arranges for Octave to be sent a forged letter in which Armance confesses to a friend that she feels obliged to marry Octave although she no longer loves him. The rival does not think of the ruse himself: it had been used in a vulgar novel, 'un roman vulgaire', that he remembers reading. It is Stendhal's way of pointing out his reliance, just this once, on a stale literary device. He even underlines its literariness by having Octave's rival engage in a lengthy discussion with his co-conspirator about Laclos's epistolary novel, *Les Liaisons Dangereuses*. One conspirator defends Laclos stoutly against the other's charge that he is no more than 'un fat', a nincompoop.[130] Octave reads the forged letter and rips to pieces the letter that he had written to Armance confessing his own secret.

Stendhal contrives a conclusion to the novel that flouts all novelistic conventions. Octave marries Armance, although he thinks of the wedding simply as one of the stupid procedures, 'démarches sottes', that society has devised to spoil a fine day, 'gâter un beau jour'.[131] But he does agree, after he has gone through the ceremony, to take his bride away on a wedding tour. The newly married couple travel to Marseilles where Octave informs his wife that he has vowed to join the Greek War of Independence. He sets sail and, as the moon rises behind Mount Kalos, takes a draught of opium and digitalis and kills himself, leaving his whole estate to Armance on condition that she remarries within a year. Armance refuses the condition. She prefers to retreat to a convent, accompanied by Octave's mother.

There is a duel in *The Ordeal of Richard Feverel* rather like the duel in *Armance*. Richard challenges Lord Mountfalcon, who has attempted unsuccessfully to seduce his wife, and, like Octave, he is wounded. But it is Richard's wife, Lucy, who dies. She has recently given birth to a son, and the shock of Richard's wound brings on a brain fever. As the novel ends, Richard is still confined to his bed, where he lies thinking of his dead wife,

---

[130] Stendhal, *Armance*, chapter 29.
[131] Stendhal, *Armance*, chapter 31.

striving 'to image her on his brain'.[132] But it is not the duel that links *The Ordeal of Richard Feverel* with *Armance* so much as the strange reluctance of their heroes to cohabit with their wives. Richard, like Octave, marries at the age of 20. Armance marries in defiance of his own resolution that he should not marry until he is 26, Richard in defiance of his father's injunction that he should not marry until he has reached the age of 25.[133] After marrying Octave departs with his wife on a honeymoon trip to Marseilles but leaves almost at once on a ship bound for Greece. Richard marries Lucy Desborough, the blooming niece of a local farmer, a young woman still less socially acceptable than Armance, and takes her for their honeymoon to the Isle of Wight, but very quickly he leaves her on the island and returns to London. His father, although he continues to support his son, has not accepted the marriage, and Richard persuades his wife that it will be easier to come to terms with his father in her absence. But he never manages even to begin negotiations. Instead he stays on in London busying himself with a project to rescue fallen women. The voice of earthy common sense in the novel is supplied by Mrs Berry, who had been Richard's nurse in his infancy: 'A young married husband away from the wife of his bosom nigh three months!' 'We all know what checked perspiration is,' she adds. At this, Richard and his young friend cannot restrain the laughter provoked by her 'quaint way' of putting things.[134] But, as Richard discovers, it is no laughing matter.

The particular object of Richard's charity is a notorious demirep known as Bella Mount. Richard's uncle Adrian understands the attraction of this kind of woman for his nephew. The problem with girls is that they are 'not like boys'. By the time they reach a certain age, 'they can't be quite natural'. They begin to 'blush, and fib, and affect this and that'. 'It wears off when they're women,' Adrian assures Richard, but until then there is a powerful attraction in 'a woman who speaks like a man', and Bella Mount is just such a woman.[135] In fact, on the night that she seduces Richard, she has dressed herself up in men's clothes, calls herself Sir Julius and insists on addressing Richard as Dick, just as if she were a roistering male companion. That masculine disguise makes her doubly irresistible when she reverts to her feminine self, when 'she sidled and slunk her half-averted head with

---

[132] *The Ordeal of Richard Feverel*, chapter 45.
[133] Stendhal, *Armance*, chapter 9, and *The Ordeal of Richard Feverel*, chapter 13.
[134] *The Ordeal of Richard Feverel*, chapter 37.
[135] *The Ordeal of Richard Feverel*, chapter 38.

a kind of maiden shame under his arm, sighing heavily, weeping, clinging to him'. It is then that he strains her to him and kisses her 'passionately on the lips'. The chapter ends with two cool narrative comments.

> Not a word of love between them!
> Was ever Hero in this fashion won?[136]

Overcome by guilt, Richard departs, not to rejoin his wife but for Germany. When he returns his wife has given birth to a son, and mother and child are staying with his father, who has been reconciled to his son's marriage almost as easily as Octave's mother is reconciled to hers. Richard comes home, gazes on his sleeping son for the first time and confesses his infidelity to his wife. By morning he has gone. He is off to France to fight the duel with Lord Mountfalcon. Richard's nurse is roused by the noise of the baby crying, and when she enters the room, she finds the young mother in a dead faint, the baby in her arms. 'O my! O my!' she moans. She had imagined, when a noise awoke her, that Richard and Lucy had been making love.[137] Richard, like Octave, survives the duel. His wife and father go to him in the wretched French inn where he is lying, but it is thought too dangerous for him to be allowed to see Lucy. She waits outside his door, contracts a brain fever, and five days later she is dead. When Richard is told the news, he 'listened and smiled': 'I never saw a smile so sweet and so sad.'[138]

When Richard leaves Lucy on the Isle of Wight, she is already pregnant. Armance is not with child when Octave sets sail for Greece and for good reason. Stendhal took the idea for *Armance* from *Olivier ou le secret*, a novel that Stendhal credited to the Duchesse de Duras. He gives a teasingly reticent account of it in one of his papers for the *New Monthly Magazine*. Olivier abandons his wife on their wedding day, leaving in explanation only a letter in which he describes himself as the unhappiest of men, which, as Stendhal notes, 'is not very explanatory'. 'Do not imagine that Olivier is too libertine,' he adds; 'quite the reverse, if you understand

---

[136] *The Ordeal of Richard Feverel*, chapter 38.

[137] At least, this is how I understand her remark: 'Oh my! oh my! ... and I just now thinkin' they was so happy!', *The Ordeal of Richard Feverel*, chapter 44. Before 1885 Mrs Berry imagined that the young couple were 'so happy that was a gender', which is obscurely expressed, but may make her meaning clearer.

[138] *The Ordeal of Richard Feverel*, chapter 45.

me.'[139] He is much more explicit in a letter to Prosper Merimée. He had intended at first, he tells Merimée, to name Octave in his own novel *Olivier*, because Octave, like Olivier, suffers from 'Babilanisme', a term for sexual impotence that Stendhal borrowed from the Italian. There are more such men than one imagines, he assured Merimée. He gives as an instance the case of Jonathan Swift. He even describes the techniques that Octave might have used to produce Armance's radiant happiness during her brief honeymoon ('une main adroite, une langue officieuse', an adroit hand, an obliging tongue).[140] But in the novel itself, Octave's secret, confessed in the letter to Armance that he later tears to pieces, is never divulged. I am not at all sure that Meredith would have guessed what it was. It seems unlikely that the young George Meredith could have unravelled a clue that escaped even the sophisticated, worldly Merimée. But it does not follow that Meredith failed to understand the novel.

Octave, 'baliban' or not, is achingly responsive to Armance's body, 'troublé' by her arm, almost naked, scarcely covered by the fine gauze of her dress, when he presses it against his breast.[141] He does not have the reputation of being a chaste young man. Armance is shocked to hear that he habitually visits low haunts where he mixes with women the sight of whom is a stain, 'dont la vue est une tache'. When Armance charges him with it, Octave at once admits that it is true and simply promises never again to patronise establishments where your friend, 'votre ami', should not be seen.[142] It may be, I suppose, that Octave visits such places to disguise his incapacity, but it seems just as likely that his 'balibanisme' afflicts him only in his relationship with Armance. That at least seems to have been Meredith's understanding. *The Ordeal of Richard Feverel* is a study of the difficulty that its hero finds in reconciling his pure love for Lucy Desborough with sexual desire. When Richard falls in love with Lucy, he takes her hand, and the hand is 'pure white: white and fragrant as the frosted blossom of a May-night'.[143] He kisses that hand, but it is not the kind of kiss that he will press passionately on the lips of Bella Mount. Love and desire, as Richard Feverel finds to his cost, are difficult to reconcile. It is a problem that Meredith addresses in his first novel and addresses again

[139] *New Monthly Magazine*, 18 (January 1826), 211–2.
[140] Stendhal, *Correspondance* (Paris, Le Divan, 1934), 6, 174–80.
[141] Stendhal, *Armance*, chapter 16.
[142] Stendhal, *Armance*, chapter 9.
[143] *The Ordeal of Richard Feverel*, chapter 15.

in his last. The Earl of Fleetwood proposes to Carinthia at a ball, even though '"wife" is one of the words he abhors': the proposal is a 'mad freak' by which he is bound because he is a man who prides himself on never breaking his word.[144] He marries, and in the long years that pass before his early death, he shares a bed with his wife just once. He leaves her on her wedding night to attend a ball, because he has given his word that he will go, but at the ball he experiences 'a headlong plunge and swim of the amorous mind, occupying a minute, filling an era', and it leads him to think how he might make his way back to the inn where he had left his wife 'at a whipping pace on a moonlight night'.[145] That stray thought is the only explanation the reader is offered of how it comes about that nine months later Carinthia gives birth to a son, 'the Amazing Baby' as Meredith's first biographer christens him.[146] Fleetwood recognises by the novel's end that 'the union of body and soul; as good as to say, earth and heaven', is to be found only in love of 'the embraced woman',[147] but for Fleetwood that recognition is hard-won, and he arrives at it too late to repair his relationship with his scorned wife. There may be physiological reasons that prevent Octave from consummating his relationship with Armance, but it is just as likely that the pathology is psychological, in which case it is a pathology with which many young men of the nineteenth century were familiar. It was the condition that Meredith explored in *The Ordeal of Richard Feverel*, his first novel, and in *The Amazing Marriage*, his last. The only reasonable conclusion is that he understood the problem so well because he recognised it in himself.

Octave asks Armance, 'mais qui est l'homme qui t'adore?', and answers his own question, 'c'est un monstre'.[148] He believes himself to be monstrous, but so does Richard Feverel after he has printed a passionate kiss on Bella Mount's lips. In horror at his own action, he runs away from his young wife to Germany. Richard confesses his sin to his wife. Octave makes confessions throughout the novel. He confesses that he lacks 'le sens intime', that he is a man without a conscience, that he has no instinctive revulsion from crime.[149] He confesses to Armance that when he was

---

[144] *The Amazing Marriage*, chapters 12 and 13.
[145] *The Amazing Marriage*, chapter 18.
[146] Ellis, 303.
[147] *The Amazing Marriage*, chapter 38.
[148] Stendhal, *Armance*, chapter 29.
[149] Stendhal, *Armance*, chapter 6.

young he was addicted to stealing; he had 'la passion de voler'.[150] Armance suspects that he has committed some great crime, that perhaps he is a murderer, and the thought serves only to fill her with 'la pitié la plus tendre et la plus généreuse'.[151] Even Octave's own mother detects in him a depth of dissimulation scarcely credible in someone of his age.[152] When Stendhal in his letter to Merimée coarsely dismisses him as a 'babilan', he manages at once to reveal the secret that lies at the heart of his novel and to disown all kinship with his hero. But the novel only works—and this is why it meant so much to Meredith—because Stendhal at once despises his hero and recognises in him his own reflection.

In 1880 Henri-Frédéric Amiel read *La Chartreuse de Parme*. He admired the novel and at the same time it repelled him. Stendhal, he writes, makes literature a branch of natural history. He does not recognise the special place of a human being in the creation, preferring to class humankind with the ant, the beaver and the monkey.[153] It is a thought very familiar to Meredith. In one of the most striking sonnets in *Modern Love*, number XXX, he mocks the notion that human 'animals' might become 'intelligences at a leap'. Human beings may have the power to understand the order of nature to which they belong, but they can never free themselves from it: all that they can do is to make themselves into 'scientific animals'. But even in this sonnet, the most cynical of the sequence, Meredith jibs against his own conclusion, and so too does Stendhal. The young men that Stendhal chooses as his heroes are at once viewed with a chilling detachment, seen from a distance that reduces them to insect size, and explored closely, inwardly, known with the intimacy with which one only knows oneself. That strange, compelling double perspective is the most important lesson that Meredith drew from his study of Stendhal's novels.

Octave dissembles habitually. He pretends to a particular fondness for the uncle that he detests. He claims to love his room, which in fact he resents because it is low-ceilinged.[154] But he dissembles because he is 20 years old, and at 20 young men can do no other than dissemble: they have not yet found or fashioned a self that they can be true to. Octave

---

[150] Stendhal, *Armance*, chapter 24.

[151] Stendhal, *Armance*, chapter 29.

[152] Stendhal, *Armance*, chapter 1.

[153] Henri-Frédéric Amiel, *Journal Intime* (Lausanne, Éditionsl'Age d'Homme, 1994), 12, 476.

[154] Stendhal, *Armance*, chapter 1.

loves Armance and pretends to love Madame d'Aumale, but for a young man like him, loving and pretending to love are scarcely distinguishable. Young men know that they wear a mask. They are much less sure as to whether or not underneath the mask there is a real face in hiding. Octave thinks himself different from all other young men, separated from them by some shameful secret. He is, he tells Armance, 'un monstre', but all young men suspect that they are monstrous. Octave is at once a case study and an everyman. He prompts a pathological interest and the more intimate, more shocking interest that one takes in oneself. The heroes of all three of Stendhal's novels are young men: Octave in *Armance*, Julien Sorel in *Le Rouge et le Noir* and Fabrice del Dongo in *La Chartreuse de Parme*. They are the most powerful models for the young men that people Meredith's novels: Richard Feverel, Evan Harrington, Wilfred Pole in *Emilia in England*, Harry Richmond, Nevil Beauchamp and the Earl of Fleetwood of *An Amazing Marriage*. But Stendhal became the most powerful influence on Meredith's novels because it was through reading Stendhal that Meredith first came to understand himself.

Meredith married in 1846 when he was just 21. He was only 18 when he met his first wife. She was almost seven years his senior, a widow, with a young daughter not yet two. Stendhal published *Le Rouge et le Noir* in 1830, but it is hard to believe that Meredith had read it before he met his future wife or even before they were married three years later. He may not have read it until his marriage was falling apart around him. That seems the circumstance that would best have allowed him to recognise his close kinship with Stendhal's hero, Julien Sorel. Mary Ellen was a widow, a legitimate object of Meredith's affection, whereas Julien's desire for Madame de Renal is quickened by the glamour of adultery. But in both cases, sentiment and social ambition work in tandem. Julien is the son of a carpenter and Madame de Renal is the wife of the town mayor. Julien remembers to his shame that when he first met her he was wearing working clothes. She presides over his sexual initiation, but just as importantly she presides over his initiation into the bourgeois world of comfortable furniture, fine fabrics and social formality to which he has always aspired. The shame that she feels when she surrenders to him is still more precious to Julien than the erotic pleasure that the encounter affords him. When Julien leaves Verrières for Paris, he realises that Madame de Renal was never more than a provincial, small-town ideal of womanhood, a precursor of Emma Bovary. He forgets her as soon as he wins the favour of the aristocratic Mathilde de la Mole. When Madame de Renal denounces him to

Mathilde's father as an unprincipled adventurer, he travels back to Verrières and shoots her. But she survives, and before he meets his death at the guillotine, Julien comes to feel that Madame de Renal was the only woman he has ever loved. The novel meant so much to Meredith, because the erotic history it relates mapped so tellingly, so chasteningly, onto his own.

Julien's seduction of Madame de Renal seems impelled not so much by love, nor even by desire, as by a sense of what he owes to himself. He approaches each stage of the seduction, taking her hand, the first kiss, as if it were a test of his manliness. We can only guess how far the novel shone a disconcerting light on the pursuit by a tailor's son of Mary Nicolls, daughter of Thomas Love Peacock, Examiner of the East India Company and daughter-in-law of Fighting Nicolls. Julien, like Meredith, is a book-devourer. He persuades Monsieur de Renal to take out a subscription to the local library. He secretly studies radical political philosophers but his tastes extend to lighter reading. The youthful lover and his timid mistress, Stendhal observes, can find all the instruction they need in two or three novels. In Paris love is the child of the novel, 'fils des romans'.[155] But even in the provinces, love is no longer innocent. After spending the evening with Madame de Renal, Julien returns to his room dreaming of only one happiness, 'celui de reprendre son livre favori', that of picking up his favourite book again.[156] Did Meredith wonder as he read *Le Rouge et le Noir* quite how literary his own courtship of Mary Meredith had been?

In 1906 Meredith read and admired a paper in two parts in *Revue des Deux Mondes* entitled 'L'Egotisme Pathologique chez Stendhal'.[157] For Ernest Seillière, Stendhal's novels are a product of Stendhal's egotism. He is a confessional writer, a true son of Jean-Jacques Rousseau, and also a man addicted to dissimulation, who lived the whole of his life as a series of masquerades. Confession itself became for him an exercise in mystification. It was a disposition with which Meredith was entirely familiar. In Stendhal's novels as in Meredith's, the two contrary impulses, the impulse to confess and the impulse to mystify, are reconciled. The young men Stendhal chooses as his heroes are his 'sosies', his other selves. They are young men who habitually mask themselves, and those young men are themselves the masks behind which Stendhal chooses to present himself before the public. In creating them Stendhal achieves a strange literary

---

[155] Stendhal, *Le Rouge et le noir*, chapter 7.

[156] Stendhal, *Le Rouge et le noir*, chapter 7.

[157] *Letters*, 3, 1553. See *Revue des deux mondes*, 31 (1906), 334–61 and 651–79.

triumph. He made his novels not by escaping from his own solipsistic tendencies but by exploiting them. Meredith's egotism was very like Stendhal's. It is a temperament that might well produce a poet, as Keats understood when he referred to 'the wordsworthian or egotistical sublime'. But Stendhal taught Meredith how, unlikely as it might seem, the same pathological egotism might serve just as well to produce a novelist. It was a lesson not lost on a writer who fashioned his most acerbic self-portrait in a book he entitled *The Egoist.*

CHAPTER 6

Sons

THE UNPARDONABLE THING

The cracks opened early in Meredith's marriage. He had not been married long when he made a mordant entry in his notebook: 'one who marries a widow, and afterwards wrote a treatise on the virtue and morality of "Suttee"'.[1] When his son, Arthur Gryffydh Meredith, was born on June 13, 1853, the marriage was already under strain. It was in the early stages of the pregnancy that Catherine Horne witnessed the ferocious row that she reported in such gleeful detail to her husband. Mary and Meredith must have hoped that the birth of a son would repair their relationship. It never does. It would have been Mary who suggested the boy's second name, Gryffydh. It was her mother's family name, and her mother had died quite recently. But it would have been welcome to Meredith too, who liked to think of himself as a Welshman even though he never set foot in the principality until 1888, when he was 60. The immediate consequence of the baby's arrival was that the young couple had to move. Peacock was 67 and, as Edith, his first grandchild, recalled, 'he hated noise'.[2] It had been bad enough sharing with Mary, her daughter and her new husband. When the new baby arrived, Peacock rented a separate house for the Merediths. It was in Lower Halliford but on the other side of the village green. One of Peacock's friends was more enthu-

---

[1] *Notebooks*, 31.
[2] *The Works of Thomas Love Peacock*, 3 vols (London: Richard Bentley, 1875), 1, l.

© The Author(s) 2019
R. Cronin, *George Meredith*,
https://doi.org/10.1007/978-3-030-32448-3_6

siastic about the new arrival. Thomas Jefferson Hogg had been at Oxford with Shelley and was writing his biography. Little Arthur, he wrote, had 'quite converted' him to babies: Arthur was 'wonderfully good and intelligent', 'sometimes he looks very pretty', and 'his mother manages him perfectly!'[3] Hogg was less impressed by Meredith, whom he christened 'the Dyspeptic'.

Before Arthur was six months old, Mary was applying to superintend a school for servants in London. She would, she proposed, stay the week in town and visit Halliford on Sundays. The Merediths began to spend much of their time at the seaside, first at Felixstowe and then at Seaford in East Sussex, where they lodged with the Ockendens. Mrs Ockenden was an excellent cook, and they became friendly with another lodger, Maurice FitzGerald, Edward FitzGerald's nephew, who was, like Mary and her father and Hogg, an exacting gourmet. He became Meredith's model for Adrian Harley in *The Ordeal of Richard Feverel*. But Meredith and Mary were not often at Seaford together. They were already beginning to live separate lives. In April 1855, Meredith wrote to Tom Taylor, the dramatist who, like Meredith and Mary, had lodged with the Macirones at The Vines in Weybridge, to explain that he would not be able to see Taylor that Sunday 'as I cannot leave my dear boy alone in the house with servants'. Mary was 'coming to Town this week, and then going to the sea-side'.[4] Little Arthur was not yet two. In December 1856, it was Meredith who was at Seaford, working hard, he tells his publisher, on his new story, *Farina*. Mary was staying with Lady Nicolls at Blackheath, and Edith and Arthur were with her. 'I am anxious,' Meredith writes, 'she should spend Christmas in town. Dulness will put out the wax lights, increase the weight of the pudding [Christmas pudding was always an alarming threat to Meredith's digestion], toughen the turkey, make lead of the beef, turn the entire feast into a nightmare, down here, to one not head and heel at work ....'[5] It is a sprightly letter, rather too sprightly. It was Arthur's third Christmas, and his father and mother planned to spend it apart. The following spring, Arthur and Edith were at Seaford with Meredith, but their mother was not with them. Her absence prompted her one surviving letter to her son:

---

[3] Quoted by Johnson, 88–9.
[4] *Letters*, 1, 21.
[5] *Letters*, 1, 29.

My own little Goldens
Have you any primroses at Seaford? See what pretty flowers they are! I send you three and a fern leaf and a Lady's Smock. I hope you will be with me before there are many more flowers to gather and then we shall all gather such lots of flowers together.
Good-bye my own Goldens—Here are ten kisses xxxxxxxxxx and coozles and cuddles from your own mother
Mary Meredith[6]

The Merediths already knew Wallis, but it was after Wallis returned from a painting trip to Europe late in 1856 that he and Mary became lovers. Mary wrote to him while he was away, but it is not a lover's letter:

My dear Mr Wallis
Your letter was a most agreeable surprise.

In July 1857, Mary was staying in Seaford alone and invited Wallis to visit her. She had laid in nine gallons of 'tonic medicine' for him, which she promised to help him drink.[7] By August Mary was pregnant. Arthur had just turned four. It had been an unusual childhood. He was the son of a mother and father who were rapidly moving apart. They remained married to one another, and they still managed at times to act as a team. Mary wrote to Charles Kent in 1856 to acknowledge a good review of *The Shaving of Shagpat*. Meredith copied into his notebook touching snatches of his son's conversation: 'Don't leave yoo baby, Mama! You bed will cry for yoo, Mama!'[8] Arthur was dearly loved by both his parents, but they were parents who preferred to spend a good deal of their time apart. Arthur's first four years were odd, and his life was soon to become still odder.

In 1858 Mary moved to Clifton, just outside Bristol, with Arthur and with Edith, who was now 13. On February 27, shortly before the new baby was born, the two children were sent off to London. Arthur travelled in Edith's care, and Edith wrote to her mother to report their safe arrival:

My dear dear Mother
We reached London at ten minutes past five quite safely: Arthur was very good all the time but he got tired at the end. Mr Wallis met us.

---

[6] The letter was first published by Nicholas A. Joukovsky, 'New Correspondence of Mary Ellen Meredith', *Studies in Philology*, 106.4 (Fall, 2009), 483–522.

[7] Joukovsky and Diane Johnson suggest she is referring to wine, but surely it must be beer. She has laid in a firkin.

[8] *Notebooks*, 37.

Wallis took the children to Aunt Kate's house (Aunt Kate was probably a relative of the Nicolls's). Arthur stayed there and Edith went on to Blackheath, to stay with her grandparents, Sir Edward and Lady Nicolls. 'Thank you very very much for the Snow drops,' Edith writes to her mother (Mary seems to have made a habit, a very charming one, of sending her children pressed flowers), and adds, 'I do not know where you put Arthurs hair but in case you can't find it I have sent you a lock of what I had.' Edith was desperately worried: 'Dear dear mother you must not fret too much and make yourself ill—I pray for you always dear Mummy.' She ends:

> Dearest mother I will come if you want me. Do not oh do not fret. Good bye my own dear mother.
>
> Your own child Edith Nicolls.
> Love to all. Oh Mamsey God will take care of Arthur. My eyes are red too—

The reason for her distress is tucked away in the body of the letter: 'Mr Wallis says George is very busy so I expect he will keep Arthur long.' She missed out the 'not' from the sentence. It was a prophetic omission.[9]

Mary's baby was born on April 18. The boy was christened Harold, but as he grew up he was always known as Felix. The child's father was registered as 'George Meredith, author'. Meredith may have agreed to this. It was the gentlemanly thing to do. It spared Felix the fate that Wilkie Collins called attention to in *No Name*, a novel published four years later in 1862, in which a young woman born like Felix out of wedlock complains of 'the cruel law which calls girls in our situation Nobody's Children'.[10] But after he collected little Arthur from Aunt Kate's house, Meredith allowed his son no further contact with his mother. On May 4, Mary wrote to Wallis, 'I hear no word of Arthur now.' She added, 'I must have Arthur for Edith's holidays.' But Meredith would not hear of it. She was not to see her son again until she was on her deathbed.

In the summer of 1861, Meredith went on a walking tour in Switzerland with his friend Bonaparte Wyse and his wife. At the last moment, he decided that he would take Arthur with him. He was away for two months.

[9] The letter survives in a transcription by Anne Ramsden Bennett, Mary's friend in the last years of her life, and the omission may be hers.
[10] Wilkie Collins, *No Name*, 'The First Scene', chapter 15.

When he came back to Copsham Cottage, the small house near Esher where he had lived with Arthur since the autumn of 1859, he learned that Mary was dying. She had moved to Grotto Cottage in Oatlands Park, Weybridge, and was living just five miles away from Meredith in the town where the two of them had set up house together just after their marriage. The daughter of his old landlady, Emilia Macirone, who was now Emilia Hornby, arrived at Copsham Cottage late one evening and demanded that Meredith allow Mary to see her son, and at last, after three and a half years, Meredith relented. On October 8, he was able to reply to Janet Ross, who had written to add her weight to the proposal, that her letter was 'based on false intelligence': 'Arthur is now at Weybridge seeing his mother daily.'[11] Meredith was saved at the last from his own intransigence by the intercession of two of his heroines, of Janet Ross, the model for Rose Jocelyn, the heroine of *Evan Harrington*, the novel that had been serialised in *Once a Week* the previous year, and of Emilia Macirone, who was an accomplished singer and the model for the heroine of *Emilia in England*, the novel on which he was already at work, although he did not publish it until 1864.

Meredith met Caroline Norton in 1859 when he renewed his acquaintance with the Duff Gordons. She was the best friend of Lady Duff Gordon, Janet Ross's mother. When Caroline Norton separated from her husband in 1836, he refused her access to her children. In September 1842, her youngest son Charles scratched himself falling from his horse and contracted tetanus. She was summoned, but before she reached his bedside, he was dead. The boy was nine years old, and she had not seen him for six long years. Her husband's refusal to allow her to see her children prompted Caroline to begin a campaign that achieved its first object in 1839 when the Infant Custody Act was passed into law. The act allowed mothers to petition for custody of their children until the child reached the age of seven, and after that it allowed a mother's right to access. But the act, as Caroline found to her cost, was difficult to enforce. In any case, it would not have helped Meredith's wife, because women guilty of adultery forfeited their rights. Meredith's friends did not blame him for removing his son from his mother's care. His first biographer, his second cousin, S. M. Ellis, records the bitterness of Mary Ellen's last years: 'Her supreme sorrow was the loss of her little son.' But he attaches no blame to Meredith:

---

[11] *Letters*, 1, 103–4.

the child 'had, of course, been claimed by his father'.[12] Meredith's decision did not trouble Ellis but it did Meredith: it troubled him all his life.
Like his upbringing as the son of a tailor, like his wife's infidelity, it haunts
his fiction.

In August 1860 Meredith succeeded John Forster as principal reader
for the publishing firm, Chapman and Hall. The £250 a year that Chapman
and Hall paid him helped to sustain him for more than 30 years. One of
the manuscripts submitted to him early in his career was Ellen Wood's *East
Lynne*. The novel was being successfully serialised in the *New Monthly
Magazine*, and it came recommended by the magazine's editor, Harrison
Ainsworth, one of Chapman and Hall's most valuable authors. Despite
that, Meredith rejected the manuscript. His verdict was brief but tren-
chant: 'Opinion emphatically against it.' He was asked to look at the novel
again, but he stuck to his opinion. In 1861 the novel was published by
Richard Bentley and became, predictably, a runaway bestseller. By 1900 it
was reputed to have sold half a million copies. When Meredith's friend,
Samuel Lucas, reviewed it favourably in the *The Times*[13] just after it was
published, Meredith was furious. He wrote to Lucas insisting that the
novel was 'in the worst style of the present taste'.[14] *East Lynne*, it is true,
exhibits a useful compendium of the qualities that Meredith despised in
the novels of his contemporaries. It had, as even Lucas recognised, 'no
motive power'. When she feels obliged to account for some especially
unlikely piece of behaviour, Wood tends simply to acknowledge her own
helplessness: 'it is more than I can tell; why do people do foolish things?'[15]
Unaccountably, Lucas admired Wood as a moralist, a role in which
Meredith would have found her manifestly absurd. 'Is it possible', she
asks, 'remorse does not come to all erring wives so immediately as it came
to Lady Isabel Carlyle?', and at once adds, 'you need not be reminded that
we speak of women in the higher positions of life.'[16] Meredith would have
hated just as much the emphatic appeals made throughout the novel for a
sentimental response. 'All our critics agree in stipulating for the pathos', as
one of the characters puts it in his unfinished play *The Sentimentalists*.[17]

[12] Ellis, 91.
[13] See *The Times*, January 25, 1862, 6.
[14] *Letters*, 1, 131.
[15] Mrs Henry Wood, *East Lynne*, chapter 12.
[16] Mrs Henry Wood, *East Lynne*, chapter 29.
[17] *The Works of George Meredith, Memorial Edition*, 22, 172.

But as even Meredith admitted, 'There's action in the tale.' There was murder, the murderer exposed on the very day on which he was to contest a parliamentary election; there was adultery, divorce, infant mortality and a train crash that providentially brands the errant wife's sin on her body by scarring her face and removing some of her teeth. When he refused Mrs Wood's manuscript, Meredith placed himself in the awkward position of Kingsley Amis's fat Englishman. Roger Micheldene is tempted to reject *Blinkie Heaven*, the manifestly excellent first novel of the detestable Irving Macher, and defend his decision on the grounds that 'there were some successes which a house of any integrity ought to be proud not to have published'. But he remembers having rejected rather recently a novel by an abrasive young West Indian as '*in love with evil*', which, when published by a rival firm, 'had not only sold half a million copies in the first six months, been accepted for translation into all Europe's major languages with Japanese thrown in and broken a record or two with the sum paid for film rights but had won two international awards and unprovoked commendations from Sartre, Moravia and Graham Greene'. *East Lynne* did not win quite so many plaudits but it sold just as many copies, and it was admired by readers such as Lucas, who was not only editor of *Once a Week*, the magazine in which Meredith had serialised *Evan Harrington*, but, to make matters still worse, had been an early admirer of *The Ordeal of Richard Feverel*. Meredith must have known (he admits as much to Lucas) that *East Lynne* was a novel perfectly designed to appeal to the popular taste, but he was still prepared to risk his standing with Chapman and Hall by rejecting it. It seems unlikely that his motives were purely aesthetic.

The disfigurement of Lady Isabel Vane, the adulterous wife, in a train crash is providential in more ways than one. It enables Lady Isabel Vane to return to her marital home and act, quite unrecognised, as governess to her own children. The only precaution against recognition she need take is to wear a pair of blue spectacles. *East Lynne* is a twentieth-century comedy, *Madame Doubtfire*, pre-written as a Victorian melodrama. Isabel Vane's upright husband, Archibald Carlyle, agrees to take as his second wife the woman who has always loved him, the blooming Barbara Hale, only when he has good evidence that his first wife has died from the injuries she sustained in the train crash. Despite his innocently bigamous second marriage, Carlyle is allowed to make his peace with his first wife before she dies. He 'leaned over' the dying Isabel, at last recognising her, and 'pushed aside the hair from her brow with gentle hand, his tears dropping on her face'.[18] Meredith rejected the novel so fiercely, surely, because he recognised in it a grotesque reflection of his own domestic circumstances. He would have thought as much even if the novel had not found place for a minor character called Mr Meredith.[19] The novel irked him because it offered him his own history rewritten as sentimental melodrama, and it irked him the more because even the moralistic Ellen Wood allowed the betrayed husband a capacity for forgiveness that the freethinking George Meredith was unable to find in himself.

The matter was still troubling him 20 years later. *Diana of the Crossways* was serialised in the *Fortnightly* in 1884 and was published in book form the following year. It follows the events of Caroline Norton's life as closely as, in his previous novel, *The Tragic Comedians*, he had followed the love affair between the French socialist leader Ferdinand Lassalle and his young lover, Helene von Dönniges. Meredith's Diana shares with Caroline Norton a disastrous marriage, a suspect relationship with a senior politi-cian much older than herself (Lord Dannisborough rather than Lord Melbourne), a subsequent relationship with a younger politician (Percy Dacier rather than Sidney Herbert), and Meredith's Diana is guilty of leaking to the editor of *The Times* a vital government secret. Caroline Norton had been accused of divulging the government's intention to repeal the Corn Laws to the editor of *The Times*, information that she had acquired because of her intimate relationship with a member of the cabi-net. She was in fact innocent of the charge. Sidney Herbert himself had been the guilty party. But Meredith had followed her life so closely that, after Caroline Norton's nephew remonstrated with him, he felt the need to add a note to later editions of the novel admitting that the 'calumny' had since been 'examined and exposed as baseless'. Diana is an embel-lished portrait of Caroline Norton. Meredith told Robert Louis Stevenson with a regrettable lack of gallantry, 'I have had to endow her with brains.'[20] But in one crucial respect, Diana's circumstances are quite different. Caroline Norton had three sons. Diana's marriage with Augustus Warwick is childless. After her husband leaves her, Diana can never suffer, as Caroline Norton had, the forced separation from her children that inspired her campaign for legal recognition of the rights of mothers. The reason is not hard to seek. Diana had to be childless if Meredith was to avoid

[18] Mrs Henry Wood, *East Lynne*, chapter 46.
[19] Mrs Henry Wood, *East Lynne*, chapter 34.
[20] *Letters*, 2, 371.

reflecting on the similarities between his own behaviour towards Mary Ellen and George Norton's vicious use of his sons as a tool in his persecution of his wife. It was almost 10 years later still, more than 30 years after Mary's death, before Meredith was able to imagine how it might have been if he had been able to forgive her.

Lord Ormont and His Aminta was serialised in the *Pall Mall Magazine* in 1893. Aminta, like the first Mrs Meredith, leaves her husband, although in this case the husband, Lord Ormont, is 40 years her senior. She settles with her childhood sweetheart, Matthew Weyburn, in Switzerland where the young couple set up a school at which Weyburn is able to put into practice his progressive educational theories, very much as Phillipp von Fellenberg had at Hofwyl, the school to which Meredith had sent his son Arthur in 1867. Seven years later Lord Ormont, who is travelling in Switzerland, hears about the school from a former pupil, inspects it and decides to send his beloved nephew there, a sickly lad called Bobby. He takes the decision without ever acknowledging that he recognises Aminta and Matthew as his own ex-wife and her lover. It is an odd, rather touching, moment, and Meredith makes it the climax of the novel. It is as if he has at last found the distance in time and the narrative distance that enables him to imagine a gesture of forgiveness that restores Arthur to the woman from whom he had snatched her almost 40 years before. In his last novel, *The Amazing Marriage*, not published until 1895, Meredith is more explicit. The Earl of Fleetwood and his wife only once share a bed, in an inn, on the night of their wedding, but nine months later Carinthia gives birth to a son that Fleetwood recognises as his own. After the birth Carinthia and her husband are alienated from one another, and all through that time Carinthia is fearful that her husband will try to gain custody of their son: 'Everything was pardonable to him', to her way of thinking, 'if he left her boy untouched in the mother's charge'.[21] She finds, when Fleetwood at last attempts a reconciliation, that she has lost whatever feelings she once had for him, but husband and wife part with mutual respect. Fleetwood has, after all, refused to do the one unpardonable thing. He has not deprived her of her son. Meredith could no more change the past than the rest of us, but he was a novelist, and novelists do have the opportunity to take the past and to re-imagine it. In his last novel, Meredith was free to separate himself from the man he had been and to consider an alternative. He was free to imagine the man he might have been.

---

[21] *The Amazing Marriage*, chapter 29.

A Poet Without a Woman

When Meredith arrived at Aunt Kate's and took away with him the four-year-old Arthur, his ambition was not just to remove him from his mother's care but to remove him from contact with all women. Meredith wanted to bring up his son in a world of men. He had entered into his misogynist years. When Mary left him for Henry Wallis, he dropped his friends and made new ones, male friends. He met Frederick Maxse who was to become his closest friend in 1859 or the year after. His friendship with William Hardman began in 1861, the same year that he became friends with Lionel Robinson, Hardman's neighbour, and with James Cotter Morison, and Bonaparte Wyse. Morison introduced Meredith to the young John Morley, who had recently left his native Lancashire and come to London intent on making a literary career for himself. These male friendships were sealed by the use of shared nicknames. Hardman was Friar Tuck to Meredith's Robin, and his wife was Demitroia because Hardman's courtship had lasted for five years, half the length of the siege of Troy. The wealthy Robinson was Pococurante, presumably after the Venetian nobleman in Voltaire's *Candide*, and Morison, as the biographer of Bernard of Clairvaux, was always St B.

Hardman best describes the social life that Meredith enjoyed in these years in his account of a walking weekend he spent with Meredith in 1862.[22] The two friends left Copsham on the evening of May 23 and walked as far as Hornsdean where they took beds at the local inn. They retired to their adjoining rooms at 11 'after large potations of soda-water flavoured with brandy' and lay awake half the night 'shouting to each other, and joking about the joviality of the whole affair'. Meredith had exchanged the fraught silences of the marital bed that he describes so feelingly in *Modern Love* for hearty badinage exchanged between men occupying separate beds in separate rooms. The nature of their exchanges can be gauged from Meredith's letters to Hardman. This, for example, on a mutual friend called Vaux, which was written after Meredith had married for the second time:

> You speak regarding Vaux. Ahem. According to his spouse's report, he, poor fellow, is Vaux et praeterea nihil. She, they say, fierily postulated or—treated her case *links und rechts*. There are some lines of Catullus

[22] Hardman, 127–37.

will describe said 'case'. May I quote them to you out of the dialogue between Janus and Catullus?—[23]

He quotes some obscene lines from Catullus about a husband incapacitated by a flaccid penis and adds the comment, 'To employ the German idiom—he had no amatory standpoint, so say the informed ... and that the lady has sofa'd her dozens, even as pancakes on the pan ... Close we those curtains.' Intimacy between men that expresses itself through salacious gossip like this has a sad ring to it. Meredith had a laughing relationship with Hardman, but the laughter can ring hollow.

A still more revealing indication of Meredith's cast of mind in these years is offered by the painter, Frederick Bacon Barwell, a close friend of Millais. Barwell met Meredith in Lynmouth in the summer of 1858. Meredith had taken Arthur to Lynmouth on holiday. It was only months since he had removed him from his mother's care. The two men spent an evening together, and Barwell remembers Meredith as 'very amusing and often witty', but what most struck him was that Meredith had employed a young man as a nurse:

> Meredith had his boy with him at Lynmouth but no nurse, for he considered that a good lad who could wash and dress the child was better than a woman. He was himself devoted to the fellow, whom I often saw with his boy-nurse.[24]

Meredith's distrust of women must have gone very far for him to prefer a young man as Arthur's nurse. When he did at last agree to take a housekeeper, he chose 'good Miss Grange', 'excellent temper, spotless principles, indefatigable worker' and, best of all as far as Meredith was concerned, extremely plain, or, as he put it, 'no sex'.[25]

In the summer of 1861, when he went on a walking tour of Switzerland with Bonaparte Wyse, he took Arthur with him. Wyse, he reported, was astonished that Meredith did not take the opportunity of a foreign vacation to 'look out for a "woman"': 'You're a pote, and I can't think how a

---

[23] *Letters*, 1, 433. I suspect the reference is to William Sandys Wright Vaux, who was a Tractarian and the first keeper of coins and medals at the British Museum. He married Louisa Rivington in 1861.
[24] Ellis, 94.
[25] *Letters*, 1, 131.

pote can get on without one. I'd go mad.' Wyse was with his wife, and the
two of them, Meredith reported, 'spoon terribly': 'I don't envy them,
though I feel a kind of emptiness—an uncared-for feeling. A good friendship would satisfy me.'[26] But Meredith was half mad on that trip. It was
always his habit to seek in physical exercise a release from his sexual frus-
trations. He was like Matthew Weyburn in *Lord Ormont and His Aminta*
who finds that 'sharp exercise of lungs and limbs is a man's moral aid
against temptation'. Matthew takes refuge from troubling thoughts about
Aminta in 'a cleansing bath of a walk along the southern hills'.[27] But on
this trip, physical exercise proved not so effective a resource. Meredith
displaced the erotic responses that he withheld from women onto the
mountains, sighing 'like Tannhäuser for the Venusberg': 'The limbs of
that lady are clean; and she is sweet and affable, and of a fair face, which
cannot be said for one woman—not one single woman hitherto encountered by me.' He was awestruck when he saw the Alps for the first time.
They had 'the whiteness, the silence, the beauty and mystery of thoughts
seldom unveiled within us', and they offered some kind of guarantee that
'in you and in me there may be lofty virgin points pure from what we call
fleshliness'.[28] Meredith claimed for himself an unusual freedom from
fleshliness. He could not be attracted to a woman, he told Maxse, if he
could not 'feel her soul'. He could only 'envy those who are attracted by
what is given to the eye;—yes, even those who have a special taste for
woman flesh, and this or that particular little tit bit—I envy them! It lasts
not beyond the hour with me'.[29] But these are the thoughts of a man tot-
tering under the burden of his self-imposed chastity. When he crossed the
Alps and arrived in Venice, Meredith admitted as much and surrendered
to the glowing erotic daydreams that the city released in him. He swam
with Arthur on the Lido every day, and in the evening 'floated through
the streets in [his] gondola, and received charming salutes from
barred windows':

> from one notably where a very pretty damsel, lost in languor, hung with her
> loose-robed bosom against the iron, and pressed amorously to see me pass,
> till she could no further: I meantime issued order to Lorenzo, my gondolier,
> to return, and lo, as I came slowly into view, she as slowly arranged her sweet

[26] *Letters*, 1, 93–4.
[27] *Lord Ormont and His Aminta*, chapter 5.
[28] *Letters*, 1, 92–3.
[29] *Letters*, 1, 105.

shape to be seen decently, and so stood, but half a pace in the recess, with one dear hand on one shoulder, her head slightly lying on her neck, her drooped eyelids mournfully seeming to say: 'No, no; never! though I am dying to be   wedded to that wish of yours, and would stake my soul I have divined it!'—wasn't it charming? This too, so intensely human from a figure vaporous, but half discernible![30]

Meredith is swooningly alert to the woman's body, but only, one suspects, because it remains at a remove from him, it remains vaporous. Women whose presence was more substantial became seductive only after he had been drinking. Some months later, in April 1862, Hardman gave a dinner party. Among the guests were Meredith and D. G. Rossetti. They 'kept it up until 2.30'. Hardman took Meredith home with him and reports the difficulty he had in piloting him through the Haymarket, 'he was so very *rampant*'.[31]

Emilia in England, the novel that Meredith began working on early in 1861, is the most revealing production of these years. Meredith was especially pleased with the callow young man of the novel, Wilfred Pole: 'The combination of sensualism and sentimentalism—of a tyrannous delicacy of imagination with the grossness of developing appetites, has not yet, as far as I know, been attempted; and no one in England has given me credit for it.'[32] Wilfred Pole falls in love with Emilia, who first appears in the novel not as a woman but as a voice, a clear contralto singing at night in the woods. When she becomes visible, Pole's sisters note 'a boot-lace hanging loose' and are still more disturbed when, as an encore to an Italian air of her own composition, she sings a rollicking comic song, a 'native British, beer-begotten air'.[33] Wilfred finds her just as disconcerting. He kisses her at last when she lifts her face to him, at night, under a virginal moon: 'Over the flowering hawthorn the moon stood like a windblown white rose of the heavens.' But Emilia has been entertaining a group of rustic labourers in a tent, and when Wilfred remembers the kiss, he is reminded that her hair was 'redolent of pipe-smoke', a circumstance that he finds all but impossible to accommodate with his notion of her, for 'nothing was too white, too saintly, or too misty, for his conception of abstract woman'.[34]

---

[30] *Letters*, 1, 97.
[31] *Hardman*, 115.
[32] *Letters*, 1, 306.
[33] *Emilia in England*, chapter 2.
[34] *Emilia in England*, chapters 12, 13 and 10.

Meredith was always adept in his renderings of callow young men, but in the early 1860s, he was able to understand Wilfred Pole so clearly because, even though he was a father in his 30s, the shock of the breakdown of his marriage had left him with feelings about women that were uncomfortably like Wilfred's. In the sequel, *Vittoria*, which was serialised by John Morley in the *Fortnightly Review* in 1866, Emilia marries the young Italian nationalist Carlo Ammiani, but it is an almost sexless marriage, as though, even five years after Mary's death, it is still the only kind of marriage that Meredith can bring himself to contemplate. 'Kissings were rare between them,' we are told.[35]

His Only Blessing on Earth

Meredith withdrew from women after his wife left him. From February 1858, when he knocked at the front door of his stepdaughter's Aunt Kate, and took his son away with him, until July, 1865, when Will Maxse was born, his son by his second wife, Marie Vulliamy, Meredith's life centred on Arthur. It was a relationship that his contemporaries, unused to so close a bond between father and son, found moving. Hardman first met Meredith in September 1861. He was, Hardman noted, 'a widower of thirty two [in fact, he was a year older], with a boy of eight years—one of the finest lads I ever saw'. Meredith was 'immensely proud of this boy'.[36] These were the years in which his son was, as he told Arthur's headmaster, the Reverend Augustus Jessopp, his 'only blessing on earth'.[37] As S. M. Ellis has it, Arthur was all through these years 'the idol of his life, the object on whom he showered all the wealth of his love'.[38] But Meredith knew from the very first that his feelings were a good deal more complex than they seemed to Ellis. He explores them in both his novels that focus on a father's relationship with his son, his first novel, *The Ordeal of Richard Feverel*, the novel that he was at work on when he first removed Arthur from his mother, and his fifth, *The Adventures of Harry Richmond*, serialised in *The Cornhill* in 1870, a novel which, because it is written in the first person, Meredith referred to as his 'autobiography'.[39]

[35] *Vittoria*, chapter 38.
[36] Hardman, 50.
[37] *Letters*, 1, 158.
[38] Ellis, 94.
[39] *Letters*, 1, 250.

The Adventures of Harry Richmond opens with the finest first chapter that Meredith ever wrote. A man hammers at a quarter to two in the morning on the door of his father-in-law's house, in which his wife has sought refuge. He asks to see his wife, but the father refuses. He protests that his daughter is 'crazed' and 'knows none of us, not even her boy'. He blames her husband for her plight. The husband retaliates by seizing the boy. He scoops up the child, who does not know him because he has not seen him for four years, and carries him in his arms, wrapped in a shawl, the seven miles to Ewling. The novel is Harry Richmond's own account of his life from the time that his father removed him from his grandfather's house. It is a first-person narrative, all except for this first chapter. The irruption of Harry's father into the life of the young boy, and his removal from the only home he has ever known, is recounted in the third person. It has to be so, because the incident has come down to Harry not as a memory but as an anecdote. That night occupies the special place in Harry's mind that the earliest childhood memories usually occupy. We cannot be sure whether they are events that we remember or events that we have been told about. The last sentence of the chapter rather wonderfully marks a transition in mid-sentence from the one to the other, from family legend to personal memory:

> So, when obedient to command he had given his father a kiss, the boy fell asleep on his shoulder, ceasing to know that he was a wandering infant; and, if I remember rightly, he dreamed he was in a ship of cinnamon-wood upon a sea that rolled mighty, but smooth immense broad waves, and tore thing from thing without a sound or a hurt.

The first chapter of the novel stands alone, separated by its third person from the novel that follows, which is exactly how Harry remembers the night that the chapter describes: 'That night stands up without any clear traces about it, like the brazen castle of romance around which the sea-tide flows.'

The father who bears Harry away like a genie in an oriental tale is a version of Meredith's grandfather, the great Mel, the chief figure in the Meredith family's legend of itself. Like the great Mel, Harry's father tries and almost succeeds in forcing the world to accept him at his own valuation. In *Evan Harrington,* in which the great Mel goes by his own name, he is apt when in his cups to 'talk largely and wisely of a great Welsh family, issuing from a line of princes'.[40] The story runs through the whole novel of how on a visit to Bath the old tailor is taken for a marquis and successfully keeps up the fiction before all the town. The claim of Harry's father is far bolder. 'Augustus Fitz-George Roy Richmond', as he introduces himself to his father-in-law, Squire Beltham, masquerades as the illegitimate son of the Prince Regent, or rather as the son of a marriage that the Prince has chosen to disown, and hence as a man who has claims not just to a title but to the crown of England itself. Harry's father is Meredith's grandfather transformed into the hero of a comic romance. But he derives from Meredith's own father, too, from Meredith's memory of the time after the death of his mother when his father was all in all to him. Little Harry sees his father for the first time framed in the doorway, 'like the giants of fairy books'. There is a 'peep of night sky and trees behind him, and the trees looked very much smaller, and hardly any sky was to be seen except over his shoulders'. This is less a description of how a father fills a doorway than of how he fills a young boy's imagination, just as Meredith's imagination had been filled by his father, and filled the more completely because he no longer had a mother. But it is surely also true that this wonderful chapter has its origin in Meredith's need to transmute into romance the night when he took little Arthur away from Aunt Kate's house and carried him back to Hobury Street. The chapter summons the possibility, perhaps one ought rather to say it entertains the fiction, that it might be possible to tear 'thing from thing' and person from person 'without a sound or a hurt'. Harry's father is modelled on Meredith's grandfather and Meredith's father, but he is also modelled on Meredith himself. When Richard Le Gallienne first met Meredith, he noted that his conversation was 'slightly theatrical, almost affectedly bravura, and made one think that he must be very like his own Roy Richmond'.[41]

Meredith and Arthur did not stay in Hobury Street for long. In 1859 they moved out of London to Esher, to a large house in the High Street, where Meredith took rooms. Arthur was running across the street one day when he stumbled and fell in front of a horse. The young woman rider picked the boy up and took him home. She was impressed by his efforts to control his tears. 'Papa says', she recalled him saying, 'little men ought not to cry.' The man who opened the door looked at her, and then opened his

---

[40] *Evan Harrington*, chapter 2.
[41] Le Gallienne, 40.

arms, 'Oh! my Janet! Don't you know me? I'm your Poet!'[42] It was Janet Duff Gordon, who had known Meredith at Weybridge nine years before. It was to Janet that he had first told the tale of the Queen of the Serpents that later found a place in *The Shaving of Shagpat*. The little girl was now a young woman of 17, a daring horsewoman and androgynously beautiful. She had 'the head' according to Meredith 'of a Roman man'. In one of G. F. Watts's portraits of her, she is crop-haired and stares out from the canvas as defiantly as one of Blake's inspired bards. Watts, her 'dear Signor', was one of a number of older men who clustered about her, amongst them A. W. Kinglake, known to her, after his most famous book, as Eothen, and Meredith himself, who was to Janet Ross always 'my Poet'. Meredith thought he understood the key to her seductive power: she gave herself 'the airs of a man, pronouncing verdicts on affairs in the style of a man, preferring associating with men; and besides she smoked'.[43] She thought that Meredith was in love with her, and so he was in the pages of *Evan Harrington*. But in 1859 Meredith could allow himself to fall in love only in the pages of a novel, and not just because his wife was still alive. He was still too damaged to love a woman in real life rather than in fiction. He could, though, bring himself to share Arthur with her. It was Janet who looked after Arthur on Thursdays, when George took his weekly trip to London, to the offices of Chapman and Hall. On those days, she recalled, Meredith 'brought his little son Arthur to me, and I taught him German. We used to take long walks together. The Black Pool in the fir woods, where a stately heron was often to be found, was one of our favourite haunts.' Janet Duff Gordon was emphatically not a 'boy-nurse', but she was little more than half Meredith's age and she was boyish. It was Janet who helped him to find Copsham Cottage, outside Esher, on the road to Oakshott, the house in which he was to live until he married for the second time.

In the summer of 1861, Meredith planned a holiday, a walking tour in the Alps with his new friend, Bonaparte Wyse, who was Irish (Meredith never tired of imitating his brogue), and, excitingly, Napoleon's great-nephew (his mother was Lucien Bonaparte's daughter by his second wife). But when the time drew near, Meredith found that he could not bear to be parted from Arthur, even though it meant delaying the depar-

---

[42] Janet Ross: *The Fourth Generation: Reminiscences* (London; Constable, 1912), 49–50.
[43] Introduction to Lady Duff Gordon's *Letters from Egypt* (1902), *Works of George Meredith, Memorial Edition*, 23, 59–64.

ture so that Arthur could be fitted with a new pair of knickerbockers. It was just after arriving home from this trip that Meredith learned that his wife was dying and, after the intercession of Emilia Macirone and Janet Ross, finally allowed her to see her son. Arthur was understandably upset when, after three and a half years, he was introduced once again to his mother in her last illness. 'My darling boy is quite well,' Meredith assured Maxse on October 19, but added, 'He has cried a little, I am told. I am afraid his feelings have been a trifle worked upon, though not by his mother so much as the servants and friends in her house.'⁴⁴ Three days later Mary Ellen was dead. Meredith was away from home and did not learn of it for a week. The news 'filled' his 'mind with old melancholy recollections which I rarely give way to'. But these were feelings that Arthur was spared: 'My dear boy fortunately will not feel the blow as he might have under different circumstances.' This was to his friend Hardman. He hints that he would like Hardman and his wife to come to him, but he has no piano, and his rooms are small, and there is the weather in November to be taken into account. Only once does he allow a glimpse into his own feelings, 'The dread of my soul is the evening!'⁴⁵ He may not really have been so crassly insensitive to the feelings of his son as he seems. It may be that he was not yet strong enough to allow himself to imagine just what his son's feelings might have been.

In 1862, almost a year after Mary Ellen's death, Meredith sent Arthur away to school, to King Edward VI Grammar School at Norwich, placing him under the care of Augustus Jessopp. Jessopp had carried out a thoroughgoing reform of the school ethos and curriculum very much after the model that Thomas Arnold had established at Rugby. He had written to Meredith in November 1861, a little more than a week after the death of Meredith's wife, to tell him how much he admired his work, and the two men became friends, even though Meredith insisted on flaunting before the clergyman his disdain for Christianity (Mrs Jessopp felt she had to ask Meredith's permission before presenting Arthur with a Bible). But, even though the focal point of school life under Jessopp was the chapel, Meredith was happy to send Arthur there. Jessopp's school offered, as the School Inquiry Commission noted, 'the highest education in the county of Norfolk',⁴⁶ and Jessopp was a personal friend, not likely to be exigent

⁴⁴ *Letters*, 1, 106.
⁴⁵ *Letters*, 1, 107–8.
⁴⁶ *Schools Inquiry Commission Report* (London: Eyre and Spottiswoode, 1868), 363.

about the fees, a matter that throughout Arthur's school career was of some moment to Meredith. Meredith escorted Arthur to Norwich in September, earlier than he had planned. He had been with Arthur on a visit to Hertfordshire when his housekeeper's niece was diagnosed with smallpox. Meredith could not take Arthur back to Copsham, and he was relieved when Jessopp agreed to take Arthur at once, even though term had already started.

Arthur and his father remained close. The school holidays became especially important. On that first Christmas, Meredith collected Arthur from the Norwich train at Shoreditch station. The two of them stayed overnight in London before travelling on to Copsham the next day. Meredith explained to Hardman that he could not accept his dinner invitation. Arthur was too anxious to get home: 'how can I possibly keep him from Copsham on Thursday?'[47] On Boxing Day Hardman accompanied father and son to the theatre, but it was, as Meredith stipulated, to Drury Lane, to the pantomime: Arthur 'will not like the Strand'. His preference was for 'a jolly clown, a pantaloon of the most aged, the most hapless, a brilliant twirling Columbine, a harlequin with a wand on everybody's bottom'.[48] Arthur did not go back to school until January 26, and then on the platform at Shoreditch station, it was the nine-year-old boy who found himself comforting the father: 'Never mind, Papa: it's no use minding it. I shall soon be back to you.'[49]

The intensity of Meredith's feelings for Arthur is best mapped in his responses to three of his son's mishaps. The first occurred just after Arthur's enrolment at King Edward VI. Meredith was staying with the Jessopps to see his son settled. In the school gymnasium, Arthur clambered up a ladder, and was meant to slide down a pole to the floor, but he missed his grip and fell, 'about sixteen feet' in Meredith's surely inflated estimate. Arthur was 'shaken and sick' but no real harm was done. He was 'jolly and ready for fresh adventures in a quarter of an hour', but Meredith confessed to Hardman, 'my parental heart beat fast under its mask.'[50] In April, the following year, Arthur came home for his Easter holiday with a bad case of measles, 'measly exceedingly' as Meredith explained to Maxse. Meredith wrote at once to Hardman in London asking him to send down

[47] *Letters*, 1, 177.
[48] *Letters*, 1, 180.
[49] *Letters*, 1, 188.
[50] *Letters*, 1, 168–9.

the appropriate medicines. He dosed the boy himself and got up 'at all hours of the night' to offer him barley water. His nursing worked wonders and a week later the spots were gone: Arthur's eyes were once more 'like two agates (in crystal currents of clear morning seas!)'.[51] Last, and most seriously, in the summer of 1863, Arthur had a riding accident. An Esher neighbour, Captain Wyndowe, came across Arthur out for a walk and thought to give the lad a ride on his horse. But he let go of the reins, the horse bolted, Arthur fell, and was dragged for 50 yards along the furze, his boot caught in the stirrup. He was taken home and, according to Meredith, though it seems unlikely, remained 'insensible' until the following morning. He had been saved serious injury because of his short stature (his head did not reach the ground), because he was wearing elastic-sided boots so that the trapped foot could slip out and because the horse bolted across heath: 'Had he been kicked, or dragged on the road, I should have had a shattered heap of all I love given to my arms.'[52] But after eight days Meredith could report that aside from a little bruising, Arthur seemed little the worse for the adventure: his recovery had been 'wonderful'.[53]

Arthur remained Meredith's 'only blessing on earth' for one more year. In April 1864, Meredith met Marie Vulliamy in Norwich. He was staying with the Jessopps; she was visiting friends. It was surely not by coincidence that they found themselves in the same city at the same time. Meredith had known the Vulliamy family for several months. They lived in Mickleham, a little more than seven miles from Copsham Cottage, in a much grander property, the Old House, a brick-built seventeenth-century mansion. Marie's father owned woollen mills in Normandy, but he had married an Englishwoman, and when he retired, leaving the business to his three sons, he moved to Surrey with his wife and his three unmarried daughters. By the time Meredith knew them, Mrs Vulliamy was dead. The family were literary and musical. They would have been interested to meet Meredith, and Meredith would have been pleased to accept their invitations. He was lonely, and the neighbourhood offered few social opportunities. By the time they met in Norwich, his attentions were fixed on the youngest of the three daughters, the 24-year-old Marie. He first showed his interest by attending a new-year ball in Esher on January 8, an unprecedented experiment. He reported the affair to Hardman while carefully maintaining what seems even for Meredith an unusually heavy disguise. He casts himself as Mr Woodhouse at the ball at the Crown in *Emma* ('The women who had danced would sit in the draughts') and also, more revealingly, as Darcy, attending the Meryton ball at which he meets Elizabeth Bennet. Darcy pretends to Bingley that, with the exception of Bingley's sisters, there is not a young woman present that it would not be a 'punishment' to stand up with. 'The young women', according to Meredith, '(saving the Clarke girls) were hideous.' But Meredith had no more interest in the Clarke girls than Darcy does in Bingley's sisters. On the Monday he went to Mickleham to see the Vulliamys again. He took Arthur with him, walking the seven miles, and carried the boy on his back on the way home, until he gave up and took a fly for the last two miles.[54] Arthur was with Meredith and Marie in April, in Norwich too. His presence no doubt made it easier for the 36-year-old novelist and the young woman 12 years his junior to find a way of talking to each other. In the train on the way back from Norwich to London, Meredith and Marie 'were alone in the carriage the whole length of the route'. Meredith was thrilled ('I say! what a charming line of Rail from Norwich to London by way of Ipswich,' he wrote to Jessopp, rather archly), but after that he admitted that had found the journey rather 'hard', 'for a young lady demands all your resources to amuse her: and I wonder whether I did?' It was a good thought of Marie's to ease the situation by asking him for 'a photograph of the little man'.[55]

In September they were married, and Marie had become, for Meredith, 'my thrice darling—of my body, my soul, my song!' Meredith was confident that Arthur would have a place in his new life. 'She is very fond of him', he tells Jessopp, 'and will be his friend.'[56] When he wrote to Maxse, he used the same words: 'she is very fond of the boy,' and he added, 'Not at all in a gushing way, but fond of him as a good little fellow, whom she trusts to make her friend.' It is Meredith who does the gushing: 'There could not be a fairer, sweeter companion, or one who would more perfectly wed with me. She tries to make me understand her faults. I spell at them like a small boy with his fingers upon words of one syllable.'[57] A man in love has to be forgiven this kind of thing, except that when the father

---

[54] *Letters*, 1, 239–40.
[55] *Letters*, 1, 255.
[56] *Letters*, 1, 263.
[57] *Letters*, 1, 263.

starts to feel 'like a small boy', his son, who was to turn 11 the following week, might well feel as if his place had been taken.

Just over a year later, on July 26, 1865, Marie gave Arthur a half-brother, Will Maxse Meredith. It was the summer holiday, but Arthur was not present for the birth. He was visiting Marie's Normandy relations.[58] Meredith asked Maxse, his closest friend, to act as godfather despite both men's 'objection to the dominant creed'. His son, he assures Maxse, is a 'prodigy', 'fair, with a fine quantity of silver hair, dark blue eyes, a very gentle look, a full chest, broad back, lusty limbs, and sonorous yell'. New fathers, like new husbands, can be forgiven their enthusiasm. But then Meredith reassures Maxse that he will not be taking upon himself any financial obligations if he agrees to act as godfather: 'There would be all good arrangements made for Boy.'[59] When Will becomes 'Boy', Arthur's exclusion from the household seems complete. It was almost six years later, in June 1871, when Marie had a second child, a girl, Marie Eveleen, known to Meredith, to distinguish her from his wife, as Mariette or Riette. Meredith wrote to Arthur to give him the news just two days after the birth: 'On the 10th your Mama presented us with a little girl; so besides a brother you have now a sister.'[60] Arthur was living in Stuttgart, studying at the Stuttgart gymnasium. Meredith had visited him in Stuttgart for eight days that summer. He was in Stuttgart again briefly the following year. After that, he was not to see Arthur again for ten years.

It seems scarcely explicable that Arthur, who, from the time Meredith collected him from Edith's Aunt Kate in February, 1858, until he declared his love for Marie Vulliamy six years later, had been his 'only blessing on earth', should have been discarded so completely. It was as if Meredith was doomed to repeat in his relationship with his first son the fraught relationship that he had had with his own father. Meredith's mother died in July 1833, when Meredith was five and a half, a year older than Arthur when Meredith removed him from his mother's care. Augustus seems to have idolised George quite as much as George was to idolise his own son, and George as a young boy returned his father's feelings. There was much to admire in the young Augustus Meredith, who was, as Ellis was told by an acquaintance, 'a perfect gentleman, and not in the least like a tailor'.[61] He was a skilled chess

---

[58] *Letters*, 1, 311.
[59] *Letters*, 1, 313.
[60] *Letters*, 1, 446.
[61] Ellis, 43.

player, and a member of the Portsmouth Literary and Philosophical Society, a man that a young motherless boy could look up to as well as love. But Meredith discarded his father from his life as emphatically as he was later to discard his son. 'My father lived to be seventy-five,' he told his friend, Edward Clodd. 'He was a muddler and a fool.'[62] When his father emigrated to Cape Town, when Meredith was just turned 21, six months before he married for the first time, Meredith broke off all contact with him. After 14 years in South Africa, Augustus returned to England and retired to Southsea, to a house within walking distance of the house where he had been born, but there was no resumption of intimacy. In October 1870, Meredith mentioned in a letter to Arthur in Germany that he had called in on 'Grandpapa Meredith' on his way to Captain Maxse's. He and his wife had asked after Arthur, he reported.[63] The visit seems not to have been repeated. On June 18, 1876, Meredith's father died and was buried in Southsea Cemetery. Ellis records that Meredith was present at the funeral and inherited a few personal effects and family portraits that he chose not to display.[64] When Arthur was sent away to school in Switzerland in 1867, Meredith withdrew his affections from him almost as abruptly as he withdrew them from his own father when he had emigrated to South Africa 18 years before. It seems a strange ending to what had been, second only to his first marriage, the most intense passion of Meredith's life.

Meredith had a strange way of referring to Arthur. He was 'Sons'. It was a term of endearment that Meredith did not share with everyone. He used it when referring to his son in his letters to Hardman but not to Maxse. Maxse was, as Meredith recognises in the manner of his letters to him, less tolerant of archness than Hardman. Maxse was, after all, a naval man. He was also less caught up than Hardman in the romance of Meredith's relationship with his son. Hardman was persuaded, it seems by the sheer force of Meredith's passion, that the young lad who had inspired it must be remarkable. He referred to young Arthur only half jocularly as his future son-in-law.[65] Arthur's mother's name for him was also plural. In her one surviving letter to him, he is Goldens. But the two names are very different. Arthur was Goldens to his mother for his hair. His hair was important to her, which is why, when Meredith removed the boy, her

[62] Clodd, 141.
[63] *Letters*, 1, 430.
[64] Ellis, 139.
[65] Hardman, 50 and 149.

daughter Edith, although she knew her mother had kept a lock, took care to send another, 'in case you can't find it'. He was Goldens for his golden curls, just as in the pantomime Buttons is named for the brass buttons running down his suit. There may be an 's' on the end of both, but the names function as singular. Meredith's 'Sons' by contrast is emphatically plural. Meredith reported to Hardman how Arthur, newly enrolled at King Edward VI, was settling down:

> Well, Sons are wonderfully *buoyant* in a jiffy. Mrs. Jessopp writes to say that she took the boys to Lowestoft yesterday. Sons were so independent that they assured her they were *exactly like the other boys* and didn't want looking after.[66]

When Meredith was expecting Arthur home for Christmas, he announced to Hardman that 'Sons come on Wednesday'.[67] When 'Sons' has the measles, his symptoms are less remarkable than the third person plural pronoun that Meredith employs: 'They are spotted like the pard. They are hot as boiled cod in a napkin. They care for nothing but barley-water.'[68] It is a strange verbal tic, and a tic that is strangely disconcerting. Domestic intimacies become somehow estranged. 'Sons' functions as a potent verbal device, enabling Meredith to embrace his son while all the time holding him at arm's length.

There is a photograph of Meredith and Arthur taken in 1862. Arthur is eight or nine but seems small for his age, slight and rather delicate. He is formally dressed in a knickerbocker suit, a handkerchief in his breast pocket, an Eton collar visible above his waistcoat, his hair has a neat high parting. Meredith, who has his arm round the boy, his hand on his shoulder, is the dominant presence. He is dark-haired and lightly bearded, his coat extends to just above the knees, and his trousers are fashionably loose. His fist rests on his hip so that his right arm forms a not quite right-angled triangle with his body, and the left leg is crossed over the right, the toe of the polished left shoe resting elegantly on the ground. It is less like a picture than a tableau of father and son, as if the pair of them were acting out their relationship for the camera. Arthur's mouth seems set into a quarter-smile, as if it were registering not so much happiness as complicity.

---

[66] *Letters*, 1, 165.
[67] *Letters*, 1, 177.
[68] *Letters*, 1, 198.

The long exposures that Victorian cameras demanded have a lot to answer for, but it is strikingly different from a photograph of Arthur with his half-sister, Edith. In this photograph Arthur can be no more than four: he is not yet breeched, and the presence of Edith shows that he has not yet been removed from his mother. Edith must be 12 or 13, a solemn, rather plain, young girl, who seems not to have inherited her mother's beauty, but she bends over the boy who is sitting in front of her so that her cheek rests on his hair, and her right hand is laid gently on his. This time it is Arthur who has his hand on his hip, the left, and he stares out at the camera as boldly as Janet Ross stares out from G. F. Watts's portrait of her. He seems very different from the boy in the photograph taken five or six years later.

Meredith's letters in these years are full of references to Sons, the little man, his darling boy, but the fondnesses, as Arthur gets older, begin to be supplemented by references of a quite different kind, cool, analytical, free from all semblance of fond parental illusion. 'At present he is not brilliant,' he tells Janet Ross, although 'he is decidedly hopeful'.[69] He was not yet eight. He was nine when he was sent to board at Norwich. His arrival at the school was preceded by a letter from Meredith to Jessopp, the head-master, introducing his son:

> This is Arthur's character. It is based upon sensitiveness, I am sorry to say. He is healthy, and *therefore* not moody. His nature is chaste: his disposition at *present* passively good, He reflects: and he has real and just ideas. He will not learn readily. He is obedient: brave: sensible. His brain is fine and subtle, not capacious. His blood must move quickly to stir it, and also his heart.[70]

If this were Jessopp's account of a pupil, it would be judged favourable, even admiring, but, coming from a father, its precisions seem affected, as if Meredith were flaunting his scrupulous objectivity. The same might be said of the letter that Meredith wrote after Arthur's first term. He warns Jessopp that Arthur is 'pre-eminently a growing boy, and has some characteristics to outgrow': 'He will never, I fancy, do credit to you by any display of acquired knowledge; but, after a period, I think you will find that his understanding is as sound as that of any fellow you have had to do

---

[69] *Letters*, 1, 80.
[70] *Letters*, 1, 160.

with.'[71] When Arthur, just arrived at the school, had his fall in the gym, Meredith told Hardman that his 'parental heart beat fast under its mask'. He means that an exterior of manly sang-froid concealed an achingly tender concern for the injured boy. But at times Meredith makes one wonder which of the two characters is the mask and which is the real Meredith. It is a question that he prompts in very many of his relationships. His second wife's sisters told him after he proposed that they had had no idea until that moment of whether his intentions had been serious. One of them thought that he might be 'studying matter for a fresh novel'. Meredith ascribes their uncertainty to his remarkable powers of self-control: 'Not a change of feature, while my heart thumped and drummed up to my ears.'[72] As when Arthur had his fall, the impassive countenance is offered as the mask for the thumping heart, but again, one wonders. In *The Egoist*, when Lady Mountstuart reveals to Sir Willoughby that she knows him to be a man twice jilted, he tries staring at her as if he has no idea what she means before quitting 'the mask for an agreeable grimace'.[73] But the point is that the grimace is just as much a mask as the stare. Sir Willoughby has no real face, only a selection of masks.

By the time Arthur was in his third year at Norwich, Meredith's expectations, which had been modest from the first, had shrunk alarmingly. His son needed a tutor 'to grind him in rudimentary Latin, hard, over and over', and he also needed a 'drill-sergeant', because he 'threatens to be as knock-kneed as any John Thomas in the kingdom'. His assessments of his son are pained:

> He ought to have a thirst for history, by this time; but the appetite in him seems to be for sensation novels. My son does not promise. I am not impatient; but he potters at everything—play and work. He's a good fellow—which must content me.[74]

The final phrase is revealing. Meredith is disappointed less for his son than for himself. He once longed for Arthur's holidays from school, but by 1866 the eagerness had cooled: 'I go to Lord Houghton's for the Easter and shall see but little of my Arthur.'[75] Two months later, still

[71] *Letters*, 1, 181.
[72] *Letters*, 1, 260.
[73] *The Egoist*, chapter 37.
[74] *Letters*, 1, 308.
[75] *Letters*, 1, 331.

before Arthur's 13th birthday, Meredith told Jessopp, in a letter apologising for his failure to attend the school gymnastics, that he was thinking of sending Arthur abroad:

> I hope my darling boy is doing well—I am nursing a thought that he should go to Switzerland and learn languages. I doubt his power to acquire a scientific knowledge of Greek and Latin. Is not our country old and worn and all in the background, greedily devouring its (coaly) heart?[76]

And that is what he did. When Arthur was 13, he was sent to a school at Hofwyl in Switzerland. Meredith had only been a year older when he was sent by his father to Germany, to Neuwied.

Meredith presents the decision as progressive (modern languages rather than Greek and Latin), and outward-looking (Germany will offer his son an escape from little England), but it was also true that the school at Hofwyl was a good deal cheaper than the school at Norwich, which was of some moment to Meredith, who had often been behind with Arthur's school fees, and now had a new family to support. By May 1866, when Meredith wrote his somewhat tactless letter to Jessopp, who would not have relished finding his school representative of a worn-out social order, Meredith had remarried and had a new son, Will Maxse, who was almost one. Arthur had played his part in Meredith's courtship of his new wife. Arthur was with them when they made their tour of Norwich cathedral and wandered through the town. A young child can be a useful accessory for a man bent on courtship. Sir Willoughby Patterne makes much of his distant relative, young Crossjay Patterne, when he is courting Clara Middleton. She finds his 'supernatural sensitiveness', his inability to free himself from a crippling concern with how she regards him (he has been jilted once before), scarcely tolerable, until she sees him scoop the boy up so that he flew aloft 'clapping heels'. She is nonplussed by the easy spontaneity of Willoughby's behaviour with the boy and thinks, 'Is he two men?'[77] But Sir Willoughby's spontaneities are never uncalculated. When Crossjay ceases to serve his purposes, Sir Willoughby casually excludes him from the narrow bounds of his affections. On one occasion, after Sir Willoughby has successfully tempted Crossjay to abandon his studies, we are told that 'he trifled awhile with young Crossjay, and then sent the boy

---

[76] *Letters*, 1, 337.
[77] *The Egoist*, chapter 7.

flying'.[78] The remark summarises the whole of his dealings with the child. It seems impossible that Meredith could have devised the episode except out of a mordant consciousness that his dealings with his own son might merit a similar judgement, and without acknowledging it as a judgement that in his more self-lacerating moods he was inclined to pass upon himself. But novelists are not obliged to form single judgements. Even in *The Egoist*, Meredith might have recognised himself too in Vernon Whitford's selfless devotion to Crossjay's best interests. Whitford loves the boy unsentimentally, and he is eager to send him away to naval college because he knows that the boy's heart is set on following his father into the service. Whitford is, as Meredith acknowledged, a portrait of Leslie Stephen,[79] but he is also a man like Meredith, who finds in a second marriage to Clara Middleton recompense for an unhappy first marriage (although Whitford's first wife, the drunken daughter of his landlady, is more like a wife of George Gissing's than the first Mrs Meredith).

A SORT OF HOMELESS FEELING

Arthur went to Hofwyl in 1867. By a strange coincidence in that same year there was some thought that Arthur's half-brother, Mary Ellen's son with Wallis, might also be sent abroad to school, not to Switzerland but to France. Felix, like Arthur, was at school in England, and his headmaster's wife wrote to Wallis suggesting that the nine-year-old Felix was too young to be sent abroad. He was doing well at school. She had been struck when he first arrived by 'a certain shrinking, frightened look about him—as if he were expecting a blow', but he has since 'blossomed out into an increased confidence and courage'. Besides, she imagined that she could detect in boys sent too early abroad 'a sort of homeless feeling'. They risk losing their own country without finding another: 'They do not regard the feelings or opinions of those among whom they live, and they are too far from their own country to feel it home, and when they return, often seem more aliens than many foreigners.'[80] It was kind, sensible advice, and it spared Felix the fate that awaited his half-brother. It may be that Meredith eventually came to the same opinion himself. He did not send his second son abroad. Will Meredith went to Westminster. Arthur never quite set-

---

[78] *The Egoist*, chapter 14.
[79] *Letters*, 2, 658.
[80] Quoted by Johnson, 173–6.

tled at Hofwyl. He showed some talent for languages. He became fluent in German and French, his Italian improved, and he started to teach himself Spanish. But Meredith remained unimpressed: 'He seems to me much the same style of boy, plodding overmuch at the book line when he should be at play; very quaint, very thoughtful, not brilliant.'[81]

'I think it just as well that you should not return to England,' his father wrote, after Arthur had been at Hofwyl for almost a year. He doubted whether Arthur had 'much desire to come home at present', and, given the letters that Meredith was in the habit of writing, he was probably right:

> Keep pure in mind, unselfish of heart, and diligent in study. That is the right way of worshipping God, and is better than hymns and sermons and incense.[82]

When Arthur was 15, Meredith decided to transfer him to a gymnasium in Germany. In the summer of 1869, he visited Arthur at Hofwyl, and he and Arthur went on a walking tour in the Alps, accompanied by Meredith's friend Lionel Robinson. After the holiday Meredith went on with Arthur to Stuttgart to settle him in his new school. The holiday started very well. Arthur was out when Meredith arrived at Hofwyl to collect him. While he waited he chatted with the headmaster's wife until Arthur 'burst into the room, pale from excitement and crying with the adolescent's voice "Oh, I am so glad; so glad! You are come at last!"'[83] It all went rapidly downhill. A week later Meredith was as excited as he always was by the Swiss Alps, but Arthur would only allow himself 'to be a little laughed out of his grimness'.[84] Four days afterwards Meredith could say only that Arthur 'stirs a little in his stiff chrysalis; a little'. He had developed an interest in philology. Meredith gave him a new nickname, 'Slouch'.[85] Being together served only to remind father and son of their differences. 'How much I long to meet you!' Meredith had written to Arthur in February, but now they were sharing a room in a Swiss inn, and they seemed farther apart than ever: 'I don't bother him. He declares he is happy, and I must accept his statement.' When he arrived at Stuttgart, after being in his son's company for almost three weeks, Meredith was relieved. 'My poor Arthur', he admitted to his wife 'is not a particle of a companion. And besides I want my half-

---

[81] *Letters*, 1, 375.
[82] *Letters*, 1, 379–80.
[83] *Letters*, 1, 387–8.
[84] *Letters*, 1, 389.
[85] *Letters*, 1, 392.

myself. I miss my Willie.'[86] The place Arthur had once held in his father's heart had been taken by his little half-brother. Meredith revealed how far his relationship with his first son had broken down in a letter to Jessopp: 'With me he was scarcely civil though I believe he had no ill-feeling.'[87] Twice more, in 1871 and 1872, Meredith paid brief visits to Arthur in Germany. The next year there was some thought that Arthur might return to England. The prospect put Meredith in a panic (panic enough to derange his prose): 'Where to quarter him is the present problem of the question—What to do with him.'[88] But in the event Arthur did not come. Instead, he found employment abroad, first in Le Havre, and then at a linseed factory in Lille. As Mrs Wicksteed, the wife of Felix's headmaster, feared might happen to Felix, Arthur's foreign education had left him with 'a sort of homeless feeling', and the feeling seems never to have left him. Meredith may have come to realise as much. *The Adventures of Harry Richmond* was serialised in the *Cornhill* in 1870. In the novel a young woman who has passed much of her life with her father in Europe describes herself as 'almost a foreigner', and then adds for no apparent reason, 'but I do think English boys should be educated at home'.[89] After 1872 Meredith did not see Arthur again for ten years.

The boy had been 'the idol of his life', but the idol was soon toppled. Meredith lost interest in his son. He may have lost interest the more readily because he suspected that the son had lost interest in him. When Meredith arrived back in England after leaving Arthur at Stuttgart, he took up a novel that he had begun to work on five years before. The most celebrated episode in *The Adventures of Harry Richmond* is the affair of the statue. Harry's father has found for himself a precarious position in one of the lesser German princedoms. The margrave's wife wagers her husband that she can arrange for a bronze equestrian statue of his renowned ancestor Prince Albrecht to be cast and ready for public inspection within eight days. The ceremony falls on the day that Harry arrives at the court in search of his father. Harry is mightily impressed by the statue when it is unveiled, so impressed that he forgets all about his quest. The prince sits astride his horse, his head bent 'almost imperceptibly … in harmony with the curve of the horse's neck':

---

[86] *Letters*, 1, 398.
[87] *Letters*, 1, 413.
[88] *Letters*, 1, 480.
[89] *The Adventures of Harry Richmond*, chapter 14.

No Prince Eugene—nay, nor Marlborough, had such a martial figure, such an animated high old warrior's visage. The bronze features reeked of battle.

After a poet recites an interminable celebratory ode, Harry, who thinks that his father might be amongst the crowd of spectators, calls out to him. The statue's head moves. The eyes, which had been 'an instant ago dull carved balls', become animated and fix on Harry. The bronze chest heaves, and a familiar voice cries out: 'Richmond! my son! Richie! Harry Richmond! Richmond Roy!'[90] Harry's father, long before it became a commonplace in every tourist city on the globe, has made a living statue of himself so that the margravine might win her bet. It is a fine example of Meredith's willingness to open up the novel to romance, so that a novel set in the early nineteenth century can accommodate an incident that might have found a place in one of those Arabian Nights that inspired Meredith's very first story. But the reason all readers remember the chapter so well is that it condenses into a single tableau the story of the whole novel, which traces the history of how a father becomes in the imagination of a young boy a bronze statue of himself, of how he is frozen into a single heroically grand posture, until, as the boy grows older, the statue starts to move, the bronze-coloured paint cracks and the father reveals himself not just as fallibly human but as someone apt to be rather ridiculous, as someone who makes of himself every now and then a public laughing stock. It had been Meredith's own experience. He had idolised his father when he was a boy only to decide as he grew older that the idolised parent was only 'a muddler and a fool'. But after that visit to his son in Stuttgart, Meredith could scarcely have evaded the suspicion that his son's feelings for him might have followed a rather similar trajectory. Harry is allowed at the very last to recover the charismatic father of his youth. He comes home with Janet, his new wife, to his childhood home only to find it ablaze. It is yet again all his father's fault. He had planned a spectacular homecoming for his son with fireworks, and the fireworks had exploded prematurely. But Richmond Roy enters the blazing house in search of Dorothy, his wife's sister and the true object of his affections. It is another of his blunders. Dorothy is not there. But it is a grand blunder, a blunder that allows Richmond Roy to die a hero, a maladroit hero but a hero nevertheless, running through the burning rooms in search of the woman he loves, a woman who happens not to be at home.[91]

---

[90] *The Adventures of Harry Richmond*, chapter 16.
[91] *The Adventures of Harry Richmond*, chapter 56.

Meredith did not manage even so comically blundering a redemption in the eyes of his son. In June 1881 Meredith heard from Lionel Robinson, who had seen Arthur in Lille, that he was ill. Arthur turned 28 that month, and he was spitting blood. Later that summer Robert Koch would at last identify the bacteria that caused tuberculosis, but there would be no cure for another 50 years. Meredith wrote at once to assure his son that there was a place for him at Flint Cottage. He had always discouraged Arthur from pursuing a career in literature, but he was now even prepared to offer his son active help: 'I am allowed the reputation of a tolerable guide in writing and style, and I can certainly help you to produce clear English.'[92] It is a claim that would have puzzled many of Meredith's readers, but the offer is friendly. It cannot, though, conceal Meredith's embarrassment. Arthur had a brother of nearly 16, at school at Westminster, 'a kindly fellow, with wits of a slow sort'. Arthur had not seen him since he was a baby. And he had a sister, 'Mariette', just turned ten and already a good musician, whom he had never met at all. He had played some part in bringing his father and his second wife together, but he had not seen Marie for many years. She was now all but a stranger to him. Arthur wrote refusing the invitation. He preferred to try the restorative effect of mountain air. Meredith suggested he might go to Davos, where he would find Robert Louis Stevenson. He is relieved that Arthur is in no immediate want of money and assures him that he has remembered his son in his will: 'you will have your share.' Arthur's ill health puts him in mind of his own:

I finished the last volumes of a novel [*The Tragic Comedians*] two years back by writing at night for three months. An attack of whooping cough followed on the lowered nerves. I have never been well since then.

He does not himself cling to life: 'While I can be of service to my children, I would stay, but no longer.' 'There is nothing saddening about death to a man of my age,' he explains (he was 53 and had almost 28 years to live), 'but the thought of a child of mine having the prospect of life extinguished in his youth, is a cruel anguish.' He may find the time to visit Arthur abroad, and may not: 'I cannot say yes, but will not decisively say no.' If he is able to come, they had best meet at Strasburg or Basle: 'You may be sure I would not walk you overmuch.' The letter is a lamentable performance. Much of it might have been written by Sir Willoughby

---

[92] *Letters*, 2, 625–6.

Patterne. But Meredith does at last bring himself to address feelingly the fact of his separation from his son: 'We have been long estranged, my dear boy, and I awake from it with a shock that wrings me.' He accepts that the 'elder should be the first to break through such divisions', 'but our last parting gave me the idea that you did not care for me'.[93] This is movingly direct but it is also very strange. It is as if Meredith thinks of Arthur not so much as his son as a younger brother.

There was no meeting in Strasburg or in Basle that year, but the next year, in August, Arthur joined his father in Switzerland, and father and son crossed the Alps together into Italy. In the ten years since he had last seen him, Arthur seemed to have improved: 'He is short, with thin black moustache and black flat sparse whiskering on a sunbrown skin, intelligent, with ready laugh, well read in modern and mediæval history, and in philosophy makes an agreeable fellow traveller.'[94] But it is as if he is describing someone he has only just met, as indeed, in some sense, he had. Arthur was on his way to San Nico in the south, but Meredith turned north at Milan and rejoined his wife, who was visiting her family in Normandy.

When Marie died in September 1885, Arthur travelled to England to offer his father his support. By then he was living on Lake Garda, trying, a little half-heartedly, to establish himself as a writer. Meredith encouraged him. 'It may amuse you', he wrote to his friend, Louisa Lawrence, 'to read an article written by my son Arthur in the *St. James's Gazette*, on the Bergamesque Alps.'[95] But in 1886 Arthur's health collapsed. He came home and was admitted to St Thomas's in Lambeth. It was his sister, Edith, who looked after him in his sickness, not his father (she was Mrs Charles Clarke by this time). Arthur's health did not improve, and early in 1889 he decided to take ship for Australia. Meredith visited him before he left and was shocked by how frail he looked. He offered Arthur money so that he might travel more comfortably, but Arthur refused it, and Meredith had to write to Edith, asking for her help to persuade him: 'you have been sister and mother to him, you will induce him not to reject from his father what may prove serviceable.'[96] But Arthur remained intransigent. In consequence he could not afford to take a first-class cabin and found himself

---

[93] *Letters*, 2, 627.
[94] *Letters*, 2, 671.
[95] *Letters*, 2, 714.
[96] *Letters*, 2, 946.

sharing with a 'mad inebriate'.[97] In June, Meredith heard that Arthur had arrived safely and reported his health much improved. In September he was thinking of going on to New Zealand, but then he changed his mind and came back to England. He arrived in the spring of 1890 and went to stay with Edith and her husband. It was not his home but it was the nearest thing to a home that he had. Edith looked after him until, on September 3, 1890, Arthur died. Edith told her father that his end had been peaceful. He had made Edith his heir, but he left his father his books. Edith had them sent on. 'The collection speaks piteously,' Meredith told her,[98] an odd expression. He may have recalled when he looked back on Arthur's short, sad life a sentence he had written into the notebook he kept during the years when Arthur had been his only blessing on earth: 'The man whose child shall fail, is himself a failure.'[99]

Meredith risked rehearsing in his relationship with his younger son the trajectory of his relationship with Arthur. When he was four, the boy was 'my half-myself. I miss my Willie'.[100] Twelve years later, Meredith described him to Arthur. He was by then a Westminster schoolboy, 'a kindly fellow, with wits of a slow sort'.[101] Meredith could on occasion be a good deal rougher. Willie was in his 20s when the poet Richard Le Gallienne was invited to dinner at Flint Cottage. He found the lad 'really a very modest and wholesome young Englishman', but he remembered Meredith's merciless teasing of the son he had nicknamed 'the Sagamore' (the reference is to Fenimore Cooper's *Last of the Mohicans*): '"Behold the Sagamore! mark that lofty brow! Stand in awe with me before the wisdom that sits there enthroned…" and so he would proceed to improvise on the sublime serenity of the Wise Youth, seated there so confidently at the top of the world, till the poor tortured Sagamore would blush to the roots of his hair.'[102] The aggression could be more direct. When Will warned his father in 1887 that his embarrassingly warm relationship with the 24-year-old Hilda de Longueil was giving rise to gossip, Meredith's reply was designed to wound: 'I charitably suppose that your poverty of language causes you to address me on such a subject so bluntly.' But Meredith did not want to risk a rupture with his second son. He wrote again three days later giving

[97] *Letters*, 2, 953.
[98] *Letters*, 2, 1017.
[99] *Notebooks*, 55.
[100] *Letters*, 1, 398.
[101] *Letters*, 2, 625.
[102] Le Gallienne, 41–2.

his son the reassurance he wanted: he had 'a warm friendly feeling' for the young woman, but he knew himself to be 'a cranky vessel quite past thought of unions'.[103] In his last years, Will acted as Meredith's literary agent, and the two were in close contact. But Meredith's letters to his son are business-like rather than loving. It was his daughter, Mariette, 'the Dearie Girl', who commanded his affections. Perhaps he found that a daughter impinged less on his sense of himself than his sons.

The Ordeal of Richard Feverel, Meredith's very first novel, the novel that he was working on when he first removed Arthur from his mother and took him into his own care, traces the disastrous consequences when a father, deserted by his wife, is 'left to his loneliness with nothing to ease his heart of love upon save a little baby-boy in a cradle'.[104] Sir Austin finds consolation in devising a perfect scheme of education for his son. For Sir Austin, Richard is 'the young Experiment'. He keeps his son under constant surveillance and, 'despite his rigid watch and ward, knew less of his son than the servant of his household'.[105] He exercises over his son an Orwellian refinement of tyranny ('I require not only that my son should obey. I would have him guiltless of the impulse to gainsay my wishes'[106]), and, predictably, the outcome is disastrous. All through the novel, Meredith maps Sir Austin's fatherly failings so deftly that it seems quite unaccountable that he should have rehearsed so many of those failings himself. Sir Austin is so anxious to safeguard his son's purity that he subjects him every night before bed to an examination in which he is asked to 'recapitulate his moral experiences of the day'.[107] Sir Austin's women friends are impressed. Lady Blandish thinks to herself, 'if men could give their hands to women unsoiled—how different would many a marriage be!'[108] But the difference, as the novel indicates, is not at all of the kind that Lady Blandish anticipates. Richard, unsoiled when he marries, rather soon embarks on an affair with the notorious demirep Bella Mount. It is a novel with a purpose according to Justin McCarthy in the *Westminster*, and its primary purpose is to raise the question, 'Are they to be sown or not, these wild oats?'[109] But when young Arthur entered his blossoming

---

[103] *Letters*, 2, 848–9.
[104] *The Ordeal of Richard Feverel*, chapter 1.
[105] *The Ordeal of Richard Feverel*, chapter 12.
[106] *The Ordeal of Richard Feverel*, chapter 16.
[107] *The Ordeal of Richard Feverel*, chapter 12.
[108] *The Ordeal of Richard Feverel*, chapter 13.
[109] 'Novels with a Purpose', *Westminster Review*, 26.1 (July 1864), 24–49, 32.

season, Meredith chose to adopt a fatherly manner that seems a rather close imitation of Sir Austin's. The day before Arthur turned 18, Meredith wrote to him in Germany, enclosing a 'tip'. Arthur should spend it on a holiday. Arthur had thought of a trip to Vienna, but Meredith is not in favour: 'As to Vienna, you are quite aware of my objections to your going there.' In Vienna there were prostitutes. His concern for Arthur's purity even overrides his objections to Christianity, a religion which has some advantages for the young: 'it floats them through the perilous sensual period when the animal appetites most need control and transmutation.'[110] Sir Austin raises his son in obedience to his own 'System'. The System seems at first to be working excellently. Richard grows up to be 'a youth, handsome, intelligent, well-bred, and, observed the ladies, with acute emphasis, innocent'.[111] When Meredith was an old man, he understood quite clearly why Sir Austin's experiment goes wrong. As he explained to his friend, the poet Alice Meynell, 'Sir Austin Feverel built a system, quite unaware, on the unforgivingness of his wife. So, though it was a pretty system, it fell.'[112] By that time Meredith's first wife had been dead more than 40 years, and Arthur, his own young experiment, had himself been dead for more than 12. But Meredith had known just as much in 1859, the year that the novel was published. It was then that he explained to Samuel Lucas: 'The "System", you see, had its origin not so much in love for his son, as in wrath at his wife, and so carries its own Nemesis.' The System was only ever 'Sir Austin's way of wreaking his revenge'.[113] Meredith did not have to wait until he was in his 70s to understand his own motives. He understood them from the first. The problem, he found, was that to understand oneself was one thing, but to change was something else entirely. He has Sir Willoughby Patterne make the same discovery. Sir Willoughby 'stood above himself, contemplating his active machinery, which he could partly criticise but could not stop'.[114] All through his career, Meredith showed himself able to arrive as a novelist at a wisdom that he could not pass on to himself as a man.

[110] *Letters*, 1, 446 and 466.

[111] *The Ordeal of Richard Feverel*, chapter 13.

[112] *Letters*, 3, 1478. Interestingly, and perhaps significantly, Meredith refers to Sir Austin's failure to forgive his wife in an expression, 'the unforgivingness of his wife', that might be read just as easily as referring to his wife's inability to forgive him.

[113] *Letters*, 1, 40.

[114] *The Egoist*, chapter 34.

Arthur, 'Sons', was the second great failure of Meredith's life. One of the minor characters in *Emilia in England* is Purcell Barrett, the disinherited son of a baronet who is reduced to scraping a paltry living as a church organist. In spite of his poverty, Barrett falls somewhat feebly in love with Cornelia Pole, one of the socially aspirant daughters of the city merchant, Samuel Pole. When Cornelia fails to keep an assignation with him, he persuades himself that she has thrown him over and shoots himself. Meredith does not treat him sympathetically. Barrett is a sentimentalist, killed by his inability to accept the world as it is. But there are aspects of his history that are familiar: 'His mother died away from her husband's roof', and the father sought subsequently to 'obliterate her entirely'. He tried to eradicate anything in his son that the son might be suspected of having inherited from the mother, even his aptitude for music. The son should have understood his father's behaviour as evidence of 'a vehement spiteful antagonism to reason'. He should have been able to regard it 'more as his father's misfortune than his own'. But he was a sentimentalist and could not bring himself to see his father clearly. In consequence he never engaged in the battle with his parent that might have enabled him to forge his own identity: 'He had been dead-beaten from boyhood.'[115] It would be very easy to think of Purcell Barrett as a ruthlessly acute analysis by Meredith of the character of his own son, except that *Emilia in England* was published in 1864, when Arthur was only 11.

---

[115] *Emilia in England*, chapter 55.

CHAPTER 7

Marie

THE CHALET

Meredith married Marie Vulliamy on September 20, 1864, at Mickleham Parish Church. The Reverend Augustus Jessopp, Arthur's headmaster, officiated, and Lionel Robinson was best man. Meredith was in raptures. 'I write with my beloved beside me,' he told Maxse, 'my thrice darling—of my body, my soul, my song.' He had until then 'never loved a woman and felt love grow in me'.[1] Bride and groom honeymooned in Hampshire. Maxse was away, travelling, and lent the newly married couple his country house, Ploverfield, with its 11-acre estate. Meredith's second marriage, J. B. Priestley writes, was 'destined to be as happy as the first was wretched'.[2] But marriages are rarely as simple as that.

Meredith chose for his second wife a woman as unlike his first as it is possible to imagine. His new wife was 24, 12 years younger than him, the daughter of Justin Vulliamy, a provincial French businessman, a hard-headed man in money matters and a man of strict and narrow principle. He was not at all like Thomas Love Peacock. It was an enthusiastically Protestant family. The eldest daughter held revivalist meetings for working men and women on Sunday evenings in a local barn. Before her marriage, to a clergyman, her younger sister supervised the Sunday school. Marie,

[1] *Letters*, 1, 279.
[2] Priestley, 31.

© The Author(s) 2019
R. Cronin, *George Meredith*,
https://doi.org/10.1007/978-3-030-32448-3_7

the youngest of the three, filled in for her on occasion.[3] Meredith had acted rather in the manner of Percy Dacier in *Diana of the Crossways*, who rebounds from Diana to Constance Asper, entranced by her difference, by her 'virgin mind and person'[4] and by her lack of interest in public affairs. Even Constance's boudoir is like a nun's cell.

Before he would give his consent to the marriage, Marie's father enquired minutely into Meredith's financial circumstances and into the circumstances of his separation from his first wife. His daughter, the woman Meredith hoped to marry, was wanting, Meredith admitted to Jessopp, in 'vitality', 'but' he added, 'the lack of it is partially compensated by so very much sweetness'.[5] The adverb is oddly scrupulous. After the marriage he made the same point more brutally: 'She is a mud fort! You fire broadsides into her, nothing happens.'[6] He and his first wife, Mary's daughter recalled, 'sharpened their wits on one another'. In Meredith's second marriage, the recreation was one-way. That may not have been a disappointment. The Earl of Fleetwood in *The Amazing Marriage* has a taste for the pleasures of 'intersexual strife and the indubitable victory' in that strife 'of the stronger, with the prospect of slavish charms, fawning submission, marrowy spoil'.[7] But Fleetwood's sadistic bent is not applauded. His friend, the writer Gower Woodseer, on the other hand, is portrayed sympathetically, and he marries an uneducated woman happy in the 'promise of life-long domestic enlivenment' that she offers him. He looks forward to teasing her mercilessly and contemplating 'a pretty face showing the sensitiveness to the sting, which is not allowed to poison her temper, and is short of fetching tears'.[8] Meredith's friend, H. M. Hyndman, the socialist cricketer, first met Meredith in 1860, when he was only 18, and kept up the friendship until Meredith's death. He got to know the second Mrs Meredith well. He was impatient with the habit that Meredith's friends fell into of 'speaking rather slightingly' of her, 'as if she were intellectually quite unworthy of her husband'. Meredith was 'not by any means an easy man to live with', and she was 'a charming, clever, tactful, and handsome Frenchwoman: a good musician, a most considerate, attentive

[3] Sencourt, 132–3.
[4] *Diana of the Crossways*, chapter 35.
[5] *Letters*, 1, 255.
[6] Sencourt, 186.
[7] *The Amazing Marriage*, chapter 35.
[8] *The Amazing Marriage*, chapter 40.

and patient wife and an excellent mother'.[9] One wonders how far the friends that Hyndman disapproved of were taking their cue from her husband. His first marriage, as Meredith reported the matter to Hardman, had been a marriage in which 'the man was eight years the junior, the woman very clever'. She 'dallied with responsibility, played with passions; rose suddenly to a height of exaltation, sank to a terrible level. And was very clever.'[10] The cleverness is mentioned twice as if it were the condition of all the other vagaries. It was not a quality that he looked for in his second wife. 'Marie knew the price of sheets and the price of towels,' Meredith's biographer, Robert Sencourt reports, 'and this Meredith felt to be most captivating in her.'[11] Like the Earl of Fleetwood in *The Amazing Marriage*, Meredith had dreamed as a boy that he might 'join hands with an Amazonian damsel and be out over the world for adventures, comrade and bride as one'.[12] But it was a dream that he had abandoned long before he married for the second time.

A year after the marriage, Marie gave her husband a second son, Will Maxse Meredith, and some years later, in 1871, their daughter, Mariette, was born. Copsham Cottage was too small for the newly married couple, and they moved to a house in Esher for six months before taking up residence in Kingston Lodge, Norbiton. Meredith did not much like Norbiton: 'no country around—brick, brick, brick; but a middling pretty little house and Marie likes it, so I submit'.[13] It was at least very close to Norbiton Hall, the house that his friend William Hardman, who would later become mayor of Kingston, had just bought for 8000 guineas. The Merediths had Kingston Lodge on a three-year lease. In 1867 they moved to Flint Cottage, the first house that Meredith had ever owned, and the house that he was to occupy for the rest of his life. On their marriage Justin Vulliamy had settled a modest income of £200 a year on his daughter. In 1870 his death brought a substantial addition to the family income. By then the family was comfortably off. But in 1884 Marie underwent an operation for cancer. There was a further operation early the following year, but that too was unsuccessful, and on September 17, 1885, she died. She had been unable to speak since May, and had suffered, but 'the end

---

[9] Hyndman, 77–8.
[10] *Letters*, 1, 262.
[11] Sencourt, 133.
[12] *The Amazing Marriage*, chapter 15.
[13] *Letters*, 1, 302.

was very quiet; in the arms of her sisters, at 10 minutes to six p. m.'[14] Meredith arrived home 40 minutes later. He had been in London, on his weekly visit to the offices of Chapman and Hall. Her hand, he reports, was still warm. Marie was buried in Dorking Cemetery. John Morley attended, to give Meredith his support.

Meredith commemorated his wife in two poems. The first, a cumbersome affair of more than 600 lines, 'A Faith on Trial', is set on May 1, 1885, when Marie was being nursed by her sisters at Eastbourne. Meredith takes his usual morning walk up Box Hill, weighed down by a private grief to which all of nature seems oblivious. The poem is loosely modelled on Browning's *La Saisiaz*. It insists that the proper response is not to flinch from the natural exuberance that Meredith sees all around him but to embrace it. Spiritual growth is only achieved by accepting nature's ordinances not by retreating into 'legends'. The same point is made more tellingly in the 24 lines of 'Change in Recurrence', a poem written soon after his wife's death. Meredith notes that the woodland creatures, the 'busy wild things' that his wife loved to watch as they went about their business in the garden, go about their business just as eagerly now that she is dead. No one is there to look at them now,

> But the blackbird hung pecking at will;
> The squirrel from cone hopped to cone;
> The thrush had a snail in his bill,
> And tap-tapped the shell hard on a stone. (21–4)

The tap-tap gives the assurance that nature's beat goes on, but the rhythm breaks just for a moment in that last line to register a catch in the speaker's throat. It is one of the very few moments in Meredith's verse that prompts a comparison with Hardy.[15]

It was a marriage of almost 20 years, far longer than the 8 years that Meredith's first marriage lasted, but what kind of marriage was it? It was happy enough, but from the first months of the marriage until Marie's last illness, it was a marriage of three people rather than of two. Mary had been dead for almost three years, but Meredith brought his first wife with him into his second marriage. He married Marie Vulliamy just after completing *Emilia in England*, and he had already made a start on the sequel *Vittoria*.

[14] *Letters*, 2, 784.
[15] Both poems were published in *A Reading of Earth* (1888).

But *Vittoria* went slowly. He was behind with Arthur's school fees, and he had the expenses of the honeymoon and of setting up house with his new wife. He broke off *Vittoria* to write *Rhoda Fleming*. It was to be a pot-boiler. He meant to write a one-volume novel, but in the end it stretched to three, and the most vivid character in it was Mrs Lovell, the widow of an army officer who had died young, and very clearly a portrait by Meredith of his first wife. Just before her final illness, Marie was helping her husband by making fair copies of the chapters of his new novel, *Diana of the Crossways*, which was a still more intimate product of his first marriage. Diana, its heroine, is a compound of Meredith himself and Mary Nicolls. The husband of Diana's best friend comes close to revealing as much when he describes Diana as 'man and woman in brains'.[16] 'I felt that she was in me as I wrote,' Meredith told an admirer of the novel.[17] Diana has Mary's wit, Mary's social confidence and, above all, Mary's recklessness, and she is also Meredith's portrait of himself as a young novelist. She is Meredith's David Copperfield, or Meredith's Pendennis, but she shadows Meredith's own career more closely. The novel that Diana cannot complete, *The Cantatrice*, is a story about a young woman 'modelled on a Prima Donna she had met',[18] just as *Emilia in England* and *Vittoria* have as their heroine an Italian contralto modelled on Emilia Macirone, the accomplished singer who was the daughter of Meredith's old landlady.

When Meredith honeymooned with Marie at Maxse's country house, Ploverfield, he wrote a poem, as honeymooning husbands often will. But the poem he wrote was 'Cleopatra', a poem inspired by an Egyptian coin bearing the queen's head. It concerns a woman who prompts the question, 'But was she lovely?' a woman who can inspire a fiercer devotion than men offer to a merely conventional beauty. 'She had her hag-like moments when she breathed/Bitterness', but despite that she had the power to sway the 'blood of men'. She may seem fickle, inconstant, but that is because 'She was divided and against herself'. She was 'an actress, not a hypocrite'. She is the most powerful female presence in all of Meredith's verse outside *Modern Love*. Meredith had written the poem to accompany Frederick Sandys's anodyne portrait of Cleopatra, an engraving of which appeared in the *Cornhill*. The poem owes more to the Egyptian coin that had probably been given to him by Janet Ross, who was living with her

[16] *Diana of the Crossways*, chapter 26.
[17] *Letters*, 3, 1578.
[18] *Diana of the Crossways*, chapter 23.

husband in Cairo but was on a visit to Britain when Meredith was married and attended his wedding. But the poem owes most of all to the memories of his first wife that were so vivid to Meredith even during his honeymoon with his second.[19]

Meredith was delighted when his second son was born on July 26, 1865, but three weeks later he joined Captain Maxse on his yacht for a trip to Cherbourg. Fathers had less to do with newborn babies then than now. The following year he wrote to Marie from town, just before starting for Fryston Hall in Yorkshire where Lord Houghton, Monckton Milnes, had invited him for Easter, signing himself 'your husband and lover'.[20] They had been married almost five years when he began a letter to Marie, who was away from home nursing her father, 'My dearest love, I kiss you.'[21] That autumn he wrote from Stuttgart where he had taken Arthur to enrol at the gymnasium, 'God bless you and give you to my arms very soon.'[22] But in 1877 Meredith commissioned a little wooden chalet to be built at the top of his steep garden. Once the chalet was built, he at last had a writing room of his own. Until then he had written in the bedroom. He was delighted with his new premises, which, he told Morley, were 'the prettiest to be found', with a view 'without a match in Surrey': 'The interior is full of light, which can be moderated, and while surrounded by firs, I look over the slope of our green hill to the ridges of Leith, round to Ranmore, and the half of Norbury.'[23] It was Meredith's den, a space rather like Captain Con's cabin in *Celt and Saxon*, the attic to which he retreats every night at 10.30 to smoke, drink and converse with his friends. The Captain is free until midnight, when his severe English wife sounds the bell that summons him back to her bed.[24] The cabin figures, a little effortfully, the nature of the union between Great Britain and its sister isle. The Captain's Irishness, like his country's, is tolerated if it confines itself to a space of which no household use can be made. But the domestic resonances seem more telling. Con's cabin is Meredith's chalet rehearsed in brogue. What it offers is a masculine space, a space free from feminine constraints. The cabin is the room in which Con's tongue is freed, just as the chalet was the room in which Meredith found that he could best exercise his creative gifts. But at

---

[19] It may be significant that Meredith chose never to publish the poem.
[20] *Letters*, 1, 332.
[21] *Letters*, 1, 384.
[22] *Letters*, 1, 399.
[23] *Letters*, 1, 537–8.
[24] *Celt and Saxon*, chapter 9.

midnight sharp, the bell rings and Captain Con goes back to his wife's bed. There were two rooms in Meredith's chalet. In one of them Meredith wrote. The other was a bedroom furnished with a dressing table and a hammock cot, a bed for one. Meredith was not yet 50 when the chalet was completed, and Marie was 37. 'I work and sleep up in my cottage at present,' he told Morley in April.[25] The month before there had been a more disturbing outburst in a letter to Maxse. 'I can't but admire Mrs. Besant for her courage,' he wrote. She had just published Charles Knowlton's *Companion for Young Married Couples* with its frank account of methods of birth control, but he added that to him the book was 'repulsive':

> I have a senseless shrinking from it. More horrible scenes of animal life can hardly be suggested. They effectually deprive me of appetite. The male—the female. Lord God!

He adds a postscript, 'By the way, I am in my Chalet: well worth a visit. The second room of it contains the hammock-cot: enviable the sleeper therein!'[26] The day after his wife's death, he gave the news to his friend Lady Lawrence. 'No longer', he wrote, 'will that melancholy light at her window speak sadly but still of life to my chalet.'[27] His wife had been bed-bound and unable to speak for some months, but Meredith seems to speak of a longer separation, as if he and his wife had for some years spent their nights separated by the length of their garden. Mariette was not yet six in 1877, but the building of the chalet marked the end, or at least the beginning of the end, of Meredith's sexual relationship with his wife.

It is, some will feel, none of our business. 'It would never occur to me', Henry James observed 'to want to know what goes on in their bedroom, in their bed, between a man and a woman.'[28] But Meredith would have differed. He agreed with John Morley who complains in his life of Rousseau that 'our fatuous persistency in reducing man to the spiritual, blinds the biographer to the circumstance that the history of a life is the

[25] *Letters*, 1, 539.
[26] *Letters*, 1, 537.
[27] *Letters*, 2, 784.
[28] *Letters of Henry James*, 3, 222. James was writing in French to his French friend, Paul Bourget, 'Jamais il me viendrait à l'esprit de vouloir savoir ce qui se passe dans leur chambre, dans leur lit, entre un monsieur et une femme.' I doubt whether he would have addressed the matter so directly in English.

history of a body no less than that of a soul'.[29] Meredith is anxious in his novels and in his greatest poem to give the history of his characters' bodies, and he knows that in order to do so he must study them in their bedrooms as well as in the other rooms of the house. In *Modern Love* he follows the estranged husband and wife into their bedroom and watches as they lie side by side in their marriage bed, the closeness of their bodies intensifying their estrangement. He did the same in the novel. Meredith is the only Victorian novelist to chart with precision the topography of a husband and wife's sleeping arrangements.

He published *One of Our Conquerors* in 1891. It was the first novel that he had written since Marie had died. Victor Radnor dearly loves Nataly, his partner of two decades, but when the daughter that both dote on reaches an age when rich heiresses are expected to choose a husband, the secret that father and mother have kept from her begins to cast a shadow on them. Victor Radnor had married early, when he was not quite 21, tempted by the wealth of Mrs Burman, a widow many years his senior, and his wife is still alive. Nataly had been Mrs Burman's companion. For two decades Victor and Nataly have been living, lovingly and entirely respectably, in sin. That is a secret that they have kept from all their friends and kept too from Nesta, their daughter. But it is a secret that begins to weigh on them ever more heavily, and as it does so it begins to come between them. It begins to inhibit their nuptial embraces. Side by side in bed, they are still conscious that 'the dividing spirit of Mrs. Burman lay' between them, 'cold as a corpse': 'They kissed coldly, pressed a hand, said good-night.'[30] Victor's sleep is disturbed by hopes that his daytime self repudiates, by vagrant daydreams that his sick and ageing wife will die, freeing him to marry again. As he lies in bed, he is conscious always of her accusing presence 'beneath a weight of darkness' as 'one heavily craped figure, distinguishable through the gloom, as a blot on a black pad'.[31] The blot constrains him in his lovemaking, and it constrains his wife too. Nataly begins to fear the 'caress' that 'would have melted her' and to feel thankful that she has a husband so sensitive to her moods that he withholds it. She becomes 'marble to sight and touch', so that when Victor embraces her he is left 'feeling her body as if it were in the awful grip of fingers from the

[29] *Rousseau*, 1, 277.
[30] *One of Our Conquerors*, chapter 18.
[31] *One of Our Conquerors*, chapter 19.

outside of life'.[32] Victor 'kissed her lips by day',[33] we are told, an expression that quietly intimates that he does not do so by night. The two begin to find reasons not to share a bed together. Nataly bids Victor goodnight and goes to her own room: 'I shall have a better chance of sleeping if I know I am not disturbing you.'[34] Or she sends him a note: 'Dearest, I go to bed early, am tired.' 'Come to me in the morning,' she adds, but the next morning she fails to respond to 'the tap of Victor's knuckle on her bedroom door'.[35] It is her daughter, Nesta, who takes her husband's place: 'Mother and daughter slept together that night, and their embrace was their world.'[36] But Nesta has not yet guessed the secret of her illegitimate birth, so that Nataly is left feeling daily 'more shut away from the man she loved' and still more sadly 'now shut away' too 'from her girl'.[37]

The charismatic Victor, shunned by the woman he loves and who loves him, becomes vulnerable to other women. In particular there is Lady Grace Halley. He squeezes her hand, and feels at once, even though 'he loved his Nataly truly, even fervently, after the twenty years of union', that 'a never so slightly lengthened compression of the hand female shoots within us both straight and far and round the corners'.[38] Meredith is the very first English novelist to explore the sexuality of lovers who have shared a bed for decades. It is one of his most striking achievements, and it had its origin surely in his own second marriage. His first wife, unlike Mrs Burman, was dead. He had no need to think of her in the way that Victor thinks of Mrs Burman, an old woman living out her life in curtained rooms, the one entertainment left her the habit of secreting herself in the back room of a pharmacist's from where she can spy on the customers.[39] But there was another sense, I suspect, in which Mary Peacock, Mary Nicolls or Mary Meredith (like Emilia or Sandra Belloni or Vittoria she had three names) was a ghostly presence that Meredith never succeeded in exorcising all through the 21 years of his second marriage.

[32] *One of Our Conquerors*, chapter 18.
[33] *One of Our Conquerors*, chapter 20.
[34] *One of Our Conquerors*, chapter 22.
[35] *One of Our Conquerors*, chapter 25.
[36] *One of Our Conquerors*, chapter 36.
[37] *One of Our Conquerors*, chapter 38.
[38] *One of Our Conquerors*, chapter 14.
[39] *One of Our Conquerors*, chapter 13.

THE PHILOGYNIST

The years of the second marriage were the years in which Meredith wrote seven of his novels, and the years in which he secured his reputation as, in Jacqueline Banerjee's words, 'one of the staunchest, most influential "male feminists" of the age'.[40] His early admirers celebrated him as the 'champion of women',[41] and they have been echoed by his most recent critics, Banerjee amongst them. It was a role that he chose quite deliberately. A deleted entry in one of the notebooks tries out titles for a book that remained unwritten, 'The Philogynist. (Champion of Woman) The Ladies' Friend'.[42] He had studied man just as deeply, he told Hugh Strong, the editor of the Newcastle *Daily Leader*, but he had studied women 'with more affection, a deeper interest in their development, being assured that women of the independent mind are needed for any sensible degree of progress'.[43] Morley memorably recalls showing Meredith a copy of John Stuart Mill's *The Subjection of Women* soon after it was published in 1869. Meredith 'fell to devouring it in settled silence, and could not be torn from it all day'.[44] It was an interest that Meredith had cultivated from the outset of his career. In 1905, looking back on his long life, he wrote, 'Since I began to reflect I have been oppressed by the injustice done to women, the constraint put upon their natural aptitudes and their faculties, generally much to the degradation of the race.'[45] In his first published story, *The Shaving of Shagpat*, when Shibli succeeds to the throne he introduces 'Laws for the protection and upholding of women',[46] and Meredith's last published novel, *The Amazing Marriage*, ends when the Earl of Fleetwood is forced to concede that the wife, whose love he has for so long rebuffed, has the right to live her life independently of him. Meredith thought of himself as a comic writer, and for him comedy, unlike tragedy, is a genre that needs to place men and women on a level with each other. In his *Essay on Comedy*, he argues that a 'state of marked social inequality of the sexes' is inimical to the comic spirit, which requires that women be

---

[40] Banerjee, 90.

[41] See Alice Woods, *George Meredith as Champion of Women and of Progressive Education*, first published in 1937.

[42] *Notebooks*, 89.

[43] *Letters*, 3, 1513.

[44] John Morley, *Recollections*, 2 vols (London: Macmillan, 1917), 1, 47.

[45] *Letters*, 3, 1513.

[46] *The Shaving of Shagpat*, 'Conclusion'.

allowed to occupy 'a station offering them free play for their wit'. Men and women, he insists in *Lord Ormont and His Aminta*, are 'equals, the stronger for being equals'.[47] Matthew Weyburn's ambition is to set up a school for both boys and girls because he knows that 'the chief object in life' is 'to teach men and women how to be one' and that the first step towards that goal is co-education. It is the most damaging consequence of the current educational system that the sexes remain 'foreigners' to one another.[48] There can be no 'advancement of the race', Meredith told a young woman who had written to him about his poem 'A Ballad of Fair Ladies in Revolt', 'till women walk freely with men'.[49]

Meredith is always alert to what he calls in *Lord Ormont and His Aminta* 'the terrible, aggregate social woman, of man's creation'.[50] He is deeply suspicious, for example, of the ideal of female innocence, detecting, as he puts it in *The Egoist*, 'an infinite grossness in the demand for purity infinite' that men impose upon women.[51] In *Rhoda Fleming* he locates only 'another side of pruriency' in 'those false sensations, peculiar to men, concerning the soiled purity of women'.[52] Sir Austin Feverel is a misogynist, but even he wonders whether women ought not to be allowed a sexual history, putting the question in his notebook, 'Wherefore are wild oats only of one gender?' In another entry he asks 'whether men might not be attaching too rigid an importance?', but venturing on such a thought frightens him and he leaves the question hanging. Meredith was bolder, at least in later life. In 1886 he advised the young Hilda de Longueuil, 'Some women as well as men require the sowing of wild oats in early life if they are to walk steady or trot zealously in harness.'[53] He understood too that equality between the sexes had to be established on economic as much as on ethical foundations. He advised a young admirer that women's independence 'must come of the exercise of their minds—the necessity for which is induced by their reliance on themselves for subsistence'.[54] Patrick O'Donnell puts it more snappily in *Celt and Saxon*. Women will only achieve equality when they 'earn their own pennies': it is

[47] *Lord Ormont and His Aminta*, chapter 16.
[48] *Lord Ormont and His Aminta*, chapter 24.
[49] *Letters*, 1, 521.
[50] *Lord Ormont and His Aminta*, chapter 15.
[51] *The Egoist*, chapter 11.
[52] *Rhoda Fleming*, chapter 30.
[53] *Letters* 2, 878–9.
[54] *Letters*, 2, 936.

'a tussle for money with them as with us, meaning power', and 'power is built on work'.[55] Hardy's Bathsheba Everdene complains, 'it is difficult for a woman to define her feelings in language which is chiefly made by men to express theirs.'[56] But Lord Ormont's formidable sister is still more forthright when she offers a spirited defence of Delilah, 'The Jews wrote the story of it, so there she stands for posterity to pelt her.' Matthew Weyburn understands her as offering 'a tolerably good analogy for the story of men and women generally'.[57] Meredith came to be a convinced suffragist. In 1876 he may have advised a young teacher that 'spreading instruction among women' would be far more productive than 'besieging Parliament',[58] but in 1889 he gently upbraided Julia Duckworth, Leslie Stephen's wife, for signing a letter in which a group of distinguished women protested against giving women the vote, and in a letter to *The Times* on November 1, 1906, after regretting the 'intemperateness' of the suffragettes' methods, he added, 'it is the very excellence of their case that inflames them.'[59] No male Victorian novelist has feminist credentials as strong as Meredith's, which makes it disquieting to call to mind that some of the most outspoken of Meredith's feminist fictions, *The Egoist* and *Diana of the Crossways* amongst them, were written in Meredith's chalet, a space to which his most intimate male friends, friends such as Morley, were admitted, but from which women were kept out, and it is still more disquieting to recall that they were written by a man whose first marriage to a woman of independent mind had failed, and who had chosen as his second wife a woman whose sweetness 'partially' compensated for her lack of vitality, a woman who captivated him not by her cleverness but by her knowledge of the price of sheets and towels.

Meredith's youngest child, the daughter that he named Marie after her mother and called Mariette, was his favourite of his three children. After his wife's death, he began looking for a governess for her. The successful candidate described her interview to Alice Brandreth: 'He talked to me for a long time, and skipped across the centuries for examples of female education, but really I don't know if he will engage me or not, and I am rather frightened at the many things he will not permit his daughter to do.'[60]

[55] *Celt and Saxon*, chapter 15.
[56] Thomas Hardy, *Far from the Madding Crowd*, chapter 51.
[57] *Lord Ormont and His Aminta*, chapter 16.
[58] *Letters*, 1, 569.
[59] *Letters*, 2, 964, and 3, 1576.
[60] Butcher, 72.

Mariette complained to Elizabeth Haldane that she was not even allowed to go into the garden without a chaperone.[61] It is hard to reconcile this Meredith with the man who shocked readers of the *Daily Mail* in 1904 by proposing that marriages should be contracts entered into only for a fixed term.[62] He suggested ten years, although Colney Durance in *One of Our Conquerors* goes further, proposing that 'marriages should be broken or renewed every seven years'.[63] It is just as hard to reconcile Mariette's father with the man who predicted two years earlier to the 26-year-old Lady Ulrica Duncombe that 'by and by' the world would 'smile on women who cut their own way out of a bad early marriage'. The 'present rough Marriage system', he advised Lady Ulrica, will persist 'until boys and girls are brought up and educated together'.[64] That was not how he brought up his own daughter, who grew up to become, according to the historian Sir John Pollock, 'the perfect embodiment of every man's imagination of the perfect Dresden China shepherdess'.[65] Meredith pauses in *Diana of the Crossways* to congratulate himself on daring to take as his central character a woman who was not a 'dolly-dolly' heroine, a woman who 'muses on actual life, and fatigues with the exercise of brains'. Such a heroine will seem to the conventional novel reader quite 'alien', a princess perhaps 'but a foreign one'. He takes pride in choosing a heroine so far from 'those ninny young women who realize the popular conception of the purely innocent'.[66] But it seems that he was determined to make his own daughter into exactly the kind of dolly-dolly woman that he refused as his heroine.

When Mariette was just turned 23, she married an American-born banker, a former Liberal MP, Henry Parkman Sturgis. He was a widower with four children, 24 years her senior, and he went on to have two more children with Mariette. Meredith reported the marriage rather simperingly to Hardman's wife. Sturgis is 'by the world's report and our experience of him, an excellent fellow, plainly devoted to Riette, young for his age'. His daughters 'take to her warmly'; the 'settlement he makes on her is generous'; his house, Givons Grove, is only 'about a mile and a half from

---

[61] Elizabeth S. Haldane, *From One Century to Another* (London: Alexander Maclehose, 1937), 164.

[62] *Daily Mail*, September 24, 1904, p. 5, under the headline 'The Marriage Handicap. Views of Our Greatest Novelist. Yen-Year Marriages: A Revolutionary Suggestion'.

[63] *One of Our Conquerors*, chapter 24.

[64] *Letters*, 3, 1438.

[65] Sir John Pollock, *Time's Chariot* (London: John Murray, 1950).

[66] *Diana of the Crossways*, chapter 39.

my cot' (Sturgis had a London house too in Carlton Terrace); and his family congratulate him 'on his alliance with G. M.' ('In America, it seems, they think I am somebody'.)[67] It sounds like a match more likely to excite a father in his 60s than a young woman in her early 20s, but Mariette showed, according to Meredith, a warm affection for her husband, 'astonishing her Dad'.[68] Mariette's marriage did not bring an end to Meredith's solicitude. In 1899 Mariette made an intervention in the Dreyfus case prompting an anguished letter from Meredith to his wealthy friend Mrs Walter Palmer (her husband was the Palmer of Huntley and Palmer biscuits): 'Pray use *at once*, either by wire or post, all your influence (mine counts for nought) with Riette to restrain her from further writings on the Dreyfus case.' He assures Mrs Palmer that the effort has 'already affected her health' and gives his recommendation that her husband should enforce his 'instant veto': 'she is not nervously constituted for such labours.'[69] Charlotte Perkins Gilman had published 'The Yellow Wallpaper' seven years before. Meredith manages to sound very like the husband in the story.

Not all novelists were so captivated by Mill's essay on the condition of women as Meredith. Anthony Trollope was no more 'a woman's-right man' than Charles Glascock, one of the most sympathetic characters in *He Knew He Was Right*. Women's rights are a pressing concern only for an intolerable American poet, Miss Wallachia Petrie, 'the republican Browning', and an equally intolerable American diplomat. The diplomat tells Mr Glascock, 'Your John S. Mill is a great man.' He is 'one of the few Europeans' able to see that 'women must at last be put upon an equality with men'. Mr Glascock responds serenely, admitting that despite Mill's high reputation, 'I don't read what he writes myself.'[70] The heroine of the novel is Dorothy Stanbury, who is quite capable of standing up to her forceful aunt and refusing the clergyman offered to her as her husband. But Dorothy refuses the clergyman not for a life of independence but because she has found another man 'whose nature was such that she could have leaned on him with a true worship, could have grown against him as against a wall with perfect confidence, could have lain with her head upon his bosom, and have felt that of all spots was the most fitting for her'.[71] Dorothy is the kind of woman that Trollope

[67] *Letters*, 3, 1162–3.
[68] *Letters*, 3, 1165.
[69] *Letters*, 3, 1337.
[70] Anthony Trollope, *He Knew He Was Right*, chapter 55.
[71] Anthony Trollope, *He Knew He Was Right*, chapter 52.

takes to his heart. *He Knew He Was Right* was published in 1869, but Trollope was 13 years older than Meredith. He belonged to a different, more old-fashioned generation. In the novel, Louis Trevelyan suspects, wrongly, that his wife has been unfaithful to him. He removes his young son from his mother's care and takes him to Italy. Meredith was the 'woman's-right man', but it was Trollope who more feelingly registers the horror of removing an infant son from his mother, and Trollope who was able to imagine how bereft that little boy must have felt. Trevelyan is not a thoughtless father. He buys his son toys, 'a regiment of Garibaldian soldiers, all with red shirts, and a drum to give the regiment martial spirit, and a battledore and a shuttlecock, and a soft fluffy Italian ball', but the toys remain unattended, and the child sits looking out of the window, frozen in a misery that he can neither understand nor articulate.[72]

Henry James was 15 years younger than Meredith, but no more of a woman's rights man than Trollope. As T. S. Eliot pointed out, he had a mind so fine that no idea could violate it, and the notion of women's rights was one of the ideas that his mind successfully resisted. In *The Bostonians* he regards Basil Ransom sympathetically, and Ransom is as susceptible to the charm of Verena Tarrant, the evangelical feminist lecturer, as he is dismissive of her views, which are to be accounted for, he feels, by the defects of her upbringing: she 'had grown up among lady-editors of newspapers advocating new religions, and people who disapproved of the marriage-tie'.[73] Basil wins his contest with Olive Chancellor for the possession of Verena—he has a masculine ruthlessness with which Olive cannot contend—and the reader applauds his victory, until it emerges that he is not Verena's corrective but her counterpart. He is in the grip of a fear that his 'whole generation is womanised; the masculine tone is passing out of the world'. His is, he believes, 'a feminine, a nervous, hysterical, chattering, canting age'. He has embarked on a mission to save his sex from 'the most damnable feminisation!'[74] The novel ends with Verena and Basil married and Verena in tears. It is to be feared, James remarks, that 'these were not the last she was destined to shed'. And that is how the novel ends. It is an ending that makes it easy to understand why it should be James rather than Meredith who was the great male novelist of women in the late nineteenth century.

[72] Anthony Trollope, *He Knew He Was Right*, chapter 84.
[73] Henry James, *The Bostonians*, chapter 11.
[74] Henry James, *The Bostonians*, chapter 34.

Unlike James and Trollope, Meredith and the two novelists he thought of as in some sense his protégés, Thomas Hardy and George Gissing, were overtly feminist novelists, but they were, all three, unlikely feminists. Meredith was, according to Hyndman, 'not by any means an easy man to live with'. The same might certainly be said of Hardy and of Gissing. Hardy was alienated from his first wife for the last 20 years of her life. He married Florence Dugdale, who had been his companion for a number of years, 15 months after her death, only to find that the shock of Emma Hardy's death had made him fall in love with her all over again. Gissing married twice, on each occasion choosing as his partner an uneducated woman of disreputable habits, prompting Henry James to ask, 'Why will he do these things?'[75] The rancour that Gissing felt when his wives persisted throughout their married lives in remaining exactly the women they were when he married them seems scarcely reasonable. He shares his own experience of marriage with many of his characters. The husband must think himself lucky, Harvey Rolfe reflects in *The Whirlpool*, 'who finds it *just* possible to endure the contiguity of his wife'.[76] Gissing arrived at a respectable domestic life only when he and Gabrielle Fleury, an educated Frenchwoman, agreed to live together unmarried. Meredith, Hardy and Gissing all knew the male urge to dominance from the inside. Even one of Gissing's women characters, Sibyl Vane in *The Whirlpool*, is inclined to the view that husbands who do not have 'the courage to beat their wives' condemn themselves to a marital misery for which they deserve no pity.[77] In this, Sibyl Vane is in agreement with Meredith's Sir Austin Feverel who holds that woman 'worships strength, whether of the physique or of the intellect, and likes to feel it'.[78]

Catherine Horne suggests that Meredith did not baulk at beating his first wife, but it was his verbal violence that those close to him had most to fear. It was not directed any more readily at women than at men. It was a merciless public humiliation of his second son not his second wife that prompted his admirer, Richard Le Gallienne, to comment that Meredith had a 'cruel tongue'.[79] Meredith's life was punctuated by violent quarrels, with Swinburne in the house in Cheyne Walk that they shared for some

---

[75] Edel, p. 534.
[76] George Gissing, *The Whirlpool*, Part the Third, chapter 1.
[77] George Gissing, *The Whirlpool*, Part the Second, chapter 11.
[78] *The Ordeal of Richard Feverel*, chapter 1, first edition.
[79] Le Gallienne, 51.

months in 1862 and 1863, with the journalist George Sala when both men were covering the Italian war in 1864. Most seriously, in 1871, Meredith quarrelled with John Morley, one of his closest friends. Morley wrote explaining his resentment of the manner in which Meredith spoke to him and the two men broke off all contact for three years. With his friends Meredith indulged in the kind of boisterous chaffing that might easily be resented, as when the unfortunate Will Meredith fell under his notice at the dinner table: 'Behold the Sagamore! mark that lofty brow! Stand in awe with me before the wisdom that sits there enthroned.' Meredith, as his friend Edward Clodd acknowledged, was 'a born tease': 'not even the discomfort of his victim could check it.'[80]

It was a manner that he adopted towards women too. Wisely, Marie chose not to respond to it, preferring to remain 'a mud fort'. She became used to it no doubt. It would have been more taxing for the American novelist, Amélie Rives, when she found herself Meredith's fellow guest at a dinner party. She had enjoyed a huge success in 1889 with her novel *The Quick or the Dead?*,[81] and Meredith chose to entertain her by developing the view that scarcely any woman had succeeded in writing 'a first-rate novel'. Jane Austen, Charlotte Brontë and George Eliot were adduced, but 'he kept to his opinion'.[82] It was as if Meredith from time to time forgot his role as 'Champion of Woman', and assumed the character of Sir Austin Feverel in his first novel. The vagaries of his wife's conduct have disillusioned Sir Austin with the whole sex. He has become a principled misogynist for whom women 'rank as creatures still doing service to the Serpent: bound to their instincts, and happily subordinate in public affairs, though but too powerful in their own walk'. Surprisingly, Sir Austin finds that a rather large group of women find his views endearing.[83] Did Meredith imagine that Amélie Rives would be charmed when he chose to entertain her with a disquisition on the inferiority of women novelists?

[80] *Fortnightly Review* 86 (July 1909), 19–31, 29.
[81] Amélie Rives, *The Quick or the Dead?* (Philadelphia: Lippincott, 1888). If he read the novel, Meredith would not have enjoyed it. It questions the propriety for a woman of a second marriage and decides against when the heroine refuses to marry the cousin of her dead husband. Oddly, the novel carries an unusually high erotic charge. It must have been this, especially piquant in the work of a woman author, rather than the effortful natural description that ensured the novel's popularity.
[82] Constance Lady Battersea, *Reminiscences* (London: Macmillan, 1923), 388–9.
[83] *The Ordeal of Richard Feverel*, chapter 1, first edition.

Meredith was encouraging to women writers on occasion. He recommended Olive Schreiner's *The Story of an African Farm* for publication
despite his anxiety about its lack of narrative momentum, and he gave the
author the rare privilege of a personal interview, an honour also granted to
Hardy and Gissing. But in 1893 Meredith rejected the manuscript of Sarah
Grand's *Heavenly Twins* out of hand. The novel was a great success when
it was published by Heinemann later that year. It was one of Meredith's
mistakes, like his rejection of *East Lynne*, if less colossal, but it had very
different motives. He pointed out Sarah Grand's weakness at 'driving a
story' with a severity that few can avoid when detecting an incapacity that
they shrewdly suspect in themselves. Meredith allows the novel 'a glimpse
of humour here and there' that 'promises well for the future', but is otherwise blind to its extraordinary and obvious merits.[84] How could he have
failed, to give just one example, not to be struck by the minor character
who returns to his room, takes off his 'clerical coat and waistcoat, and puts
on a coloured smoking jacket, which had the curious effect of transforming
him from an ascetic looking High Churchman into what, from his refined,
intellectual, clean-shaven face, and rather long straight hair, most people
would have mistaken for an actor suffering from overwork'.[85] The two
writers later became friends, but the rejection must have been particularly
galling for Sarah Grand because she is a novelist so clearly indebted to
Meredith. The impresario who wants to put her tenor on the stage appears
only briefly, but Meredith must surely have recognised him as a German
relative of his own Mr Pericles, the patron of the soprano in *Emilia in
England*, and *Vittoria*: 'Oh, have I found you? What a *Lohengrin*! Ach
Gott! it is the prince himself.'[86] Angelica, who escapes at night dressed as
her twin brother, owes something to Meredith's dissolute Mrs Mount who
is in the habit of masquerading in the character of Sir Julius, although
Sarah Grand's character is far more wholesome. But the real debt to
Meredith is not to be found in her characters. It was Meredith who had
given Sarah Grand the confidence to reintroduce romance into the novel,
so that *Heavenly Twins* can seem to anticipate the Virginia Woolf of
Orlando, or an even later novelist. The heavenly twins themselves, Angelica

[84] For a full discussion of Meredith's rejection of the novel, see the introduction to *Sex,
Social Purity and Sarah Grand*, ed. Ann Heilmann and Stephanie Forward (London:
Routledge, 2000).
[85] Sarah Grand, *Heavenly Twins*, Book 2, chapter 3.
[86] Sarah Grand, *Heavenly Twins*, Book 4, chapter 12.

and Diabolo, might have been invented by Angela Carter. Meredith saves his wittiest hit for Sarah Grand's Evadne, who would be enough, he claims, to 'kill a better work with her heaviness', but it is Evadne who most clearly articulates Sarah Grand's themes. The minor theme of the novel is that the sexual double standards of the nineteenth century will persist so long as women agree to forgive in the men that they marry sexual histories that would never be condoned in a bride. Again it is a Meredithian thought. It is Meredith's Lady Blandish in *The Ordeal of Richard Feverel* who thinks to herself, 'if men could give their hands to women unsoiled—how different would many a marriage be!'[87] When Evadne discovers the disreputable history of her first husband, the surprisingly and rather admirably tractable Colonel George Colquhoun, she insists that their marriage remain sexless. Grand's major theme is that the very best women will continue to live unhappily unless they are allowed to take up the public work, especially the work on behalf of their own sex, that needs to be undertaken. If women are obliged to spend their days, like Evadne, sitting at the window, sewing, they will run mad. Meredith should at least have been alert to the implications of that position for the novelist. The novel was still at the end of the nineteenth century the literary form that women had most successfully colonised. Not to allow Grand to use the novel to express her ideas would leave her sitting like Evadne, on display, but on display pursuing an activity that is only recreational, an activity like sewing. Meredith was a champion of women, but, as his response to Sarah Grand's manuscript indicates, a champion who was likely at any moment to reverse his character and become their taunting antagonist.

Maxse outdid Meredith in his admiration for John Stuart Mill. In 1870 he described Mill as 'the greatest thinker of the age', and his failure to be elected for Westminster 'a national disgrace'. But four years later, Maxse published another pamphlet, 'Reasons for Opposing Woman Suffrage', in which he explained that Mill was in this matter mistaken. He had been misled because 'he formed his idea of women generally' from his knowledge of his wife, and Harriet Taylor had given him a false idea of women's capacities. Maxse prophesies rather wildly that the extension of the suffrage to women would result in civil war, but his real objection is that women are inherently conservative. If women were allowed to vote, the

[87] *The Ordeal of Richard Feverel*, chapter 13.

effect would be to entrench the Tories in power.[88] It seems not to occur to him that Mill could not change his mind on this matter without abandoning the whole of the political philosophy that Maxse professes so much to admire, and it does not occur to him because Maxse never brings to his own political views the test of consistency. Meredith often disagreed with Maxse, but Maxse, the model for Nevil Beauchamp in *Beauchamp's Career*, was for many years his closest friend. He was the friend in whom Meredith found it easiest to recognise another self, and the extreme unpredictability of Maxse's opinions was one of the things that bound the two men together.

For many of these years, Meredith divided his affections between Maxse and William Hardman. He placed himself rather in the position of Cecilia Halkett, the 16-year-old heiress in *Beauchamp's Career*, who swithers between Beauchamp and Blackburn Tuckham, the characters modelled on Maxse and Hardman. Beauchamp like Maxse is a fiercely patriotic radical and Tuckham like Hardman is a Tory. It is usually represented as an oddity that the two newspapers that Meredith, who liked to think of himself as radical, wrote for most often, the *Ipswich Journal* and the *Pall Mall Gazette*, should both have been solidly conservative, but it might be better thought of as a proper expression of Meredith's mobile personality. He was after all a radical who during the American Civil War was an outspoken supporter of the Confederacy. He was even inconsistent about the journalistic profession itself. For eight years, beginning in 1860, he wrote two pieces every week for the *Ipswich Journal*, one of them a leading article. The one thing to be said in favour of Richard Rockney, the journalist in *Celt and Saxon*, is that he did away in his journalistic prose with 'the Biscay billow of the leading article'.[89] Meredith reserves a special contempt for leader writers. 'I feel such a spout of platitudes that I could out with a Leading Article,' says Dartrey Fenellan in *One of Our Conquerors*.[90] When Victor Radnor awakens from a dream in which he almost remembers the idea that occurred to him when he had his fall on London Bridge, he retains only a sense of how shrunken it seemed, 'like a paragraph in a newspaper, upon which a Leading Article sits, dutifully arousing the fat worm of sarcastic humour under the ribs of cradled citizens'. Meredith

---

[88] See Captain Maxse R. N., *Our Political Duty* (London: W. Ridgway, 1870), and *Objections to Women's Suffrage* (London: W. Ridgway, 1874).

[89] *Celt and Saxon*, chapter 16.

[90] *One of Our Conquerors*, chapter 7.

wrote leading articles for the money, of course. As a journalist he was a hack, and hacks are prone to self-contempt. But it was not just that. For Meredith it was not so much a predicament as the condition of his whole existence to be divided against himself.

It was a trait that he lent to his characters. In the first novel, Sir Austin Feverel uses his family crest rather than his name to sign his book, 'a griffin between two wheatsheaves'. Some of his women readers take the crest to signify that the author is hermaphroditic, 'a double-animal, and could do without them'.[91] But Sir Austin is remarkable throughout for his double-ness. He has a hard exterior that he has cultivated to protect his inner softness. It is, as Mrs Berry notes, a temperamental hermaphroditism: 'He keeps his face and makes ye think you're dealin' with a man of iron, and all the while there's a woman underneath.'[92] One chapter of *Emilia in England* is entitled 'Of the Double-Man in us'.[93] The chapter focuses on Wilfred Pole, the novel's representative double man. The philosopher values 'oneness of feeling which is the truthful impulse', but the novelist is different. He finds his truth in doubleness. He is more like Luigi, the spy in *Vittoria*, who insists that although he is a spy he is honest, because in becoming a spy he has remained true to his natural duplicity. A man who cannot 'deal double' is 'imperfectly designed':

> Here are two eyes. Were they meant to see nothing but one side! Here is a tongue with a line down the middle almost to the tip of it—which is for service.

He has two arms, two hands, but, Luigi insists, he has only one heart.[94] Meredith would have known better. The heart has its left side and its right. Harry Richmond, torn between Janet Rivers and Ottilia, the German princess, feels 'divided by an electrical shot into two halves'.[95] The first chapter of *The Adventures of Harry Richmond* is entitled 'I Am a Subject of Contention', but more important than the contention over Harry in which his father and grandfather engage is the contention that is waged within Harry himself. Nevil Beauchamp's problem is that 'he was trying to be two men at once'. His is 'a composite structure like the kingdom of

---

[91] *The Ordeal of Richard Feverel*, chapter 1, first edition.
[92] *The Ordeal of Richard Feverel*, chapter 38.
[93] *Emilia in England*, chapter 30.
[94] *Vittoria*, chapter 5.
[95] *The Adventures of Harry Richmond*, chapter 50.

Great Britain and Manchester'. He walks through the world 'in the complete form proper to his budding age, that is in two halves'. In *The Tragic Comedians* Sigismund Alvan is a house of many chambers but a house that is pulled down because the 'two men' who inhabit it cannot be reconciled.[96] After the failure of 'The Cantatrice', Diana begins a novel with the working title 'The Man of Two Minds', and as she develops the idea, she begins to think of herself as 'the woman likewise divided'. She is, she decides, 'the Woman of Two Natures'.[97] It is her predicament, but it is also a predicament without which she could never have become a novelist, because novels, at least in the later nineteenth century, are written out of the divisions within their authors. As Diana recognises, to be a novelist means 'living the double life of the author'.[98] Meredith sometimes speaks as if it is the young, and more specifically young men, who are divided against themselves. In *Emilia in England* the 'period of our duality' is the time of 'opening manhood'. Every young man sets out as a 'double-man', but in the course of time, circumstance will fuse the two men composing us into one 'who is commonly a person of some strength'.[99] It is out of the 'conflict of sensations' within him, we are told in *The Adventures of Harry Richmond* that a young man 'becomes gradually enriched and strengthened, and himself shaped for capable manhood'.[100] Then, to borrow the terms that Meredith uses in 'The Woods of Westermain', blood, brain and spirit will be fused. But in Meredith's writings, and, the evidence suggests, in Meredith himself, blood, brain and spirit remained perpetually at odds.

All through his career, Meredith mocked the need to idealise women evident in young men such as Wilfred Pole in *Emilia in England*: 'Nothing was too white, too saintly, or too misty, for his conception of abstract woman.' In his novels he set himself conscientiously to re-attach women to their bodies. He allows them, for example, a sexual history. Rose Jocelyn makes a great deal of not allowing a young man to kiss her (kissing carries a metonymic weight in the novels of the later nineteenth century) until she is sure that he is the young man that she will marry, but in the end she kisses Ferdinand Laxley, goes on to marry Evan Harrington and seems none the worse for it. A scene in *The Egoist* makes the point more intimately.

[96] *The Tragic Comedians*, chapter 19.
[97] *Diana of the Crossways*, chapter 38.
[98] *Diana of the Crossways*, chapter 15.
[99] *Emilia in England*, chapter 30.
[100] *The Adventures of Harry Richmond*, chapter 50.

Vernon Whitford finds Clara Middleton soaking wet at the railway station
and takes her to the station inn to dry her clothes. He insists that she take
a glass of brandy and water, a daringly earthy drink for the heroine of a
novel, and then she and Vernon share the glass. When she hands it to him,
she notices that he turns it in his hand unthinkingly before putting it to his
lips. It makes her 'shrink and redden'.[101] But Meredith was just as horrified
by Zola and the French naturalists as Wilfred Pole would have been.
Reading a novel by Catulle Mendès gave him the sensation of 'passing
down the *ventre de Paris* and out at anus, into the rat-rioting sewers,
twisted, whirled, tumbled amid the frothing filth, the deadly stench, the
reek and roar of the damned'.[102] Meredith liked to think of himself as
steering a middle course between French obscenity and English idealism,
but the prose suggests that his responses were a good deal more erratic,
more insecure. Insecurities may be the things that make us human, but
they can also make us cruel. Meredith knew and liked Oscar Wilde, but
when Frank Harris asked him to sign a petition calling for Wilde's early
release from prison, Meredith refused: 'Abnormal sensuality in a leader of
men, he said was a crime, and should be punished with severity.' He
insisted that 'immorality and, a fortiori, abnormal immorality was a proof
of degeneracy'. He became 'emphatic, loud, rhetorical'.[103] It was not his
finest moment.

Meredith might have been happier had he succeeded in fusing blood,
brain and spirit, but he would have been left with nothing to write
about. He liked to give the impression that he had outgrown his youthful self, more particularly that he had drowned it in a burst of volcanic
laughter. Laughter in Meredith, even in his very first story, *The Shaving
of Shagpat*, is what frees a man from himself (women, as Meredith
observes in *The Egoist*, are still forbidden 'the gift of humorous fancy'[104]), and almost all those who have left a record of Meredith bear
witness to the explosive quality of his laughter. It is one of the things
that distinguishes Meredith from Sir Willoughby Patterne, who laughs
'with a mouth that would not widen'.[105] But Meredith's laughter was
so uninhibited, his head thrown back at such an angle, his eyes so

[101] *The Egoist*, chapter 27.
[102] *Letters*, 2, 889.
[103] Frank Harris, *Contemporary Portraits* (New York: Mitchell Kennerley, 1915), 205.
[104] *The Egoist*, chapter 9.
[105] *The Egoist*, chapter 3.

streaming with tears, that one suspects that laughter may have been one more manifestation of the mask he wore so habitually rather than a sign that he had removed it. As he remarks in *Rhoda Fleming*, 'perfect candour can do more for us than a dark disguise'.[106]

Meredith is a peculiar, perhaps a unique, instance of a man who contrived to become a celebrated novelist despite an unusual inability to pay much attention to the world outside him. Henry James asked Edith Wharton to consider how little of the 'baggage of the authentic novelist' was in Meredith's possession. The absence from the novels of all the 'prosaic details' that the reader had a right to expect was so complete that one was often at a loss to determine 'in what country and what century they were situated'. The novels left him 'always at a loss to know where he was, or what causes led to which events, or even to discover by what form of conveyance the elusive characters he was struggling to identify moved from one point of the globe to another'.[107] In *The Bostonians* James introduces a Miss Birdseye who 'had only a bare, vulgar room, with a hideous flowered carpet (it looked like a dentist's)'.[108] Miss Birdseye is only a minor character, but her carpet is more palpable than any item of furniture in any of Meredith's novels, and it is through the carpet that the reader is made to feel all the meagreness of Miss Birdseye's life. In most novelists Meredith's would be a damning deficiency. But the novels retain their value for all that, because Meredith, despite his failure to attend to the world outside him, was a close observer of the world within. On first reading, *The Tragic Comedians* disappoints. It has little of interest to say about Ferdinand Lassalle, or about French politics in the 1860s, not to speak of French social relations and French furniture, with all of which Meredith was entirely familiar. But six years after its publication, Meredith offered an unintended tutorial in how best to read it when he embarked on his relationship with Hilda de Longueil, and acted out in his own person the tragi-comedy of the infatuation of an ageing man of genius with a young woman many years his junior, whom he dimly suspects, despite his feelings for her, to be entirely banal.

Meredith could write novels without compromising his egotism only because he was a divided man. He did not have to look outside himself to find a whole cast of characters. In his first novel, for example, he appears

---

[106] *Rhoda Fleming*, chapter 6.
[107] Wharton, 232–3.
[108] Henry James, *The Bostonians*, chapter 20.

as Sir Austin Feverel, betrayed by his wife with his friend, and as his son, Richard. He is Richard in the romance of Richard's youth and still more when Richard so abruptly and so properly cuts loose from the father who is devoted to him. He appears as Adrian Harley, the Wise Youth, who looks on life simply as material for his epigrams, as a farcical comedy put on for his cool amusement, and he appears too as his cousin, Austin Wentworth, who shares Meredith's moral values and republican sentiments. Even Hippias Feverel, uncle to Adrian and Austin, who, like Meredith, had the misfortune of having both 'strong appetites and a weak stomach',[109] is a self-portrait of a kind. But it was not enough for Meredith to be a divided man. He would not have written as he did had he not been a man divided against himself, had he not been, like Sir Willoughby Patterne, the 'Laocoon of his own serpents'.[110]

He was a champion of women who recognised in himself the disposition he gives Nevil Beauchamp, who found it impossible 'to think that women thought'.[111] He could find a place for Caroline Norton in a novel, he claimed, only by endowing her with brains.[112] Still more alarmingly, he knew that women fed in him an urge to dominate, holding out to him 'the prospect of slavish charms, fawning submission, marrowy spoil'.[113] Without that particular instance of self-division, the novels, already without a gripping story, would have been left without a plot. Meredith made his novels out of his quarrel with himself. He read other people's novels in much the same way. He was provoked to decline Sarah Grand's *Heavenly Twins*, I suspect, precisely because he recognised how Meredithian a novel it was. He refused Samuel Butler's *Erewhon* too, incited to disapproval by a novel which so closely echoed his own religious beliefs. The Erewhonians pretend to worship an air-god but reserve their true devotion for ydgrun. Their true religion is Grundyism. He rejected Shaw's *Cashel Byron's Profession*. A novel in which a cultivated woman with an income of £40,000 a year chose to marry a prizefighter struck as self-evidently preposterous a reader who had allowed Rose Jocelyn of Beckley Court to marry Evan Harrington, a tailor. *Cashel Byron's Profession* had the additional disadvantage that it dealt so largely with the brutalities of the ring, material that

[109] *The Ordeal of Richard Feverel*, chapter 1.
[110] *The Egoist*, chapter 39.
[111] *Beauchamp's Career*, chapter 27.
[112] *Letters*, 2, 371.
[113] *The Amazing Marriage*, chapter 35.

Meredith already knew would figure largely in *The Amazing Marriage*. Some of Meredith's most surprising decisions as a publisher's reader are best explained by the irritation he felt with his own novels. His fiercest quarrels were almost always quarrels with himself. 'I do not think Mr. Meredith liked the company of very rich people,' Alice Brandreth remarks. He puzzled her (she was quite rich herself) by observing that 'the vision of rich people was limited to their personal possessions, and that their mental horizon was bounded by their own park gates'.[114] But he made his way into those park gates in almost every novel he ever wrote, and he did just the same in life, regularly accepting the invitations of his rich friends such as Monckton Milnes or Mrs Walter Palmer of Huntley and Palmer biscuits. Like Luigi in *Vittoria*, Meredith could only be himself by dealing double. The prose he admired was prose the least like his own, 'pure sweet Thackerayan English'.[115] But Meredith's novels could not be written in prose like that, only in Meredithian prose, in the prose that still makes his novels all but impossible for so many to read, because that prose is the perfect vehicle for a writer who was so deeply uncomfortable with himself.

Why it should have been so is plain enough to see. It had its origins in shame, shame at his humble origins as the son of a tailor and shame that his first wife should have left him for another man. Those things would in themselves have put a strain on Meredith sufficient to leave a mark on his prose, but the prose was further contorted by Meredith's need at once to confess his shame and to conceal it. When Meredith married for the second time, he was 36, an age by which we have almost all of us become the people we are going to be, for better or for worse, for the rest of our lives. Meredith remained the man he was, the man that those early experiences of his had made him. In *Farina*, Meredith's second tale, published in 1857, the German students who admire the beauty of Margarita Groschen, the White Rose of Germany, form the White Rose Club, a band of young men who take it as their task to protect Margarita's honour, and in 1895 in Meredith's very last novel, *The Amazing Marriage*, he recycles the same episode. Twenty-four Welsh squires form themselves into a company for the protection of the Earl of Fleetwood's wife on her progress from Wales into Kent. He was the same man when he wrote his second story and when he wrote his last.

---

[114] Butcher, 7.
[115] Nicoll, 15.

By 1864, when he married again, Meredith already had the materials out of which he continued to make his fiction for the rest of his life. He made his novels out of his own experiences as a son, as a husband and as a father. These were the experiences that formed him, or deformed him as some might say. In *L'Homme qui rit* Hugo mulls over the Chinese habit of manufacturing monsters by placing a child of two or three in a porcelain vase that has no top or bottom. The child stays there for many years until at last the vase is broken and the child emerges shaped exactly like the vase, 'ayant la forme d'un pot'.[116] As Hugo knew very well, the Chinese practice is universal. That is how we are all brought up, except that the porcelain vases in which we are enclosed are metaphorical. In the nineteenth century at least people began to think as much. In *Notre-Dame de Paris* it is Quasimodo that every reader recognises as his brother, because Quasimodo, whose body is like one of the gargoyles that adorn the church he loves, reminds us that we are all of us deformed by the circumstances life has allotted us. In *L'Homme qui rit* our representative is Gwynplaine, still more monstrous than Quasimodo, his face carved into a permanent rictus to equip him for a professional future in a raree show. We all of us resemble, as Hugo reminds us, those captives who are malformed because they have been imprisoned beneath the leads of the Doge's palace in cells too low to allow them to stand up, too narrow to allow them to lie down.[117]

Over the years Meredith's deformities became more and more visible. As he grew older and his prose became more and more eccentrically idiosyncratic, the social mask that he chose to assume in company became ever more fixed and exaggerated. When H. M. Hyndman first met him in 1860, he seemed to Hyndman, when he was at his best, 'quite at home with the men around him', his conversation 'without effort or artifice', but afterwards, even 'in the bosom of his own family', his talk seemed as 'artificial, not to say stilted' as his prose: 'you could hear the clank of the machinery all the time.'[118] Henry James found that there was no coming into contact with the man, only with the 'impenetrable shining scales' that he had evolved as a defensive armour.[119] In his conversation he no longer reached out to other people. In 1894 he struck W. S. Blunt as 'a queer voluble creature, with a play-acting voice, and his conversation like one

[116] Victor Hugo, *L'Homme qui rit*, Book 1, chapter 4.
[117] Victor Hugo, *Notre-Dame de Paris*, Book 4, chapter 3.
[118] Hyndman, 70–1.
[119] Letters, June 1893.

dictating to a secretary, a constant search for epigrams'.[120] His talk was no longer a way of communicating. It had become a system of self-defence. In my last chapter, I will focus on the aspect of the novels that most fully expresses Meredith's difficult, rebarbative, compelling personality, the aspect of the novels that makes them for so many readers as unreadable as they are for John Sutherland. All the most significant novelists of the later nineteenth century are stylists, but in the case of Meredith, it is most emphatically true that the style is the man. Meredith was an odd man, and his oddities are nowhere more visible than in the oddities of his prose.

[120]W. S. Blunt, *My Diaries: Being a Personal Narrative of Events 1888–1914*, 2 vols (London: Martin Secker, 1919–20), 1, 143.

CHAPTER 8

Meredith and the Meredithian

BECOMING AN ADJECTIVE

For four years, between 1905 and 1909, Henry James busied himself pre-paring the New York edition of *The Novels and Tales of Henry James*, an edition that would collect in 23 volumes all of the fiction that he wished to be remembered by. James furnished the edition with 18 prefaces in which he outlined the art of the novel as he understood it, and before reis-suing the novels, he revised them once again, some, such as *The Portrait of a Lady*, extensively. James was already a celebrated novelist, but in the New York edition, he recreated himself as a Jamesian novelist. In *The American* Christopher Newman had been 'clean shaved' 'save for a rather abundant moustache'. In the New York edition 'save for the abundant droop of his moustache he spoke, as to cheek and chin, of the joy of the matutinal steel'.[1] It is as if James were coming forward as his own most accomplished parodist. Meredith, like James, like Hugh Dencombe in James's story 'The Middle Years', was 'a passionate corrector, a fingerer of style'. He published his first novel, *The Ordeal of Richard Feverel*, in 1857. He revised it for the Tauchnitz edition of 1875, revised it again for the collected edition of his novels in 1885 and revised it yet again in 1896 for a new collected edition. By then, as he reported to Edward Clodd, people had begun to describe 'this or that as Meredithian': he had, even before

---

[1] Henry James, *The American*, chapter 1.

© The Author(s) 2019   245
R. Cronin, *George Meredith*,
https://doi.org/10.1007/978-3-030-32448-3_8

Henry James managed the feat, 'become an adjective'.[2] The word Meredithian was in common use from the 1890s. It referred to a prose style remarkable for its 'elaborate artificialities'. It referred to Meredith's 'manner', and it was a manner that, according to many commentators, 'had better be left alone'.[3]

In an essay for *The Yellow Book*, John M. Robertson suggests that it is a style characteristic of a number of nineteenth-century writers, of Browning and Swinburne in verse and Carlyle in prose.[4] But for Robertson its most flagrant exponent is George Meredith. All four stand convicted of a literary vice that Robertson calls 'preciosity', by which he means the habit of 'twisting the face of speech into every shape but those of beauty and repose'. It is a literary vice associated with 'egoism'. It is the expression in Meredith of his 'individual self-will, defiance of censure, persistence in eccentricity, and self-absorption in isolation'. Unhappy with the reception of his early work, he responded by cultivating a 'defiant idiosyncrasy' of manner. It was his way of registering his contempt for the judgements of the literary public and for the 'common speech' that it preferred. Robertson reports that he could only read Meredith's later novels by translating the prose into ordinary English. 'Instead of desperately construing endless paragraphs of gritty perversity', he trained himself to skip lightly over 'every mound in the path, content to follow the movement of a striking story behind a style that in itself has become a mere affliction'.

Swinburne claimed that he had read a first draft of *Emilia in England* written in 'pure sweet, Thackerayan English', but found, when the novel was published, that 'Meredith had translated it into his own peculiar language'.[5] It seems an improbable story. It is surely more likely that when Meredith had shown Swinburne the manuscript of the novel he had, like Robertson, successfully translated it in his imagination into the kind of English that seemed more appropriate to it. When he revised his novels for the New York edition, James made them more Jamesian, and as Meredith grew older, his prose became ever more emphatically Meredithian. But in the later nineteenth century, the process might operate in reverse: a writer might draft a book in a peculiar language and then successfully translate it into the common tongue. Meredith's friend, James Cotter Morison, had

[2] Clodd, 146.
[3] *The Athenaeum*, 3581, June 13, 1896, 777; *The Academy*, 1106, July 15, 1893, 48.
[4] John M. Robertson, 'Concerning Preciosity', *The Yellow Book*, 13 (1897), 79–106.
[5] Nicoll records Swinburne making the claim, 15.

such a success with his *Life and Times of St Bernard* in 1863 that Meredith ever afterwards addressed him as 'St. B.' The book's success owed much to Morison's limpid prose. The book is dedicated to Carlyle, which is entirely appropriate because St Bernard is for Morison the historical counterpart of Carlyle's fictional Abbot Samson in *Past and Present*, but in the first draft of the book, Carlyle had infected Morison's style. The whole book was written in 'Carlylese'. Morison succeeded in thoroughly disinfecting his prose before publication, and he undertook the revision, strange as it may seem, on the advice of George Meredith.[6]

Swinburne claimed that *Emilia in England* was first drafted in 'pure, sweet, Thackerayan English'. Morison's life of St Bernard might, had it not been for Meredith's intervention, have been presented to the world written in Carlylese. It is characteristic of late Victorian writers that they were unsure as to how they their books ought best to be written. The writers of the period had an uneasy relationship with their own styles. As Robertson recognises, the uncertainty came out of the increasingly fraught relationship between writers and their audience. In January 1895 when Henry James was beckoned onto the stage on the opening night of *Guy Domville*, his appearance, as James explained to his brother, instigated a contest of cheers and boos in which 'all the forces of civilization in the house waged a battle of the most gallant and sustained applause with the hoots and jeers and catcalls of the roughs, whose roars (like those of a cage of beasts at some infernal zoo) were only exacerbated by the conflict'.[7] In the theatre James came face to face with his audience. As a novelist he was spared such direct confrontations, but he knew, just as Hardy knew, that those who read novels just as much as those who attended theatres were very likely to 'say harsh heavy things—/Men with a wintry sneer, and women with tart disparagings'.[8] At such a time style had two functions: it was not just the means by which writers communicated with their readers, it might also function as the means by which writers chose to defend themselves against readers with whom they were out of all sympathy. The contest between the two impulses can be detected in much of the writing of the period, but it is nowhere waged so fiercely as in the Laocoönian contortions of George Meredith's prose style.

---

[6] Hardman, 249.
[7] *Henry James Letters*, 3, 508.
[8] 'Wessex Heights', 12.

One rather common effect that Meredith's style had on its readers was to foster a wish that he would get rid of it. Frank Burnand, the popular dramatist, sitting with Meredith on the beach at Seaford, idly throwing pebbles into the sea, was so charmed by Meredith's conversation that he exclaimed, 'Damn you, George, why won't you write as you talk?' Henry Hyndman was sitting with them. He 'understood well what Burnand meant'.[9] So did Meredith. He recycled the remark many years later in *Diana of the Crossways* when Diana is advised by a newspaperman, 'Write as you talk and it will do'.[10] But Meredith's reputation for conversational ease may itself have been a by-product of his tortuous prose style. The way he talked seemed the more beguiling because it was so different from the way he wrote, just as Swinburne's delusion that he had read an earlier draft of *Emilia in England* written in 'pure sweet, Thackerayan English' may itself have been produced by the convoluted prose of the published novel. The belief in the ease of Meredith's conversation was not shared by everyone. John Morley reports that Meredith 'missed ease' in his conversation as much as in his prose: 'Even into his best talks there came now and again a sense of strain.'[11] Unlike Frank Burnand, Richard Le Gallienne found that Meredith's 'talk was exactly like his books, elaborately fanciful yet knotted with thought, a thicket of thorn-bushes hung with sudden starry blossoms'.[12] When Katharine Bradley and Edith Cooper, the two women who wrote together under the name Michael Field, first visited Meredith at Flint Cottage, they remembered him greeting them with the extraordinary sentence: 'I must come forth to bid you welcome.'[13] J. C. Squire reports that another of Meredith's guests was asked before sitting down to lunch whether he would like to 'lave' his hands.[14] The closest Meredith ever came to introducing himself as a novelist into one of his books was in the character of Diana Warwick in *Diana of the Crossways*. An editor thinking to employ her as a journalist advises, 'write as you talk', but the renditions of Diana's conversation in the novel make it seem as artificial as Meredith's seemed to at least some of his friends.

[9] Hyndman, 71. Hyndman found that Meredith's conversation became artificial and affected as he grew older.

[10] *Diana of the Crossways*, chapter 18.

[11] John Morley, *Recollections*, 2 vols (London: Macmillan, 1917), 1, 40.

[12] Le Gallienne, 40.

[13] *Works and Days: From the Journal of Michael Field*, ed. T. and D. C. Sturge Moore (London: John Murray, 1933), 76.

[14] Squire, *Life and Letters*, 66.

Diana's closest friend is only persuaded after reading her private letters that 'she had the gift of writing'. Meredith points out that such sentiments are 'usual with those who receive exhilarating correspondence from makers of books'. The private letters make the prose of the novels seem painfully artificial by comparison. When she reads the novels, Emma Dunstane finds that she 'condemned the authoress' by comparison with the letter writer.[15] Meredith allows her at that moment to give voice to his own rueful understanding that his style was a thing that many of his readers, many even of the readers that he counted amongst his friends, regretted. They shared a feeling that his novels would have been the better if he had not bothered to put them into prose. Diana admits that she 'wrote laboriously'. When she writes she is tormented by the urge to 'prune, compress, overcharge'.[16] Diana is surely speaking here for Meredith, who was more inclined to overcharge his prose than any other novelist of the nineteenth century.

Meredith sometimes defended his own practices. He could complain bitterly of the British resistance to literary experimentalism. In *Beauchamp's Career* he denounces the activities of 'the self-appointed thongmen, who walk up and down our ranks flapping their leathern straps to terrorize us from experiments in imagery', and in *The Amazing Marriage* he reprehends the habit of setting 'literary police' upon any 'audacious experimenters' who do not find the language as it is currently spoken and written adequate to their purposes.[17] In these passages he is speaking on behalf of the literary malefactor, but on other occasions he is ready to assume the role of the thongman or the policeman himself. 'She wrote as she talked,' he said of Janet Ross, and that was why she was to be trusted: 'Readers growing familiar with her voice will soon have assurance' that 'she would not have blotted a passage or affected a tone for the applause of all Europe'. He is a still more fervent admirer of Alice Meynell, and he admires her writing because no one could detect in it 'the library's atmosphere'. Hers is a prose free from 'doctorial pedantry'. She is a writer so averse from 'the packed phrase or the smart' that Meredith fears on her behalf the verdict of those who prefer a more aphoristic manner. Characteristically he goes on to quote from her a particularly elegant aphorism against aphorisms.

[15] *Diana of the Crossways*, chapter 15.
[16] *Diana of the Crossways*, chapter 1.
[17] *Beauchamp's Career*, chapter 34; *The Amazing Marriage*, chapter 45.

Her father, she writes, 'never lifted a pen except to write a letter': he was possessed of 'an exquisite style from which to refrain'.[18]

Meredith rarely took example from Alice Meynell's father: he never learned to refrain from his own prose style. But the writers he most admired were those who did. He was an admirer of the 'pure, sweet Thackerayan English' that he did not write. Thackeray, he told Eyre Crowe, is 'the most perfect Artist in Prose that I know of'.[19] This was in 1858, before he had published his first novel, but throughout his life he admired writers whose language achieved a 'beautiful translucency'.[20] From 1878 when Robert Louis Stevenson sent him his first book, *An Inland Voyage*, Stevenson replaced Thackeray in Meredith's estimate as the exemplary artist in prose. After reading *Catriona* he wrote to Stevenson, 'As for the writing I say nothing more than I trust it may be the emulation of young authors to equal it.'[21] It is a generous and proper tribute, and Meredith offers it in a sentence remarkable for an entirely un-Stevensonian awkwardness. Meredith approved of Stevenson as a theorist of style as well as a practitioner. He admired his essay 'On Some Technical Aspects of Style in Literature'.[22] But Stevenson insists that prose writers should achieve their effects 'unobtrusively', and that is not an adverb that Meredith's prose invites. When he advised a young admirer in 1900 that the ideal style could be defined as 'a noble matter in an easy manner',[23] the remark suggests an odd ignorance of the character of his own prose, the difficulty of which was remarked on by almost all of his critics and reviewers. For J. M. Robertson *One of Our Conquerors* was 'the hardest novel to read that I ever met with'. Despite this, when his son Arthur confessed an ambition to 'embrace the profession of Literature', Meredith was confident that he could help him: 'I am allowed the reputation of a tolerable guide in writing and style, and I can certainly help you produce clear English.'[24]

---

[18] George Meredith, *Miscellaneous Prose*, *Works of George Meredith*, *Memorial Edition* (London: Constable, 1910), 23, 59 and 136.

[19] *Letters*, 1, 32.

[20] The phrase is used in the 'Essay on Comedy'.

[21] *Letters*, 3, 1153.

[22] *Letters*, 2, 791.

[23] *Letters*, 3, 1362. Cline reads 'a noble manner in an easy manner', but that is surely either a misreading or a transcription of a slip by Meredith.

[24] *Letters*, 2, 625–6.

As Thomas Hardy remarked, Meredith was in the habit of giving, 'no end of good advice, most of which, I'm bound to say, he did not follow himself'.[25] When his friend Captain Maxse was at work on his second novel, Meredith wrote to remind him how important it was to devise a strong plot: 'Where there is no plot, no story, the author generally maunders.' Maxse should trust the judgement of his readers: 'The best critic is the Many, in matters of human nature'. Last, he should 'aim at being concrete rather than abstract'.[26] This is all very sensible, but scarcely what one would expect from a novelist who was, as J. B. Priestley put it, 'one of the worst narrators in the history of the English Novel',[27] who consistently expressed his contempt for the opinion of the general reader and who was so little concerned with the concrete that he left Henry James at a loss 'even to discover by what form of conveyance the elusive characters he was struggling to identify moved from one point of the globe to another'.[28] Such remarks might suggest that Meredith was a writer curiously ignorant of the character of his own books, but Meredith, as so often, was beforehand with the thought. 'Do I give advice I do not myself pursue?' he asked Maxse: 'None the less do I see what should be.'[29]

Meredith's admiration for writers such as Thackeray and Stevenson who wrote so very differently might be understood as the admiration that socially awkward people tend to feel for those who are habitually at their ease. J. C. Squire imagines Meredith reviewing a foolish novel by an intelligent author:

Come we now to Mr. Timms, ambushed by all the sprites, an eye, distinctly, nay, desperately, intelligent still gleaming darkly amid the weedy abysms of the sentimental brake.

Squire has Meredith reading over the passage and substituting 'ambuscadoed' for 'ambushed' before settling on 'embuscadoed'.[30] Meredith's style is so odd that it prompts the reader to imagine, as Squire does here, how he came to arrive at it. Swinburne's illusion that he had read a draft of *Emilia in England* written in sweet, simple English serves to underline

[25] Quoted by Stevenson, 174.
[26] *Letters*, 1, 41–2.
[27] Priestley, 147.
[28] Wharton, 233.
[29] *Letters*, 1, 50.
[30] Squire, 62–3.

how sensitive a reader Swinburne was. He registers that the Meredithian style is a disguise, and like all disguises it tempts the reader to imagine what it would be like if the disguise were doffed. That is why it is so fitting that *The Shaving of Shagpat*, Meredith's first prose fiction, should pretend to be a translation, a tale from the *Arabian Nights* that had not found a place either in the French version of Galland or the English version of Lane. George Lewes and George Eliot admired it, but even George Eliot admitted to feeling 'rather a languishing interest towards the end of the work', and she was a far more patient reader than the story is likely to find these days. This is a typical sentence:

> Now, while Shibli Bagarag gazed on Shagpat kindled by the beams of Aklis, lo, the Genii Karavejis and Veejravoosh circling each other in swift circles like two sapphire rings towards   him, and they whirled to a point above his head, and fell and prostrated themselves at his feet: so he cried, 'O ye slaves of the Sword, my servitors! how of the whereabout of Karaz?'[31]

Whether prose such as this excites interest or a yawn, it is very evidently exotic. 'How of the whereabout of Karaz?' is a question translated out of some unknown tongue by a writer who has only a limited grasp of English idiom. *The Shaving of Shagpat* is a special case, of course. It is an Eastern tale, and it is as traditional for the writers of such tales to dress up their prose as it is for Aladdin and the Genie to be given fancy costumes in the pantomime. But in Meredith the foreign disguise was habitual. He describes Matthew Weyburn, the young hero of *Lord Ormont and His Aminta*, as 'un-English, profoundly so',[32] and he seems to have thought the same of himself. As the French critic, Marcel Schwob, put it, Meredith's novels seem translated into English from some other language, a previously unknown language that he calls 'meredith': 'Meredith ne pense ni en anglais, ni en aucune langue connue: il pense en *meredith*'.[33] It was a disguise that, according to Henry James, he was as likely to assume at a dinner party as at the writing desk. Henry James detected in Turgenev 'a peculiar sense of being out of harmony with his native land—of his having what one may call a poet's quarrel with it'.[34] Meredith's quarrel with

[31] *The Shaving of Shagpat*, 'The Plot'.
[32] *Lord Ormont and His Aminta*, chapter 3.
[33] Marcel Schwob, *Spicilège* (Paris, Société du Mercure de France, 1896), 91.
[34] Henry James, 'Iwan Turgeniew', *North American Review*, 118 (1874), 326–56.

England was, James found, still less restrained: 'He hates the English, whom he speaks of as "they".'[35]

Meredith would have been addressing James as a Welshman. It was a character he assumed so often and so convincingly that an old colleague of mine, Welsh herself, always pronounced his name in the Welsh manner, with the accent on the second syllable. There is no evidence that Meredith favoured that pronunciation himself, and there was little reason for him to have done so. He may have had a Welsh name, but the Merediths had lived in Portsmouth, where Meredith was born, at least since the middle of the eighteenth century. He paid his first and only visit to Wales in 1888, when he was 60, after Will, his son by his second marriage, had taken a position with an engineering firm in Llanelli. Yet his novels are stocked with affectionate portraits of his 'fellow-countrymen'. The name Feverel is a trumpet call that issues from 'the Conqueror's ranks', but the Feverels married into 'the royal blood ap Gruffudh', from which they derived their Welsh estates.[36] Welshmen feature prominently in the novels and are usually exemplary. In *Vittoria* there is Merthyr Powys, and in *The Amazing Marriage* there is Owen Wytham. Much of the unfinished *Celt and Saxon* takes place in the Adister family's Welsh seat, Earlsfont. Meredith was so confident in his Welsh identity that in *The Tale of Chloe* he introduces the word 'rhaiadr' without bothering to explain that it is Welsh for waterfall.[37]

Meredith's mother was the daughter of a Portsmouth innkeeper, but she was a Macnamara, which allowed Meredith to describe her as 'pure Irish'. Through his mother he could also claim as compatriots the Irish characters who appear in the novels almost as frequently as the Welsh, from Diana Merion, daughter of 'the famous Dan Merion' in *Diana of the Crossways*, to the romantic young Irishman Patrick O'Donnell of *Celt and Saxon*. The habit of clinging to a Celtic ancestry is common enough in England and even commoner in America (in 1889 Meredith, who thought himself better appreciated on the other side of the Atlantic, told a friend, 'I feel that I am an American writer'[38]), but for Meredith it served a special purpose. It allowed him to present himself as an outsider in the world of English letters, a Celtic interloper resistant to the oppressive arrogance of the colonial power, or, perhaps still more often, as a writer for whom the

---

[35] *Letters of Henry James*, 2, 199.
[36] *The Ordeal of Richard Feverel*, chapter 2, first edition.
[37] *The Tale of Chloe*, chapter 9.
[38] *Letters*, 3, 1709.

battle between the Celtic insurgent and the Anglo-Saxon literary police was internal, a struggle that took place within himself.

Meredith's sense of himself as a foreigner was instigated by a family romance that imagined the Merediths as descended from royal Welsh ancestors. It was a romance that Meredith realised when he, like the Feverels, married into 'the royal blood ap Gruffudh' by taking as his first wife Mary Ellen Nicolls, whose mother was Jane Gryffydh, daughter of the rector of Maentwrog. When he was 14, he was sent to a school run by the Moravian fathers at Neuwied on the Rhine. He was only there for two years and most of his schoolfellows were English, but he brought back with him to England a sense of himself as a displaced person that remained with him all through his life. It was not at all a peculiar situation. It was the perspective that was all but demanded of the late Victorian writer. Swinburne and Wilde underlined their sense of displacement by writing on occasion in French. Hardy's early novels are written from the perspective of a man who is at once a citizen of London and a resident of a west country village and who feels at home in neither, and James's early novels trace the fortunes of Americans transplanted to Europe, or, in *The Europeans*, of a brother and sister who cross the Atlantic in the other direction and feel equally out of place. But in Meredith much more obtrusively than his contemporaries, the sense of his own displacement manifests itself in the way that he writes. His prose invites remarks such as Victor Radnor attracts in *One of Our Conquerors*. Radnor is, his guests are wont to say, 'not quite English' even though he is 'not at all foreign'.[39]

The effect is at its most extravagant in the late poetry, in the *Odes in Contribution to the Song of French History* (1898), for example, in which we meet line after line such as these:

> For this at our nature arises rejuvenescent from Earth,
> However respersive the blow...[40]

Or this from *The Empty Purse* (1892):

> Not as Cybele's beast will thy head lash tail
> So præter-determinedly thermonous...[41]

[39] *One of Our Conquerors*, chapter 21.
[40] 'Alsace Lorraine', Bartlett, 2, 62–3
[41] *The Empty Purse*, 585–6.

Respersive (something like shattering?) and thermonous (hot-headed, presumably) are words likely to give pause even to experienced readers of nineteenth-century verse. Meredith rather frequently deploys a vocabulary, the one purpose of which seems to be to dumbfound. John Sutherland points out in *Beauchamp's Career* 'the amazing word "obmutescent"' (speechless) and wonders not unreasonably why Meredith introduces such a word, 'Does he do it to annoy?'[42] The habit might best be explained as an expression of Meredith's playfulness. He admitted to MacNeile Dixon, Professor of English at Glasgow, that he was sometimes 'guilty of tricks of literary humour': 'There is no defending it, I can only say that it is a relief to me.'[43] He expects his reader to laugh with him when he uses these odd words, which is why he is especially keen on using them when he is writing about laughter. In the 'Essay on Comedy', those without a sense of humour are 'agelasts', and those whose laughter is as explosive as his own are 'hyper-gelasts'. Meredith was after all the son-in-law of Thomas Love Peacock who was widely credited with having coined the longest word in the English language, floccinaucinihilipilification.[44] But if Meredith's use of this vocabu-lary is humorous, it is a belligerent humour, a humour likely to remind his readers of the meagreness of their own vocabularies. It is a vocabulary that seems designed to exclude rather than to communicate, and amongst those excluded were a rather large majority of ordinary novel readers, especially women readers, most of whom did not have the benefit of a classical educa-tion. Readers of *The Egoist*, which was better received when it was published in 1879 than any of Meredith's earlier novels, encountered 'basiation' for kissing, 'bradypeptics' for sufferers from indigestion and the adjective 'per-coct', which is witty after a fashion because it means something like com-monplace. Readers of the novel are asked to swallow 'deglutition' as a word for swallowing, and there is also a lengthy list of slightly more easily deci-phered words such as 'cloacaline', 'emulgence' and 'esotery'. The Egoist himself, Sir Willoughby Patterne, enters a protest against the use of 'modern barbarous words', but it is somehow predictable that the example he gives is the only barbarous word in the whole novel to have entered into general usage, 'sociology'.[45]

---

[42] *Beauchamp's Career*, chapter 4; John Sutherland, 'A Revered Corpse: The Peculiar Unreadability of George Meredith', *Times Literary Supplement*, September 5, 1997, p. 5.

[43] *Letters*, 3, 1275.

[44] The habit of describing things as worthless; there are in fact precedents for Peacock's use of the word.

[45] *The Egoist*, chapter 14.

Meredith was not alone in his predilection for out-of-the-way words. It was a habit that he shared with his contemporaries. In Henry James's *Roderick Hudson*, Rowland Mallet is impressed when he views the Coliseum by the 'chance anfractuosities of ruin' visible in the upper tiers.[46] Hardy, perhaps a more surprising exponent of a recondite vocabulary, invites his reader to consider how Eustacia Vye's lips when she is seen in profile form 'with almost geometric precision, the curve so well known in the arts of design as the cima-recta or ogee' (he was a trained architect, of course, but his readers, he must have known, were not).[47] In *Far from the Madding Crowd*, Bathsheba Everdene laying down the law to her employees is a 'small thesmothete'.[48] Even the exemplary Stevenson, as he paddles his canoe on his *Inland Voyage*, relishes a tedium that allows him to feel 'dignified and longævous like a tree'.[49] In his essay on style, Stevenson laments that the writer has to work only with the words that the language supplies and that this limits the possibilities available to him almost as much as the set of building blocks that the child finds in the toy box limits the virtuosity of his designs. Late Victorian writers search out recondite words on the hunt for a few new building blocks, as a way of escaping from 'the finite and quite rigid' lexicon that constitutes, as Stevenson points out, 'the acknowledged currency of our daily affairs'. None of them took the practice quite so far as Meredith, and just as significantly none of them entered such impassioned protests against it. He very often sides with his own Mrs Chump, the widow of a rich merchant in *Emilia in England*, who complains of those who use 'great cartwheels o' words that leave a body crushed'. Even Adela Pole who insists that she is 'not uneducated' protests against Sir Twickenham Pryme's habit of introducing her to words that 'seem monsters'. The protest is prompted by his use of the word 'eclictic'.[50] The advice Meredith offers to a young writer, Sidney Royse, is rueful. Much as he admires Lysaght's 'Lexiconizing', he advises him to 'renounce all classic compounds' when writing a novel: 'They puzzle readers, irritate reviewers' and are appropriate only in the work of 'learned humourists'.[51] Elsewhere he doubts even this. In the *Essay on Comedy*, he suggests that 'the trick of employing Johnsonian

---

[46] Henry James, *Roderick Hudson*, chapter 7.
[47] Thomas Hardy, *The Return of the Native*, chapter 7.
[48] Thomas Hardy, *Far from the Madding Crowd*, chapter 10.
[49] Robert Louis Stevenson, *An Inland Voyage*, 'Changed Times'.
[50] *Emilia in England*, chapters 33 and 34.
[51] *Letters*, 2, 1056–7.

polysyllables to treat of the infinitely little' stifles laughter rather than exciting it. In *Vittoria* Carlo Ammiani's journalism is not the more impressive by dint of a style in which 'words of six syllables form the relief to words of eight'[52] (Meredith restrained his own verbal playfulness when writing for the newspapers: like the journalist Rockney in *Celt and Saxon*, his preference then was for 'an armour in which he could walk run and leap—a natural style'[53]). In the novels it is blusterers such as Harry Richmond's father, Augustus Fitz-George Roy Richmond, who are in the habit of using 'threatening polysyllables'.[54] Squire Beltham, Harry's grandfather, who exemplifies everything that is best in the English squirearchy, is even suspicious of his son-in-law's use of the word veracity: 'I don't want any of your roundabout words for truth.'[55]

John Robertson got though *Lord Ormont and His Aminta* only by trying Lynaght to follow the story whilst ignoring so far as he was able 'a style that in itself has become a mere affliction', but in the novel itself, Meredith sometimes seems to share his point of view. He praises the language of stable boys who speak to each other in a 'blunt and racy vernacular, which a society nourished upon Norman-English and English-Latin banishes from print, largely to its impoverishment, some think'.[56] He knew very well that the objections to his own English were not at all to its blunt raciness. He was much more like Gower Woodseer, the apprentice writer in *The Amazing Marriage*, who, in the opinion of the representative Englishman, Mr Chumley Potts, 'speaks foreign English' and 'talks like a Dictionary Cheap Jack'.[57] Meredith guyed the reviewers of his own books when he summarises the reception of Diana Warwick's novels in *Diana of the Crossways*. Reviewers complain of her 'tendency to polysyllabic phraseology' and her neglect of 'vigorous, homely Saxon'.[58] But Meredith was capable of making the complaint himself. 'Words big in the mouth', he remarks in *Rhoda Fleming*, 'serve their turn when there is no way of satisfying the intelligence.'[59] In his thoughts on diction, as on most other matters, Meredith is remarkable for holding his own practice in deep

---

[52] *Vittoria*, chapter 5.
[53] *Celt and Saxon*, chapter 16.
[54] *The Adventures of Harry Richmond*, chapter 51.
[55] *The Adventures of Harry Richmond*, chapter 51.
[56] *Lord Ormont and His Aminta*, chapter 19.
[57] *The Amazing Marriage*, chapter 23.
[58] *Diana of the Crossways*, chapter 21.
[59] *Rhoda Fleming*, chapter 22.

suspicion. He is in this and in much else a writer divided against himself, which is one reason why his novels offer so shrewd an insight into literary culture in the late nineteenth century. It was a period in which writers tended to despise the readership they appealed to, a period in which ambitious novelists were in the grip of two contradictory impulses, to write for the general public and to write in a way that pointedly excludes that public as unfit to appreciate their merits.

But it was not the use of out-of-the-way words that most struck Meredith's readers. His lexiconizing is characteristic, but it is 'Meredithian' only because it is a habit that Meredith at once indulges and vigorously condemns. His contemporaries tended to reserve the epithet for two other of his stylistic traits, 'conciseness of epigram' and 'unexpectedness of metaphor'.[60] Meredith drew attention to his skill as a maker of aphorisms repeatedly and from the very first. *The Ordeal of Richard Feverel* is punctuated by quotations from 'The Pilgrim's Scrip', the collection of aphorisms that Richard's father, Sir Austin, published after the breakdown of his marriage. In the last novel, *The Amazing Marriage*, Captain Kirby, 'the Old Buccaneer', father of Carinthia Jane and of Chillon, is another aphorist, author of 'Maxims for Men', which, like 'The Pilgrim's Scrip', is repeatedly quoted from all through the novel. In *The Egoist* there are quotations from the Book of Egoism, an imaginary collection of aphorisms, and in *One of Our Conquerors* the narrative is frequently interrupted by epigrams fashioned by the mordant social satirist Colney Durance. Meredith introduces characters who are aphorists because they allow him at once to advertise and to excoriate the aphoristic tendencies of his own prose. In his notebooks, as in the novels, Meredith worked at his aphorisms, and never harder than when he was chiselling out an aphorism denouncing aphorisms: 'A brilliant saying arrests thought: a simple observation instigates it: an idea that fixes the mind to itself cannot be of entire truth: one that leads it forth, altho' it be into darkness, is the better guide.' Which was perhaps a little long-winded, and so he tightens the thought: 'A brilliant saying is a shot in the dark: a simple observation is the use of the eyes by daylight.'[61]

Meredith allowed an American admirer, Mrs J. B. Gilman, to make a collection of aphorisms drawn from all his published novels, and she published it in 1888 under the title *The Pilgrim's Scrip*. She took as her

[60] *The Academy*, 1106 (July 15, 1893), 48.
[61] *Notebooks*, 50.

epigraph Coleridge's remark in *Aids to Reflection* that 'the largest and worthiest portion of our knowledge consists in aphorisms'. It was a bold decision to use the very same title that Sir Austin Feverel had chosen when he published as a slim volume a collection of his own aphorisms. Sir Austin's wife had run away with his best friend, leaving him to publish 'in this bashful manner' his 'bruised heart to the world', and the aphorisms return repeatedly to the misogynistic feelings that his wife's betrayal has inspired in him: 'I expect that Woman will be the last thing civilized by Man.'[62] It seems scarcely conceivable that Meredith would have wished Sir Austin's sentiments to be taken for his own, especially given that the domestic circumstances in which Sir Austin put together his volume and in which Meredith wrote his novel were so nearly identical. But the aphorism of Meredith's that has achieved widest circulation, oddly uncollected by Mrs Gilman, is an aphorism ascribed to Sir Austin, 'Who rises from Prayer a better man, his prayer is answered',[63] and Meredith's notebooks reveal that long after the novel had been completed and published, Meredith continued to devise aphorisms that he assigned to 'The Pilgrim's Scrip'. It is entirely characteristic that the aphorisms in Meredith's first novel should bring together items that demand to be understood as symptoms of an understanding perverted by a domestic mishap and items intended as contributions to 'the largest and worthiest portion of our knowledge'. It is the expression of an ambivalence that Meredith extended from the content of his aphorisms to his feelings about the aphorism as a literary form. It would be possible to assemble from Meredith's writings an impressive collection of aphorisms against aphorisms. 'There is more in the world than the epigrams aimed at it contain,' he remarks in *The Tragic Comedians*.[64] The aphorist, according to Gower Woodseer in *The Amazing Marriage*, produces 'pellets instead of flowing sheets'[65]: the thought comes to him when he re-reads his own notebooks. Pithy sayings have a value, but it is a modest one, a thought that Meredith frames in a notebook as an aphorism: 'Proverbs are chalk-eggs, from which nothing is hatched, but which tempt the hen to sit.'[66]

---

[62] *The Ordeal of Richard Feverel*, chapter 1.

[63] *The Ordeal of Richard Feverel*, chapter 12.

[64] *The Tragic Comedians*, chapter 8.

[65] *The Amazing Marriage*, chapter 18. Woodseer's notebooks seem to be identical to Meredith's. This thought occurs to him when he comes across the long-winded aphorism and the pithier revision of it that Meredith had transcribed into his own notebook.

[66] *Notebooks*, 62.

Those of Meredith's characters who share his own gift for phrase-making rarely inspire much affection. Richard Feverel's uncle Adrian has a wicked tongue and is much the most entertaining character in the novel, but he regards his fellow human beings with chilling detachment, as if their lives were a play performed for his amusement. In *The Egoist* it is Mrs Mountstuart Jenkinson who has the gift for saying 'the remembered, if not the right, thing'. She terrifies Sir Willoughby Patterne, because he knows that when she coins a phrase 'it stuck to you': it became a placard that, whether you would or not, you were obliged to carry around with you for the rest of your life. Laetitia Dale, the young woman who loves Sir Willoughby and succeeds in marrying him at the last (a rather dismal success, as she knows only too well), never escapes Mrs Mountstuart's casual notice of her: 'Here she comes with a romantic tale on her eyelashes.'[67] It is not an amiable gift, but it is a gift that, as Meredith knew, was by the nineteenth century expected of the novelist. Gower Woodseer acknowledges the writerly pleasure of arriving at the exact phrase, a pleasure 'such as entomologists feel when they have pinned the rare insect'.[68] It is Dickens's pleasure when he finds the phrase that Mr Turveydrop will carry with him through eternity, 'the Master of Deportment'. But Dickens was a model that Meredith both revered and reviled. He had much the same mix of feelings about himself.

'Conciseness of epigram' is one constituent of the Meredithian style; the other, and the more remarkable, is 'unexpectedness of metaphor'. The predilection for epigram was one of the things that gave Meredith's novels their foreign character, which made them read as if they had been translated, most likely from the French—as Mrs J. B. Gilman points out in the introduction to her collection of Meredith's aphorisms, the writers most celebrated for aphorism are French: Pascal, Bruyère, Rochefoucauld.[69] The metaphorical vivacity makes Meredith's prose still stranger, but he arrives at it not by crossing the frontiers between nations but between genres, by asserting in his prose the right to linguistic experiment that the English poets he most admired, the Elizabethans and the Romantics, had claimed as the special mark of the poet. In *Diana of the Crossways* Diana's admirer, the rising politician Percy Dacier, gazes as evening falls on the

---

[67] *The Egoist*, chapter 2.

[68] *The Amazing Marriage*, chapter 10.

[69] *The Pilgrim's Scrip: or, Wit and Wisdom of George Meredith* (Boston: Roberts Brothers, 1888), x.

towers of Caen, and a phrase from Diana's novel comes into his mind: 'thoughts that are bare dark outlines, coloured by some odd passion of the soul, like towers of a distant city seen in the funeral waste of day.' His 'bluff English anti-poetic training' would ordinarily have led him to dismiss the sentiment as a typical 'modern specimen of romantic vapouring'.[70] But evening is falling, and he is in France, and he is half in love with the writer, and just at that moment the words seem to him a magical anticipation of his own mood as he stands gazing on the darkening towers of Caen. Meredith offers very few quotations from Diana's novels, and he has no need to, because she is a novelist whose prose style is indistinguishable from Meredith's, and she is most like him not just in recognising that her prose will arouse mixed, conflicted feelings in even her most sympathetic readers, even in readers such as Percy Dacier, but in sharing those mixed feelings herself.

Like the poets, Meredith resorts to figures of speech in an effort to break free from the shackles that confine us to our habitual ways of seeing. In a fine phrase in *Beauchamp's Career*, he refers to 'the unlettering elusive moon'.[71] The moon unletters quite literally, by emitting a light that you cannot read by, but its real work is to do away with the alphabet that we use to read the daytime world, an alphabet that has become so familiar that it obscures rather than reveals the things it names. Figurative language like moonlight has the power to restore to the world its proper strangeness, to make it once again a thing of wonder. When Evan Harrington, in danger of missing his father's funeral, hires a fly, he acts out with the postillion a little play that neatly addresses the novel's theme of how the idea of a gentleman ought best to be defined. Is it a matter of how much money one has or of how one behaves? The postillion is comically torn between his contempt for Evan's lack of cash and his admiration for his gentlemanly bearing, and as he suffers this quandary, he and Evan 'jogged easily on the white highway, beneath a moon that walked high and small over marble clouds'.[72] The journey is by night, under moonlight, and that is what makes the episode not just a simple moral fable of the kind that Fielding might have written: the night sky bathes it in romance. But Meredith knows very well that most figurative language fails to illuminate. As Alvan, who is himself addicted to such language, puts it in Meredith's

---

[70] *Diana of the Crossways*, chapter 22.
[71] *Beauchamp's Career*, chapter 23.
[72] *Evan Harrington*, chapter 6.

Tragic Comedians, metaphor is more commonly 'like the metaphysician's treatise on Nature: a torch to catch the sunrise'.[73]

Meredith's similes sometimes make vivid the object they are describing. In *Beauchamp's Career*, Beauchamp's imagination is seized when his uncle's housekeeper mentions that she has in her possession a lock of Cecilia Halkett's hair. The thought of it 'hung in his mind': 'He saw the smooth fat curl lying secret like a smile.'[74] The simile does not simply note the curve of the tress; it perfectly fixes its plump complacency. Cecilia is a wholly amiable young woman but she is an heiress. Self-satisfaction is not a quality peculiar to her so much as an inevitable appurtenance of her class, and it is perfectly embodied in that lock of hair. But just as commonly figures of speech get in the way of the objects they are supposed to be presenting. In *The Amazing Marriage* Gower Woodseer is intended as a friendly portrait of Robert Louis Stevenson, but he writes in a manner much more likely to remind the reader of Meredith. When Woodseer reads over one of his manuscripts, he tends to be displeased, and 'for the best of reasons: because it racked our English; signifying, that he had not yet learnt the right use of his weapons'.[75] When he tries to recall a beautiful woman he has met in a casino, he thinks of lying on a bank of 'silvery cinquefoil' gazing on the evening star, or of Persephone rising at dawn to gather 'an early bud of the year', or of a lake 'that curls part in shadow under the foot of morning', and after all this effort he finds that the woman herself has been lost 'in a ring of dancing similes'. He can remember what her eyes look like only when he can forget that he is a writer and escape for a moment from 'his coil of similes'.[76] It is a habit he has inherited from his father, a shoemaker and a nonconformist minister, who 'hauls women into his religion, and purifies them by the process', or imagines that he does. He 'worships them in similes', which amounts to 'running away from them, leering sheepishly'.[77] Lady Mountstuart in *The Egoist* is an aphorist and therefore untrustworthy, but her aphorism on similes is at least worth thinking about. When a young woman reaches for a simile to express her surprise on having received a proposal, Lady Mountstuart advises, 'Defer the simile ... If you hit on a clever one you

---

[73] *The Tragic Comedians*, chapter 4.
[74] *Beauchamp's Career*, chapter 44.
[75] *The Amazing Marriage*, chapter 18.
[76] *The Amazing Marriage*, chapter 9.
[77] *The Amazing Marriage*, chapter 37.

will never get the better of it'.[78] The problem with figures of speech is that they are insubordinate: they are forever distracting the attention from the object to themselves. In 1903 Meredith gave some rueful advice to Harold Owen, a young reporter for the *Manchester Guardian* who had written a pamphlet: 'The large use of metaphor bewilders the public, and leads to the idea that imagination, his best servant, commands him.'[79]

Metaphors have a life of their own, often to the discomfort of their framer. In *Beauchamp's Career* Beauchamp's political mentor is Dr Shrapnel, a man whose prose style, like Carlyle's, is as disturbing as his extreme radical views. When the housekeeper of Beauchamp's uncle calls, he gives her tea but then invites her to consider the likeness between despotism and the church organ and between the 'Constitutional bourgeois' and the piano. The government that the doctor favours is best figured by a full orchestra: 'That is our republic: each one to his work; all in union!' Rosamund is left perplexed:

> It was perceptible to her that a species of mad metaphor had been wriggling and tearing its passage through a thorn-bush in his discourse, with the furious urgency of a sheep in a panic; but where the ostensible subject ended and the metaphor commenced, and which was which at the conclusion, she found it difficult to discern—much as the sheep would be when he had left his fleece behind him.[80]

Meredith writes the passage out of a wry awareness that many of his readers will share her perplexity. Even in this, fairly lucid passage, the sheep seems to have escaped its explanatory function before the sentence ends leaving the animal holding together in a single gaze its shorn body and the fleece that it has left on the bush and wondering where its true identity is situated. Most of Meredith's metaphorical flights end similarly. He takes up a metaphor in an effort to reveal something about the world in which he finds himself and leaves it only when it has brought him to a place in which the world has been jettisoned in favour of a puzzled self-contemplation. As usual he knows as much himself. As he points out in *Vittoria*, 'All similes followed out are mazes: they bring us back to our own face in the glass.'[81] Meredith's prose is remarkably mannered, and still more remarkably it is almost always ruefully aware of its own mannerism. His writing is richly

---

[78] *The Egoist*, chapter 35.
[79] *Letters*, 3, 1479–80.
[80] *Beauchamp's Career*, chapter 12.
[81] *Vittoria*, chapter 36, first edition.

metaphorical in part because he thinks of himself as a Celt. Even the English 'concede the use' of metaphor to 'the Irish and the Welsh'. The thought is Squire Adister's in *Celt and Saxon*. Meredith writes like a Celt, but a Celt who has a bluff Englishman like Mr Adister looking over his shoulder, whose preference is for 'undecorated plain speech' and who thinks of metaphorical writing as 'fool's froth'.[82] Meredith is, for a novelist, a remarkably literary writer, and he is also a writer remarkably apt to hold literature in suspicion.

The Plush of Speech

Meredith's style is an expression, V. S. Pritchett suggests, of his class-consciousness: it has its origins in his 'shame' at being the son of a tailor.[83] It is not an idle thought. Meredith's habit of writing English as if it were a foreign language allies him with Evan Harrington, the hero of his second novel who is, like Meredith, a tailor's son. Evan is introduced to the reader as he stands on the deck of the Jocasta, the ship on which he travels back to England from Portugal. He wears a 'dusky sombrero and dangling cloak, of which one fold was flung across his breast, and dropped behind him' so easily that he might have been taken for 'a wandering Don', Byron's Don Juan perhaps. 'The line of an adolescent moustache ran along his lip', completing a foreign disguise that would have been perfect had his eyes not been 'blue and of the land he was nearing'.[84] In Portugal Evan has been under the tutelage of his older sister, the Countess of Saldar, who has married a Portuguese nobleman and has perfected her removal from the tailor's shop by learning to speak English as if it were a foreign language. She speaks English like a native only in moments of excitement. At other times she speaks a carefully 'foreignized' idiom that establishes her as a woman 'alienized' from her own country. When she mixes with the English gentry, the women mock her habits of speech, what they call her 'euphuisms', but the men are beguiled. Her language is the most potent item in the foreign disguise she assumes the better to conceal her lowly origins. Meredith mocks her, but he admires her too, and, still more remarkably, he recognises himself in her. He shares with her, for example, her euphuistic turns of phrase, so that the anecdotes through which she

---

[82] *Celt and Saxon*, chapter 3.

[83] V. S. Pritchett, *George Meredith and English Comedy* (London: Chatto and Windus, 1970), 33.

[84] *Evan Harrington*, chapter 4.

flaunts her intimacy with the Portuguese nobility become her 'Lusitanian *contes*'.[85] When Meredith invents such phrases, he is mimicking her habits of speech perhaps, but it seems almost as likely that she is mimicking his.

Robertson accuses Meredith of twisting the face of speech. The charge carries the implication that it is ungentlemanly to cultivate so mannered a style. The secret of aristocratic bearing, Meredith explains in *Vittoria*, is to render heart and brain 'positively subservient to elegance of limb'.[86] 'High social breeding', he remarks, 'is an exquisite performance on the instrument we are.'[87] But the performance must be effortless. Plutarch records that Alcibiades refused lessons on the flute because it was an instrument that could not be played without discomposing the features. Hazlitt recalls the anecdote in his essay 'On the Look of a Gentleman'. The gentleman identifies himself by declining 'to put himself into any posture, that is not perfectly easy and graceful'. The ease is even more important than the grace. Sir Charles Bunbury 'as he saunters down St James's' 'presents nothing very dazzling, or graceful, or dignified to the imagination'. He is wearing perhaps 'an old shabby drab-coloured coat, buttoned across his breast without a cape,—with old top-boots, and his hands in his waist-coat or breeches' pockets, as if he were strolling along his own garden-walks, or over the turf at Newmarket', and yet anyone can tell even from a distance that he is 'a gentleman of the first water'.[88] Byron makes a very similar point when dismissing Keats for the vulgar cockneyism of his poetic style. For Byron Keats's style is the verse equivalent of an apprentice walking the streets in his Sunday best. A gentleman might seem slovenly in comparison, but there would be no mistaking him for the apprentice for all that the apprentice's clothes might be the 'better cut and his boots the best-blackened of the two'.[89] Style is the dress of thought, and in Britain dress codes always mark class differences. In *Beauchamp's Career* Colonel Halkett walks onto the terrace 'trailing a newspaper like a pocket handkerchief'.[90] Even the easy, negligent ease with which he holds his newspaper marks him the gentleman, and just this once Meredith handles

---

[85] *Evan Harrington*, chapters 3, 4, 17 and 21.

[86] *Vittoria*, chapter 17.

[87] *The Amazing Marriage*, chapter 46.

[88] William Hazlitt, 'On the Look of a Gentleman', *The Complete Works of William Hazlitt*, ed. P. P. Howe, 21 vols (London: Dent, 1930–4), 12, 210–11.

[89] Lord Byron, *The Complete Miscellaneous Prose*, ed. Andrew Nicholson (Oxford: Clarendon Press, 1991), 159.

[90] *Beauchamp's Career*, chapter 47.

the simile almost, although not quite, as easily as the Colonel holds his paper. As a reviewer in *The Spectator* observed, Meredith's prose style more often positively '*gasps* with effort',[91] and the effort betrays in itself Meredith's consciousness of his own lowly status as the son of a snip. In *Diana of the Crossways*, Diana remarks that a 'plush of speech haunts all efforts to swell and illuminate citizen prose to a princely poetic'.[92] Plush is a rich fabric, but it is also, as in Thackeray's *Yellowplush Papers*, the fabric from which the liveries of servants were traditionally cut.

Henry James's prose may seem almost as mannered as Meredith's, especially as he rewrote it for the New York edition, and Henry James became a novelist after reading *Evan Harrington*. In *The American* Christopher Newman is denied the opportunity to marry the Countess de Cintre by her mother and her brother. Christopher is too 'commercial': he is a millionaire but his fortune has come by way of trade. So too had the fortune of the James family. But there is no trace in the novel of the painful, humiliating recognition of a shared identity that links George Meredith to Evan Harrington. It was James's grandfather rather than his father that was besmirched by his association with commerce, and the James family, unlike the Merediths, were successful. Meredith felt branded all through his life by the knowledge that his name had appeared on the board over a tailor's shop in Portsmouth, whereas there were streets in Albany and Syracuse named after Henry's grandfather, not to mention the town Jamesville. But a still more important difference was that James was an American. The Countess's family may despise Christopher Newman, but he is, by his own reckoning, a good fellow, as good or better than the family he aspires to ally himself with. *The American* is an absurd enough novel. Madame de Cintre yields to her family's insistence that she give Newman over and enters a Carmelite convent, and her mother murders her father to protect the family name. It is all, as Newman recognises, 'like a page torn out of a romance, with no context in his own experience'.[93] But in his most characteristic gesture, as he sits when in company, Newman stretches out his legs, confidently and easily asserting his ownership of the social space.[94] It is what makes him so different from Evan Harrington and what makes Henry James so different from George Meredith. Meredith, as he

[91] Quoted in Ellis, 191.
[92] *Diana of the Crossways*, chapter 4.
[93] Henry James, *The American*, chapter 24.
[94] As when he is introduced, in the first paragraph of the novel.

writes, never stretches out his legs. The prose is always tense, always on edge. James, by contrast, whatever his anxieties about himself, was always socially easy. Roderick Hudson may be refused by the Princess, but he is never abashed in her presence any more than was Henry James at the dinner tables of Rome or Paris or London. It was quite different for George Meredith and the difference is most marked in their prose. James's prose even in the New York edition never quite loses an easiness that Meredith never quite arrives at.

But Meredith was far from the only nineteenth-century novelist whose talent was born out of shame. There was Dickens, never able to forget the blacking factory. Hardy found his own lowly origins almost as productive. In *The Hand of Ethelberta* Hardy clearly recognises himself in his heroine who becomes a famous poet and is invited to fashionable dinner parties, at one of which she finds her own father serving as butler. There was George Gissing whose career as a novelist began when he was expelled from college for stealing cash from a fellow student. Meredith's prose style can be explained as a response to his particular social circumstances, but it is also the most complete expression of a very particular personality. Meredith was an unusually self-absorbed man, and he had a painfully acute sensitivity to what other people thought of him. He had, in other words, a sensitivity to others that was a symptom rather than a mitigation of his self-absorption. He inhabited his own life with unusual intensity, and he had an unusual ability to contemplate that life as if it were someone else's. He developed a prose style that became an exact reflection of the man. It is mannered and yet it remains ruefully conscious of its own mannerism. It is Meredith's style that reveals him most completely, and it reveals him as a man anxious at once to conceal and to expose himself. His prose is excessively figurative, and, as Hugo puts it in what Meredith thought the greatest of all nineteenth-century novels, a prose rich in figures is the mark of a writer 'qui veut tout dire et tout cacher',[95] who wants to tell everything and to conceal everything. Meredith writes in metaphors because the metaphor can offer such wholly unexpected revelations, and he is fond of metaphors too because, as his own Nevil Beauchamp points out, 'There's nothing like a metaphor for an evasion'.[96] But Beauchamp should perhaps have added that it is precisely in our evasions that we reveal ourselves most nakedly.

[95] *Les Miserables*, Tome 4, Livre septième, chapitre 2.
[96] *Beauchamp's Career*, chapter 16.

From its first publication in 1891, *One of Our Conquerors* was widely regarded as the most Meredithian of all Meredith's works, the novel in which he began not so much to practise as to parody his own manner. Max Beerbohm, who ranked Meredith as a writer second only to Shakespeare, was also his most accomplished parodist:

> It is recorded that the goblins of this same Lady Wisdom were all agog one Christmas morning between the doors of the house and the village church, which crouches on the outskirt of the park, with something of a lodge in its look, you might say, more than of celestial twinkles, even with Christmas hoar-frost bleaching the grey of it in sunlight, as one sees imaged on seasonable missives for amity in the trays marked "sixpence and upwards," here and there, on the counters of barter.[97]

But in *One of Our Conquerors*, Meredith outdoes Beerbohm's parody. It was known by then that Meredith liked to supply his novels with a first chapter that functioned as a warning, a chapter designed to deter the reader rather than to offer a polite invitation to proceed. The young men in the novels have to undergo an ordeal before they arrive at maturity, and Meredith's first chapters acted as a rather similar ordeal through which all those who wished to read the novel were required to pass. But the opening of *One of Our Conquerors* proved an ordeal too severe for even Meredith's experienced readers to endure without protest. Very little happens. A rich businessman, unnamed until the last paragraph, dressed in a tailcoat and resplendent white waistcoat, slips as he crosses London Bridge and is upended. He is helped to his feet by passers-by, his hat is recovered, and he seems none the worse. But he is discomposed when a mild altercation breaks out with one of those who have assisted him, and as he goes on his way across the bridge, he tries and fails to recall an idea that came to him as he fell. He tries to recover that idea all the way through the novel and never quite manages to do so.

On the face of it, the chapter introduces *One of Our Conquerors* as a condition of England novel. The white waistcoated gentleman, Victor Radnor, is the central character. The grimy passer-by who helps him to his feet takes offence at a casual remark of Victor's and the fragility of the bond between the classes stands revealed. When Radnor walks on, looking

---

[97] See 'Euphemia Clashthought' in Beerbohm's *A Christmas Garland* (London: Heinemann, 1912).

over the parapet of the bridge and contemplating 'the hundreds of masts rising out of the merchant river', he finds the scene sublime, but it is a sublimity that the nation's poets have refused to recognise. His own friend, the satirist Colney Durance, prefers to caricature the Anglo-Saxon race 'in the modern garb of liveryman and gaitered squire' busily engaged in 'blacking Ben-Israel's boots and grooming the princely stud of the Jew'. The picture drawn by Durance 'in literary sepia' of 'the Jew Dominant in London City' and the British populace tugging its forelock to 'the Satyr-snouty master' is deeply unpleasant. Even in its own time, its virulence was unusual. But it works within the novel to expose Victor Radnor's suspicion that he might have much in common with the alien figure of the Jew that his friend Colney finds so upsetting. He is a fabulously wealthy financier and uses his wealth to ensure that the world gives him back 'the splendid reflections' of himself that he demands,[98] but even his own beloved daughter is unsure whether he is more properly a 'merchant' or a 'speculator'.[99] 'He is not quite English, yet he is not at all foreign,' his guests observe, neither a native nor an alien.[100] Radnor demands to be recognised as the heroic representative of London, the great merchant city, but he cannot quite rid himself of the suspicion that he might really only be an interloper, a symptom of the city's degeneracy, which is why the sublimity of the view from London Bridge that he contemplates is always on the verge of collapsing into bathos. Victor's insecurities are not confined to his professional life. He is a devoted husband to his wife Natalia, and a devoted father to his daughter Nesta, but he and Natalia, although the daughter does not know it, are not married. When Victor was a young man of 21, he had married a rich widow, Mrs Burman, unable to resist 'the pounds of barley sugar in her pockets'.[101] When he left her for her young companion, she refused to divorce him. His daughter, although she does not know it, is illegitimate. That secret threatens the rich life that he has made for himself and his family. A word from the old widow, the wife that he has abandoned, and everything would collapse, the lavish entertainments, the musical parties, the respect and the affection in which he is held by all his friends, even the unthinking trust of his beloved daughter. As Victor Radnor walks over London Bridge, he slips on some

---

[98] *One of Our Conquerors*, chapter 27.
[99] *One of Our Conquerors*, chapter 8.
[100] *One of Our Conquerors*, chapter 21.
[101] *One of Our Conquerors*, chapter 8.

vegetable matter and takes an undignified tumble. The novel will reveal that he lives his whole life in daily fear of a similar but still more calamitous mishap.

The first chapter maps Victor Radnor's inner life. As he walks across the bridge, the novelist accompanies him, seeing what he sees, and thinking his thoughts, and the first and overwhelming impression is what uncomfortable companions the two men are. Men of wealth and men of letters had a prickly relationship in the nineteenth century. The Cheeryble brothers in *Nicholas Nickleby* are businessmen and as benevolent as their name implies. The Cogglesby brothers in Meredith's *Evan Harrington* are their close (rather too close) relatives. But as the century wore on representations of the wealthy darkened. The type of the rich man became the speculator, Dickens's Mr Merdle or Trollope's Augustus Melmotte. Mr Dombey's wealth comes from trade rather than speculation, but he too is an empty shell of a man. 'I do not think Mr. Meredith liked the company of very rich people,' Lady Butcher recalled.[102] But in the novels he made a point of treating the rich more generously. Mr Pericles in *Emilia in England* and *Vittoria* is a millionaire, but he cares for music more than for all his millions. The Earl of Fleetwood in *The Amazing Marriage* is the richest aristocrat in all England, but, for all his failings, he is a man of some substance. Meredith refuses to offer him as a simple illustration of the dictum that the more you have, the less you are. Given the reputation of the railway speculator George Hudson, who may have offered Dickens and Trollope a model for Merdle and Melmotte, it is striking that Meredith allows Thomas Redworth to win the fortune that allows him to become the second husband of Diana of the Crossways through speculation in railway shares. Redworth is bracingly unapologetic about the fortune he has won. 'Money', he tells Diana, 'is of course a rough test of virtue,' but, he adds, 'We have no other general test.' He snorts in disdain when Diana suggests that 'there is more virtue in poverty'.[103] And yet Meredith, whose financial necessities had tied him to his desk all his adult life almost as tightly as if he had been one of Victor Radnor's clerks, knew little enough of the fabulously opulent life that Victor lives. Victor invites his friends to extravagant musical weekends at his mansion outside London: Meredith had to content himself with invitations from the Miss Lawrences, the unmarried sisters of the local MP, to the modest musical evenings that

---

[102] Butcher, 7.
[103] *Diana of the Crossways*, chapter 27.

they organised in their London house. George Meredith and Victor Radnor have little but their taste for music in common. In literature their tastes are quite different. Victor's preference is for what his friend Colney Durance calls 'the brandy novel': 'I can't read dull analytical stuff or "stylists" when I want action.'[104] A quarter of a century before, Meredith had remarked that his own son had a taste for 'sensation novels'.[105] It had not seemed to him a hopeful sign. The reader struggling through the first chapter knows none of this, except that it is all present, all thoroughly laid bare, in the extraordinary prose.

The presence of the banana skin on the pavement, if banana skin it is, is easily explicable. Radnor is crossing the river from the north, walking towards Borough Market which in the late nineteenth century was the principal fruit and vegetable market for the whole of London. It is the manner of referring to the banana skin that is odd. Radnor slips on 'some sly strip of slipperiness abounding in that conduit of the markets', upended in his dignified progress by a piece of litter too low for him to notice or to name. But does Meredith's refusal to name the item mock Victor's loftiness or share it? It is impossible, we are told, to look north-eastwards from the bridge without noticing 'the glow of whitebait's bow-window by the riverside', the window, that is, of one of the establishments offering whitebait suppers, the preeminent cockney delicacy before the onset of pie and eel shops. Meredith seems to be Victor's accomplice here in the attempt to forge from the view from the bridge a new, urban picturesque, but he abandons the task almost at once. The window becomes the 'frontispiece of a tale to fetch us up the out-wearied spectre of old Apicius; yea, and urge Crispinus to wheel his purse into the market for the purchase of a costlier mullet!' The only function of these stale ('out-wearied') classical references (Apicius was a legendary Roman gourmet and Crispinus buys a mullet for 6000 sesterces in Juvenal's fourth satire) is to belittle the Londoner comfortably sitting down to his plate of whitebait, who would be unable to make anything of them. In the oddest of all stylistic flourishes in the chapter, Victor imagines how it would be if the nation's poets rather than satirise his devotion to the goddess of Commerce were to share it. He imagines poet and alderman sitting side by side at a city dinner, sniffing the soup appreciatively before one after the other plunging into the 'turtle tureen': 'Heels up they go, poet first—a plummet he!' The wildly surreal

---

[104] *One of Our Conquerors*, chapter 18.
[105] *Letters*, 1, 308.

fantasy would be entirely gratuitous except that it imagines the equally bizarre relationship that the whole chapter explores, between Victor Radnor, the hugely successful financier, and George Meredith, the under-appreciated poet who tells his story.

It is Victor Radnor's habit on the first day of spring, no matter the weather, to assume his summer wardrobe and put on a white waistcoat. The altercation that discomposes him is prompted when he is helped to his feet and looks down to find 'absurd blots of smutty knuckles distrib-uted over the maiden waistcoat'. 'Oh, confound the fellow!' he says, qui-etly enough, addressing the remarks to the waistcoat rather than to anyone in particular. But the man who has helped him to his feet, 'who knew himself honourably unclean' and had a lively sense of 'the view taken of honest labour in the mind of supercilious luxury', takes offence: 'Am I the fellow you mean, sir?' Radnor responds 'by way of amiable remonstrance', 'Ah, well, don't be impudent', and the unclean workman silences Radnor with a crushing retort, 'And none of your dam punctilio.' Radnor knows that he has no gift for repartee, but he is especially helpless in the face of the remark because he has no idea what the word 'punctilio' might mean. None of the usual senses seems quite to fit: 'was it a London cockney crow-word of the day, or a word that had stuck in the fellow's head from the perusal of his pothouse newspaper columns?' (and what is a crow-word, the reader might wonder, a word useful to those wishing to pluck a crow with someone, or a word with which to crow over a vanquished antagonist?). If 'an odd word engrosses our speculations', Victor thinks to himself 'we *are* poor creatures'. But Meredith has made quite sure that his attentive readers have no choice but to allow the odd use of the word punctilio to engross their speculations. As it happens I think I know where Meredith had come across the word. It was not an instance of cockney slang, and it did not stick in his head from his reading of newspapers. It came from Stendhal, the novelist that he most admired. In Stendhal's preface to *La Chartreuse de Parme*, he points out that the Italians are little given to vanity but that, when the mood takes them, they are passionate in its display, and in such moods they refer to it as *puntiglio*. If I am right, it is a striking instance of Meredith's perversity. He ascribes to a represen-tative specimen of the metropolitan unwashed a word taken directly from the Italian for which a novelist with whom only the most erudite of his readers would have been familiar could find no French equivalent. It is as if Victor Radnor's discomfiting encounter with a member of the London labouring classes concealed within it an encounter just as discomfiting between the common reader and a supercilious Francophile English novelist. John Sutherland has written of 'the peculiar unreadability of George Meredith',[106] and the first chapter of *One of Our Conquerors* is as peculiarly unreadable as anything he wrote. The entire chapter seems written as a confession of Meredith's extreme discomfort with his subject matter. It painstakingly and painfully traces the workings of a mind, Victor Radnor's, that Meredith finds quite foreign. And yet that style works all the while to reveal Radnor's principal characteristic. He is a man ill at ease in his own skin, and the prose, bizarre as it so often is, always succeeds in giving a powerful impression of someone at odds with himself and at odds with his world. Victor Radnor is a man always in danger of suffering a tumble that will make him all at once the kind of absurd public spectacle that he most dreads becoming. When the accident happens and Radnor finds himself flat on his back, laughing in the way that people do who fear that they have made themselves ridiculous, Meredith recognises an odd complicity with him. His own first chapter, he knows full well, is very likely to attract from his reader a rebuke rather like the rebuke Radnor is offered by the unwashed workman: 'And none of your dam punctilio.' The gleaming white pages of the new novel are just as likely to be besmirched by unsympathetic attention as Radnor's white waistcoat. To many of his readers, it will seem as if he has not so much started his novel as performed in public, just like his hero, an agonisingly slow-motion pratfall. But the complicity that links Meredith and his hero goes deeper than this. If Radnor is a man with a private history that he dreads becoming public, so is Meredith, and if Meredith can trace so accurately the lineaments of a man uncomfortable in his own skin, it is because he knows very well that he suffers himself from the same condition. Meredith, for all the differences between the two men, is exactly the right person to tell Victor Radnor's story because Meredith, as J. C. Squire understood, writes the prose of a man who 'was not so much afraid to be himself; he positively disliked to be himself'.[107]

The opening chapter of *One of Our Conquerors* is written in 'meredith' rather than in English. By 1891 Meredith had become an adjective. The face that he turned to the world had by then become as fixed as a mask. His prose had undergone the same evolution. The prose style had become the

---

[106] John Sutherland, 'A Revered Corpse: The Peculiar Unreadability of George Meredith', *Times Literary Supplement*, September 5, 1997, p. 5.
[107] Squire, 69.

exact equivalent of the 'impenetrable shining scales' with which, according to Henry James, Meredith repelled any advance towards intimacy. And yet it is a prose that, however mannered it became, still contrives to lay bare the man whose private face it seems intent on concealing. It is a face that many readers will find unsympathetic. Meredith could be a harshly unforgiving man, ruthlessly cutting off from his affections one after another his father, his first wife, his oldest child. To trace that behaviour to its source, to locate its origin in the sensitivities of a man born a tailor's son, whose first wife left him for another man, does little to excuse it. In Meredith's first novel, Mrs Berry says of Sir Austin Feverel, 'He keeps his face and makes ye think you're dealin' with a man of iron, and all the while there's a woman under-neath.' But the woman underneath, as Mrs Berry found, might exert her influence only to make the exterior man still more unforgiving. When Mrs Berry surprises Sir Austin weeping over his son's cot, he instantly dismisses her from his service. Meredith was often wounding even to those he loved, which is not a more attractive trait because it was a consequence of being himself so easily wounded. But if it is not more attractive, it is at least a characteristic that many of us can, at odd moments, guiltily recognise in ourselves. And Meredith, unlike most of us, was capable of exercising a pitiless self-knowledge. He was, to give just one example, himself a harsher critic of the literary manner that he cultivated than all but the most extrava-gant of his calumniators. His novels are punctuated by protests against every aspect of the Meredithian prose style, and the self-knowledge he arrived at was only the more complete because it accommodated the suspi-cion that such knowledge did not bring with it any magic power to change even those aspects of his behaviour that he most regretted. Meredith found, like his own Sir Willoughby Patterne, that he was able to stand 'above him-self, contemplating his active machinery', but for all that he might 'criticise' it, he could do nothing to bring it to a stop.

Meredith, as even his contemporaries tended to agree, is hard to read, but he remains worth reading for several reasons. First, his novels, in their prose as much as in their plots, offer the liveliest demonstration of the development during the later nineteenth century of the literary novel, that is, of the kind of novel defined by its difference from the novels that the reading public preferred. The literary novel characteristically has an embattled relationship with its readers, and Meredith's are the novels that chart that embattled relationship most precisely. They can do so because Meredith's relationship with his readers was so accurately reflected in his embattled relationship with himself. Second, Meredith's novels reveal with unusual clarity the two impulses that govern the novel in the later nineteenth century, and perhaps throughout its history, the impulse to address the world as it is and the impulse to escape from it. In Meredith's novels realism is finely poised against romance. They maintain that balance so expertly because the novels allowed their writer as much as they allowed their readers an escape from the self, but an escape that is repeatedly foiled. Meredith knew that he was at his best as a painter of 'morbid emotion' and he regretted it, but his fascination with 'cobwebs in a putrid corner'[108] is repeatedly countered by a love of open spaces, snow-covered alpine scenery or night skies lit by a white moon. Third, Meredith offered his literary successors a way of holding a character at a contemptuous distance that does not prevent the character from being known inwardly and intimately. Amiel was horrified by Stendhal's way of making the novel a branch of natural history, but Meredith, who learned so much from Stendhal, knew that a character such as Sir Willoughby Patterne might at once be studied as a striking example of an inferior species and explored as an only too recognisable version of the self. Meredith is an awkward novelist just as he was an awkward man, never able to free himself from the painful self-consciousness evident in all of his life and in all of his fiction. It is always a relief to turn from Meredith to more socially easy novelists, to Thackeray, for example, whose 'pure, sweet, Thackerayan English' makes him so delightful a companion. But Meredith, in his awkwardness, in his embarrassments, in the strain evident in so much of his prose, can engage his reader with an intimacy that more comfortable writers such as Thackeray cannot match. Meredith will never be amongst the more popular of nineteenth-century novelists, but he is amongst the most distinctive. It is not for nothing that, as he remarked to Edward Clodd, he had 'become an adjective'. His novels offer their readers an experience that cannot be found elsewhere.

[108] *Letters*, 1, 322–3.

BIBLIOGRAPHY

Amiel, Henri-Frédéric, *Journal Intime*, 12 vols (Lausanne, Éditions l'Age d'Homme, 1976–1994).

de Balzac, Honoré, *Le Curé de village* (Paris: Calmann-Lévy, 1891).

Banerjee, Jacqueline, *George Meredith* (Tavistock, Devon: Northcote House, 2012).

———, 'George Meredith and Emilie Maceroni: Part of the Background to "Modern Love" and the Italian Novels', http://www.victorianweb.org/authors/meredith/emilie.html.

Bartlett, Phyllis, ed., *The Poems of George Meredith*, 2 vols (New Haven and London: Yale University Press, 1978).

Battersea, Constance Lady, *Reminiscences* (London: Macmillan, 1923).

Bayley, John, review of *The Poems of George Meredith*, ed. Phyllis Bartlett, *Times Literary Supplement*, October 7, 1978, pp. 1246–1248.

Beer, Gillian, *Meredith: A Change of Masks: A Study of the Novels* (London: Athlone Press, 1970).

Beerbohm, Max, *A Christmas Garland* (London: Heinemann, 1912).

Blunt, W. S., *My Diaries: Being a Personal Narrative of Events 1888–1914*, 2 vols (London: Martin Secker, 1919–1920).

Broughton, Rhoda, *Cometh Up as a Flower* (London: Guildford, 1867).

———, *Alas!* (London: R. Bentley, 1891).

Buchanan, Robert, *A Look Round Literature* (London: Ward and Downey, 1887).

Bunbury, Selina, *Our Own Story* (London: Hurst and Blackett, 1856).

Butcher, Lady (Alice Mary Brandreth), *Memories of George Meredith, O. M.* (London: Constable, 1919).

© The Author(s) 2019
R. Cronin, *George Meredith*,
https://doi.org/10.1007/978-3-030-32448-3

Buxton Forman, Maurice, *A Bibliography of the Writings in Prose and Verse of George Meredith* (Edinburgh: Bibliographical Society, 1922).

Byron, Lord George Gordon, *The Complete Miscellaneous Prose*, ed. Andrew Nicholson (Oxford: Clarendon Press, 1991).

Caine, Hall, *The Prodigal Son* (London: Heinemann, 1904).

Carroll, Lewis, *Through the Looking-Glass* (London: Macmillan, 1872).

Charnock, Richard, *On the New Bankrupt and Insolvent Acts* (London: Owen Richards, 1845).

———, *Bradshaw's Illustrated Hand-book to Spain and Portugal* (London: W. J. Adams, 1865).

———, *Ludus Patronymicus; or, the Etymology of Curious Surnames* (London: Trübner & Co, 1868).

———, *The Origins of the Etruscans and their Language* (London: 1875).

Charteris, Evan, *Life and Letters of Sir Edmund Gosse* (London: Heinemann, 1931).

Clodd, Edward, *Grant Allen: A Memoir* (London: Grant Richards, 1900).

———, 'George Meredith: Some Recollections', *Fortnightly Review*, 86 (July, 1909), 19–31.

———, *Memories* (London: Putnam, 1916).

Collins, Wilkie, *No Name* (London: Sampson Low, 1862).

———, *Man and Wife* (London: F. S. Ellis, 1870).

Coustillas, Pierre, *The Heroic Life of George Gissing*, 3 vols (London: Pickering and Chatto, 2011).

Curle, Richard H. P., *Aspects of George Meredith* (London: Routledge, 1908).

Dickens, Charles, *Nicholas Nickleby* (London: Chapman and Hall, 1839).

———, *The Old Curiosity Shop* (London: Chapman and Hall, 1840).

———, *Little Dorrit* (London: Bradbury and Evans, 1857).

———, *Great Expectations* (London: Chapman and Hall, 1861).

Disraeli, Benjamin, *Henrietta Temple* (London: Henry Colburn, 1837).

Dumas, Alexandre, *La Dame aux camélias* (Paris: Gallimard, 1975).

Edel, Leon, *Henry James: A Life* (London: Collins, 1987).

Ellis, S. M., *George Meredith: His Life and Friends in Relation to His Work* (London: Grant Richards, 1920).

Farley, Paul, and Michael Symmons Roberts, *Deaths of the Poets* (London: Jonathan Cape, 2017).

Field, Michael, *Works and Days: From the Journal of Michael Field*, ed. T. and D. C. Sturge Moore (London: John Murray, 1933).

Fletcher, Ian, ed., *Meredith Now: Some Critical Essays* (London: Routledge and Kegan Paul, 1971).

Forster, John, *Life of Charles Dickens* (London: Chapman and Hall, 1893).

Galland, René, *George Meredith: les cinquantes premières années* (Paris: Les Presses Françaises, 1923).

Gilman, Mrs J. B., *The Pilgrim's Scrip: or, The Wit and Wisdom of George Meredith* (Boston: Roberts Brothers, 1888).

Gissing, George, *The Unclassed* (London: Chapman and Hall, 1884).

———, *Isabel Clarendon* (London: Chapman and Hall, 1886).

———, *The Odd Women* (London: Lawrence and Bullen, 1893).

———, *In the Year of Jubilee* (London: Lawrence and Bullen, 1894).

———, *The Whirlpool* (London: Lawrence and Bullen, 1897).

Grand, Sarah, *The Heavenly Twins* (University of Michigan: Ann Arbor Paperback, 1992).

Haldane, Elizabeth S., *From One Century to Another* (London: Alexander Maclehose, 1937).

Hammerton, J. A., *George Meredith: His Life and Art in Anecdote and Criticism* (Edinburgh: J. Grant, 1911).

Hardman, Sir William, *A Mid-Victorian Pepys: The Letters and Memoirs of Sir William Hardman, M. A., F. R. G. S.*, ed. S. M. Ellis, revised second edition (London: Cecil Palmer, 1928).

Hardy, Thomas, *Desperate Remedies* (London: Tinsley Brothers, 1871).

———, *A Pair of Blue Eyes* (London: Tinsley Brothers, 1873).

———, *Far from the Madding Crowd* (London: Smith, Elder & Co, 1874).

———, *The Hand of Ethelberta* (New York: Henry Holt, 1876).

———, *The Return of the Native* (London: Smith, Elder & Co, 1878).

———, *The Trumpet-Major* (London: Smith and Elder, 1880).

———, *A Laodicean* (London: Sampson Low, 1881).

———, *Two on a Tower* (New York: Henry Holt, 1882).

———, *The Woodlanders* (London: Macmillan, 1887).

———, *Tess of the d'Urbervilles* (London: James R. Osgood, McIlvaine & Co, 1891).

Harris, Frank, *Contemporary Portraits* (New York: Mitchell Kennerley, 1915).

Hazlitt, William, *Complete Works of William Hazlitt*, ed. P. P. Howe, 21 vols (London: Dent, 1930–1934).

Heilmann, Ann and Stephanie Forward, eds, *Sex, Social Purity and Sarah Grand* (London: Routledge, 2000).

Hopkins, Gerard Manley, *The Correspondence of Gerard Manley Hopkins with Richard Watson Dixon*, ed. Claude Colleer Abbott (London: Oxford University Press, 1935).

Hugo, Victor, *Notre-Dame de Paris* (Paris: Flammarion, 1923).

———, *Les Miserables* (Paris: Gallimard, 1951).

———, *Les Travailleurs de la mer* (Paris: Gallimard, 1975).

———, *L'Homme qui rit* (Paris: Flammarion, 1924).

Hyndman, H. M., *The Record of an Adventurous Life* (London: Macmillan, 1911).

Henry, James, *The Novels and Stories of Henry James*, 35 vols (London: Macmillan, 1921–1923).

———, *The Letters of Henry James*, ed, Leon Edel, 4 volumes (London: Macmillan, 1974–1984).

———, *The Complete Letters of Henry James, 1878–1880*, ed, Pierre A. Walker and Grag W. Zacharias (Lincoln, Nebraska: University of Nebraska Press, 2015), 72.

———, 'Iwan Turgeniew', *North American Review*, 118 (1874), 326–356.

———, *The Future of the Novel: Essays on the Art of Fiction*, ed. Leon Edel (New York: Vintage Books, 1956).

James, William, 'A World of Pure Experience', *The Journal of Philosophy, Psychology and Scientific Methods*, 1 (September 29, 1904), 533–543.

Johnson, Diane, *The True History of the First Mrs. Meredith and Other Lesser Lives* (New York: Alfred A. Knopf, 1972).

Jones, Mervyn, *The Amazing Victorian: A Life of George Meredith* (London: Constable, 1999).

Joukovsky, Nicholas A., 'According to Mrs Bennett: A document sheds a kinder light on George Meredith's first wife', *Times Literary Supplement*, October 8, 2004, 13–15.

———., 'Mary Ellen's first affair: New light on the biographical background to *Modern Love*', *Times Literary Supplement*, June 15, 2007, 13–15.

———., 'New Correspondence of Mary Ellen Meredith', *Studies in Philology*, 106.4 (Fall, 2009), 483–522.

———., '"Dearest Susie Pye": New Meredith Letters to Peacock's Natural Daughter', *Studies in Philology*, 111.3 (Summer 2014), 591–629.

Keats, John, *The Letters of John Keats*, ed. Hyder Edward Rollins, 2 vols (Cambridge, Mass.: Harvard University Press, 1958).

Kingsley, Charles, *Yeast* (London: John W. Parker, 1851).

de Kock, Paul, *Le Cocu* (Paris: Librairie Trémois, 1925).

———, *La Bouquetière du Chateau d'Eau* (Leipzig: Auguste Schnée, 1854).

Lawrence, D. H., *Study of Thomas Hardy and Other Essays* (Cambridge: Cambridge University Press, 1985).

Le Gallienne, Richard, *The Romantic 90s* (London: Doubleday, Page and Co., 1925).

Maceroni, Emilie, *Magic Words: a tale for Christmas time* (London: Cundall and Addey, 1851).

Manning, Anne, *Some Account of Mrs Clarinda Singlehart* (London: Arthur Hall, Virtue & Co., 1855).

Marryat, Frederick, *Peter Simple* (London: Routledge, 1856).

Maxse, F. A., *Robert Mornay* (London: Chapman and Hall, 1859), published under the pseudonym Max Ferrer.

———., *Our Political Duty* (London: W. Ridgway, 1870).

———., *The Causes of Social Revolt: A Lecture* (London: Longman, Green, Reader, and Dyer, 1872).

———., *Objections to Women's Suffrage* (London: W. Ridgway, 1874).

McCarthy, Justin, 'Novels with a Purpose', *Westminster Review*, 26.1 (July, 1964), 24–49.

Men of the Time: A Dictionary of Contemporaries, containing biographical notices of eminent characters of both sexes, 10th edn (London: Routledge, 1879).

Meredith, George, *The Works of George Meredith, Memorial Edition*, 24 vols (London: Constable & Co., 1909–1911).

———, *Notebooks of George Meredith*, ed. Gillian Beer and Margaret Harris (Salzburg: Salzburg Studies in English Literature, 1983).

———, *Letters of George Meredith, collected and edited by his son* (London: Constable, 1912).

———, *The Letters of George Meredith*, ed. C. L. Cline, 3 vols (Oxford: Clarendon Press, 1970).

———, *Selected Letters of George Meredith*, ed. Mohammad Shaheen (Houndsmills, Basingstoke: Macmillan, 1997).

Meredith, Mary, 'Soyer's Modern Housewife, or Ménagère', *Fraser's Magazine* 44.260 (August, 1851), 199–209.

Milner, Viscountess (Violet Maxse), 'Talks with George Meredith', *National Review*, 131 (1948), 449–458.

Mitford, Mary Russell, *Atherton* (London: Hurst and Blackett, 1854).

Moffatt, James, *George Meredith: a primer to the novels* (London: Hodder and Stoughton, 1909).

Morgan, J. H., *John, Viscount Morley* (London, John Murray, 1925).

Morley, Henry, 'Ten Years Old', *Household Words*, 7 (May 14, 1853), 245–248.

———, 'Brother Mieth and His Brothers', *Household Words*, 9 (May, 27, 1854), 344–349.

Morley, John, *Rousseau*, 2 vols (London: Chapman and Hall, 1873).

———, *Recollections* (London: Macmillan, 1917).

Müller, Max, *German Love: from the Papers of an Alien*, trans. Susanna Winkworth (London: Chapman and Hall, 1858).

Murdoch, Iris, *The Sovereignty of Good over Other Concepts* (London: Routledge and Kegan Paul, 1970).

Myers, F. W. H., *Essays Classical and Modern* (London: Macmillan, 1921).

Nicoll, W. Robertson, *A Bookman's Letters* (London: Hodder and Stoughton, 1915).

Norton, Caroline, *Lost and Saved* (London: Hurst and Blackett, 1863).

Periodical accounts relating to the missions of the Church of the United Brethren, established among the heathen (London: 1844).

Peacock, Thomas Love, *Halliford edition of the works of Thomas Love Peacock*, ed. H. F. B. Brett-Smith and C. E. Jones, 10 Volumes (London: Constable, 1924–1934).

———, *The Letters of Thomas Love Peacock*, ed. Nicholas A. Joukovsky, 2 vols (Oxford: Clarendon Press, 2001).

————, *The Works of Thomas Love Peacock, with a biographical notice by his grand-daughter, Edith Nicolls* (London: Richard Bentley and Sons, 1875).

Photiadès, Constantin, *George Meredith: sa vie, son imagination, son art, sa doctrine* (Paris: Librairie Armand Colin, 1910).

Pollock, Sir John, *Time's Chariot* (London: John Murray, 1950).

Priestley, J. B., *George Meredith* (London: Macmillan 1926).

Pritchett, V. S., *George Meredith and English Comedy* (London: Chatto and Windus, 1970).

Proust, Marcel, *A la recherche du temps perdu*, 4 vols (Paris: Gallimard, 1987–1989).

Renan, Ernest, *Vie de Jésus* (Paris: Michel Lévy, 1863).

Ritchie, Leitch, *Wearyfoot Common* (London: Bogue, 1855).

Rives, Amélie, *The Quick or the Dead?* (Philadelphia: Lippincott, 1888).

Robertson, John M., 'Concerning Preciosity', *The Yellow Book*, 13 (1897), 79–106.

Ross, Janet, *The Fourth Generation: Reminiscences* (London: Constable, 1912).

Sand, George, *Mauprat* (Paris: Calmann Lévy, 1883).

Sassoon, Siegfried, *Meredith* (London: Constable, 1948).

Schreiner, Olive, *The Story of an African Farm* (London: Chapman and Hall, 1892).

Schools Inquiry Commission Report (London: Eyre and Spottiswoode, 1868).

Schwob, Marcel, *Spicilège* (Paris, Société du Mercure de France, 1896).

Scott, Walter Sidney, ed., *The Athenians: Being Correspondence between Thomas Jefferson Hogg and His Friends Thomas Love Peacock, Leigh Hunt, Percy Bysshe Shelley, and Others* (London: Golden Cockerel Press, 1943).

Seillière, Ernest, 'L'Egotisme Pathologique chez Stendhal', *Revue des deux mondes*, 31 (1906), 334–361 and 651–679.

Sencourt, Robert, *The Life of George Meredith* (New York: Charles Scribner, 1929).

Shaheen, Mohammad, *George Meredith* (Houndsmills, Basingstoke: Macmillan, 1980).

Shelley, Mary Wollstonecraft, *The Letters of Mary Wollstonecraft Shelley*, ed. Betty T. Bennett, 3 vols (Baltimore and London: Johns Hopkins University Press, 1983).

Shelley, Percy Bysshe, *Letters of Percy Bysshe Shelley*, ed. F. L. Jones, 2 vols (Oxford: Clarendon Press, 1964).

Smith, Peter C., *Per Mare Per Terram: A History of the Royal Marines* (Photo Precision, 1974).

Squire, J. C., *Life and Letters* (London: Hodder and Stoughton, 1920).

Steele, Anna, *So Runs the World Away* (London: Chapman and Hall, 1869).

Stendhal, *Armance; ou, quelques scènes dans un salon de Paris en 1827* (Paris: Hazan, 1949).

————, *De l'amour* (Paris: Garnier, 1964).

————, *La Chartreuse de Parme* (Paris: Gallimard, 1973).

————, *Le Rouge et le Noir* (Paris: Gallimard, 1994).

Stevenson, Lionel, *The Ordeal of George Meredith* (New York: Charles Scribner's Sons, 1953).

Stevenson, Robert Louis, *An Inland Voyage* (London: Kegan Paul, 1878).

———, *Prince Otto* (London: Chatto and Windus, 1886).

———, *Essays in the Art of Writing* (London: Chatto and Windus, 1905).

Sutherland, John, 'A Revered Corpse: The Peculiar Unreadability of George Meredith', *Times Literary Supplement*, September 5, 1997, p. 5.

Trevelyan, G. M., *The Poetry and Philosophy of George Meredith* (London: Constable, 1906).

Trollope, Anthony, *He Knew He Was Right* (London: Strahan and Company, 1869).

———, *Lady Anna* (London: Chapman and Hall, 1874).

———, *Letters of Anthony Trollope*, ed. John H. Hall, 2 volumes (Stanford: Stanford University Press, 1983).

Wallen, John, 'The Cannibal Club and the Origins of 19th Century Racism and Pornography', *The Victorian*, 1.i (August, 2013), 1–13.

Wharton, Edith, *A Backward Glance* (New York: Appleton-Century, 1934).

Williams, David, *George Meredith: His Life and Lost Love* (London: Hamish Hamilton, 1977).

Williams, Ioan, ed., *Meredith: The Critical Heritage* (London: Routledge and Kegan Paul, 1971).

Wilt, Judith, *The Readable People of George Meredith* (Princeton: Princeton University Press, 1975).

Wood, Ellen, *East Lynne* (London: Richard Bentley, 1861).

Woods, Alice, *George Meredith as Champion of Women and of Progressive Education* (Oxford: Basil Blackwell, 1937).

Yonge, Charlotte M., *The Heir of Redclyffe* (London: John W. Parker, 1853).

———., *Heartsease, or the Brother's Wife* (London: John W. Parker & Son, 1854).

Index[1]

---

[1] Note: Page numbers followed by 'n' refer to notes.

© The Author(s) 2019
R. Cronin, *George Meredith*,
https://doi.org/10.1007/978-3-030-32448-3

CPSIA information can be obtained
at www.ICGtesting.com
Printed in the USA
LVHW051512131220
674072LV00016B/1826

9 783030 324506